Alba Branca

Muse

MACMILLAN

First published 1998 by Macmillan

an imprint of Macmillan Publishers Ltd
25 Eccleston Place London SW1W 9NF
and Basingstoke

Associated companies throughout the world

ISBN 0 333 69879 7

1 3 5 7 9 8 6 4 2

A CIP catalogue record for this book is available from
the British Library.

Phototypeset by Intype London Ltd
Printed and bound in Great Britain by
Mackays of Chatham plc, Chatham, Kent

Acknowledgements

I would like to thank the following people: Marc Stevens, Suzanne Jackson, Noga Arikha, Elizabeth Winkelman, Anne Atik, Ariadne Calvo-Platero, Francesco Venturi, Janine di Giovanni, Filippo del Drago, Stephanie Cabot, Arabella Stein, and my husband Guido Branca.

For Guido

The heavens often rain down the richest gifts on human beings, naturally, but sometimes with lavish abundance bestow upon a single individual beauty, grace and ability, so that, whatever he does, every action is so divine that he distances all other men, and clearly displays how his genius is the gift of God and not an acquirement of human art.

Giorgio Vasari
The Lives of the Painters, Sculptors and Architects:
Leonardo da Vinci,
Painter and Sculptor of Florence (1452–1519)

One

DANTE OMEGA AT TADEUS LAUDMAN

The Italian realist Dante Omega claimed that when he picked up a brush for the first time, at the age of seventeen, it seemed to him as simple a gesture as drinking in order to quench his thirst. The result was the birth of his 'Mythology' series, now exhibited, thirty years later, alongside his recent works, at the Laudman gallery, in Manhattan.

Why it is that this artist took so long to achieve recognition is a mystery. The vigor of his lustrous brush strokes, the ethereal light which pours on to the canvas, the ardent and almost insistent way in which his models stare at the viewer through the canvas (in some cases achieving the 'Mona Lisa' effect, where, from whichever angle one stands, the sitter's gaze always seems to be directed towards the viewer), all these attributes render Omega's work so powerful, it is difficult to look at his paintings without feeling magnetically drawn into them.

Having achieved full artistic maturity at the Accademia di Belle Arti in Rome, under the watchful eye of Andrea Di Fatto, it is no surprise that much of Omega's later work bears some of his master's influence, especially when it comes to the Ingres-like renditions of faces plastered against a dazzling background of

1

primary-colored landscapes, a device which brought Di Fatto instant fame in the 1920s.

Where Omega's early work betrays a certain grappling to find his own style – clearly demonstrated in his painting *Cupid and Psyche*, his ambitious technique resulting in an awkward combination of Soutine and Balla – the later works, especially exemplified in his 1954 painting, *Aphrodite and Hephaestus*, show a rapid maturity and sophistication which set the path for his 'Mythology' series, depicting gods and goddesses in a natural environment. There are more traditional works as well, such as several pastels of his wife Isabella, one in which she is looking out of a rainy window with a melancholic gaze in her eyes (the pastel is aptly called *Sadness*) and two views of Rome, entitled *Dawn* and *Sunset*, which, through the various soft pink, red and blue hues and tones the artist uses, manage to perfectly and beautifully capture these distinct moments in the Roman skyline.

As for the drawings he executed between the ages of eighteen and thirty, not only can we delect ourselves in following the artist's gradual development, but we can view his first five drawings, so technically proficient that for one moment this author doubted the artist's veracity as to his claim to have never picked up a brush before this later age. But the artist's comment was quickly corroborated when the gallery owner, Tadeus Laudman, a long-time friend of Omega's, confirmed this amazing revelation, and added jokingly, 'he must have been an artist in another life. Perhaps Caravaggio, who knows . . .!'

Who knows is right. And whoever wishes to know more. must rush to see these exquisite works. on view until November 30th.

Laura Miller. in *Art Wave* magazine, November 1988

I found this article the other day, under a pile of old letters and various paraphernalia I had stuck in my bottom drawer. Reading it moved me indescribably. Not because it was a particularly outstanding article – it actually struck me as being rather naive – but because it brought back memories of those days when the name Dante Omega was almost mythical to me, and where I could not imagine him ever being part of my reality.

Today, this man is not only part of my life, but he has invaded it to such a degree that I have trouble focusing on anything that does not pertain to the sensitive topic of art, the people who create it, enrich themselves with it, immerse themselves in it, and occasionally die for it.

I live alone now. A pleasant but small apartment in a brownstone, tucked away in a tree-lined street near the Hudson River. I don't know my neighbors, except for the overly perfumed woman who lives right next door to me and who speaks so loudly on the telephone that if I leave my front door open even a crack, I can hear all of her conversations.

I've been working on my book for seven months. The pressure to finish it has been such that I hardly go out during the day, except to buy groceries or walk around the block in order to stretch my legs.

I sometimes go out at night. But usually I'm so tired, that by eleven o'clock I'm already in bed. I like my new way of living. It is quiet and monotonous. My few desires seem to have shrunk to bare necessities such as food and an occasional piece of clothing, and my one time greg-arious lifestyle seems to have disappeared somewhere far away in time, a phenomenon I attribute to my having just turned thirty.

My days are unvarying. I'm at my desk by nine in the morning, a cup of coffee in my hand, my thick and ugly glasses on my nose (the ones which Otto hated so much), and my red kimono with holes around the elbows and a black Japanese character on the back, tightly knotted around my waist.

I don't always eat lunch. Sometimes I just forget about it and go on writing until the phone rings and I'm immediately brought back to reality: 'Laura,' a desperate voice asks me, emphasizing my name as if I were a long-awaited savior, 'we don't know what to do: Andrew just left Mandy, no one knows where he is and she's driving me crazy, do you have any idea of where he could be?'

Last week my friend Sandra called me at one o'clock in the morning in a frenzy; her boyfriend was supposed to call her from Mexico that night and he hadn't, did I think that this meant that he could have met some woman on the plane or God knows where, or did I think that everything was fine and she should just relax?

I still try to keep in touch with my close friends, although perhaps with less dedication than before. I think they sense this, especially Sandra and my old college friend Rebecca, who refuse to accept it and invite me constantly, luring me out by mentioning some man they claim would be just perfect for me. I seldom accept these matchmaking invitations, and when I do, it's only to come back feeling that I have just wasted four hours of my life.

Therefore, I have been focusing primarily on my book. Perhaps it is the impending deadline that is making me nervous, or the realization that I haven't proved to be especially successful in mixing business with pleasure, but the selfish decision to concretize my ambitions has over-ruled that of remaining a loyal friend.

The person who calls me most often is my mother. She lives in Palm Beach, and is remarried to a man who smokes menthol cigarettes and who seems to spend most of his time laughing at his own jokes. His name is Oscar, and I have great trouble concealing my dislike of him. My mother married him shortly after my father died of cancer, almost ten years ago. She left New York one month after the funeral, claiming she couldn't stand being in the same city, or in our old Riverside Drive apartment. At the time I felt there must have been an ulterior motive for this move, because I remembered my mother speaking rhap-sodically about the city and vowing never to leave it.

She always insisted that this action was not triggered by anything or, more specifically, anyone. It was just, she said, a desire to turn over a new leaf. Palm Beach seemed to be the right place to do so. And as for Oscar, she claimed to have met him six months later, at some cocktail party.

I was then nineteen years old, and a sophomore at Barnard College. My mother's departure caused me much pain, as I felt abandoned and betrayed. It took me many years to forgive her, and for a long time, I refused to talk to her.

I therefore found myself with no one to turn to, except to my aunt Edna, my mother's sister who lived in a grandiose apartment on Fifth Avenue. Edna and her husband Sidney, a rich entrepreneur, went through great trouble to make me feel better. They suggested I give up my room at the Barnard dorms and live with them, which I did for a short while, until I moved into an apartment with Rebecca, on west 113th Street.

My mother had always been jealous of Edna's wealth. I suspected her unexpected marriage to Oscar (nicknamed, in Palm Beach, 'the king of real estate') to be some kind of childish retaliation against her younger sister. My father being a college professor, and my mother a failed actress, I had grown up surrounded with books, not money.

Scattered throughout our three-bedroom apartment, were old photographs of my mother in her film heyday. Whenever I'd have friends over (and I still recall this with great embarrassment), she'd give them a tour of the apartment, pointing to the photographs with her perfectly manicured red nails. She recounted her short life as a Hollywood actress, where she could have succeeded if it hadn't been for one film director whom she couldn't name because it would be too dangerous, but who refused to cast her as the star in his film, which she couldn't name either, unless she slept with him, so of course she said forget it honey, and the film went on to be made with Lauren Bacall instead, who lived happily ever after.

None of us ever knew if this was true, especially because in her story, Lauren Bacall was often replaced by

Ava Gardner or Rita Hayworth. But we never brought our suspicions out in the open, since she evidently revelled in the story.

I was a frustrated child, mostly, I think, due to the fact that I spent many years trying to get close to my father, a man I admired and feared at the same time, and who, although he may have kept his love for me tucked away somewhere in his soul, kept me at a distance for as long as I can remember. Only when he became ill did he gradually soften. He would call me into his room and we would have long conversations, usually about literature and his favorite writers, Joseph Conrad and Aldous Huxley among others. Books and words were his universe, the one he felt most comfortable in. He didn't like to talk about himself, or about my mother, as if they simply did not need to be discussed. The subject of his illness was never brought up. It was more of a mirage or a dream; so when the time suddenly came to face the truth, I wasn't at all prepared for it. It was a gray summer afternoon. My mother was out, and I was keeping my father company. I remember that he was wearing a light-blue shirt and an old pair of brown trousers. Even though he was so ill, he could not bear the idea of being in pajamas during the day. 'It makes me feel as if I've surrendered to my condition. And I haven't,' he once told me, one of the few comments he ever made in relation to his illness.

That day, we were talking about his classes, and the fact that he missed teaching, missed some of his students, several of whom I got to meet, since they came to visit him, sometimes spending so much time with him that my mother gently had to ask them to leave. As we started talking about one of his favorite students, I found myself asking my father if he knew what courses he would be teaching in the fall semester. Again, I couldn't accept the fact that he was sick with cancer. To me it was evident that he would be cured, and would soon be back on his feet. It almost didn't make sense to see him lying there with his sunken eyes and dried out lips. But his response to my question was unexpected. 'There won't be another semester, Laura,' he said steadily.

'What do you mean?' I asked, still not wanting to believe the truth.

'I won't be teaching in the fall because I'll be dead by then,' he answered, avoiding my gaze. 'Now, please leave the room, I'm feeling a little tired. And tell your mother not to disturb me.'

I closed his door quietly, my body shaking as if I had just been knocked over, my eyes swelling with tears. I went into my bedroom, and after crying for what seemed to be an eternity, I started remembering how my father used to be.

He was a very tall and serious man who was not known to have a particularly good sense of humor. He was twelve years older than my mother, often got impatient with her, and threatened to leave her several times. Now, at the end of his life, when he was very sick and unable to walk, my mother would serve him meals on a platter and sit by his bedside in silence, until he'd fall asleep. Several times I passed by their bedroom door, and saw my mother kissing his forehead with her eyes closed.

My father died that fall, without my ever knowing if

he loved my mother. And to this day I mourn all the things I never got to say to him.

Since she moved to her white and coral pink mansion in Palm Beach, my mother traded her fantasy of living like a glamorous actress, for the life of a glamorous wife. She entertains constantly, and her husband lavishes clothes and jewels on her. Every two months they are off to some faraway resort, and every four months she tries to convince me to join them, something which I've managed to avoid until now.

As her once frequent trips to New York diminished, my mother's newly acquired lifestyle, which she had pre-viously kept as subdued as possible in my presence, suddenly increased in its ostentatious display. On her last trip to New York, where she showed up at my apartment with a larger-than-life diamond necklace, a new face, and a new mink coat, she insisted on driving around the city in a rented limousine, letting out little cries of recognition every time we'd pass a familiar building or street. She brought me to Bergdorf-Goodman's where she bought me clothes I have yet to wear, and made me wait for her for practically an hour as she tried on lipsticks and perfumes, morning and night creams, speaking loudly and reminding me of my childhood days when I was so ashamed of her.

But despite her eccentricities, I must admit that in the last few years, my mother surprised me in many pleasant ways: she was so present and supportive during and after my separation from Otto, that I can honestly say that without her, I'm not sure where I would be standing today. Not that I had any desire to kill myself, but my self-esteem was so low that it took someone with great strength and patience to help me rise again above the surface. The analysis I undertook with a respected New York psycho-analyst was successful insofar as I was able to fit certain pieces of my past and present together like a puzzle, slowly beginning to understand what had motivated my decisions in the first place. But my mother was more efficacious because she knew exactly where I was coming from: she had lived more or less the same experiences herself, with my father, and as she often told me, 'self-destruction is regrettably part of our family's genes. It's like a disease. You'll get rid of it by paying attention to it. Not by ignoring it. Be strong, and be patient, and you'll see, you'll even-tually feel much better.'

I got my life back on track and settled into my new apartment. I tried to look for a job in a publishing company, or writing for a magazine, a fruitless venture. I decided to take up Italian classes. Whereas I had never bothered doing it with Otto, I now felt it was time to perfect the little that I knew. Besides being useful pro-fessionally (I was often given material in Italian which I had trouble understanding), I saw it as a challenge in relation to my past; I reasoned that if I was able to learn the language and not necessarily associate it with Otto, then this would mean that I was over him, and could now face the future sanely, dissociating past events with present undertakings.

I learnt faster than I expected, after enrolling in an intensive conversation class where the teacher, Michele, a tall and rather pale Venetian, took me out a few times after classes to his local restaurant. Although Michele clearly had romantic feelings for me, I could not reciprocate them. Thankfully this happened at the end of the term, and although from then on Michele deliberately cut me out of the dialogues he urged the other students to engage in, his callow retaliation had no consequences whatsoever: I had learned what I needed to.

When I was asked to translate an article about an Italian art dealer, I was able to do so without too much difficulty. This filled me with pride, a healthy sign that my life was back on track again.

Now that I was strong again, my mother went back to being her old self; we started bickering again, and she began to criticize me and the fact that I had chosen to write about art, of all things. 'Why don't you go to law school?' she repeatedly asked me. 'At least you won't be broke when you come out of there, and you'll be sure to find a job. And of course plenty of eligible young men go to law school. Plenty of nice Jewish boys who come from good families.'

'Thanks but I'm not interested in law school or nice Jewish boys,' I answered her. 'I'll eventually be interested in a nice and intelligent man, not boy, and that's certainly not going to be in the near future. So please let's refrain from bringing up the whole topic once again. It's becoming really tedious.'

My mother did not discontinue her diatribes until I landed the Omega book contract; since then, she's been treating my writing with utmost respect. It is a relief to her that my life has taken on such a positive and, moreover, lucrative turn, especially after my disastrous marriage to Otto, whose name she will not utter, for fear that the devil will once again erupt in my life. Unlike my mother, I don't mind bringing up the past; where she seldom talks about her difficult and painful marriage to my father, I have chosen to empty myself out, so to speak, of the events I witnessed and lived through during the one year of my marriage. I have managed to get over the queasiness these recollections used to cause me (like spitting out sour remnants), and can now deal with them for what they are: misfortunes, some periods of great happiness, others of torturous unhappiness, a lot of wasted time, but overall, no regrets. I learned that suffering makes one mature. The French didn't invent the words 'erreurs de jeunesse' for nothing; we've all been through them one way or another. After all, clichés exist for a good reason.

The book I am writing is about Dante Omega, the elusive and outlandish Italian contemporary painter. Within two months I must submit it to my editor, Ensor Mason. He is a frightfully unpleasant albeit perceptive man I prefer to have the least possible contact with, an obviously reciprocal feeling considering the minimal number of times he actually picks up his telephone to speak to me directly.

I cannot wait to finish this book. Although I have enjoyed researching and examining the artist's work, I have lately fallen into a state of stagnation where I just don't seem to have anything left to say. For the past ten days I have remained on page 185, unable to formulate my conclusion, my eyes fixed on the words until they become black meaningless dots which start buzzing around my head like angry flies. Last week, not daring to tell the man who commissioned this book, Alain Jaurel, about my problem, I found myself obliged to call Ensor, something which I was not supposed to do without Jaurel's accord. I told Ensor about my block. 'I'm stuck,' I said. 'Give it to me as it is,' he answered. He actually liked it. But not Jaurel, whom I showed it to immediately after. 'Your conclusion is foggy and sloppy,' he said, 'do it over again.' I threw my arms in the air in dismay. 'Monsieur Jaurel,' I said, 'I am going to ask you this for the last time: if you'd only let me write about the erotic aspect of some of his works, it could be the greatest conclusion of all. Listen to this: "After years of portraying scenes from Greek mythology, Dante Omega has finally stripped down to the bare essentials: the rendering of female bodies in their most explicit and crude forms." How's that?'

'Ridiculous,' Jaurel answered. 'And please, let's not bring it up again. I'm starting to find it very tiresome. I am sure, Mademoiselle Miller, that you'll be able to find several other things that interest you in the artist's work, besides those naked bodies.'

I dropped the subject. But I think about those crude lithographs very often. I saw them at Omega's studio three months ago, and they have stuck with me ever since. The first time I told Jaurel about my discovery, he told me he'd think about it. The second time, his answer was definitive: 'Let's not mix Greek mythology with anything else. The artist is known for his powerful rendering of those mythological scenes, so let's not confuse the public with what sounds like mediocre erotic works.' I gave up. What could I do? I had to follow his orders.

So here I sit today, watching those same dots, with even less to say. It is a warm autumn day, the central heating is on for no apparent reason, making my apartment unbearably hot, and my long, tangly dark hair badly needs to be washed. I go to the refrigerator and take out some black olive paste and some goat's cheese which I spread on a piece of French bread. I pour some olive oil over it and add a little pepper. I recline in my kitchen chair and stretch out my legs. I am wearing a white T-shirt and flowery shorts my mother used to wear in the sixties. I look down at my elongated body, and decide that considering the inordinate amount of time I spend indoors, my body does look rather healthy. I stand up and look at myself in the dirty kitchen mirror. My usually large blue eyes look unbearably small, my bony face looks tired, and I have a pimple forming on my forehead; I look awful, and decide that as soon as this book is finished, I am going to take a long vacation.

This thought gives me some encouragement. I sit back down and quickly finish my snack. I look at the computer screen blankly and my thoughts start drifting off. 'Cut it out,' I say out loud, hitting the computer keyboard, 'get back to work.'

The idea then hits me that I should fly back to Rome, in order to interview Omega one last time. After all, I only interviewed him twice, discounting brief and unfruitful phone conversations, and a third time could inspire a thought provoking conclusion. But then again, he is such a difficult man to deal with, do I really want to go through with it one last time? And would Jaurel agree to pay for it? Probably not, considering the amount of money he's already given me. But then again, I don't have anything to lose by asking him.

Alain Jaurel, a Frenchman who's been living in New York for nearly twenty years, is the owner of the New York based Jaurel Gallery, which represents Dante Omega. He is of medium height, with large heavy-set eyes, and wears his thin brown hair perfectly parted on the side, thus revealing an undeniable dandruff problem. I met Jaurel on several occasions, mostly openings and cocktail parties, when I was still involved in writing for various fashionable magazines about the art world.

Jaurel is a very energetic man. He is known to possess an unquenchable thirst for very young women, while keeping up a very convincing front with his wife and four children (or so the rumors go).

How could I have ever predicted that one day I would be so heavily involved with this man? The story is quite simple, and unfortunately, not over yet.

I have been a fan of Omega's work for a long time. It started six years ago, when I saw a series of his watercolors in Paris. They moved me to such an extent, I went out of my way to find out more about this then unknown artist. Around one year later, as I was reading *The Herald Tribune* during one of my long lunch breaks from the Ecole du Louvre (I was living in Paris and finishing a degree in nineteenth-century art history), I read to my delighted surprise, that Dante Omega had just been taken on by the Laudman Gallery (which became the Jaurel gallery in 1989, after Tadeus Laudman died), one of the most powerful and important galleries in the world. A show of his work was due to open in the following months. Later on, when I discovered that my talent was more journalistic than curatorial, I wrote the short article about the show for *Art*

Wave magazine (the one which is reprinted here), but the article went unnoticed, as did the exhibition. It took four more years (by which time I was back in New York with Otto) and two more exhibitions before Dante Omega was called one of the most important figurative painters of our century.

After his series of paintings entitled *The Twelve Trials of Heracles* was shown at the Venice Biennale, I again tried to draw attention to him, deploring the unjustifiably long amount of time it had taken for him to be recognized as a true master. The five-page article was published in *Art in America*, and helped launch my career as an art critic.

One early morning, several articles later, the telephone rang. It was Alain Jaurel. He spoke fast and breathlessly, and I wasn't able to get a word in edgewise during his whole monologue. 'Good morning Mademoiselle Miller,' he said in his thick French accent. 'This is Alain Jaurel on the telephone. I am planning a fall show of Dante Omega's work. I need something like a *catalogue raisonné* of his work, or better yet, a monograph. I'd like you to do it. I've read many of your articles, I like the way you write. I especially like the latest one you wrote about our friend; you seem to understand his work quite well. I also understand that you speak Italian a little bit. Is that right? Good, good, this could be very useful to us. I will therefore go straight to the point: are you interested in writing about Dante Omega? If you are, I'd like you to know that I'm willing to pay you a very generous sum of money as an advance. We can of course discuss all of these details when we see each other. Think about it for a few days and call me back at the gallery. Thank you and goodbye Mademoiselle Miller.'

That was it. Needless to say, being in a financial rut as well as being a fan of Omega's prompted me to call him back rather quickly, and before I had time to say anything, he suggested we meet in order to talk about it. I consulted various friends on the matter, and all seemed enthusiastic about it. 'Do it,' they all said, 'it's the opportunity of a lifetime.'

I agreed to meet Alain Jaurel at Bice, a trendy midtown Italian restaurant. I wore a dark gray suit with a pink silk shirt, and my hair up in a bun. I looked professional and serious, which was exactly the image I wanted to project.

Alain ordered a bottle of white wine, insisting I have the risotto, and once our first courses had arrived, carpaccio for me, calamari for him, he began talking. 'This is what I would like from you,' he said, crossing his hands resolutely. 'I'd like you to write a monograph on Dante Omega. Talk about his childhood, a little bit about his family, his art studies, what prompted him to paint, etc . . . Nothing too complicated, just your usual biography. I'd like its publication to coincide with the retrospective I am planning to have in October, a year and seven months from now. Here, taste these calamari, they're delicious.'

'No thank you,' I answered, fidgeting with my napkin.

'The person who will publish this book is Ensor Mason, whom you may or may not know, of Babylon Press. They're excellent publishers of art books. Have you heard of them?'

I nodded my head. Of course I had. But Ensor Mason, no, I had never heard of him.

'Ensor is an old friend of mine. He's crazy about Omega's work. He loves the whole idea.'

I was suddenly confused. Who was in charge of all of this? The Jaurel Gallery or Babylon Press? And why was Jaurel asking me to write a book on the artist? There were so many other people whose names were firmly established in the art world, and who were obviously more experienced than I was, a young journalist who had never written a book before, and whose authority rested solely on the publication of a few reviews and articles. I admit that the prospect of breaking new ground was very tempting, so I put aside my suspicions about Alain Jaurel and his approach, and listened to him intently, as he proceeded to explain more about his gallery and how, if it were not for him, Omega would have remained a virtual unknown, which, as I probably knew, he was far from being today.

After a lengthy self-congratulatory monologue that glorified the virtues of his sharp eye and his ability to prophesize success, I decided that it was time for me to ask him exactly how much he intended to pay me. I was determined to refuse his offer unless it was, as he had implied, very generous.

'M. Jaurel,' I ventured, 'this whole idea sounds very appealing to me. As you know, and as you rightly observed, I feel very close to Dante Omega's work. It would obviously be an honor for me to write this book, but before we start talking more in depth about it, would you mind telling me more about the financial aspects of it?' I sighed heavily and felt my cheeks turn red; I had never been good at negotiating deals.

'I see you like to get straight to the point,' he remarked

with a large grin on his face. 'I like that. I like women who get straight to the point. Well, it's as simple as this Mademoiselle Miller,' he said, taking a loud sip of his wine. 'I am financing part of this book, namely one hundred proofs signed and numbered, which will include fifty color reproductions, and two or three original etchings signed by the artist. This will greatly increase the price of the monograph, as you can well imagine. The commercial version will only include reproductions, and, as you have probably figured out since you seem to me to be an intelligent girl, the circulation for that book will be much wider. Mason is in charge of all of that. As for you, all you have to do is write the text, and we take care of everything else.'

Alain Jaurel took a cigarette out of a golden box, stuck it between his teeth, and kept it in his mouth without lighting it. Then, he gravely removed the cigarette from his mouth and placed it next to his plate. He waited a while before saying anything further, his face having taken on the expression of someone who has just made an important decision.

'Now, Mademoiselle Miller,' he said, clearing his throat before continuing, 'for the advance I promised you, here is how it will work. You are to get a total of fifty thousand dollars, yes I know it's a large sum but let me explain: it will be paid to you in installments, at the completion of every chapter you submit. Let me explain further. You are to write five chapters. You show me the chapter, I like it, I pay you a certain sum. I don't like it, I will not pay you and you do it over. Do you or do you not follow me, Mademoiselle Miller?'

'I follow you,' I said, feeling overwhelmed by this

information, 'but what about Ensor Mason? When do I show him my chapters?'

Here, Alain Jaurel raised his voice and appeared nervous.

'You are never, and I repeat, *never* to show him anything before you show me first. Do you follow me?'

I nodded silently.

'You come to me with the facts, Ensor will take care of the rest. It is very simple. You will be paid in installments: divide fifty thousand dollars into five, and there is your advance which will be deducted from any royalties that ensue, until, of course, the full amount is recovered. After that, you are to get six per cent of the retail price as royalties for the gallery edition, twelve per cent for the commercial edition. Do you follow me?'

'Yes, M. Jaurel, I follow you,' I answered, although by now I was lost in a cloud of numbers and wonders.

'Good,' he said. 'You will have a couple of months per chapter, giving you approximately ten months to finish this book. I trust that your non-negligible advance will permit you to live quite well without any need for additional income, therefore allowing you to invest all of your time in this undertaking. Am I, or am I not, correct?' he asked, his unlit cigarette back in his mouth.

I started to feel pure contempt for this man, whose Napoleonic way of talking was becoming more and more offensive. Despite his generous offer, I felt tempted to turn the whole thing down. Why, once again, was he asking me to carry out such an important task? What did he see in me that he didn't see in others? And how could I ever work with a man who finished every sentence with an ultimatum?

Jaurel must have sensed my discomfort, for he softened his tone. 'Now Laura – can I call you Laura? – let me add the following: all your expenses relating to this book will be paid for, as well as any additional expenses you may incur during the course of your research; all you have to do is submit receipts. Very important the little receipt. Now. This exhibition is scheduled to open next October. The book must be ready by December, so that we can quickly send it off to the printer and have it on the stands the following year at the opening, and in the bookstores.' He then paused for a moment and looked me straight in the eyes.

'Okay, Mademoiselle Miller, you are a beautiful girl, you will surely understand what I am going to tell you. I know I sound authoritative. I don't mean to be. All I am trying to say, is that this book has to be finished by December 1st at the latest. That gives you, as I already stated, ten months to write it. I will be honest with you, Mademoiselle Miller. I need this book. Omega needs it for his career to become even bigger. The public needs it in order to realize that Omega is a giant. A genius. Mason needs it for his publishing company. And you could use it for your career. I doubt, Mademoiselle Miller, that any art magazine will pay you along the same lines for an article hardly anyone will read. Is that correct?'

'Yes, that is correct,' I sighed. 'But M. Jaurel, I need time to think about all of this.'

'You need time to think about all of this,' he said, mocking my comment, glancing at me with ice-cold eyes.

'I like quick decisions, Mademoiselle Miller, not people who need time to think.'

'But—' I started, faltering on my words, feeling that I had just lost the deal then and there, 'I—'

'You nothing,' he interrupted brusquely. 'You have one day to think about it. You can call me at the gallery. As you can well imagine, I have several capable people interested in this project.'

I sighed with relief. At least he was capable of some compassion. And his comment seemed an appropriate entry to the question that was burning on my lips. 'Since you brought this up, I must ask you a question, M. Jaurel,' I said, trying to keep my voice steady. 'Pardon my indiscretion, but how come you want me? As you implied, there are plenty of well-known, sought-after and able people who would be more than willing to do this, so I was just wondering...' Here I blushed, realizing my modesty could be interpreted as self-disparaging, a trait I did not want to project, and one I suddenly feared would make me lose the job just as fast as I had been offered it. I nervously clutched my glass as I awaited his response.

M. Jaurel wiped his mouth with his white napkin, once again took the cigarette which was lying on the table and finally lit it. 'Mademoiselle Miller,' he said, blowing a cloud of smoke in my direction, 'I think there is one thing you should know about me. I like to give people chances. Being experienced doesn't always mean you're good. On the contrary. I think that a fresh eye can sometimes be more rewarding than a trained one. Do you follow me?' Here his face took on a serious expression, as he set his elbows on the table, clasped his hands tightly, and brought his face a little too close to mine. 'I need a fresh eye for this venture. As you may or may not know, M. Omega is a difficult man, an impatient man, and to be honest with you, most people who interview him get fed up rather quickly. Only someone young, ambitious and open-minded will be able to deal with him, and to look at his work in an original way, which, Mademoiselle Miller, is why I was interested in you in the first place. I feel that you have an innovative and interesting way of looking at the artist's work, and, most important of all, I feel that you understand it, and convey its meaning quite eloquently in your articles. Also, you speak Italian and he doesn't speak any other language, besides very poor English. In one word, I think you are the ideal person for this job. Now, does that answer your question?'

'Yes, it does,' I answered diffidently, wanting to feel reassured and flattered by his laudatory speech, but unable to put aside the gnawing suspicion that he had another reason for hiring me, one which he was keeping to himself. It was imperative that I make the decision right then and there. Either I was going to turn down his offer, or I would have to look at this venture as an opportune challenge to consolidate my position in the world of art criticism. I chose the latter, with one goal in mind: I would break through. Never mind my suspicions and my paranoia. I needed the money; the challenge, and the opportunity.

'Yes, it does,' I repeated, this time loudly and firmly. 'It does answer my question, M. Jaurel.'

'Very well then,' he said, folding his napkin and leaning back in his chair, 'now that we've finished talking about business, let's enjoy our meal, and tell me a little bit more about yourself.'

This is how it all started. How I began my book on Dante Omega, born Ruggero Lombani, in 1934 in Naples. I cannot include everything I have learned about his life in my book, because it is supposed to be a monograph and not a biography, and deals mainly with his work. But I have devoted a small section to his tragic upbringing and his younger years, a task which proved to be quite daunting at first, because the painter refused to discuss his personal life in any way, prompting me to gather information from various unreliable sources. I submitted the material to Jaurel, who must have said something about it to his client, because a few days later I received an unpleasant call from Omega, during which he firmly stated that he did not wish to have his childhood or younger years discussed in any way. 'It's about my art,' he said angrily, 'not about my life.'

I told him that his life set the path for his art, and after a long and tiresome debate with him in which I tried to convince him that people also wanted to know about the man behind the artist, he finally acquiesced to having 'a few crumbs,' as he put it, of his personal life revealed in the book, as long as it was accurate, and didn't outweigh the subject he cared the most about, his work. He suggested I call his old friend Fabio Falucci, who, he promised, would be able to tell me anything I needed to know about his childhood.

I complied with his orders. I called Fabio up, and got rid of everything I had written until then. This was obviously the man I should have talked to from the beginning, and I cursed myself when I thought of all the useless trouble I had gone through. Fabio was Ruggero's closest friend in school, and a key eye witness to the events that unfolded before young Ruggero's eyes. The material I gathered through Fabio is extensive, therefore I only incorporated a small portion in my manuscript. Here are several of those passages which, though I consider them crucial to understanding Omega, I wasn't able to incorporate in my manuscript, because the artist strongly objected to them, even threatening Ensor Mason to sue Babylon Press if they went against his will.

The only child of a grocer and a seamstress, Ruggero grew up in a modest section of Naples, until the age of ten. Then, increasing financial difficulties drove the family to move to an even poorer section of town, the Forcella district. He had trouble making friends in his new school, and was often teased and tormented, on account of his lisp, and his weight problem.

Few people remember Ruggero from that period, mostly because he was very reserved and kept to himself most of the time. His teachers remembered him as being a mediocre student, except in history where he displayed a keen interest, particularly in that of the Hellenistic and Roman periods. According to Fabio, if there was one thing that made Ruggero suffer most, it was his lisp. He was so self-conscious about it that he deliberately tried to avoid words which carried the letter s or z in them. As a result, he talked less and less, and his teacher held a private meeting with his parents, which ended up with Ruggero's father lashing his son's back furiously, because he was failing in school and bringing shame to the family name.

'I'll never forget the sight of his back the next morning,' Fabio recalled, as we spoke on the phone from his apartment in Rome. 'It was as if someone had combed his back, leaving red and purple parallel lines. And it's not as if he deliberately showed it to me. On the contrary: It so happened that we would walk to school together each morning, and that day I noticed that with every other step he took, his face would take on a painful expression. I asked him what the matter was and he told me his foot hurt. I let it go at that. But that afternoon, during recess, Paolo, one of those awful boys who took pleasure in tormenting him, came up to him with a large grin on his face. "Come stai oggi Lombani," he asked, winking at his friends, and, faithful to the ritual, giving him a ferocious slap on the back. What happened next was unexpected: Ruggero let out a slight sound and fainted. The boys laughed. They thought he was faking it. "Fifone!" they roared in unison. "Scaredy cat!" But I could see that this was not a game. I became very angry and told them to shut up and to run and get help. They stood there, shrugged their shoulders, and Paolo told me to go get help myself. But the other boys in the class went to get the teacher, and she ran over to see what had happened. She immediately called a doctor. They took off Ruggero's shirt, and everyone gasped – including Paolo. It was rather shocking, I must say. The teacher ordered us to wait for her in class. The doctor and our teacher looked *at each other with such concern that I became worried. "Is he going to die?" I cried out. "No Fabio, he's not going to die, but he's been badly hurt."*

They didn't ask me if I knew how it had happened. They obviously didn't need any explanation. All I remember is that later on Ruggero's parents were summoned again to the school. The teacher and the director of the school took Mr and Mrs Lombani into a separate room and asked them questions for a very long time. Ernesto, a good friend, and I spied from behind the door, and tried to hear what was going on, but all we could see was Ruggero's mother wiping her eyes and blowing her nose. Then the director went to talk to Ruggero alone, and asked him what had happened that night at home. While I was keeping guard in the hallway, Ernesto heard Ruggero say he had fallen down the stairs.

The next day, Ruggero didn't come to school at all. I interpreted it as a good sign. He was probably recuperating at home. But the following day he didn't show up either, so I decided to drop by his house after school to find out if he was doing better.

The Lombani family lived in a large apartment building where one could hear the neighbors upstairs and downstairs and where there were all kinds of different cooking odors. I guess they must have been surprised to see me, for when I knocked on the door and asked to see Ruggero, Antonella looked very distraught. She said that he was sleeping and not feeling well. Ruggero's father, a stout and big man with an ugly face, was drinking a beer and joking with one of his friends. I told Antonella I had brought his home-work, and could I possibly leave it by his bed. She replied that it was probably best for me to let him sleep, but she would tell him I had stopped by. She was very pale, Antonella, and looked terrified. She was about to close the door in my face when I heard Ruggero. "Mamma!" he cried out, in a strained voice, "chi c'è?" She didn't know what to answer. She tried to smile, and said, "Oh! he must have just woken up." She turned towards Silvio, her husband, and told him I was here to see Ruggero who had just woken up. She was obviously distressed about something, and at that point I was starting to get worried about my friend. I was deter-mined to see him. Silvio looked at me and asked me what I wanted. "I want to find out if Ruggero is better. I know he fell down the stairs, and I want to know if his back is better." I said timidly, not only because the man was intimidating, but because I knew I had more to gain by playing stupid. Silvio lost some of the color in his face when he heard me say that. "How do you know he fell down the stairs?" he asked me. "Everyone knows!" I exclaimed. "I mean that's what he told the director who told us and—"

"Fine," the father vociferated. "Go ahead and see him."

But his tone of voice betrayed a certain uneasiness about something; I quickly found out what it was.

I entered Ruggero's room. The curtains were drawn, and it was dark. He was lying on his bed, and when he saw me, he said, "Ciao Fabio," in a very thin and trembling voice. I turned the light on. "No!" he implored. But I ignored his plea. His body was tucked under the covers. Only his head was noticeable. He looked sickly. His eyes were swollen, and his skin greenish. I asked him what the matter was and he said he didn't feel well. I asked him if the doctor had come to see him and he shook his head. "My father doesn't like doctors," he said. I told him he looked awful. He tried to smile and said he'd be better soon. I asked him to get out of bed. I was a smart kid. He refused. "I don't want to get up." But I insisted. I told him that if he didn't get up I'd bring a doctor over. He got scared and got out of bed.

Here Fabio paused. I waited, breathless, for him to continue. He finally said that up until today, he cannot forget the sight of that boy. Even the memory of it makes him shudder, and it's no wonder that Ruggero is such a strange and difficult man today.

I encouraged him to go on. He cleared his throat and resumed where he had left off.

'He got out of bed, and this time I had to cover my eyes with my hands. His legs were beaten to the core. There was dried blood all around his knees, and an open wound that gaped at me like the eye of a Cyclops. It was too awful to look at. "Why did he do that to you?" I asked in a whisper, "why?"

Ruggero lowered his head. "Because he thinks I told the director that he beat me the other day. And I didn't. I said I had fallen down the stairs. But he won't believe me."

He kept his face down. As he turned around to get back into bed, I noticed that the back of his legs looked like they had been slashed as well, and this time I knew what to do.

I ran out of the apartment. I went to get my father who had just come home from work. I told him every-thing. He listened carefully, asked me if I was sure and called the police. As you may know, Miss Miller, we respect children a great deal in Italy. Child abuse is not common in Italy. Back then, in the forties, people who committed such crimes were immediately sent to jail. It was considered outrageous. So when I told my father what I had seen, he took it much to heart. He waited for the police to come over, and they all drove together to the Lombani household. I, of course, was not allowed to be part of the expedition, but I heard later on what had happened.

They knocked on the door and Antonella answered it, as she had for me. When she saw the police and the detective she immediately started shouting. "What do you want from us? We're good people!" and Silvio told her to be quiet. My father later told me that it was quite obvious that Silvio had no idea what the police were there about. Not only that, but his first reaction was to say something like "What did my son do now?" and when they told him they were there to see his son, he went to get him immediately, and pulled him out of his bed by the ears, because he was so convinced he had done something wrong. The police heard the father holler in the bedroom, and ran in. "You can have him," Silvio shouted, "I can't deal with him anymore."

My father, as well as the policemen and the detective, were shocked by what they saw on Ruggero's legs. They asked Silvio why he had done such a thing to his own son, and he told them he didn't know what they were talking about. The detective pulled the boy's shirt off and had to pretend to cough (so said my father) in order to avoid showing his true feelings. Then, he looked at Silvio, and told him they were going to arrest him for child abuse. Silvio looked shocked. "Are you crazy?" he said, "and why don't you ask my son first before sticking me in jail?"

The detective asked Ruggero who had done all of this to him. Silvio glared at him, as a last attempt to intimidate him, while Antonella cried in a corner. Ruggero didn't answer. The detective asked the question again, and Ruggero lowered his eyes towards the floor. Suddenly, and most unexpectedly, Antonella cried out, "Tell them Ruggerino! Tell them the truth! Don't be afraid of him!"

That was it. Ruggero pointed towards his father and nodded. "He did it to me."

Silvio Lombani was arrested immediately and the story was on the front page of the newspaper the next day. People talked about it a lot, especially because at first the authorities hesitated to leave Ruggero with his mother. They were worried she'd return to her husband once he was out of jail (which was to be five years later), and her reputation as a weak and simple woman was not in her favor. It was rumored that Ruggero would be placed in an orphanage, but his mother made such a fuss about keeping him, that finally the authorities gave in, checking up on Ruggero's welfare periodically.

Ruggero was once again sent to a different school, and my family moved to Florence. We lost touch for many years, until we were seventeen and we were both finishing high school. One day, as I was going to visit my aunt who still lived in Naples, I bumped into Ruggero on the street. He looked the same. A little overweight, the same friendly smile. Like mine, his voice was now much deeper, and he had acne on his face. He still didn't have many friends, and it appeared, from what he implied, that people still teased him about his lisp. I asked him about his father. He told me he had died in jail, a few weeks before his due release. I found out later that the circumstances of his father's death were unknown. Rumors implied a Mafia hit. But whatever the real causes were, Ruggero did not seem to want to dwell on the topic. There was something new in his life, he said, something exciting. He had discovered painting, and it had become his passion.`

What follows is information I gathered from several of Omega's colleagues in art school:

After he had completed high school, Ruggero won a prestigious scholarship to the Accademia di Belle Arti in Rome. He read the *Odyssey* that summer, and became obsessed with Greek mythology. He decided to change his name to Dante Omega, the former being the first writer in the Florentine tongue, the latter being the last letter of the Greek alphabet. He didn't want to bear his father's name, and instead wanted to create a new identity for himself in order to start a new life that was as far removed from the slums of Naples as possible, where his only tie was to his mother, who wrote to him every week, though many of her letters remained unanswered.

Dante became the star pupil of the school. His talent was unanimously recognized, and his mentor, Di Fatto, a one-time futurist who had turned to realism, predicted a great future for him. The small amount of scholarship money he had won enabled him to find a room in a boarding house, after which he was lucky enough to find himself a job as a teacher's assistant in the Accademia. He was a good teacher, I was told, although not the most popular.

That same year he met Maria. She was a fellow student in his painting class, and she was very beautiful. Dante, who had never been in love before, found himself falling for her. He attempted to talk to her on several occasions, even found the courage to ask her out for a cup of coffee, but she didn't seem interested in reciprocating his advances. He became very depressed. At around the same time, he befriended a fellow student named Vanni Tulsa (whose claim to fame was established around twenty years ago, when he started to paint on the back of postcards and exhibited one thousand of them).

It took me a long time to track Vanni down. I found him living in Saint-Paul de Vence, with his wife and children. He doesn't speak English, and has contributed the following information, which I translated from the French:

It seems that Vanni became Omega's confidant. The latter, who had never had any experience with women, was impressed by his friend's notoriety as a ladies' man. He consulted him on the matter of Maria, and confessed to being in love with her. He saw her as a Greek muse, he told Vanni. She was Erato and Euterpe, poetry and music combined, and her beauty equaled that of the goddess Aphrodite.

Vanni tried to demystify her instantly, but Dante was adamant. 'I love her,' he said, 'and I'm ready to marry her right now, even though I've barely said a word to her.'

Vanni told Dante that if he really wanted to seduce her, he should start by improving his appearance, perhaps lose some weight, and shave his beard.

Dante followed his friend's advice scrupulously. He almost starved himself to death, managed to scrape up a little money to buy himself a new shirt, and finally the day arrived when Vanni told him he should go ahead and ask her out.

Dante went over to her after painting class. She barely recognized him. 'You look different,' she remarked. He asked her if she would be interested in having coffee, or perhaps a drink with him later on, and she said yes.

'I've rarely seen a man be so emotional,' Vanni told me. 'He kept laughing, and prancing about the room, lighting cigarette after cigarette. The more nervous he was, the more pronounced his lisp became. He must have asked me about a hundred times if and how he should kiss her that night. He even wanted me to practice with him, and I had to push him away several times. It was quite moving to see him like this, and I *wished from the bottom of my heart that their evening together would be successful. But to tell you the truth, I was nervous. Maria was a sophisticated girl. Her upbringing had been very different from Dante's. She came from a rich Roman family. She was indeed very beautiful, and had many men after her, men who were more socially adept and better looking than Dante, who was, quite frankly, very clumsy in his demeanor and looked much younger than his age. Poor boy . . . But I hoped that she would at least grant him a kiss, or some form of attention that would boost his fragile ego.'*

Vanni didn't hear from Omega until the next morning. And when he did, he quickly found out that the news was bad. Maria didn't want him. She had talked all night about the school, her friends, her family. Dante, nervous as he was, drank too many glasses of wine in an attempt to be more eloquent. As a result, he stumbled on his words, and made a total fool of himself. He kissed her on the way out, in the middle of the street, and she gently pushed him away, telling him he stank of wine. 'Puzzi di vino,' she said.

Vanni reassured Dante that it wasn't the end of the world. 'There'll be other chances,' he told him. 'You're going to have to try again.'

The same night, Dante wrote her an apologetic letter, and included a poem by his namesake. It must have had some effect, because she consented to see him again.

'Dante didn't give me all the details of that evening. All I know was that she basically made it clear to our friend that she wasn't interested in him. When he asked

her why, she said something to the extent that she wasn't attracted to him. I think he even asked her to marry him and she laughed. The poor boy was devastated. I did everything I could to make him feel better, to no avail. He became a recluse, and spent long hours painting in the studio that had been placed at our disposal. He didn't let anyone see what he was painting. If anyone approached him, he would brandish his brush and shout. 'Don't come near me!' He had a become a different man, an angry man, who was wounded by love for the second time in his life.

But finally, after two weeks, Dante let me see his painting. There was not only one of them, but two. Two portraits of Maria, and they were absolutely stunning. He had represented her as a Greek goddess. On one, she was sitting down, surrounded by a circle of young men. The landscape was suffused with color. The painting was simply called, Helen and her Suitors. *For each of these masterpieces, he had used a model who looked somewhat like Maria, and finished off her face as he remembered it.*

The second painting was entitled, Aphrodite and Hephaestus. *Here, the landscape was bleak, painted in gray and black tones. Beautiful Aphrodite, adorned with jewels and her feet painted in gold, lay on a bed, with a sad look on her face. Her husband, portrayed as a hunchback, held her hand.'*

In addition to disclosing a previously unrevealed sense of irony, Dante had probably felt empathy towards Hephaestus, the ugliest and least graceful of the Gods, whom Aphrodite, considered to be of utmost beauty, and besieged by hoards of men, had consented to marry. According to Vanni, besides the fact that these two paintings set the ground for a whole new style which eventually became his trademark, they also managed to liberate Dante, and he was able to pursue his activities, spending the majority of his time reading the classics and painting.

'He never mentioned Maria again,' Vanni told me. 'It was very painful for him, mainly, I think because she had obviously rejected him on account of his looks, and, as he often said (though I doubt the truth of this), also on account of his lisp. From the few things you told me about his childhood, Miss Miller, and mind you he never ever told me a word about it, this was probably connected to his school days, and to those terrible memories of his monstrous father, and of feeling small, weak and ugly. I'm sure that's what he felt then, as a child, and what he felt with Maria, as an adult. The only difference was that when he was younger, he didn't have an outlet. When he was older, he did. Painting saved his life. I really believe it. And one can feel it in his work. There is this incredible energy, this sense of victory and triumph over adversity, that radiates from his canvases.'

I asked Vanni if he knew what happened to Maria. He told me that she married some rich Italian, he couldn't remember whom, and had died a few years ago of cancer.

After finishing art school, Omega started working as a part-time teacher, while painting during his spare time.

This went on for two years. He had several shows, which slowly but surely established him on the local art scene. Once he had accumulated some money from his sales, he quit his job, and focused solely on his painting. There is some controversy as to what Omega did during the following fifteen years, until he met Isabella in 1975, at the country house of a friend of his. Vanni moved to Ferrara shortly after the completion of his studies, and married his childhood love. He tried to keep in touch with Omega, exchanging letters with him, occasionally had coffee with him when he would pass through Rome; but after a while, he lost touch with him altogether, to the relief of Vanni's wife who found Omega unbearable.

'He had become an extremely difficult man to be with,' Vanni told me in our last conversation. 'He always appeared to be tired and irritable. He looked unwashed, often got drunk, and boasted about women he had seduced, women whose names he couldn't remember. I found this hard to believe, but didn't let on. He didn't seem to have many friends. His mother had just died that year, I think it was 1960, or 61. I took pity on him, and offered to put him up at my house in Ferrara, where he could rest and paint at his leisure. He refused, even appeared surprised and offended by my invitation: "I'm doing fine. I'm having a show soon, I have some money, so why would I come to rest at your house? I don't need rest." And he got up and left. I have no clue as to what became of him after that.'

Several people have ventured their own speculations as to what Omega's activities were during those fifteen years: his aunt Rosa (an eccentric old woman whom I tracked down in a ramshackle apartment in Naples, and who requested that her answers be remunerated or else she wouldn't talk), claimed that he spent lots of time 'running after girls and doing nothing,' whereas his paternal uncle claimed that he was living on the streets, just like a beggar. One of his neighbors, a certain Andrea Carracio, claimed he spent most of his days and nights indoors, painting and reading. Based upon my deductions about Omega's complex personality, I am thoroughly inclined to believe Carracio. Nevertheless, these enigmatic and solitary years came to an end when he met Isabella Dell' Aquila, the shy daughter of a rich Calabrian art collector with a dubious past.

Isabella's father had taken a passionate interest in Omega's paintings, boasting a collection of nine of his works, thus starting a cycle among other competing collectors, which gradually led the name Omega to be associated with soaring prices, establishing him at first as a national hot commodity, and eventually consecrating him as nothing less than an institution.

The courtship between Omega and the virgin Isabella was brief, the marriage lavish, according to Dell' Aquila's wish. They were married in 1975, and she bore him one daughter Maria, who died of meningitis four months after her birth, in 1976. Isabella's father died one year after his grandchild's birth, of a burst appendix. I have been told that it is around this time that Omega's behavior started to show ominous signs of what was to come. He kept his grief hidden away until time decomposed it into bitterness.

He became subject to frequent bouts of irritation and outbursts of anger, which eventually spiraled into violence. It was very hard for his wife, a simple and good woman, who had never asked anything more than to be married to a decent man, and who found herself exposed to a violent husband, who often denigrated her. She came to view her plight as a curse from God.

These last painful bits were gathered recently, after I visited the Omega residence, and needless to say, I have not included them in my book. Instead, to please the artist and the editors, I have focused on the essentials, and I must admit that until now, it has been going rather smoothly, actually much better than I anticipated. After checking each chapter for accuracy, Jaurel sends me to Ensor Mason for editorial purposes. This has become a monthly routine which I have come to despise, mostly because of Mason's irritatingly perspicacious comments, which often lead me to rewrite whole sections, reducing the amount of time I have left.

I realize only now how easy writing this has been, especially in comparison to this block I've been having lately. How am I to finish this if I have nothing left to say?

I sit back at my desk and stare at the ceiling. As Jaurel keeps emphasizing, half of the art world is anxiously awaiting this book. The responsibility is on my shoulders, and the burden of it is starting to weigh unusually heavily on me. My eyelids slam together like the abrupt closing of a door, and I am swept into a labyrinth of semi-conscious dreams, sweet and sour images of two men dancing endlessly on a tightrope in a deserted circus.

*

I moved into this apartment a year ago. Three years after I had left Otto. My favorite photograph of him (the one where he's sitting on a rocking-chair with his hair slicked back and his blue eyes softly gazing at me) still lies somewhere amongst the dusty boxes that are piled up in my storage closet. I don't need to look at the photograph; it's enough for me to know that it's there.

I met Otto when I was living in Paris. Having been fascinated with French culture from an early age, I had always had romantic visions of myself living and working there, perhaps spending the rest of my days in a farmhouse in Provence. Two years after I had completed my degree at Barnard College, I packed my suitcases and flew to the yearned-for city of lights, where I had been guaranteed admission at the Ecole du Louvre.

It is in Paris that I married Otto, at the age of twenty-five. Though we separated one year later, the period of our engagement, during which we were living together at his apartment on the Ile St Louis, and our first married months together, in New York, were no doubt among the happiest, so far, of my adult life. While at first I could not fathom the reason for this happiness, I have since realized, many years and tears later, that I loved Otto because he was so exotic to me, so much more worldly and sophisticated than anyone I had ever encountered in my sheltered New York life. While most people I knew saw the world as a threatening and dangerous place, Otto plunged right into it, immersing himself in its wonders and dangers, always re-emerging on the surface, seemingly wiser and stronger every time, and always ready to condemn my vulnerability. 'You live too much in fear,' he often told me, 'you should just go for it, like I do. Get tougher, embrace what life has to offer; don't shy away from it.'

Otto seemed invincible to me. He knew how to appreciate life without the daily neurosis which afflicts most of us – or so I believed until I realized that he was afflicted with a neurosis that was far greater than mine. But as far as I knew back then, his energy and often exhausting enthusiasm made him more appealing to me: here was a man who wasn't afraid of anything, a man who was willing to cross dangerous frontiers for the sake of his art – most of his photographs were taken in precarious conditions (wars, revolutions, danger zones) – a man who could hold a conversation with practically anyone, always maintaining an equal level of grace with his interlocutors.

These traits made me love him even more, although today they merely make me scoff. There were also his dashing looks and his impeccable sense of style, his smooth way of resolving what seemed to be insoluble difficulties. And of course there is the fact that Otto was rich, and contributed to making my life very comfortable as well as exciting.

These are all attributes which seem quite superficial today. But I was twenty-five at the time, and back then, these things seemed not only as bright as the Parisian lights, but challenging and enticing, virtually irresistible. And most important of all, I was convinced that I could change this man, better him. I would help him get rid of his frequent need to use drugs, encourage him to work more assiduously, and teach him how to face life in a more salubrious way: I was going to mold Otto into the perfect man.

These grand ideas were short-lived, and far more quix-otic than I realized. The downfall came slowly, the gruesome slide towards destruction which landed him in a recovery center somewhere in Minnesota. I chose not to go see him, nor did he ask to see me, although he did express a wish to be divorced as quickly as possible. I acquiesced and hired an expensive lawyer. The divorce was settled two and a half years ago. I was left with a substan-tially smaller amount of money than my lawyer had led me to expect, which made me wonder if I hadn't been swindled by Otto who could have hindered the process by concocting some ingenious scam or other, such as under-reporting his assets, something I wouldn't put past him. But perhaps this is mere paranoia on my part, a leftover of the slippery slope I had to follow him through, a selfish slide where my presence in his life was but a mere reassur-ance that he wasn't alone on board, and that whatever he did to himself, I would be there to save him. 'Death is the only limit to the dark side,' he repeatedly told me; 'any-thing short of that is only exploration.'

I was the one who found him lying in the tiled stall of our Mercer Street bathroom, the shower on, blood dripping down his nose, his face blue, his fingers limp. I stared at his naked body, letting the water run over him, a last call for purification – a pathetic attempt no less.

I was told later on that he had suffered a massive heart attack, and that the cause was cocaine abuse. It was a miracle he was still alive, the doctor confessed to me later on, as I sat in the waiting room of St Vincent's hospital. 'He's got a sturdy heart,' he added, a comment which left me surprisingly cold.

I chose to leave that day. I packed my belongings from the Mercer Street loft, said goodbye one last time to the creaky bed, the tiled bathroom, the enormous living-room that we had entertained in so often, the skylight in the kitchen, and the dying ficus trees. I stood on the street with several suitcases, hailing a taxi with tears pouring down my cheeks.

I stayed with my friends Thea and Adam. I plodded through *The New York Times* real-estate section, and within five days found a small apartment in the West-Village. I went to see *Splendor in the Grass* with them at the Thalia Soho Theater, and cried so much at the ending that Adam gently kissed my lips in sympathy, Thea took offense and I had to calm them both down as Thea pressed Adam to explain why in the world had he felt the need to kiss me and Adam shrugged his shoulders and repeatedly answered, avoiding my gaze, that he couldn't explain why. I suspected that one of the main reasons, disregarding a certain empathy he must have felt for my then desperate state of mind, was related to that memorable evening we had spent kissing through a Cassavetes film and later on my kitchen floor, kissing languorously as Otto slept soundly in the next room, dead drunk. As Adam slipped off my shirt, whispering tantalizing things in my ear, we both heard a sharp noise coming from the bedroom. Adam sprung up, fastened his belt and dashed out of the loft like lightning. I never found out what the noise had been. But this unresolved moment between us left a certain exciting tension which, for one reason or another, we never dared indulge in. Soon after that he met Thea, a frail freckled redhead from NYU Film School who dyed her hair black two weeks after meeting him. I liked Thea. She was bright and pretty in an unusual way, and blushed profusely when she laughed. The spectacle of her adoration for Adam, an extremely good-looking and mediocre painter, was so painful to behold, I chose to stop seeing them for a while after I left their shabby Bowery apartment.

I moved into my present apartment on a rainy day. I clutched the brand new keys in my hands feverishly, feeling the sweat stick to my palms like honey. As I entered my new space, a sudden childish freedom overtook me, and I had to sit on the bare wooden floor, my legs crossed, my head resting against the freshly painted white walls. I remained there for a long time, listening to light raindrops fall on the leaves of the oak tree outside, as the summer sun gave way to dusk, a pink glow in the sky, smooth shadows around me, and a dreamlike vision of hope overwhelmed me.

There is a Greek myth about the sculptor Pygmalion, which goes as follows: although he scorned the society of women, he did admire Aphrodite, the goddess of love. He made a marble statue in her effigy, of such beauty that he fell in love with it. Alas, a statue being a statue, it did not reciprocate his love. Aphrodite was moved when hearing this story, and she decided to act upon her emotion. So one day, while Pygmalion was hugging the lifeless statue, it suddenly started moving and reciprocated his kisses; it was alive.

Omega's two paintings of Pygmalion are probably among his most striking. In the first one, entitled *Pygmalion I:*

The Despair, an old man wearing dark shabby clothes, squeezes a marble statue of a young woman. His head is jerked backwards as he holds her, his eyes are semi-open, his cheeks pale, and there are creases folded on his forehead like pleats. His hands, entwined around the woman's waist, betray an almost surreal strength, as the fingers clutch the lifeless material, the bones and muscles curved in an eagle-like position.

Besides the masterly technique in which the painting is done (the poignancy of the moment, the harmony of the bright yellows, greens and pinks, the disconcerting way in which one is drawn into the painting and the artist's world), the sense of desperation and blind hope that emanates from the work is truly remarkable.

In *Pygmalion II: The Metamorphosis*, we notice that the statue has moved. The young woman is now resting on one foot, as the other one is bent backwards, pointing graciously upwards. She is laughing, her hair looks slightly disheveled, and she is seemingly offering herself to Pygmalion, her arms stretched out towards him in amused surrender.

Pygmalion stands upright, motionless. The lines on his forehead are now gone, his hands are tightly clasped together as if in prayer. He seems to be crying, given the way in which his lips curve downward, and the room in which both stand now shines with an uncanny light.

Omega paints from life, except for a few of the settings in his renditions of mythological scenes, which he copies from illustrations. Although it was once rumored that he used a projector for the totality of his work, the contention was quickly dropped when a television program on him was nationally broadcast, showing, besides an in-depth interview, the artist concentrating on a life-size painting he had been working on for a few months. As a woman and child sat for him, his paint brush slowly swept the canvas, producing with near perfection, a cheek, then a nose, pink lips and the soft and creamy white face of the infant, all this in an unusually fleeting lapse of time.

Most of Omega's work deals with Greek mythology; images of gods and goddesses, ancient cities and battles. He has also painted still-lifes and landscapes (notably a strikingly detailed one of Rome which he took five years to finish), and a few portraits of friends and family: his wife Isabella standing next to a window on a rainy day; Isabella sleeping on a burgundy couch; the writer Matteo Salesi smoking a pipe and holding the newspaper *Il Tempo* in a disgruntled way. There is also a self-portrait of the artist looking at himself in a mirror, one hand cupped around his gray beard, the other holding a paint brush. His stony brown eyes seem to stare directly at the viewer, and his mouth is slightly open, as if he were about to smile.

Omega's paintings are mostly large-sized canvases (varying from three to eight feet in height, and from five to ten feet in width) which he stretches himself. The man is, to say the least, eccentric and difficult to bear. The two occasions I've managed to interview Omega have revealed, as I had been led to expect, an impatient and often aggressive man, who, after twenty minutes or so, would end his sentences by turning his back and walking away, all the while grumbling to himself. Merely getting him to come back and sit down with me has proven to be a highly stressful process, which, during my first trip to his studio, included a whole array of insults, ranging from 'you do not understand artists' to 'please leave my place now'.

Needless to say, I do not have much sympathy for the man, and if it weren't for his art, and for the terrible childhood and misfortunes he endured, I would probably have utter contempt for him. But I have remained quite patient with him, and as I got to know him better, I decided he must be treated like a child; it is always easier to forgive a child. Especially an unloved one.

Omega's English is barely rudimentary. He still lisps, although very slightly, and continues to be overweight. I imagine he looks quite similar to the way he did as a child, except of course for his beard and the striking gravity of his face. His way of dealing with the world is basically to ignore it. Some of his friends I interviewed for the book claimed jokingly that not only does he paint the Ancient Greeks but he lives with them as well. 'Not only that,' one of them added, 'but he doesn't own a watch and can tell the time by looking at the sun and the stars.'

Though I cannot help but admire the results this constant and imperturbable obliviousness have produced, I did suffer additional bouts of impatience in his presence, especially the day I landed in the heat of a Roman August, and arrived at his apartment sweating profusely, only to find that he wasn't there. This day has stuck with me since then, not only because of his unexpected absence and because it was the last encounter I had with him, but also because it was during that stay that I discovered his erotic lithographs.

Not only did this discovery lead me to believe that I

had witnessed something I was not necessarily supposed to see (or broadcast, as far as Jaurel was concerned), but the eeriness and mystery that seemed to surround the discovery made me realize that I had stumbled upon something of utmost importance, and that if brought to the public eye, these lithographs would shed a whole new light on this man's work.

Let us begin in Rome. I arrived around 9.00 a.m. at the Hotel Victoria, near the Via del Corso. I ordered some breakfast, took a cold shower, applied some make-up, and jumped into a cab to the Omega residence, a large and cluttered apartment in the Trastevere quarter.

Isabella, a short and stubby woman with rosy cheeks and tired eyes, led me to the living-room and told me I could wait there if I wanted to, he would be back shortly. She offered me some peach juice and I sat silently in the airy room, my legs stretched out on the worn out and stained white carpet.

After a long half-hour, Isabella came back into the room and started to speak very fast, her arms darting about the room, her cheeks red.

'Dante just called on telephone, he no come back,' she said in her broken English, 'Dante busy in another città for printing.'

'What?' I exclaimed, already imagining Jaurel's discombobulated face at the end of the line as I broke the news to him, 'What do you mean? What city?'

'He far away. Not come back today. Tomorrow. Yes. Tomorrow. He very sorry. Me too very sorry,' she said, embarrassed.

'Please Signora Omega,' I said in a softer voice, 'what

if he doesn't come back tomorrow? What am I supposed to do if that happens?'

'I said, he will come tomorrow. He in other città.'

'Well, which città is that, Signora Omega? Tell me, which city is your husband in? I could go and meet him wherever he is. You see, I've got to be back in New York in three days, this is very important, I have to finish this book. You understand, don't you?'

At that same moment, there was a knock on the door. Isabella hurriedly went to open it, mumbling to herself on the way. She opened the door, her back turned to me, her corpulent body lodged in the doorway, obstructing my view of her interlocutor. I heard a cough and a demure female voice. Isabella responded to it quickly and in a low voice, so that I couldn't hear a word of what she was saying. A sudden impulse made me get up and walk discreetly towards Isabella. What I saw in the next fleeting moment, remains to this day vague and indistinct. Before she turned and ran away, I caught a glimpse of a female profile with long dark hair. I do not recall what the face looked like, but I know that it belonged to a young girl with dark skin and long legs. The way the young girl ran was odd: her arms were stretched out in front of her, as if she were about to take flight, or perhaps playing some obscure game. I also remember thinking that her hair looked as if it hadn't been brushed in a long time.

When Isabella closed the door, I asked her who the girl was. Her answer was brief. It was the neighbor's daughter, she said. I didn't ask any further questions, but felt that something was amiss. I didn't have time to pursue that thought since Isabella's voice came floating back to my ears, reiterating that it would be better if I dropped by tomorrow, I would be sure to find her husband. 'Could I at least talk to him on the telephone?' I asked, 'Just to remind him that I'm here?'

She shook her head, and this time I saw she was getting impatient. 'Per favore signorina, non è a Roma. I don't know where he is. I can't tell you nothing. I don't know nothing. You come back tomorrow.'

It was obviously of no use. I went back to my hotel and slept soundly until that evening. I called up my friend Sarah, an old Parisian acquaintance now living in Rome whom, despite the rarity of our meetings, I always delighted in seeing.

Sarah told me to meet her in a restaurant on Piazza Farnese, right behind the Campo dei Fiori. She arrived nearly a half-hour late, and apologized profusely, blaming it on her newly acquired Italian habits.

She looked older than the last time I had seen her, and had gained some weight. Her long curly hair was tied into a braid. She wore an unflattering dress, no make-up, and I suddenly felt awkward with her. It didn't feel like it used to, when, after our Ecole du Louvre classes, we would linger in cafés and restaurants, drinking carafes of red wine and smoking too many cigarettes. So many years had passed, or so it seemed.

We reminisced about old times, and she asked me about Otto. I told her I'd prefer not to talk about him. She smiled and said she understood perfectly. I ordered pasta then veal, and I noticed that she had barely touched her salad; I did not say anything.

Later on, after we had practically finished a bottle of

red wine, she told me she was pregnant. Her eyes were shining, but it wasn't from happiness. It was from too much wine and what seemed to be despair. The father, she said, had been a one-night stand. His name was Giuseppe, she had tried to find out where he lived, but to no avail. She had tried to call him and let him know, but he had left her a wrong number. And to make matters worse, she had recently found out why it was so hard to get in touch with him: he was rumored to be some kind of a con-artist. Everything about him was fake. His address, his phone number, his profession. For all she knew, his name was fake as well.

I shook my head in disbelief, and told her how sorry I was.

'There's no need,' she attempted to smile, 'it's life. I always suspected life was a game, a game of compromises, and here is my proof.'

I remained silent and put my fork down; I had a knot in my stomach.

'Well,' I asked, overcome by a sudden curiosity, 'tell me at least what this guy pretended to be?'

She tried to smile as she explained; he had claimed to be working in an advertising company. How could she have known? He was good-looking, very well dressed, drove a nice car. He had implied that he was interested in settling down, so of course, naive as she was, she took it as an indirect compliment. 'And most of all,' Sarah said, finishing her glass of wine, 'he was probably one of the greatest lovers I ever had.'

She slammed her glass back down, and lowered her head.

'Sarah,' I said softly, 'if I can be of any help to you . . .'

She lifted her head, and I noticed her eyes were full of tears. 'It's okay Laura, it's my choice. I'm doing this to myself, I've got to deal with it.'

'Are you sure you want this child?' I asked.

'Yes, I do.'

'And you want to bring it up alone?'

'What other choice have I got?'

I paused. Then I asked her if she ever bumped into him again, would she tell him that she was bearing his child? Of course not, Sarah answered. And what if she told him and he decided to recognize the child? I asked, realizing that I might be treading on dangerous ground.

'God, Laura . . .' Sarah answered, looking at me strangely, 'let's not totally delude ourselves. And besides,' she added, 'do I really want my child to grow up with a con-artist as a father? No. I don't.'

'Sarah, how are you going to support this child?' Now I was starting to feel aggravated by what I perceived as her irresponsibility. 'I have some money of my own. You know, my family and everything . . . And I've always wanted a baby.' She shrugged her shoulders, and I felt a deep wave of pity for her. 'Sarah,' I said, taking hold of her hand, 'Sarah, it may not be too late! How many months pregnant are you?'

'Eighteen weeks,' she answered.

There was nothing left to say. I ordered the check, dropped her off at her apartment in the Trieste quarter on the other side of town, and promised to call her the next day.

I wished I could help Sarah, but I didn't know how. I

cared for her, despite our intermittent meetings, and swore to myself that I would keep in touch with her. I had let her down, as I had many of my other friends; I would have to find the time to call her regularly and make sure she was okay.

I tossed and turned until the sun came out. I felt overwhelmed by the events of that evening. It seemed that I was suddenly, in the space of those twenty-four hours, regaining some lucidity which I had lost during the course of this last year.

Life was dirty, unruly, tough. Happiness and success were strangers to most of the population. I had been a lucky and spoiled child. I obviously had more to learn. And as for mature lucidity, perhaps I hadn't ever reached that point, perhaps reality was starting to seep into my brain for the first time; it was a germ, an incurable disease that I would have to learn to live with. Like everybody else. Or almost.

The next day, I was back at the Omega residence. As I had suspected, Dante was nowhere to be seen. Isabella fretted about the house, begging me to just sit there patiently and he would show up, but one hour later I lost patience. After being once again denied a phone call on the grounds that she didn't know his phone number because he had never given it to her (something I had trouble believing), I finally coerced Isabella into telling me where her much feared husband was. He was in a printing house in Pomezia. He did not like to be bothered there, and would probably be angry at her for revealing, his whereabouts. I thanked her profusely and promised never to bother her again. I jumped into a taxi, and half-an-hour later I was standing on a train platform on my way to Pomezia.

The train ride was fifteen minutes. I got off in a modern station, and asked someone for directions to the printing house. It was three minutes away, I was told. As I walked, I noticed the hills were lower and drier here. It was a mixture of the country and an industrial town, which, I learned, had its boom in the 1960s, when a lot of Roman industries moved here, later abandoning their warehouses to artists.

I found Omega, thanks to the help of an American woman I met in a caffé right next door to the train station.

'It's in there,' the woman said, a fake blonde who wore a tight green dress and a straw hat. She pointed her long silver nail towards the tiny battered door of a shabby building and announced that she was actually waiting for her boyfriend who worked there. If I bumped into him his name was Peter, I should tell him that she had brought him what he wanted, and she was getting very hot waiting for him in this bloody caffé with wasps all over the place.

I remarked on the fact that the place looked decrepit. 'Well, what do you expect,' she snickered, 'with all the shit that's been going on in there these days . . .'

This remark puzzled me. 'What do you mean?' I asked.

She looked at me, and shrugged her shoulders. 'Never mind what I mean. The usual shit I guess.'

When I asked her once again to elaborate on her remark, she looked at me impatiently, took a loud sip of her limonata, and informed me that the printing house was on the fourth floor with no elevator, after all what did I expect this was Italy not America, people didn't take as many things for granted here.

I walked slowly up the long staircase, wondering if this statement was intended to be an indirect apology for the state of the elevator industry in Italy, or a defensive and somewhat patronizing attitude, rather typical of those foreigners who have spent lots of time abroad, and who feel a guilty patriotism towards their adopted land.

Then it occurred to me that it simply could have been a quick and easy way to change the topic of conversation which had evidently taken an unwanted turn. I pondered this last thought, wondering what she had meant about the 'usual shit' that was happening at the printing house. My thoughts were interrupted by the realization that the sleeves of my white summer dress were getting stained on the way up, as the banister was coated with fresh varnish. By the time I got upstairs I was not only mumbling at the sad state of my attire, but I was so hot and thirsty, my mouth felt drained of all its saliva.

I found Omega in the back, drinking tea with a tall, elegant man who stopped talking when he saw me. 'Can I help you?' he asked, raising a bushy eyebrow.

'Mr Omega,' I said, speaking breathlessly, 'I am Laura Miller, we were supposed to meet yesterday at your house, I came all the way from New York, I'd really like to talk to you.'

He frowned and stared at me incredulously. 'How you found me?' he asked, 'Who told you I'm here?'

'Your wife,' I said, 'she told—'

'My wife!' he roared, 'I tell her always *never* to say where I am, *never*!'

He rose out of his chair and darted out of the room, leaving me and the elegant man slightly bewildered.

'Jean-Pierre Malat,' he said, shaking my hand. 'I suppose you are used to our friend's habits,' he said revealing a polished white smile.

'Well, not quite,' I said, smiling for probably the first time in the whole day.

'I understand you are writing about Dante,' he said politely.

Then ensued a long and tedious conversation about our mutual friend, whose disappearance was beginning to irritate me to such an extent, that I had to cut Jean-Pierre Malat short. 'I'm sorry,' I said, 'but I really have to go and find him.'

I found Omega standing in the other room, looking out of the window and talking to himself in a low voice. I remained still behind him, not daring to interrupt, wondering when I was going to faint from dehydration. He was speaking fast, almost chanting. It sounded like an Arabic prayer, especially in the way that he tilted his body forward every so often. I couldn't understand what he was saying, but from the teary and monotonous tone of his voice, it was clearly not something he was joyful about. I cleared my throat after a short while, and decided to interrupt. After all, this could go on for hours, and I did not have that much time to spare.

'I'm sorry Mr Omega,' I said, 'but I do need to talk to you.'

He turned around and stared at me blankly. 'Yes,' he said slowly, 'what do you want?'

'I came all the way here to talk to you; as I mentioned

before, we had made arrangements to meet yesterday in Rome.'

I knew my voice sounded irritated, my American accent in Italian was probably very noticeable, but I didn't make any effort to conceal any of it.

He shook his head and motioned me to sit down. He then slapped his thick hands against his knees and yawned. 'Please, go ahead, Miss Laura, I am listening.'

As I bent down to get my tape-recorder and my note-book, I felt suddenly dizzy.

I asked him for some water in a polite voice, and he pointed towards an old stove, atop which stood a pot of fresh tea. I didn't dare ask for anything else, so I found myself drinking hot mint tea in the heat of the day.

'That is how Bedouins do it,' he explained in his Nea-politan Italian, 'they wear wool and drink hot tea in summer. It is very good for you. Stops thirst.'

I drank in silence. The tea was, I had to admit, thirst-quenching. After an awkward moment of silence, I turned my tape-recorder on, and began interviewing him. He answered all of my questions, as if it were some admin-istrative duty or a multiple question exam. His answers were short, elliptical, and, I was almost glad to hear, arro-gant; at least his apparent obliviousness contained more than met the eye, considering the abrupt way in which he reacted to some of my thoroughly researched questions.

As one hour ticked by, he became more and more impatient, until he finally got up and said that was enough, he wanted to go home. He clumsily tucked his jeans shirt into his orange shorts, and managed a painful smile. 'Goodbye Miss Miller,' he said. His eyes sent me an enigmatic spark, and I was suddenly left alone, with the sound of his footsteps resonating against the bare and cold floor.

I rewound the interview, and walked around the printing house. Compared to the previous rather disastrous meetings I had had with him, this one had gone very well. I felt content.

As I walked towards the exit, I noticed that everybody seemed to have gone home, and there was an eerie silence about the large and airy room. Three color lithographs were tucked into a corner of the room, and I picked them up gingerly, mumbling to myself about how careless certain people can be. One of the lithographs was unfinished; a bearded man on a small boat (probably Odysseus), waving to a woman with hair down to her feet.

The other lithograph struck me, not only because of its subject matter, but also because it was unlike any other work of Omega's. It represented a naked young woman, lying on a wooden floor. Her legs were spread out. Her right hand was curved, her wrist touching her pubic hair, her fingers seemingly inside her vagina. Her left hand was clutching her left breast. The young woman's hair was somewhat covering her face, but one could tell that her mouth was open and her eyes closed. The lithograph was erotic in a vulgar way. It made me shiver and I put it down quickly, as if I had just burned my fingers. I looked at it again as it rested on the press. Its title was *Muse III*. The date was fairly recent; the artist proof number was listed as 14/100. There was no signature to be seen, except for a little sign at the bottom right hand side of the painting which looked like this: α

I picked up another lithograph. The same young

woman (recognizable only from her body) was sitting on a wooden chair, her arms tied upwards, her feet attached by white ribbons to the legs of the chair. Her head was bent backwards (concealing her face once again), her legs spread apart, revealing drops of blood which trailed along her thighs onto the chair and the floor, forming a small puddle at her feet.

It was an extremely disturbing lithograph, which verged on the pornographic. For one brief moment I wondered whether this could be the same hand that had painted all those arresting themes from Greek mythology. I looked at it closer. The title was the same, although the serial number and Roman numeral were different. This one was called *Muse IV.* Although none of these works were signed, they all bore the same symbol on the right hand side of the lithographs. The technique was the same, removing any immediate doubt I had concerning the artist's identity; this was the hand, the unmistakable style that I knew. It was Omega in all his splendor, his inhibitions released on paper, a jumble of erotica, pornography, and raw talent.

As I put the lithographs back down, taking a last look at them, a strange feeling came over me. I couldn't help but feel that notwithstanding their erotic content, the model in the lithographs seemed to betray a tender intimacy with the artist that was not merely professional, a thought I quickly dismissed as irrelevant. The pornographic and disturbing aspect of the lithographs were redeemed by the poignancy of the work, and that was the most important quality. The means that the artist had used to achieve that poignancy were none of my business. I pulled out my notebook, grabbed a red pen out of my bag, and wrote down, '<u>ask</u> <u>Jaurel about Muse</u>,' underlining it heavily.

I closed my bag shut, and was about to step out the door when a strongly built man suddenly appeared on my left side and grabbed my arm.

'Chi sei, che fai qui?' he asked me with a heavy foreign accent.

I started abruptly and told him my name. 'I was here interviewing Mr Omega,' I said, trying to keep my voice firm and professional.

He let go of my arm. 'Nobody's allowed in here after hours,' he said in a perfect American accent. 'I'm sorry I scared you, but I'm not supposed to let anyone in, it's the rule here,' he added apologetically.

'I came in here a while ago, I just finished interviewing Mr Omega. I was on my way out,' I said coldly, looking at the man straight in the eye.

'Okay, that's fine, I didn't realize. I guess everybody left much earlier today, it's a holiday here, they're all going away, so I'm on duty for the next twenty-four hours.'

I smiled. 'I understand,' I said. 'Well, good luck.'

As I was about to walk out the door, the man suddenly extended his hand, introduced himself as Peter, and began to ask me questions about my American origins. I had to stop him short, explaining that I didn't want to miss my train, and by the way his friend was waiting for him downstairs in the café, she'd like him to come down. He shrugged his shoulders and said let her wait, a comment I chose to ignore, mainly because his tone betrayed a desire to open up to me, something I had no intention of encouraging.

I quickly said goodbye, and rushed out the door before he had time to ask me anything else. As I walked outside I sighed with relief. I noticed empty spaces and smoke coming out of some of the huge factories around me, adding yet another sinister dimension to this industrial town; I couldn't wait to get back to Rome.

As I accelerated my pace, I could feel a subtle and pleasant breeze caressing my neck, a welcome occurrence in the heat of August. I let my hair down, took out my compact, added some chapstick on to my dried-out lips. As I was about to put the compact back in my bag, I heard a noise behind me. I turned around. No one was there. Just the bleak landscape and a few rusty cars. But for some unexplainable reason, I didn't feel alone. I had the suspicion that I was being followed. I looked around again. There was no one around me. I attributed my fear to the eeriness of my immediate surroundings, and when I saw the train station looming in the close horizon, I felt reassured. Once on the train I fell asleep, and fifteen minutes later was awakened by a portly woman who smelled of fish. 'Roma, Signorina,' she said, shaking me rather violently, 'Stazione Termini.'

Two

I met Otto when I was living in Paris, in a small one-bedroom apartment on the top floor of a building on the Rue Tournefort, right by the Mouffetard Market. I found that apartment through an American student who took classes with me in nineteenth-century painting at the Ecole du Louvre.

I painted the walls myself, and despite the limited size of both rooms, I managed to create a homely and rustic atmosphere, brightened by the direct sunlight and view of the Parisian rooftops, adding a cheerful note to my new-found feeling of independence.

Around six months after my arrival, my money started to run out. Instead of calling my mother up (which I had done until then, perpetually bemused and spoiled by the extravagant sums of money she would wire me) I decided to fend for myself and to get a job. My French was fluent by now, and I decided that there was no reason why I shouldn't try.

I found a job almost immediately. I was having coffee with some Ecole du Louvre friends, when a girl who had been sitting silently until then, the girlfriend of one of my fellow students, Jean-Luc, started to complain about her job, the fact that she hated her boss so much, and that, thank God, she only had two more weeks to go. She said she had just quit that morning, and hoped she would find another job soon. The girl's name was Sophie. She wore torn jeans, cowboy boots, and a tight red lycra shirt which revealed large breasts. She looked older than she probably was, somewhere between twenty and twenty-two years old. She had long golden hair, a perfectly proportioned body and an arrogant look on her face. She was undeniably beautiful, despite the excessive amount of make-up she wore around her eyes. As she raised her hand to light a cigarette, I noticed that her nails were bitten to the quick.

I had heard about Sophie before. She was said to be madly in love with Jean-Luc, a handsome and bright young man whom I had been infatuated with for a short time, though I gave up once I realized that my interest was not reciprocated. Jean-Luc was said to be unfaithful to Sophie, although that rumor was never corroborated. Actually, both of them seemed to elicit rumors wherever they went, so I chose to disregard all of them when I moved my chair closer to Sophie's, and asked her to tell me more about her job.

'Are you looking for work?' she asked immediately.

'Yes, I am. I'm planning to quit the Ecole du Louvre.

'Why would you want to quit?' She looked at me from behind her long eyelashes and took a drawn-out drag on her cigarette.

'I just don't feel that I'm really learning anything. The classes are so impersonal, the teachers all seem to be per-petually stressed out, and I figure I could learn just as much from reading books. Plus, I'm really sick and tired of taking exams.' (I later regretted this impulsive whim of mine; I could have easily completed my year there. And although my reasons for quitting were convincing enough, the truth of the matter was that I was young, and much more interested in taking advantage of the Parisian social and night life, than its crammed classrooms.)

My answer to Sophie's question prompted her to list a litany of complaints and grievances she held against her parents, who, if she ever did quit school 'would freak out and never talk to me again. You're really lucky you have open-minded parents,' she said in an envious voice, 'mine are real stiff asses.'

We went on to talk about various topics pertaining to parents, boyfriends and broken hearts, until I veered the conversation to what I was most interested in, namely her job.

'Do you know anything about that job you're giving up? I mean, do you know if she's looking for someone or—'

'If you want my job you can have it. With open arms. Yes, my boss is looking for someone, so why not drop off your resumé? It's the Moher Gallery, you've probably heard of it, it's pretty famous. Anyway, I'll be leaving next week, so there you go! But I have to warn you, she's a real bitch.'

Then she laughed, and pushed her mane of hair away from her face. 'Well, she's not that bad,' she said apologetically, 'she's just a real pain in the ass. But you'll get used to her. You have working papers, right?'

I told her that I had a special visa which enabled me to work twenty hours a week. If Madame Moher was willing to compromise and pay me the rest 'under the table', I would consider myself lucky. If not, well, tant pis, a part-time job would be better than nothing.

'I don't know,' Sophie said, looking skeptical, 'Madame Moher is not exactly the most flexible person . . . But you never know, right?'

'Right.' We both laughed, and switched to other topics, and by the end of the conversation and a last cup of coffee, she left me her phone number and wished me good luck. 'If I don't see you when you drop by, give me a call, and tell me what happens,' she said, as we kissed goodbye and parted ways.

Three weeks later, I was working at the Moher Gallery on the Rue Mazarine. Not only did she hire me on the spot, but she agreed to bending the rules a little, and paid me my remaining twenty hours in cash. At first, my job consisted of menial duties such as answering the phone and typing letters for Madame Moher. As for lunch breaks, they were rather short, too short for my taste, but I never dared bring up the issue. I got used to gobbling down a quick croque-monsieur at La Palette, the café next door which had become my second home.

Madame Moher was a tall and lanky woman in her early fifties, who wore no make-up, and whose thick gray hair was pulled into a tight bun. Her thin lips always seemed to be chapped, and she seldom smiled. Her glasses often slid down to the tip of her nose, and would remain there sometimes for hours, a sight that drove me crazy. She liked to wear loose dresses and skirts, usually with plain dark silk shirts, closed off by a large gold pin which she wore too frequently.

Despite her rather unattractive features and stingy habits, Madame Moher was overall a nice woman. Her husband, Hervé Moher, the founder of the gallery and, as rumors went, a formidable and quite impressive man in his heyday, had died in the late seventies, leaving her the job of running his widely successful enterprise.

Rumors were that she had continued her late husband's business halfheartedly. But being a devout and loyal woman who seemingly still mourned her husband's death, she took over the business with resolute stoicism, and managed, though with some financial difficulties, to maintain its reputation.

I admired her dignity, and that is one of the many reasons why I stuck it out with her, despite the fact that some of my Parisian friends warned me that she was an embittered old witch who would only take advantage of me.

I attributed their prejudices to Sophie's slandering of Madame Moher. And when I asked the latter how she had gotten along with Sophie Werther, her face seemed to drop, and her mouth took on a bitter expression. 'We did not get along,' she answered superciliously, 'I needn't say more.'

By the time I had been working there for three months, I was promoted to the position of assistant, and Madame Moher announced in her usual dry and mingy way, that I now had the 'luck and great fortune' of becoming a salesperson in her gallery. She then was quick to add that it was a title I should not take lightly, considering the responsibility such a bestowal can entail. And as for a commission on the works, well, we would have to discuss that later. For now, all I had to concentrate on was working as hard as possible, 'sans plaintes et sans problèmes,' and she would be glad to address the financial issue when the proper time came.

The proper time did come (I apparently fulfilled her wish to keep problems and complaints out of her way) not without my surprise and to my friends' bewilderment. After five months, she offered me a 10 per cent commission on all works I sold, and after eight months, she took me out to the brasserie Lipp for lunch, to celebrate my first major sale, a de Chirico painting.

I was pleased to notice the attentiveness of the waiters and the maître d'hotel towards her. I asked her if she came here often, and she answered, in a firm voice, that this was the restaurant where Hervé used to lunch. It was the first time I had heard her utter his first name. I attempted a compassionate smile, but was quickly rebuked when she cleared her throat and admitted that she attributed the success of the de Chirico sale to the length of my skirt.

This non-sequitur surprised me; bluntness was not an attribute Madame Moher was wont to display; and the fact that it was tinted with humor made it even more unusual. I was taken aback a second time when she suddenly burst out laughing, the wrinkles around her face magically relaxed, her eyes sparkling with a new light. She raised her glass of white wine and proposed a toast to our success. 'It's fine,' she said, 'you did a good job. Keep on wearing those skirts of yours.'

I nodded my head and raised my glass, unable to say a word. I put the glass down and nervously played with some bread crumbs, while, as was her custom, she quickly changed the topic of conversation to how good the 'harengs pomme à l'huile' were. I muttered something to the effect that I was sure they were (although I've always had a profound aversion to herring), and finally sighed with relief; I felt as if she had finally let me in on one of her most intimate secrets, this one being that not only did she have a heart, but she cared about life's little comforts, and for some reason I imagined to be a painful one, did not let herself take advantage of them. Perhaps I acted as some kind of a catalyst, in that my youth and ambition reminded her of her early days. Or perhaps she merely felt comfortable with me. Whatever it was, I felt her relax in my presence that day, as well as during the following weeks and months, and that set off a complicity between us which lasted until Otto arrived.

He walked into the gallery on a rainy spring afternoon. He wore a black leather jacket over a pair of jeans and a white shirt. His long dark hair was slicked back, his blue eyes sparkled in the gray afternoon, and his lips bore a familiar pout, this being a defensive trait seemingly common among those artists seeking gallery representation. He was undeniably handsome, although in a chameleon-like way. His expressions added charm to his manner. On the other hand, and much to my relief, some of his features were unattractive as well, such as his stout hands and the space between his two front teeth.

He introduced himself in a low Italian-accented voice, pronouncing his name very clearly, so clearly that for one short moment I wondered whether I should have known of his existence beforehand. 'You probably don't accept slides or portfolios,' he immediately plunged in, 'but I brought mine anyway. I know that the best entrance to a gallery is through another person, you know, the whole connection thing, but this is where it stands right now; I need representation and I know I'm good.'

'If you're so good,' I couldn't help but retort, 'why don't you have anyone?' I immediately blushed at the sound of my own voice, principally because I rarely used dry sarcasm with anybody, especially not at a first encounter, unless I was either attracted or put off by that person. I decided that in this case, I was most definitely put off.

'I do have someone,' Otto answered with a smirk on his lips, 'she lives in Caracas. I'm going to see her next week actually.'

Then he burst out laughing at the sight of my unamused face, and said something to the effect that this was a joke, didn't I have a sense of humor and what was my name anyway. I muttered my name under my breath. He lit a cigarette and sat on my desk. He told me about himself, about how this was the first gallery he had stopped in, he knew Hervé a long time ago, in the good old days, and as a matter of fact Hervé had almost offered him a show, but had died before anything could be done about it. And to be honest, that is why he stopped by today, he wondered if he could talk to Monique.

His speech sounded so fake and presumptuous, I vowed to throw away his portfolio as soon as he had his back turned. I called Madame Moher in her office. 'There's a photographer here with his portfolio,' I said, knowing that not only the comment itself but the drawling and exacerbated tone of my voice would be largely sufficient to dissuade her from popping her eagle-shaped head out of her office. 'Tell him we're not interested,' she quickly responded. 'And by the way,' she added, 'how many times do I have to tell you that I do not like to be bothered about wandering artists who—'

'I know Madame Moher, I know,' I interrupted, 'But this man here asked to see you.'

'I'm busy,' she snapped.

'I'm sorry Mr—' I said, hanging up the phone.

'Stamballo,' he repeated in that clear voice of his, seemingly unperturbed by the situation. 'Don't bother telling me what she said, I think I can figure it out on my own,' he smiled. 'Needless to say, may I add, that had you sounded even a little more thrilled about me she just might have asked you what my name was, but then again . . .'

'Then again she never asks for names,' I answered, returning a polite smile. 'Now if you'll excuse me, I have a lot of work to do. You can of course leave your portfolio with me, and I'll hand it over to Madáme Moher as soon as possible.'

'Of course,' he repeated, the smile as if frozen on his face, 'it will be quite an honor to leave my portfolio in the company of your charming self.'

'The honor shall be mine,' I answered sweetly. 'Now. Again. I'm busy, you'll have to excuse me.'

At that same moment Madame Moher called me. 'Ask him for his name,' she said. I lifted my head up, looked at Otto, and faltered. 'Otto . . . ?'

'Stamballo,' he repeated again.

'Otto Stamballo,' I muttered, but to my surprise there was no one left on the line.

Madame Moher came rushing into the gallery, waving her hands emphatically. 'Monsieur Stamballo, Monsieur Stamballo, it's been a very long time since I've seen you, please, come into my office, I'm so sorry, my assistant didn't tell me your name, you know how it is with all these artists these days, you have to be choosy, really. Mademoiselle Miller, I hope you were nice to Monsieur Stamballo, his father was an old friend of mine.'

'Mademoiselle Miller was just delightful,' Otto was prompt to reply, 'she seemed very concerned.'

'Very good, very good. Now, please follow me Monsieur Stamballo.'

As they walked away, Otto turned around, waved his portfolio and smiled at me, this time clearly condescendingly.

I ignored him and went on typing a letter, trying to determine the exact nature of my thoughts, wavering somewhere between ridicule and contempt. After realizing that Otto and Madame Moher had been in her office for almost an hour, I decided that I definitely felt contemptuous towards them, and that any feeling of ridicule I had was short-lived. The fact of the matter was, I did not like this man. And if the attention Madame Moher demonstrated towards him did make me feel slightly embarrassed at first, it quickly turned into contempt for her as well; if she was able to appreciate such a phony individual, as he appeared to be, well, that was her problem. Not mine.

By the time both emerged from her office, I had managed to calm myself down. But the sight of Madame Moher led me to believe that something of the utmost significance had taken place in that office of hers. Her cheeks were flushed as she approached my desk. Her breathing was rushed, as if she had been running, and I noticed that she squeezed her hands tightly together, as if trying to stop them from trembling.

I didn't dare ask her if she was all right, but I felt concerned. She asked me to get both of them a cup of coffee, actually no, I should make it water for her, she didn't want to get more agitated than she already was. I took it as a clue and asked her if she felt all right.

'Of course I do,' she answered, attempting to smile, 'it's just been such a long time. You see, Monsieur Stamballo's father was an old friend of mine.'

'So you mentioned before,' I ventured politely.

'Yes, well, I haven't seen his father in years, and Monsieur Stamballo and I were just catching up on all these years which have been cruelly cut short I'm afraid . . .'

As I tried to understand the meaning of her cryptic statement, Otto cleared his throat and told me that his father had just died. I expressed my condolences to both of them. 'Well, Mademoiselle Miller, what about that coffee?' Madame Moher suddenly asked, regaining her composure. 'And by the way, please call Jean Tarjean and confirm our lunch appointment tomorrow. One o'clock at the Balzar. Now Monsieur Stamballo, please leave your portfolio here and follow me.'

I made the phone call, all the while determined to find out exactly what had happened between her and the recently deceased Monsieur Stamballo. As I was trying to figure out a subtle way to broach the topic, Jean Tarjean answered the phone, and that quickly distracted me from my previous thoughts. I powdered my face before I got up, and went to the espresso machine at the other end of the gallery. As I came back carrying one cup of coffee and one glass of mineral water on a wooden tray, Madame Moher was giving Otto a tour of the gallery. I heard their voices drifting away as they climbed the winding staircase to the upstairs storage room, and it was then that it hit me. An overwhelming and violent certitude, like a sharp and unexpected cramp. I suddenly had the profound conviction that this voice I was hearing for the first time in my life, was going to become very familiar to me. Not only that, but it would become part of my life. And perhaps the most frightening element of that certitude was its inexplicability. How could a voice I already despised become part of my life? Unless, of course, but no. It couldn't be. It was not possible. Strictly impossible. How could I? And why should I? Yes, why should I learn how to love it? Was there a reason? A need?

I opened the portfolio he had left on my desk. The photographs were all black-and-white. Images of caged teenage prostitutes in India. Bombed-out buildings in Beirut. A starving family in Bangladesh. A Mafia hit in Sicily. True, the images were riveting, but it was more because of their distressing subject matter than the beauty of the photographs themselves. They were suffused with a dim, almost ethereal light, that shone from the foreground of the photograph, leaving the background in semi-darkness. In terms of effect, it worked. In terms of emotion, it failed. I felt manipulated; the strength of his work lay mainly in its voyeuristic aspect. I even had to brush aside the idea that he had lured these people into posing for him. I closed his portfolio and found myself sighing with relief; this ruled out any possibility of my ever being attracted to him. At that same moment their voices drifted back downstairs, and this time Madame Moher came straight at me, her glasses on the tip of her nose.

'Mademoiselle Miller,' she said gravely, 'I would like you to know that I have decided to exhibit Monsieur Stamballo's work. We should plan for an October show and see how that goes, although I'm quite confident that everything will go very well. The show should take place right after Moltansko and before Eugenie Narbonne, who, by the way, I'd like you to call, her paintings were supposed to arrive a long time ago, ask her when she sent them, I don't like this at all, not at all. And give Monsieur Stamballo his cup of coffee, will you?'

I proceeded to do so while he looked through various catalogues, commenting all the while on different exhibitions, with a scorn and arrogance which I found extremely uncalled for, considering that he had just been taken on by us. On the other hand I couldn't help but agree with some of the things he said about a few young artists that I myself held in low esteem, artists whom I had always suspected Madame Moher had taken on more for their reputation than for their artistic merit. I asked Otto what he thought about Moltansko, a successful artist Madame Moher seemed to be very attentive to, a suspicion that was further confirmed when I noticed that whenever Moltansko was expected, Madame Moher switched from her usual sober way of dressing to bright colors and a little bit of lipstick. Moltansko being a notorious homosexual, I deduced that she performed this little act for business reasons rather than seductive play, something which redeemed Madame Moher in my eyes; the term 'rat race' was after all not that foreign and despicable to her, as she had once told me in one of our few long conversations.

Otto's answer to my question was quick and to the point. No, he didn't like Moltansko. And not only did he not like his work, but he hated the person as well. I asked him why; he didn't reply, but went off on a discourse about contemporary art and forsaking high standards, which lasted until later on that afternoon, after the closing of the gallery, when I finally agreed to join him for a cup of coffee at La Palette. 'Don't worry, you don't have to be nice to me,' he laughed, as we sat down at an outdoor table. It had stopped raining, and several people were in short sleeves, although it was April, and quite fresh outside.

'Not that I know you well enough to say this,' I retorted coldly, 'but disregarding any feelings of animosity I may or may not have towards you, I am now obliged to be, if not nice, at least courteous towards you. You have become one of our artists, and I should treat you with the respect a client, or should I say an artist, is entitled to.'

Otto looked at me amused. 'Talk about professional! Besides, I'm not one of your artists yet. I think our friend wants to give my work a trial run before she decides to represent me exclusively. If you want to be rude to me, you have until October, so please be my guest!' Here Otto burst out laughing, as I remained cold and stern, unaffected by his joke which I found silly. 'And by the way,' he added smiling sweetly, 'I do hope to find out one day what it is I did to you,' he said.

'Maybe you will, maybe you won't,' I answered tentatively, not quite sure myself what it was that bothered me so much about him.

'Well. Let's get back to business,' he said in English, admitting that it was a language he felt more comfortable in than French. His Italian accent was less noticeable in English, and he indeed seemed to speak the language with greater speed and ease. I asked him how long he'd lived in New York. 'For the past twelve years,' he said. 'My French used to be better. I used to spend more time in Paris, especially as a child and then during school holidays. Also, my mother's French, so I often speak French to her. But mostly Italian. My father's Italian, and I speak it with my whole family.'

'So you never lived here?'

'Well, yes, when I was a child, and I also lived here for one year right after college.'

'Oh? What were you doing?'

'I lived with a woman. Until we broke up and I went to New York. She stayed here. Actually,' he added, 'I found out a couple of months ago that she was married and had two children. It felt kind of strange, you know. I was totally crazy about her. Beautiful girl. Frigid but beautiful. A Ford model. Her name was Tana, short for Antananarive. Her parents chose the name by spinning a globe and then pointing at it randomly with their eyes closed. When they opened their eyes, the father's index finger was on the capital of Madagascar. Cute isn't it?'

'Very,' I answered curtly.

'You're a funny girl, you know that?' He said, his eyes sparkling. 'I find your nonchalance extremely sexy.'

'First of all, I hate being called funny,' I snapped,

'especially because for me there's nothing more unsexy than being called funny.'

'I disagree,' he smiled. 'What would you like to drink?'

'An espresso.'

'Un express, un petit-créme,' he called out to the waiter.

'And besides,' he added, taking evident pleasure in the turn the conversation was taking, 'notwithstanding the fact that I do find you funny, I find you extremely attractive as well. And not only because of your apparent indifference to me.'

'I'm sorry to say this Monsieur Stamballo,' I retorted, deciding once and for all that the main reason why I didn't like him was because he got under my skin, 'but not everyone can find you fascinating.'

He looked amused, and bent his thin and long body towards me. 'You know, I think we're going to get along very well. I like you. And by the way, please call me Otto. I'd prefer it if you did. Although I am now a client and I am ten years older than you, the difference between us is not that great.'

'How do you know how old I am?'

'I don't, I'm guessing. Twenty-four, twenty-five?'

'Twenty-five,' I sighed. I wished I hadn't followed him out for coffee. Despite the fact that my initial curiosity about him had triggered in me an urge to know him better, this was curbed by his pompous suaveness and arrogant convictions which I found unnerving.

'Well, what's the difference anyway . . . So. Let's get back to our previous discussion.'

'Yes. Let's,' I replied firmly, remembering that I had to

call my friend Baptiste in order to confirm dinner for the following evening.

'We were talking about the present state of the art world . . .'

'Yes, we were,' I answered absentmindedly.

'Well, I see the art world today as the following,' he said, sipping his petit-créme. 'Statements have nowadays become as important (and sometimes more important) than the creations themselves, with the exception of a few young artists who have managed to transgress this reverse conformism, and who have followed their own fire, so to speak.'

'Who do you think are those lucky ones?' I asked, crossing my legs and pulling down my blue dotted dress, suddenly self-conscious about the piece of thigh I had been inadvertently showing off. He named a few artists, among them Clement Narfesco and Cedric Shilfe, both of whom I held in high esteem. I shared my enthusiasm with him, agreeably surprised about what I deemed were among the best choices the art world currently had to offer. I even revealed to him that I was very well acquainted with Cedric Shilfe (I emphasized the 'very well,' hoping he'd understand I'd been romantically involved with him), and if he wanted to, I could arrange a meeting between both of them. He smiled. 'That won't be necessary,' he said. 'Cedric and I are good friends. But thanks anyway.'

I felt like a fool. I had tried to impress him, and had failed miserably. Not only that, but if he and Cedric were such good friends, the latter had probably told him about our short love affair, which ended when his wife found out about it. The whole event had left much awkwardness between us, and I cut off all relations until I bumped into him, his wife, and his new baby boy, Leonard, named after the actor who plays the Vulcan hero in *Star Trek*. This did set off a renewed 'strictly coffee' so to speak, relationship between us, which lasted until my departure for Paris, over a year ago. Since then I hadn't heard from him, and decided that I didn't really care. In order to avoid further embarrassment, I switched the topic back to Otto and the gallery.

'How come you want to show in Paris, if you live in New York?' I asked him, in a detached tone of voice.

'Because I want to come and live here for a little while,' he answered, lighting another cigarette.

'Why?' I asked again.

'You are inquisitive aren't you?' He observed.

'You don't have to tell me,' I rebutted, 'anyway I just realized I don't have much time, I've got to go home and get changed. I have an appointment tonight.'

'Oh, I'm sorry, I didn't realize. Let's get the check.'

If there was one thing Otto knew how to do, I decided right there and then, it was how to manipulate me into feeling bad. I did want to know about his reasons to show in Paris. But any form of curiosity seemed to lead him to think otherwise.

'Is anything wrong?' he asked, pulling money out of his pocket.

'No. It's just . . .' I hesitated.

'What is it Laura?' It was the first time he had used my name. The way he pronounced it made it sound fresh and melodic.

'No, it's just that . . . how should I put it. Despite what

you may think, I am honestly interested in your reasons for showing in the gallery, and it seems that—'

'What do I think?'

'Excuse me?'

'You said, "despite what you may think". What are you referring to?'

'Forget it!' I exclaimed, wishing I had kept my mouth shut once and for all, and wondering what it was about this man which prompted me to say all the wrong things.

'That's quite all right, Laura. We've got plenty of time. Plenty. A whole lifetime perhaps.'

I had no desire to hear him elaborate on this unexpected comment. I lowered my head, feeling my cheeks burn with embarrassment. He asked me if I wanted another coffee, and I heard myself say sure, why not.

'So do you want to hear about Paris?' he asked me cheerfully. 'I'd be glad to tell you.'

'Go ahead,' I sighed, lifting my head up, and meeting his bright blue glance.

'Well, it's as simple as this,' he said. 'As I mentioned before, I want to come and live here for a little while.'

'Were you represented by a gallery in New York?'

'Yes, I was. But I ran into a couple of problems with one of the owners, which led me to decide that I couldn't stay there any more.'

I refrained from asking him the reasons for his departure. But my silence must have prompted him to disclose that he had gotten involved with that same owner, and the involvement had ended up creating a rift between them. She had left her current boyfriend, who had once been a friend of Otto's, for him, at which point he fell in love with another woman, the same one he was about to visit in Caracas.

'Poor boy, how you must have suffered . . .' I said sarcastically.

Here, Otto laughed uncomfortably, as though surprised by my comment. He took a sip of his coffee, and continued.

'I packed my bags,' he said, 'and came here. I've always had a special fondness for Paris. I was born here, you see, and despite the fact that I went back to Italy at the age of eight, I've been coming here very frequently ever since. My father was actually born here too. Lived here until he was ten, then his family shipped him back to Rome. My grandfather was very involved in politics, he even ran twice for President, and ended up Minister of Labor some years later. My grandmother was a Venetian Countess, a very haughty and disagreeable woman, so they say. She died when I was three. Anyway. My father finished a doctorate in philosophy in Bologna, then decided to get involved in politics, just like his father. He started off quite well. He was brilliant, witty, and had all the foundations for being a great politician. It was at that time that he met my mother. He was twenty-nine.'

'Where did he meet her?' I asked, getting slowly engrossed by his story.

'He met her in Rome, at the French Embassy. She was the daughter of the French Consul. She was very young then. Must have been eighteen or nineteen. She was very beautiful, and my father claims to have fallen in love with her right there and then. They started a romance, he asked for her hand three months later and her father refused.

He disliked my father. He didn't trust him. He felt that he would hurt his Hélène, his one and only daughter, and he wanted the best for his child, which is quite understandable.'

'Quite,' I repeated, amused by this paternal conscience.

'You see, my father had quite a reputation, even at that early age. He was quite dashing. A real "tombeur," a real charmer. He was said to have slept with this and that one's wife, and the Consul was a rather conservative man, in all senses of the word. His suspicions were not only increased but confirmed when the scandal happened. That really did it for my poor father.'

'What scandal?'

'At about the same time, my father was awakened in the middle of the night by a friend of his who worked for the Press. This friend told him the following news. My father had supposedly impregnated a Roman Senator's seventeen-year-old daughter, who had to run away to Switzerland in order to have the child. The poor girl died at childbirth, and my father was held responsible for this tragedy. It was a big scandal. But they had no proof. They couldn't even try him. Not only that, but no one had ever seen them together except for one of the Senator's cooks who wasn't even sure it was him. So to this day no one knows who the father really was. My father certainly denied it all of his life.'

'So what happened? Did he end up marrying her? I mean your mother?'

'They finally eloped. Hélène's father refused to speak to his daughter until I was born. By then he was no longer Consul and had settled back in Paris. Imagine; they lived in the same arrondissement, yet he wouldn't speak to her. But when I was born, he sent a telegram asking her to come see him. She went over to his apartment and he forgave her. They loved each other tremendously. His wife had died when Hélène was thirteen, and as is often the case, he saw not only the young girl in Hélène, but his wife as well. He was a very sad man. I don't think he ever got over his wife's death.'

Here Otto paused, and took another sip of his coffee. His gaze drifted slowly somewhere on to the street, as if trying to focus on those long forgotten memories. I didn't say a word. 'My parents moved back to Rome when I was small. But my mother was unhappy there. She missed Paris, and she wanted to be near her father. My father refused. He was involved in politics again, and had great hopes of becoming the next leader of the Christian Democrats. She stayed in Rome until I was eight. By that time my sisters Alessandra and Stefania were born. Then my mother found out that my father had been sleeping with the maid and she left him almost immediately. She took my sisters but left me behind; my father insisted I stay with him. And so I did. I often visited my mother, and I know the separation was traumatizing for her, but somewhere along the line I was angry at her for having left me behind. We had a number of difficult years together, where we didn't communicate very well. The anger dissipated with time, and now we get along fine. She still lives in Paris, and believe it or not, so does my grandfather; he's ninety-seven now! As for my sisters, since they were brought up here we didn't see each other too often. In a way I feel like I grew up as an only child. You know; they visited, I visited, but still, it wasn't the same. My sister Stefania lives in New York now, she's married to an American.'

'And your other sister?'

'Alessandra? She's in Italy. In Milano. She loves it there. Anyway. Next time we see each other I'll tell you more. There's lots more to tell. Lots more. And I want you to tell me all about your life. How come you're here, where you grew up, all of that.'

'Believe me,' I laughed, 'my life is not half as interesting as yours. Not even close to half.'

'So what? Every life is interesting. Privilege doesn't make it more so.'

'Oh yes it does,' I answered categorically.

'Why do you think so?' he asked, pulling his money out for the second time.

'Because when money gives you greater access to the world, you're obviously going to experience and live through much more than just anyone—'

'Depending, of course on how you make use of this greater access,' he ventured. 'There are some privileged people who lead very sheltered lives. Others who live it up and live well. Then there are others who feel they have a debt towards society because of their position. A form of guilt, I suppose . . .'

'Of course,' I answered, 'you set your own rules. I suppose you can either give something back – call it guilt if you like – ignore your privileges, make the most of them, or abuse them. It seems to me that most people abuse them.'

'Do they really? You must know many restless people

then,' he said in an icy voice which made me feel so uncomfortable I wanted to bury my head under the table.

We both got up to leave. As we made our way out of the crowded and smoky café, I caught a glimpse of myself in the mirror. I was astonished to see that my cheeks were flushed, my eyes were shining, and I bore all the signs of a woman hopelessly denying her feelings of undeniable attraction and infatuation, a staggering revelation which turned to utter embarrassment when I noticed that not only was my hair falling in every direction, but the white scarf around my pony-tail was threatening to come undone at any moment, which I instinctively remedied by pulling it off altogether and letting my hair loose. I noticed Otto looking at me. I looked downward, then up again. He was still staring, his eyes focused on my face, scrutinizing me in a way which made me uneasy. 'What's the matter?' I asked him, trying to keep my voice steady.

'I wish I wasn't going to Caracas,' was his only answer, as he jotted down my phone number, promised he'd call sometime in the next couple of days, and left me on the Boulevard St-Germain, staggering as if I were drunk.

I called Baptiste from the street, and suggested that we have dinner that same evening, hoping he would be available. He agreed. I saw a lot of Baptiste in those days. He was a film editor, who had traveled all around the world, and introduced me to many interesting people. I met him in a small restaurant on the Quai de la Tournelle, and he remarked on my appearance, saying I was looking very good. I shrugged my shoulders: 'I must have slept well for a change,' I muttered.

We ordered prawns and a cool bottle of white wine. I

tried to focus my attention on what he was saying, but found myself drifting back to the afternoon, and to Otto's lemon-scented aftershave. As Baptiste poured my third glass of wine, I was suddenly overtaken by horrendous stomach cramps. Baptiste had to rush me to the bathroom, where I threw up so violently my face turned livid. He drove me home, insisting on staying with me until I felt better. He looked very concerned, and suggested we call a doctor. 'It looks like you have food-poisoning. You don't want to mess around with that, especially if the prawns are the cause of it.'

He then went into a whole diatribe about fish and how you can tell if it's fresh or not, he learned that on a fishing trip he took in Alaska, a memorable trip, I should try and take it one day. I told Baptiste it was actually the last thing I wanted to think about at that precise moment, and that really, he could go now, I was going to be fine.

'Are you sure?' Baptiste asked, 'you still look rather pale.'

'I'll be fine, I promise,' I answered, 'now if you don't mind, I'd like to wash my face and get into bed.'

'Fine. Go ahead. I'll wait here,' he said, sitting down on a chair, and holding his coat. 'Once you're in bed I'll leave.'

I brushed my teeth, sprayed some Evian water on my face, put on a long T-shirt and climbed into bed. As I lay down, the bed started to rock under me, as if I were in a boat. I closed my eyes and tried to focus on anything but that queasy sensation. I thought about Otto; there was no doubt about it. Not only was the man a pompous cynic, but he had managed to irritate me to the point of physical illness. This was a man I should surely forget about, and the sooner the better.

'Your color came back,' I heard Baptiste say from somewhere across the room. I opened my eyes and smiled at him. 'I'm feeling much better,' I said, 'You can leave now. Really. And thank you so much for taking care of me.'

'Are you sure?' he asked, unconvinced.

'Yes, I'm sure. I think I'm going to fall asleep very soon.'

He made me promise I would call him the following day and left me lying on my bed, my arms straight against my sides, ready to spring up if I felt nauseous again.

I woke up in the middle of the night with my cheeks and forehead wet with sweat and my mouth tasting like warm sand, reminding me of the beach I played on so long ago (was it fifteen, twenty years ago?) with my mother and father on a small island in Greece, jarring in me the memory of that woman who drowned that summer trying to save her two little girls who were caught in the undertow.

After Zeus realized he had been duped by Prometheus (who was known to favor mortals over the gods), he decided to take revenge on his brother. He ordered Hephaestus, the god of celestial fire, to create a woman out of clay and water. Her beauty was to be such, that it would rival that of immortal goddesses. Her name was to be Pandora. All the divinities, except for Hermes (the god of travel and eloquence) were to lavish this newfound beauty with gifts. But Hermes did otherwise: he followed Zeus' order to teach her guile and treachery.

Pandora was sent off by Zeus, as a gift to Epimetheus, Prometheus' foolish brother. Pandora brought a sealed jar with her, and kept it close to herself. Little did she know that the jar contained all the plagues of mankind.

Although Prometheus had warned his brother never to accept a gift from Zeus, Epimetheus, transported by her beauty, invited her to join the mortals and to be his bride. After their marriage, Pandora, overcome by curiosity, opened the lid of the jar, out of which flew all the terrible ills that had been placed there, dispersing themselves all over the earth. Only the spirit of hope remained, trapped inside, thus unable to alleviate the afflictions that were to plague mankind from then on.

Omega's painting of Pandora is riveting. A young woman with jet black hair, a diaphanous face, and wearing a suggestive long white robe draped around her body (giving the impression that she's floating) clutches an imposing magnificent oval-shaped vase. It is decorated with mosaics and leaf-like pieces of gold, around which are painted intaglios of gods and goddesses sharing grapes and playing the harp.

Pandora stands in the middle of an empty field, surrounded by a crowd of men. One of her hands is wrapped around the jar, the other holds the base against her chest.

Next to Pandora stands Prometheus. There is an expression of apprehension on his face; his back is turned to the men in the background who are clapping their hands with joy and rapture, obviously unaware of the contents inside the vase.

The colors in the painting are so brilliant and fresh, they seem to have just been painted, and explode on to the canvas in various hues of blue, green, red and yellow. The deep purple of the thick and plump grapes stands out as one of the darker colors of the painting. Despite its tragic denouement, there is something extremely positive and joyful about this work, suggesting the artist was in a particularly good state of mind when he painted it.

The trustees of the Museum of Modern Art purchased this piece last year. I went to look at it the other day. I stood in front of the painting for a very long time, scrutinizing it from every angle. I felt glued to it, mesmerized by its beauty and its strength. I tried to interpret the work according to what I knew about Omega's life. He had painted it approximately sixteen months before, at a time when I knew he was having some financial difficulties. I thus dismissed the idea that he probably felt secure in his life, and found myself wondering whether the cause of this optimism could have been love. Was he having an affair? Or was he merely projecting the love he felt for his wife? I dismissed the latter as unlikely, considering his obsession with privacy – but then again, I had come to expect anything with Omega . . .

As I stood there, barely noticing the crowds of people that came and went beside me in waves, I was suddenly hit by a puzzling and unaccountable intuition: Could he have been in love with 'Muse', the woman in the erotic lithographs? The date on the bottom of those crude works was approximately two months prior to the execution of this painting, indicating a possible parallel. Who was that woman? How did he get to know her? How did he convince or lure her to sit for him in such a lewd way? The answer was simple: only love or money would prompt a woman to do so, therefore rendering the possibility of an affair even more probable. I left the museum in a daze, and as I walked down Fifth Avenue, decided to keep these thoughts to myself. After all, I could be wrong; over-interpretation can sometimes hinder the search for truth.

I wrote about Pandora that night. I wondered what would have happened if she hadn't succumbed to her curiosity, and had let those evils lie where they were, leaving someone else the task of revealing them to the world. I wondered how mankind suddenly faced its own mortality.

Four days after my return from Italy, I had lunch with Jaurel. He was tanned, having just come back from a business trip to Mexico, and looked rested. Before I showed him my notes from the interview, I explained how hard it had been to get in touch with Omega. He laughed and shook his head. 'These artists, they have egos the size of the Eiffel Tower.'

He continued to joke about various artists from the gallery, and for the first time, went so far as to expose intimate details about his private life, boasting about his wife and children, and what a wonderful family he had. 'My youngest baby said her first word today: perro. That's what you get when you hire Filipino nannies. Your children end up learning Spanish, not English!'

We both laughed, and he continued to tell me anecdotes about his precocious children, and how his second eldest son Jean-Guillaume had just been admitted to the school for gifted children.

'My oldest son Matthieu wants to be a pilot,' Jaurel continued. 'He decided that when he was five years old, and he hasn't changed his mind since. I have strong-willed children. I believe they will all go very far in life,' he added with a determined look on his face which I couldn't help but find touching.

'Like father like son,' I remarked in French, a comment which brought a gloating smile to his lips, and made him chuckle with content.

Jaurel was obviously in a good mood that day. When I showed him my notes, he went over them carefully, nodding his head in approval, hardly making any critical comments, which he usually did.

When he came to the end of the page, he suddenly frowned, and looked at me. 'What does this mean?' he asked, showing me the red underlined 'ask Jaurel about Muse'.

'Oh.' I blushed. 'It's actually something I wanted to talk to you about.'

I recounted my meeting with Isabella, described my trip to Pomezia, and to the printing house, and told him about my discovery of the lithographs, which I found very powerful, but unlike anything I had ever seen of Omega's before. I confessed how ambivalent I felt about categorizing them as pornographic, especially because it brought up the whole question of pornography qualifying as art, which I usually answered in the negative. But perhaps this was an old stereotype that needed to be redefined?

He didn't respond and I squirmed in my chair as he

continued to read my notes with a frown on his face. I adjusted my black tights and my suede mini-skirt, and caught sight of myself in the mirror on the right side of our table. I decided that I liked my new shoulder length haircut. It made me look younger, and made my blue eyes look wider. I was also surprised to see that I hadn't lost the golden tan I had acquired in Italy, and I looked rested, as if I had just returned from a beach somewhere in the Caribbean. It was almost worrisome, because I didn't want Jaurel to think that I wasn't working hard enough. Then again, his attitude throughout this meeting, until I mentioned 'Muse', projected satisfaction rather than discontent, so I decided not to worry about it for the time being. Instead, I immediately focused my attention back on my previous thoughts. 'What do you think of this, M. Jaurel?' I asked, crossing my legs. 'Do you think these erotic lithographs are something I should bring up in the book?'

Jaurel pursed his lips together. This was obviously the wrong question to ask him. As for my views on the topic, he did not seem in the least interested. 'Are you sure these lithographs were his?'

I nodded. Of course I was sure. I recognized his style.

'Well Laura,' he said, a fake smile forming on his heavy-set face, 'let's put this erotic issue on the side for now. That is, do not include it in the book. I first need to make some inquiries about it. Then we'll talk about it. And I count on you to keep all this to yourself, do you understand me Laura, all to yourself.'

The old wolf was back in his territory again. What could I do but smile back and obey his commands. I was after all, as he had once explained to me, a mere art critic, and not a psychologist. The psychologist explains and interprets. He doesn't describe. The art critic describes and explains, without too much interpretation; just enough to render his or her point of view. If something appears to be out of his league, then it is best to leave it be. The psychologist will take care of it.

This limited point of view of Jaurel's gave me a good idea of the kind of literature he was used to reading. It also betrayed his profound insecurity about studying certain matters in depth, including his own. Could this insecurity, I wondered, be used to my advantage?

I did not pay much attention to what Jaurel told me. As I wrote my book, I brought up every topic I could think of (though following Jaurel's order to leave out any mention of the infamous lithographs), quoting as few sources as possible, but taking various liberties with, as Jaurel had called them, psychological hypotheses. It was enough that I couldn't incorporate what I really wanted to, and what I felt was a revealing aspect of the artist's work. Instead I had to make a compromise. I was writing what I deemed to be an average book, for which I was getting paid a lot of money. I had no choice. I needed the money.

Three

Otto called me two days after our first meeting. He told me to meet him in front of the Picasso Museum. It was another one of those sunny spring days, which bathes Paris in majestic splendor, as if it has just risen from its seasonal sleep. As I was reflecting upon the beauty of my immediate surroundings, Otto arrived on a motorcycle, his hair slightly disheveled, a dimpled smile on his handsome face. He commented on my gray-striped pant suit (which I had bought for the occasion), and apologized for being five minutes late. He smiled and said that it was nice to see me again. I nodded my head in agreement. I was too overcome by his presence to say anything.

After we checked our coats, we walked around the museum, paying exaggerated attention to the paintings, my body and my gaze carefully avoiding his, for fear of giving away my real sentiments, which I preferred to keep somewhere tucked away until the proper time arose.

That time proved to arrive embarrassingly soon. After a long lunch following our seminal museum viewing, Otto suggested we walk around the Marais and the Place des Vosges. He took a last sip of his coffee, threw his black leather jacket across his sparkling white shirt, and as we left the restaurant he put his arm around my waist, eventually sliding it down towards my nervous cold hand, the warmth of his fingers acting like a sedative against mine. 'By the way,' he said out of the blue, 'I want you to know that I've canceled my trip to Caracas.'

I didn't answer. We walked around the Place des Vosges hand-in-hand. I could feel myself oscillating between feelings of self-consciousness and bliss: one part of me yearned to be thrust into his arms, the other one urged me to stay away.

In my previous relationships, I had tended to display a certain patterned reaction towards any kind of rapid demonstrations of lust. They were an ephemeral easy sexual quenching with no future whatsoever, which had proved too often to be merely a waste of time and instilled many false hopes. So as of late, I stayed away from mawkish eagerness, choosing apathy instead.

That proved to be an equally big mistake. After several unfruitful tries, I decided to give up men for a little while. It was a good time to do so, since my job at the Moher Gallery demanded many hours of hard work. My responsibilities had increased drastically; Madame Moher seemed to have a lot of faith in me, and I gave her good reason to maintain it; if there was one thing I did not want to spoil it was my relationship with her.

My reaction to Otto astonished me no end. I attributed my conflicting feelings towards him to the realization that this was probably the first time in my life that a man had had such an effect on me.

So when he gently rested my head against a tree in the garden of the Place des Vosges, and started kissing me in such a way that I later swore my feet rose off the ground,

I gave up. I pushed to a side all rational voices, and focused on his lips and his strong arms around me, a delicious sensation enthralling me. Later on, in an apartment somewhere in the Ile Saint Louis, I yielded to his hardened desire, as he explored and savored each part of my body as if it were a newfound treasure, sending me to such spheres of ecstasy that I finally broke down in tears, because the sensation was too overwhelming for me to bear.

I was awakened by the smell of fresh lilacs by my side, around which a note was attached. 'I forgot I had an appointment. I couldn't wait for you to wake up. I'll call you later. You are the most beautiful woman I've ever made love to.'

I looked at my watch. It was noon. I called Madame Moher up and told her I was sick. I looked around the bedroom. It was beautifully decorated, with colorful drapes hanging as curtains on the large bay windows, Indian saris hung on the wall, a Biedermeier chair, and various different pieces that testified to good and expensive taste.

I walked around his apartment which was covered with oriental textiles and antique wooden furniture. The living-room was large and airy, with beams covering the walls and ceiling, an old fireplace, and an impressive array of books, paintings and photographs. There were oriental carpets and Indian Buddha sculptures strewn about the room. His kitchen was rustic, with garlic strands and copper pots dangling from the wall. When I looked through the kitchen cabinets, I found them to be mostly bare, as was his refrigerator. I wasn't surprised. Otto had not struck me as someone who liked to cook, considering his heavy social schedule, and the fact that he seemed unable to sit in one place for any long period of time. But of course this was all based on assumptions. I couldn't say I knew Otto well. Actually, I hardly knew him at all. And despite that, I felt so close to him, as if I were experiencing some kind of déjà-vu, as if everything about him was familiar, even predictable. After reflecting on these uncanny thoughts, I left the kitchen and wandered down the hallway, where I found his office. I cast a quick glance over the neat desk and various filing cabinets, but did not dare enter. I took a jacuzzi and a shower in his Turkish blue tiled bathroom, and opened every apothecary jar that lined the sink: One was filled with colored cotton balls. Another with blue bath salts.

I went back into the bedroom, wearing Otto's white fluffy bathrobe, and started skipping around his room, like a child who cannot control her happiness. I lay on his bed and closed my eyes. I could almost feel the touch of his silky skin against mine, the grip of his arms around my waist, the sound of his purring voice as he glided in and out of me that morning, and I found myself clutching him when a violent gust of wind and rain suddenly knocked his window wide open, startling us at first, until we both started laughing, our bodies wet with sweat, and he covered my face and neck with long kisses which sent a shiver down my spine, so I closed my eyes again and indulged in my newfound pleasure.

Although I still had trouble admitting it, there was no doubt that I was falling in love. I was ready to do anything for him. He was the most interesting and challenging man I had ever been with, and I felt a childish desire to prove myself to him.

I got dressed and devoted the rest of the afternoon to shopping. I spent a fortune on clothes and shoes, justifying my expenditure by my being in love and wanting to look good. It was a lame excuse, but at that point I wasn't too concerned about acting rationally. An impulsive whim was dragging me from store to store, and when I finally got back to my apartment, later on that afternoon, I ran myself another bath and tried on my new outfits, all the while imagining my next meeting with Otto, and wondering why he hadn't called me yet.

My thoughts were interrupted by the strident ringing of the telephone. I answered it in a new short gold dress and high heels. It was Otto, asking me to come over. One hour later I was back in his arms, and when he whispered in my ear 'I hope you realize that one day you'll be my wife,' I couldn't find the proper words to answer him. I thought that either this was a joke, or the man was crazy. Only later did the real meaning of the sentence hit me.

He left at seven the next morning. He was working on a shoot for *House and Garden*. I tried to wake up when he did, but was unable to. When the alarm rang at nine o'clock, I had trouble remembering where I was. I got out of his bed drowsily, and quickly got dressed; I couldn't afford to be late for work. I rushed to the Métro station, and as I was about to sit down in the carriage, I felt something heavy in my jeans pocket. I plunged my hand in, and pulled out an unknown set of keys; they were his. Around each key, he had attached a sticker: 'Top', 'bottom', and 'mailbox'.

I used the keys that same night. I only went back to the Rue Tournefort for clean clothes. After two weeks, I moved in with Otto. I did not rationalize the move. It was a necessity. Almost a primal one, like eating or sleeping; it provided no explanation other than immediate gratification.

After the first few days, what had been genuine impulses turned into insecurities. I suddenly felt shy, as if I had been offered a gift I didn't dare open, for fear of what it held inside. What if I didn't like it? Or, what if I liked it so much I wouldn't want to let go of it? And what if he didn't like me enough to let me keep it?

But my fears proved to be unfounded. Otto displayed such passionate feelings towards me (more so than I towards him), that in my self-protective way, I reasoned that he had more to lose than I did.

But as his feelings about me became ever more demonstrative, so did mine. I felt myself slowly sinking into true love, and after trying to fight it for a short while, decided to just let it be; if our relationship was to become a memory, I pondered, it would be a nice one. And if it was to become an actuality, well then, it was all for the better.

I started missing more and more days at work, mostly due to the late hours at which we would get home, making love until dawn and the lifting of the sky. Around noon we would wake up, and Otto would slip his jeans on and run downstairs to get the last of the morning's croissants. He would then serve them to me in bed on a silver platter, complete with café au lait and raspberry preserve, and every two days, a fresh bouquet of lilacs.

Otto made me feel like a queen. I basked in luxury without too much thought, except for perhaps the resigned notion that this would not last forever. This notion, as it had so many times before, strengthened me. Despite its neurotic and negative implications (was I so wary of happiness, of being hurt?) it served two purposes: to protect me from any disappointments, if there were to be any, and on the outside, it seemed to lead Otto to mistake my insecurity for coldness. This, in turn, led him to increasing outbursts of love and paranoia, such as, 'I'm not sure you're in love with me,' or 'I'm afraid you'll leave me.'

The irony of these declarations was that they could have easily been uttered by me, but instead, I chose to listen with a half-smile on my face, caressing his hair, and assuring him that no I would not leave him, and yes, I thought I was in love with him although I wasn't sure, I needed more time to think, it usually takes me a long time to fall in love.

I do admit that this little game of mine gave me plenty of satisfaction. It was a cheap thrill to see Otto pleading for my love, his muscular arms wrapped around my body, as I once pushed my face away in fake annoyance, pretending to be too tired to make love, whereas in the bottom of my fragile heart, I knew I would do anything for him but wasn't yet sure that this feeling would be reciprocated. I didn't trust him entirely. I made a mental calculation in my head. If his behavior proved to be constant throughout the following month, I would drop my shield and reveal my true feelings. Until then, I had to be cautious.

Today, four years later, when I look back at this period of my life, I realize how hard Otto must have been trying. I could have spared myself many false insecurities had I known how deeply he actually felt about me, mostly because I think he saw some kind of savior in me, and imagined that I would rehabilitate his life into a normal and healthy one; indeed, I later realized, throughout our first month together, Otto was in the throes of trying to kick his cocaine habit. Perhaps out of naiveté, or because this lifestyle was all new to me, it took me an unusually long time to figure out how deeply Otto was entrenched in this habit. But once I understood it enough, I realized that I had never even had a chance. Where I could have helped him I failed; I arrived on the scene too late, with no possibility of a retake. And up until this day, I still wonder whether my marriage could have been different had Otto and I met sooner.

Money was Otto's greatest asset, but also his greatest liability. He spent it too freely: on me, on himself, on his friends, and last but not least, on cocaine. This order was quickly reversed once we moved to our Mercer Street loft in New York. There, our social life reached frenzied proportions, much more so than in Paris. I found myself playing the role of the wife of a much sought after socialite, who, despite his bad habits, continued to attract people wherever he would show his handsome face. I became aware that charm was another key to his success, as well as the glamorous coterie of people he knew, many of them childhood friends; his mother and sister were also regularly featured in social columns, especially Alessandra, a famous beauty whose endless list of prospective husbands was always a source of gossip. As Rebecca pointed out, I had not married into a discreet, average family. 'This family makes noise, and not all of it is sweet music. I hope for your sake that you get used to it,' she added, a warning that I did not dwell on.

Just after our return to New York, Otto rented a studio space on Lafayette Street where he could be found in his darkroom working diligently. But once he re-established contact with his old friends and acquaintances, invitations started pouring in once again, reaching such an apex of activity that it didn't afford me much spare time for job-hunting, and Otto became more lackadaisical about his work. He was occasionally called on shoots outside the country, but once he started up his cocaine habit again, he turned many offers down, claiming he was too busy. 'It's no big deal,' his argument was when I criticized his laziness, 'it's not like I really need the money.' We entertained lavishly, went out practically every night, and the frenzy and excitement around our life was such that I occasionally found myself indulging in those same substances from which I later tried to keep Otto away. But as I painfully learned, while this was an infrequent pasttime I indulged in at parties, and not one I could admit to particularly enjoying, it was definitely not so for Otto: this was his security blanket which kept him warm and secure. And when it was pulled away from him, a nasty draft blew forcefully through the cracks in his personality. The few times I attempted to seal those cracks for him, he threatened to leave me. Or he would comply, only to continue doing it behind my back, carefully erasing any traces that would reveal his defeat. But the truth of the matter was that my earlier participation in this activity, however infrequent, was enough to undermine my vehement opposition to his increasing consumption. Where he would listen to me at first, he eventually turned a deaf ear to my harangues, and towards the end of our relationship, he gave up trying to hide it from me altogether. He spent more and more time at home, lying awake at night, indulging in the drug throughout the day, the tip of his fingers red with blood, his eyes glazed over with the look of someone who's adopted an attitude of utter indifference to the world.

Through my friend Sandra, who was away in Brazil for half of the year Otto and I spent in New York, I met and became closer to Adam Selman, an ex-boyfriend of Sandra's, with whom I shared a love for film. I started to spend a lot of time with Adam. We went to see old films at the Thalia SoHo, or at Theater 80. There was nothing we enjoyed more than going to see double features, sometimes even seeing three films a day, followed by a drink or a bite, and an extensive conversation about what we had just seen.

I liked Adam. He was a breath of fresh air compared to Otto's friends, and his presence always imbued me with a nostalgic feeling for those days before I knew Otto, days when the word celebration was carefully used, and never abused. Besides our mutual love for film, I didn't have much else in common with Adam. I didn't like his painting (a poor imitation of German expressionism), and didn't particularly agree with his views on deconstructionism and his constant quoting of Derrida. But none of this really mattered. At first, he was a pleasant diversion from my life. Then, he became my solace; he was always available when I needed him, and I could always rely on him when things got too difficult for me to bear at home.

I would not go as far as to categorize Adam's behavior as purely generous. He was in fact attracted to me, and waited patiently for many months, hoping he could kindle an equivalent fire in me. He eventually did. One evening, as Otto had gone out with his sister Stefania and her husband (I had refused to join them on account of a persistent headache), Adam called and suggested we go to see the eight o'clock show of *The Killing of a Chinese Bookie*. 'It will make your headache go away instantly,' he promised. As we were watching the film, he grabbed my hand and kissed it. I laughed awkwardly, and before I knew it he pulled me against him and started to kiss me. I mumbled something about my being married, but the combination of his good looks and the fact that he was a great kisser somewhat detracted me from the grim reality of the situation, and we ended up keeping our eyes closed throughout the entire movie.

Once we left the theater and found ourselves fidgeting with our spring rolls in a Chinese restaurant, I had to tell Adam the truth. 'We can't do this. I'm married. I really like you, but there's no way I can start having an affair on the side. I have to focus on my life with Otto, and try to make it better. I really want to make it better.'

Then, as suddenly as the words I had just uttered, I started to cry. I couldn't control myself. I was practically sobbing, as Adam held me in his arms and tried to comfort me. 'Laura . . .' he kept saying, 'Laura . . .'

It was as if for the first time in many months, I

realized the extent of my love for Otto, and how painful his addiction and lifestyle were for me. I longed to go back to our first days in Paris, to the freshness and excitement of those days when we couldn't seem to keep our hands off each other. I longed to see him sober, active, vibrant and funny. We didn't laugh anymore. We now fought, sulked, or stayed away from each other for hours on end. I still loved him in the same way, but our relationship was wilting away, and I felt, right then and there with my head buried in Adam's arms, that if I didn't attempt one more time to restore our natural energy, Otto might languish away and die. I didn't share these thoughts with Adam. I asked him to take me home, and as we got to the front door he tried to kiss me again. I gently turned my cheek, and told him I just wanted to be friends. He said fine, no problem, and asked me if he could come in to use the bathroom. I had no choice but to let him in. As I pushed the front door open, I realized that Otto was home; the bedroom light and television were on. I showed Adam where the bathroom was, and went into the bedroom to say hello to Otto. He was lying on our bed, flat on his back with all his clothes still on. I called his name out twice but he didn't hear me. All my previous tender feelings towards him stiffened into hatred. It was eleven o'clock at night, and he was already in this state. I went into the living-room where I found Adam looking at Otto's photographs on the walls, and praising them extensively. 'He's really good,' he said. 'He was,' I retorted.

Adam looked at me, and probably responding to the angry look on my face, asked me what the matter was. I told him Otto had passed out on our bed, and apologized for my sentimental behavior in the Chinese restaurant. 'I'm really sorry,' I said, 'I don't know what got into me.' Our eyes rested on each other. Adam took hold of my hands gently, and wished me a good-night. 'Take it easy Laura,' he said, in a compassionate voice.

As this time he bent down to kiss my cheek, I placed my lips on his, and next thing I knew we were rolling on the floor kissing passionately. 'I really like you,' he whispered in my ear. 'I've been wanting this to happen for the longest time.'

That's when we suddenly heard the sharp noise coming from the bedroom and Adam leapt out of the apartment. I didn't see much of him after that evening, especially since he met Thea and fell in love with her.

Around that same time, Otto started to reach frightening levels of substance abuse. He would sit by the window for hours and ask me if the cops were coming to get him. He thought someone was hiding behind the curtains of the living-room. He shouted at me for no reason and one morning I found him on the telephone, screaming 'fuck you bitch' to his mother when she volunteered to get him some help. He would force me to sit next to him as his whole body would contort itself from cocaine excess. He wouldn't talk. He would sit by the window in silence, his mouth dry like sawdust, chewing monotonously on some invisible ingredient, his arms clutching his body in desperation, as if afraid he would lose his balance altogether. Occasionally, his nose would bleed, and I would have to wipe off the blood.

I felt an increasing amount of guilt seep into me because of my infidelity with Adam. It had been a weak and easy way out, not a solution. It was unlike me, and showed a side of myself I had trouble facing up to: instead of confronting my marital problems, I was running away from them, perhaps because of the sad certainty that it was a lost cause. I interpreted my having chosen Otto as a reflection of my state of mind: A woman who sought a challenge in order to affirm her identity, and who needed love so badly as to become reckless.

I wouldn't go as far as to say that the outcome of my marriage wasn't a surprise to me: it was. Its slow descent accelerated without warning when we returned from our glorious honeymoon and settled in New York, a city whose temptations were too enticing for Otto to resist. In Paris, decadence required a certain amount of civility, and had to be performed with grace. If one went beyond moderation, insidious exclusion was instantaneous.

In New York, things were different. Civility was not imperative, and decadence had no boundaries. One could go very far, without worrying about social stigmas or labeling. It was a personal choice, and whether or not others agreed with it was not an issue.

There was no doubt that Otto felt more comfortable in New York. Where in Paris, he could stop himself before he went too far, here he did the opposite. He went so far, he couldn't stop himself any more. His friends started to change their attitude towards Otto. They gradually stopped coming by, either because they didn't know how to help or didn't want to. I always suspected this was because a number of them partook in the same activity, and usually at his expense. And when they would dare make comments such as 'you look like a wreck, you should really slow down Otto,' he would laugh and tell them to stop exaggerating, implying that I was the one who set them up to say that. The only person we heard from regularly was Ted, Otto's drug dealer. The few times I heard his nasal voice on the phone, I was surprised by how abrupt it sounded. The voice was one of a harried man, who wanted to get down to business immediately, not waste any time on unnecessary words. He was the man who provided; a name without a face, which would make me cringe every time I heard it.

The last two weeks before Otto's overdose, I noticed that neither of the two men seemed to be in contact. At first I rejoiced in this, envisioning Otto back on the right track, thinking that after all our marriage might indeed survive the last unbearable four months, when our physical intimacy was non-existent, and the complicity we had once shared as man and woman, husband and wife had disappeared.

After a long talk with my friend Rebecca, I reached the conclusion that instead of fruitless cogitation, I needed to resort to action: unless he made a concrete effort to change, and allow himself to be helped, I would have to leave Otto. It was no longer a question of saving our marriage, but of saving myself. Otto's excess was his own choice, and he obviously didn't care enough about our future to do something about it. I would have to act with strength and lucidity, and give him one last chance. I wished, from the bottom of my heart, that he would finally yield to my demands; there was nothing I wanted more than to find the Otto I once knew. The Otto I loved, for better or for worse, as declared during our marriage ceremony, the man who had demonstrated unconditional love for me, until the hatred he felt for himself destroyed all our chances for happiness. But there was hope; small, yet present, and I could almost feel it sitting in the palms of my hands as I entered our bedroom around noon one morning, the time when Otto would usually wake up.

'Hi,' I said to him as he yawned and stretched his arms out. He was lying naked on the bed, and the television was on without the sound. 'How did you sleep?'

'Fine, why do you ask?' He turned his handsome face towards me, and the look he gave me then was that of a complete stranger; it was a hardened and weathered look, which seemed to imply that whatever I wanted to say to him, as I stood shyly by the entrance door, was not worth bringing up. The damage was done, the look seemed to say, and there was no going back.

'Otto,' I murmured, as I sat down on the edge of the bed.

'What is it?' He sat up and crossed his arms around his legs, looking at me enigmatically.

'I miss you,' was the only thing I could say.

'I'm right here, Laura, how could you miss me?' he said calmly.

'You're not here Otto. Only part of you is. You've turned into a different human being.'

'Oh God not that again,' he said irritated, getting up and putting his kimono on.

'Otto, we've got to talk, I can't go on like this anymore.'

He sighed loudly. 'Fine. Let's talk. What do you want to talk about?'

He was intimidating me and he knew it. I had to

swallow hard and take a deep breath before I plunged in, as if I were diving into an ocean whose waves might engulf me.

'I want to talk about you, Otto.'

'Stop using my name every goddamn sentence, it drives me crazy.' His tone was snappy and dry.

'Fine. In one word, I want to go back to the way we were—'

'That will never happen,' he interrupted, 'you can never go back.'

'You can go back to being happy. Right now you're unhappy, and you're making me unhappy.'

'Who says I'm unhappy?' He turned his back to me and started fumbling with something in his drawers.

'I say you're unhappy. You pack almost two grams of coke a day into your nostrils. Doesn't that mean something about your state of mind?'

I knew I shouldn't have uttered the words so brusquely, but I could think of no other way to broach the subject. I had to confront him and be direct about it, because no one else dared to. And besides, this was not the first time I had brought this up. But it was the first time that he reacted to me so violently: he turned around so quickly it startled me. Before I knew it, Otto was grabbing my arm forcefully and screaming at me. 'You're so fucking stupid!' he screamed, 'You're such a fucking stupid bitch!'

He pushed me against the wall and I let myself fall down, tears running down my cheeks. 'I love you, Otto, that's why I'm saying that, I want to help you, I want you to stop destroying yourself like this, please do it for me, for you, for us, please . . .'

I was sobbing uncontrollably, my hands covering my face, and I didn't hear him bend down next to me. My whole life was falling apart in front of me, and there was nothing I could do about it. 'Laura,' I suddenly heard him say, 'Laura look at me.'

I looked up at him, and saw his gentle eyes gazing at me, his hand clutching mine. 'It's happened to me before Laura,' he said in a near whisper, 'it's happened before and I got out of it on my own. All by myself. You've got to let me be for it to happen again.'

'But it's been months Otto, months! How can I let you be?'

'Believe in me,' he said, looking at me and wiping the tears off my cheeks, 'Trust me.'

'I can't, I can't . . . You've hurt me too much, you won't listen to me, you won't try and change and get help.'

'I don't know what to say,' he muttered, his gaze now avoiding mine.

'Do you admit you have a problem?' I asked in between my tears, 'Do you admit this is destroying our marriage, our love for each other?' As I was asking him this question, I realized that his answer was going to determine the outcome of this marriage. By admitting he had a problem, he was taking that first step towards recovery. By denying it, he was going to stay where he was and destroy us forever. The word 'forever' lingered in my mind as I awaited his answer, my hands trembling, my tears sticking to my cheeks, my pulse beating rapidly.

'I admit our marriage isn't going well, that I'll admit,' Otto finally answered, standing up and leaving me crouched on the floor. I felt nauseous. I stood up slowly and went to sit next to him on the bed, where he had resumed his original position. I brought my face close to his and kissed him. His tongue felt cold, his body stiff. I started speaking frantically, as if this was the last moment we would be sharing together, as if he was going away on a long trip, and I had to cram all the words I could think of before his departure. I was desperate, but I didn't care. At this point, I had nothing left to lose. 'Will you give me a last chance, will you love me and stand by me, will you let me love you and stand by you, will you take me back to Paris and to all our great memories, will you ask me to marry you all over again, will you please let me help you, or give you the number of someone who could help you get out of this?'

He shook his head. 'No,' he said in a clear voice.

'Do you want to change, do you Otto, do you want us to be together and happy?' I clutched him against me, and started kissing him everywhere, in a frenzy. I took my clothes off, he let me go through the motions although he remained impassive. I placed his hand on my breast, then brought my lips close to his member, but quickly came to the realization that all of this was useless. He couldn't make love, and didn't even seem to care. His mind, his body was numb. He looked at me and said in a strained voice, 'You'd better get dressed, Laura.'

I slowly put my clothes back on. He started humming to himself and turned up the volume on the television. There was a commercial for face cream on, and he directed his gaze towards it as if this was something of great importance to him. I hadn't been able to reach him. I wasn't even sure he still loved me. All I knew was that we were no longer part of the same world.

I stopped by the door before leaving. 'Bye Otto,' I said in a murmur. He didn't seem to hear me. I called his name out again and he turned his head towards me. 'What is it?' he asked.

'This was your last chance,' I said, my last wish for a reaction on his part.

'I know,' he answered, focusing on the television screen again. 'I'm sorry. Please close the door behind you.'

I left. I stood behind the closed bedroom door, the sound of the television drifting through the cracks, my tears blurring my vision. I had never felt so alone, so abandoned. I closed my eyes and leaned against the wall. At that moment the bedroom door opened again and Otto came out. Seeing me he suddenly pressed me against him. We clutched each other breathlessly, our bodies leaning against each other in the dark hallway, our tears melded together, our lips sealed into one long kiss. We didn't say anything to each other. We remained in that position for many long minutes, perhaps even hours, and in that same position we said our final goodbyes, knowing there would be no turning back, and that we were from then on following our own separate destinies.

After I found Otto lying in the bathroom two days later, and after answering draining and exhausting questions about him to the police, I sought the help of his sister Alessandra, and together we sent him to a rehabilitation center in Minnesota. I set out to change my life that day, cleanse it of all the suffering it had been through, and attempted to start all over again. I did it all with the name Ted engraved in my mind, and the sound of his harried voice when he would ask, 'Is Otto there?' a voice whose face I was determined to find, a face I blamed for destroying my marriage. I knew this feeling was not entirely rational since Otto was responsible for his own habit, but I couldn't help thinking that had it not been for Ted, and the increasingly large amounts of cocaine he provided to his client, things could have been different.

Today, I occasionally wonder about Ted. But not in the same way. I wonder how he lives, how aware he is of the number of lives he's destroyed (I doubt Otto's is the only one), or even if he ever thinks about it. But I no longer blame him as I used to. I now believe that all of us were to blame, all of Otto's entourage, including myself, who watched and witnessed it with a disapproval that wasn't loud enough. I sometimes dream of Otto, and often think of our first glorious months together, where my love for him was boundless, as if it could never cease to flow, and where every rush of feeling I had for him gently brushed against my heart with the delicacy of a white silk glove. But there is no use in lamenting over the past. My memory has become selective, and only certain events stayed with me, particularly the early events which were to eventually set the tone of our short-lived relationship:

Approximately six weeks after I had moved in with Otto on the Rue Saint Louis en L'Ile, something unexpected happened. We were soaking in a bubble bath, when Otto stepped out of the bathtub and told me to wait for him there.

He came back approximately five minutes later, lifted

my wet body out of the bath, and told me to follow him into the bedroom.

'It's always good to do these things when you're relaxed,' he said, toweling me dry, and putting a fluffy white bathrobe over me.

'What things?' I asked him, 'What are we going to do?'

'You'll see,' he answered, with a sly smile on his face. As he gave me a quick kiss on the lips, I noticed his eyes were shining brightly, and made a comment about it. 'My eyes are shining?' he laughed, 'Well, yours will be too, in a few minutes.'

I followed him docilely into the bedroom, not knowing what to expect. He turned on some music, told me to lie on the bed, and handed over a mirror to me, on which rested two lines of cocaine.

'Would you like some?' he asked me, as if he were offering me a slice of cake.

'I don't know,' I smiled, embarrassed.

'Have you ever done it before?' he asked, this time in a more concerned tone of voice.

'Yes, twice,' I answered. I had indeed tried it while I was at Barnard, attending one of those Columbia fraternity parties where being under the influence seemed to be 'de rigueur', especially amongst the crowd of enviable young men who dominated the room with their imposing presence and intimidating manners, as they roamed around in their rented tuxedos, in search of new numbers to dial and fresh lips to kiss.

But that was a long time ago. Today, five years later, I did not feel the urge to conform or impress in order to belong somewhere. I had my own life, my own rules, and I didn't sense the need to change them.

But, to my own surprise, I found I was thinking otherwise. As I looked at the gleaming white powder, at Otto's irresistible smile, I found I was saying to myself, 'After all, why not?'

We each did a line, after which Otto put the little mirror back in his mahogany chest of drawers, turned the music on even louder, and looked at me, his sparkling eyes as blue as the Atlantic ocean, his cheeks flushed, and as he pulled his shirt over his head and opened my bathrobe, exposing my yearning body and covering my damp skin with hurried kisses, I said to myself that I had never felt happier before in my life, that this man made me feel beautiful and irresistible, and that there was nothing I would ever deny him.

I felt his tongue against my breasts, then later deep between my legs. When he lifted his head up, he bore a magnificent smile on his face, his teeth white like ivory, and he made me repeat after him, I love you, I love you, I love you.

Otto had many friends in Paris. Wherever he went, and whoever he was with, he exhibited his undeniable charm, a trademark he only parted with during his darkest days.

We went out every night. To dinner parties, nightclubs, parties, openings, screenings. I stopped seeing many of my friends, such as Baptiste, or some of the people from the Ecole du Louvre. Otto didn't get along with them, and neither did they with him. The only person he seemed to like was Jean-Luc, Sophie's boyfriend, but even that only lasted a while. So I cut off my relations with them as well, all this for the sake of love. Needless to say, I was to strongly regret this later on.

Virtually every time we went out, Otto found another reason to buy me clothes, so much so that I started to accumulate a substantial wardrobe which required my getting a closet of my own in his bedroom.

He liked me to wear short skirts and high-heels. He claimed it brought more attention to my legs, and made my neck look longer. He encouraged me to wear more jewelry and less make-up, and it came to the point where I rarely got dressed without seeking his approval of my attire. I had never met a man for whom physical appearance mattered so much, and the truth of the matter was, I didn't mind it. I complied with his orders willingly. And when my friend Sarah remarked that he seemed to like 'playing doll' with me to a point which made her worry about me, I had to disagree. 'He makes me feel great,' I said. And it was true. It was as if Otto had dug deep inside me, exposing qualities in me which I hadn't fully taken advantage of: my looks, and my sexual power.

So once he had helped unleash these once dormant attributes of mine, I allowed myself to indulge in them. After all, I reasoned when I did have small pangs of conscience, all it would take for this to stop, was for me to put an end to it; but then again, was that really imperative, considering the amount of joy it gave both of us, when Otto would watch me trying on clothes in a store, sometimes sneaking into the dressing-room where he once leaned me against the wall and circled my legs around his waist as he clasped me tightly, when suddenly the saleswoman who was helping us called out that she had found the size 36 I wanted, and she burst into the dressing-room uninvited. Upon seeing us she let out a quick cry, dropped the skirt she was holding, and kicked us out of the store, yelling that her shop was not a brothel, and didn't we feel any shame, any shame at all.

As my new self-assurance grew, so did the discovery that I could flirt and be just as charming as any other woman who might have intimidated me previously. The more I forced myself to be aggressive and assuming, the more powerful I felt, and I gradually became part of Otto's social entourage, and felt the world paying more attention to me than it ever had before. A segment of society which had once seemed unattainable to me (well known artists, showbiz personalities, European socialites and aristocrats), was now not only within my reach, but had included me as one of its members. I was introduced as 'Laura the art critic and Otto's girlfriend'. The term art critic was certainly far fetched at that point, but Otto's friends all seemed to have the need to label people in one way or another. I couldn't merely be Laura with no further explanation. I had to either do something, be someone, or come from somewhere. I had never worked in an investment bank, had a show, modeled, or acted in a movie. My family was neither powerfully rich, landed nor titled. I didn't travel extensively and vacation in St Tropez, Cortina or Gstaad. My father did not own a 'little island with its own area code' in Greece or in the Caribbean. And when I did travel, I didn't stay in castles and five-star hotels, but in little pensions and youth hostels. These drawbacks, however, made me more endearing in these people's eyes, which, despite the absurdity of it (they probably attempted to view my being part of the majority of the world as exotic in its normality) was to their credit. And on top of it all, I was an American. That in itself was a questionable trait. Not all these socialites liked Americans. But I was supposedly different, as a Spanish girl named Soledad once told me in the bathroom of a fashionable night-club, as I was applying lipstick and she had just finished snorting cocaine in one of the empty stalls (cocaine, I quickly learned, was ubiquitous in these circles). Soledad looked at me in the mirror and told me I looked European. Then she also added that I dressed well and spoke good French, and asked me whether I had ever thought about modeling, because I had the figure and the look, and if ever the idea sounded tempting to me I should tell her because she knew everybody in the fashion world. I smiled and told her I would think about it.

As Otto told me one day with a mixture of jealousy and pride, it also seemed that I had made quite an impression upon certain members of the male contingent of this entourage, including Dimitri, a Russian Prince, and especially Luca, Otto's oldest childhood friend from Italy, who reportedly found me very alluring. Although this compliment didn't leave me indifferent (Luca, a publisher, was practically the only one of Otto's friends whom I found intelligent, attractive and interesting), I did feel as if I had just been flattered for the wrong reasons. Was this Otto's way of justifying his pampering me, as if he felt a certain amount of guilt about it? Or was it merely self-satisfaction that thanks to his dexterous hands and sense of style à la Professor Higgins, I had now been molded into a 'Duchess' like Eliza Doolittle in *My Fair Lady*? I decided that as long as he didn't make me do something against my will, I would not let this preoccupy me. Instead, I would continue to have fun. It was no doubt the most entertaining and exciting time I had ever had. The phone never stopped ringing, we seemed to be invited everywhere, so after two months of this intense socializing, it was no surprise when Madame Moher announced that I was fired, and that she wished me good luck for the future. She then asked to speak to Otto, and told him that his October show would have to be postponed until a later date, a statement that made Otto furious, since he felt that she was involving her relationship with me with his career. She retorted that she had been doing him a favor because she liked his father so much, and if he didn't appreciate that he should go to seek representation elsewhere, but he should be aware that not all gallery owners hire pretty assistants.

This made matters worse. Otto jumped into a cab and rushed to the gallery. While I sat in the living-room waiting for him, I realized that Madame Moher was probably very hurt about what had happened, and was projecting her disappointment with me on to Otto. This realization increased my feelings of guilt towards Madame Moher; we had established a nice relationship together, and I had heard from several people that she had taken a strong liking to me. She obviously viewed this whole episode as a betrayal on my part, and the only explanation I could find for my selfishness and irresponsibility was that I was in love, a justification I couldn't imagine she would deem worthy of forgiveness.

I called her up to apologize. I tried to explain the situation to her, but she seemed cold and uninterested. I finally asked her if she was very angry with me. 'I'm disappointed in you,' she answered, 'you were doing good work until this Stamballo came along. For me, my private life and my work are two different things. Obviously not for you. Unless of course you were just not taking your work seriously.'

'But I was!' I exclaimed, 'and I really feel bad about all of this . . .' I felt like crying, but held my tears back.

'Mademoiselle Miller,' she said, 'it is not enough to feel bad. You must do something about it. And one last word of advice: if Stamballo "fils" is as bad as Stamballo "père" was, I can assure you that your life will be difficult. Very difficult. Goodbye Mademoiselle Miller, your boyfriend has just arrived.'

It was only later that I understood what Madame Moher had meant by my doing something about feeling bad. It was her way of giving me a last chance and I hadn't even picked up on it when I should have. It was now too late. There was nothing I could do about it. And actually, I wasn't even sure I wanted to do something about it. Stepping back again might put an end to this fairy-tale I was living.

Otto came home looking dour, and although he refused to elaborate on the details, he told me his show was indeed postponed, and he was now reconsidering whether he wanted to show his work there in the first place. We left for New York without seeing Otto's photographs displayed on the walls of the Moher Gallery.

I recovered from this double disappointment much

faster than I expected, and this convinced me that my new style of life was obviously more appropriate for me at this time than pursuing a career. As for Otto, he dismissed the importance of the event with a wave of the hand, and assured me that he could find plenty of other places that would be more than happy to show his photographs. 'For example,' he said with some urgency, 'the Stone Gallery in New York. I happened to talk to the owner last week, he's really interested in meeting me. And since we're thinking about moving there together, it could really work out.'

'I hope it does,' I responded before switching the topic of conversation altogether.

I had come to have ambivalent feelings about Otto's photography. Although I loved the recent work he had done, a series of photographs taken in several French train stations, and some portraits of his friends, I often had the unsettling feeling that he had chosen this career for himself not out of love or need for it, but because there was nothing better for him to do. He didn't seem to passionately care about it, and often days or weeks would pass without him picking up his Leica.

I did not bring up the topic with Otto. But one day, after more than a month had gone by, I decided that it was time to face the facts. We had just taken one of our endless afternoon naps and were about to get dressed for the evening, when I remarked on the fact that he hadn't gone near his camera in a long while. Otto did not take this comment lightly. 'Can I know why you ask?' he asked me, his voice painfully cold.

'I'm asking because I'm wondering if there is a reason or if—'

'Do I ask you what you do all day?' he started shouting at me, his voice echoing against the stone walls, 'Do I?'

'No, you don't,' I answered, trying to keep my voice from trembling.

'So why not do the same for me? My life is my business. Not yours.'

'Is that so?' I snapped, 'So please tell me what the hell I'm doing here then.' I couldn't control my sudden anger, and in a way it served its purpose. Otto looked at me strangely, obviously surprised by my reaction, and launched into a short speech in which he tried to explain his position in relation to the world he lived in, his voice calm again, as if there hadn't just been an altercation between us. 'Most of the people I know don't work,' he said slowly, as if weighing the impact of his words. 'You see, I'm one of the few who actually does something constructive with his life. Something other than partying, traveling, and spending many nights in different beds. I take photographs because I like to, not because I have to. I chose to do this and I love doing it. To tell you the truth, having my first show in New York was one of the highlights of my life, and I hope I have many more. But like most artists, I have my own pace and you have to realize that. I'm sorry I blew up at you before, and I hope you understand what I'm trying to say.'

I did, but I was only partially convinced. I realized that Otto may have had the desire, but he didn't have the discipline. And as I got to know him better, this failing proved to be the main impediment to our relationship, the one that would finally destroy us altogether. But in the meantime life went on, and the issue of work was set aside.

The week after our discussion, as I was about to get dressed for a Brazilian dinner party, Otto came into the room, put his arms around me, and once again, told me to close my eyes. My body froze up, as if the temperature had suddenly dropped. 'No Otto, not again,' I said, praying that he wouldn't pull out cocaine from his chest of drawers. 'Relax!' he laughed, 'It's not what you think! I do that stuff very rarely. Come on Laura, don't get so uptight . . .'

I closed my eyes. I felt something cold against my left hand, sliding towards my finger. 'Open your eyes,' he said. On my fourth finger lay a thick golden ring, mounted with a deep sapphire stone, surrounded by little diamonds. 'Otto,' I gasped.

He looked at me and smiled, then, in a sudden gesture clasped me tightly against his chest, and whispered in my ear, 'I love you, I want you to marry me, I want you forever by my side.'

I looked up at him. His eyes were filled with tears, and as I answered 'Yes, I'll marry you,' he lifted me up, so high I started shouting, and as he brought me back towards him we both started laughing, and tears swelled in my eyes as he clasped me tightly against him. He reached for the telephone, wiping his tears as he broke the news to his mother. His voice changed when he talked to her. It sounded lower, less exuberant, more cautious. He spoke briefly, recounting our meeting, mentioned Madame Moher's name, and brought up his father. 'Papa would have loved her,' he said, 'it's a pity he's not here to share this moment with me.'

After he hung up, we talked about his father. Otto told me about the last time he had gone to visit him, around three months ago, a week before his death. 'He was in perfect health. Eating out all the time, dragging me to cocktail-parties, running after women like he always did. He actually introduced me to a woman whom I suspect was more than just a fling. A very good-looking woman. A musician I think. Cristina was her name. But who knows... My father was such a ladies' man, you could never keep track.'

'And what about Madame Moher in all of this? How did she know your father?'

Otto smiled. 'Monique? She was madly in love with him. I think they had a brief affair, many, many years ago, and I think she's still sour about the fact that it didn't work out. But why don't you first call your mother before we get into this, and then I want to call Luca to tell him the good news. I'd like him to be my best man.'

'Forget it! My mother can wait!' I exclaimed, more out of apprehension than for any other reason. 'Tell me more about this! I can't believe it. Your father and... Madame Moher! Well what do you know,' I mumbled dumbfounded by the news. 'I gather that she was better looking than she is now,' I added, trying to envision what Madame Moher might have looked like twenty or thirty years ago.

I called my mother up. She responded with shock, at first coldly, then vainly attempting to dissuade me from doing such a rash and hasty thing. 'You barely know him,' she said, 'how can you marry someone so fast?'

'I love him,' I answered categorically.

'That's not enough,' she replied.

'Then what is enough?' I asked.

'Certitude. Right now you don't know what you really think. You're just blinded by love. Call me in a few months and we'll talk again.'

'I've already made my decision,' I said firmly. 'I know him, and I love him.'

'Okay. Then I have nothing else to say to you, except for this: I have a bad feeling. From what I can see in the photograph you sent me, I don't like the way he looks, and I don't like the style of life you both lead. It's vapid and non-productive, and I'm not sure this man is right for you.'

'Oh, I see. I suppose your Palm-Beach way of life is more productive, I suppose Oscar is right for you,' I said, boiling with anger and wishing I hadn't called her in the first place.

'I'm fifty-seven years old my dear, and you're twenty-five. Let's keep things in perspective here. I've lived longer than you. I know one or two pointers about life which you don't. And I'm your mother. Let's not forget this. You owe me some respect.'

'Fine. I'm sorry. But first of all, I happen to know that you're sixty years old, not fifty-seven, and second of all I want you to know that nothing will stop me from getting married, not even your motherly wisdom.'

'All right. Then I have nothing else to say. Goodbye.' She hung up before I was able to say anything else, and the conversation was left at that. I felt too embarrassed to tell Otto what she had said. He appeared to get the gist of it though, and tried to reassure me. 'She'll get used to it,' he said, putting his arms around me, 'don't worry. After no time at all, she'll be asking for grandchildren. Just wait and see.'

'I don't know, I hope you're right,' I said, trying to hold back my tears. However angry I was at her, I still valued my mother's judgment, for whatever it was worth. I felt a sudden indecision creep into me, and for perhaps the first time since I'd met Otto, I wondered if I should recant and reconsider my decision. But Otto didn't give me time to pursue this thought. 'I love you Laura,' he said, 'I can promise you that I will make you a very happy woman. I want to have children with you, I want you forever by my side. You're like a breath of fresh air in my life.'

He placed his two hands around my face, and kissed the whole of it, from my hair to my eyes, to my cheekbones and to my lips. I had to surrender. This was all too sweet to give up.

That night, Luca took us out to dinner. He was about to move to London, and wanted to celebrate the happy event with us.

'I'm very happy I'm going to be Otto's best man,' he told me as the waiter poured us some wine, 'and if you don't mind my saying so, I hope I manage to find someone as equally attractive as you are. I mean if Otto is getting married, then it is time for all of us to re-evaluate the status of our love life, is that not so Othello?'

Otto smiled. 'Yes, it's so, but please don't call me Othello anymore, that's kid stuff.'

'Va bene Othello, va bene Othellino.'

We all started laughing. It was a joyful occasion, full of champagne, good food and inebriated jokes. As the dessert arrived, Luca made a last toast to us and asked if he could kiss the future bride. 'Be my guest,' Otto said, smiling gleefully, 'but watch where you kiss her.'

Luca rose from his chair and placed his arm on my shoulder. But instead of kissing me on the cheek, as I was expecting him to, he took my hand delicately in his, and gently placed his lips on the back of my hand, leaving a troubling warmth on my skin which seemed to linger for too many minutes.

When he sat back down I noticed his cheeks were flushed, a reaction which Otto seemingly ignored; Luca brought up his new job in London, and the conversation took on a professional turn.

After dinner, Otto and I walked around the empty streets of the sixth arrondissement. The red wine felt heavy in my body, and the champagne light in my head. When we arrived at the Place Furstenberg, we stood still, the half moon lurking above us. We listened to the nocturnal sounds, our hands clasped together, our heads touching. There was nothing to say. It all seemed perfect. Our love rose above all, indestructible, eternal.

The next morning I met Otto's mother for the first time. Recently remarried to a certain Baron Pierre de Valors, she bore on her face the expression of a harried person, as if the time she was spending in one's company could have clearly been better spent elsewhere. (Later on, I realized that this was her own way of protecting herself from exposing her own feelings of vulnerability.) As Otto had explained to me, walking up the Avenue du President Wilson towards her apartment, she kept very busy with her husband's social schedule, chairing charities and gala benefits, and, being a music lover, was heavily involved with the Paris Symphony Orchestra, of which she was an important benefactor.

Hélène de Valors was, confirming all accounts, an extremely attractive woman. She was fairly tall, with small bones and an angular figure. She had blonde hair held back with combs, tanned skin, enviable cheekbones and almond-shaped blue eyes, just like Otto's. She wore a cream-colored silk shirt, with tailored woolen pants and a heavy gold necklace around her neck. She extended a stiff hand to me, and led us into a ballroom-sized living-room. The decoration was similar to Otto's, except that in this case the furniture was much more elaborate and grandiose, from the crystal chandeliers, to the Louis XV furniture and the Delacroix drawing right above the plush red-velvet sofa chair I was sitting on.

Conversation was strained. I couldn't figure out if it was that she didn't care about her son, or his accomplishments, but whatever Otto seemed to say she took with utter calmness and near indifference. When he told her a little about me and the fact that we wanted to get married as soon as possible, she merely said, 'that sounds like a nice idea,' rang a little bell, and ordered the maid to bring in some more tea and perhaps some pastries. Her comment startled me. If my mother had been there, she would have immediately asked how come we wanted to get married so soon, was I pregnant, were we sure this was the right thing, especially after such a short period of time. But as far as I could tell, those thoughts didn't seem to occur to the Baroness. After she asked to see the ring, and looked at it with approval, especially after Otto reassured her that he had bought it at Cartier, where his mother was an old client, she hardly paid any attention to me, and spent a lot of time talking about Otto's two sisters. 'Alessandra is in love with some English fashion designer, she's not sure she's coming to Paris next weekend, she's busy traveling around the country with him. She's had her hair cut, it looks magnificent. You should call her more often Otto, really, she'd be delighted to hear from you.'

'I call her. She's the one who never calls me . . .' Otto smiled at me, and took a sip of his tea.

'And did you hear about Stefania and George? They're thinking about moving to Spain, he's been offered a good position there.'

'Where in Spain?' Otto asked.

'Madrid,' she answered, pouring herself some more tea.

'Great city,' I said. 'And great museums.'

'Indeed,' she answered, with a forced smile.

I felt very ill at ease, especially because Otto didn't help the situation. He didn't seem aware of my discomfort, and went on talking to his mother as if I weren't in the room.

Then, as if he suddenly remembered I was there, Otto grabbed my hand and kissed it. 'Mother, I'm madly in love with Laura,' he announced, as he held my hand in his. 'I can't wait to get married.'

Hélène's painted lips finally extended into an earnest smile. 'Well, she's a beautiful girl,' she said in a kind voice. 'I wish you both all the luck. Now, when were you both thinking of getting married?'

Her voice suddenly sounded uplifted, as if Otto's de-claration had greatly reassured her.

'We're not sure. We're thinking June or July.'

'That's in two months. Well, although it seems rather sudden, I suppose it's possible. What does your mother think about all of this?'

'Oh,' I blushed, 'well, she's a little taken aback.'

'I understand,' Hélène answered, as the maid came back in with a tray of petits-fours and a fresh pot of tea. 'Well, she shouldn't worry,' she added, as I picked a rasp-berry tartlet off the tray, 'my son is very trustworthy. He always displayed good taste, and he's always behaved like a gentleman.'

This sentence struck me as awkward. But there was no use in pondering it, since the family dynamics were obvi-ously much more complex than I had anticipated. But at this stage, it seemed fruitless to try and piece the family puzzle together; I had a lifetime to do it, I reasoned, a conclusion which, little did I know, never even had a chance of concretizing.

We left Hélène's house with the promise that we would be back for dinner the following week. Otto was quiet on the way back, and I avoided mentioning the meeting. Finally, as we reached home, I asked Otto about his relationship with his family. 'Do you get along? I mean, do you get together and talk about things?'

'Like what?' He frowned.

'I don't know,' I shrugged my shoulders. 'Anything.'

Otto was silent for a short while. 'No,' he finally answered, 'I can't really say we get together and talk. I mean yes we get together sometimes, but we don't talk.'

'You seem to have rather strained relations,' I ventured.

'You could call it that, yes. But that's the way it's always been. In your world, not communicating in a family is seen as a strain. In mine, it's taken for granted.'

'I see,' I answered, realizing how wide the gulf between our two families was, and how unlikely it was for them to ever tread on the same territory.

'My family is not a warm family. It never was.' Otto added, as he opened our front door and let the machine pick up the phone which had just started ringing. 'My mother has always been this way. She had a difficult life with my father. She knows she didn't spend enough time with us when we were young, at least not with me, and instead of doing something about it now, some thirty years later, she has decided to just let it be. And I don't blame her for it. It wouldn't make sense for her to suddenly try to be closer to me. It's not in her character. At least she's consistent and doesn't let it get to her anymore.'

'I see. And what about me? Do you think she liked me?'

'She'll get used to you. And once she does, she'll be much warmer towards you. Now if you don't mind, I'm going to go downstairs and get myself some cigarettes. I forgot to buy a pack on the way home ... I'll be right back. Do you need anything?'

'No.'

'See you in a minute.'

As I heard him close the front door, I threw myself on the bed, crying. It was enough that my mother had reacted so negatively to the news. The fact that his mother seemingly felt the same left me at a loss. What about me, I kept thinking, what about my feelings in all of this? Was Otto really the man I wanted to marry? Would he make me happy?

A little while later, I heard the key in the door and quickly wiped my tears. As he stepped into the room, I noticed he was carrying a large mixed bouquet of flowers. 'I'm sorry,' he said, kneeling down towards me. 'I'm so sorry. I know it's not easy for you. I guess we just come from two different worlds and it will take time for both of them to meld together, or for us both to make sense of it all.'

We made sense of it three months later, with a civil wedding at the Mairie of the sixteenth arrondissement, on the Avenue Henri-Martin. I wore a low-cut short white dress, and my hair up in an elaborate bun, circled by a row of white and pink flowers, revealing heavy-set diamond earrings offered by my new mother-in-law. Twenty people attended, mostly family and close friends. Sandra and Rebecca flew in from New York, Luca from London, where he played his role of best man with all the poise it required. We invited two hundred people to celebrate with us that night, in a night-club near Les Halles. My mother took me aside, held my hand in hers, and told me she wished me much happiness. 'I'm sorry about all those things I said about Otto. I guess I was wrong. He seems like a nice boy. He sure seems to love you, and he's really quite handsome. Much better looking than that awful photograph of him you sent me. And it's clear that he comes from quite a family. At least I don't have to worry about that. Of course he could have been Jewish but then again, I gave up on that one a long time ago.'

'Let's not forget Aaron Steinberg,' I reminded her smiling, as the memory of Aaron suddenly came to my mind, a short and gawky teenage book-worm, who had a voracious appetite for the classics, and who displayed his affection by buying me a book a day, assuring that by the end of our short-lived relationship I could boast a small but impressive library.

'How long did that last? Four months. And besides, you were sixteen, for crying out loud.'

'All right. But he still counts. And what about Michael Waldberg? He was an important one in my life. I was totally in love with him,' I said, blushing at the sound of my words. I had never been so honest with my mother before, certainly not in discussing any of my feelings about the men I dated.

'You were? Well, what do you know. I never thought you liked him . . .'

'Oh, I liked him all right. The problem was him. He didn't like me enough. He left me for that Sharon girl, you remember her? The plump one with the braces?'

'Sure. Sharon Lipsky. Now Sharon Waldberg. She married Michael three years ago.'

'No way,' I retorted.

'Why not? She became pretty and thin, and as you can imagine she doesn't wear braces anymore. I was invited to the wedding but I couldn't make it.'

'You were? Why on earth would you be invited to Sharon and Michael's wedding?' I said, genuinely bewildered and slightly irritated that Michael had chosen to invite my mother and not me.

'Her mother was a good friend of mine, a nice woman. We went to high school together in Brooklyn.'

'You did? I never knew that!' I exclaimed, winking at Otto who was dancing with his sister Stefania.

'Sure. Brenda Dovel. She was a beauty. All the boys were after her, while I would sit and watch. Sometimes I would sit and cry. She married early and divorced. Sharon she had with her second husband who happens to know Oscar. The world is so small, I swear . . .'

She took a loud sip of her champagne, and straightened her pink and gold strapless dress. 'I got fat. Can you tell?' she asked me, a childish and touching grin on her face.

'No mother, I can't tell. You look beautiful,' I answered, giving her a kiss on her perfumed and tight cheek.

'Really? You think so?' she asked, with a sound of relief in her voice, 'I wish you could have been there this morning when Oscar gave me hell about this dress. He said it made me look like a Christmas tree.'

'It does not,' I objected, 'Oscar doesn't know what he's talking about. And this dress really flatters you. You look great. Tanned, healthy, and I like your hair up.'

'All right. You're a good girl. Don't overdo it.'

'I'm not overdoing it. I mean it! You look great!'

'Well, so do you, Mrs Stamballo. You look like an angel.'

My mother's acceptance of Otto meant a lot to me. I hugged her and gave her another kiss before she strolled over to Oscar with a belligerent look in her eyes.

My happiness was unbounded, and continued to remain that way all throughout our honeymoon in the

Maldives, where we rented a sumptuous villa on the beach, and where Otto opened himself up to me in all his splendor, exhibiting a love for me and expressing a desire to achieve success, which could have fooled anyone, including himself.

Four

I am sitting in Kennedy Airport, waiting to board my plane to Rome. No one knows I am doing this except for my mother. I called her last night, just so she'd know where I was in case of an emergency. I have decided to do this after deliberating about it for a long time. Ever since my last visit to Italy, I have not been able to put aside the conviction that there is more to be uncovered about Omega, and that I am the only one who can do it. This thought was obviously triggered by the discovery of the lithographs at the printing house, and later grew in proportion to Jaurel's interdiction of my revealing their existence. My curiosity was aroused, and, combined with my desire to find an original conclusion for my book, prompted me to pay for my own round-trip ticket: I am on a mission of discovery.

Yesterday I phoned Jaurel at the gallery, and was put on hold for an exceedingly long time before I could talk to him. 'I think I need to interview Omega one last time,' I said, speaking fast and breathlessly, as I often did when he made me nervous. 'It might help me out with my conclusion, which, as I've told you, I've been having some trouble with . . .'

'I know. So what? What additional information do you need? You know everything there is to know.'

'I don't. He's a difficult man to talk to, as you know too well. And besides, I'm stuck, and I feel that the only way out for me is to interview him one last time.'

Jaurel cleared his throat before responding: 'Mademoiselle Miller,' he said, slowly, dragging down each syllable, 'you will get out of this block of yours because you have no choice. I don't care what you write about. Just write. As long as it's not about the lithographs, of course. You have exactly six weeks to complete this book. How exactly do you intend to keep your word, if you suddenly fly off for a week, just because Mademoiselle would like to? How, *how*? We are serious people here, not dreamers. You do your work on time, and that's all there is to it. *On time!*'

Here his voice rose to a roaring crescendo, and I found myself acquiescing against my will. 'You're right M. Jaurel, you're right. I'll do my best. And you don't have to worry about having the work on time. That goes without saying.'

'Good. Now. I'm very busy, I will talk to you next week. Goodbye Mademoiselle Miller.'

'Goodbye,' I sighed. What could I do? I certainly couldn't call Ensor about it. I was left with only one solution: to pack my bag and fly off to Rome the next morning.

So here I am. I couldn't sleep all night. The plane is late, it is raining outside, and I'm awaiting the trip with a mixture of trepidation and anticipation. I took a substantial amount of money out of my savings account, and booked myself a room in a five-star hotel on the Via Bocca di Leone, in the center of town. I reasoned that in the event that I encounter some obstacles during my short business trip, they should not interfere with my few pleasures, namely Italian food, roaming around the city, stopping in cafés, going to the Galeria Doria Pamphili, and most importantly, staying in a grand hotel, something I did not have the satisfaction of indulging in last time, since Jaurel, never renowned for his generosity, put me up in a three-star hotel, which, though it was very comfortable, did not match my dream of staying in a luxurious palazzo, a wish I have granted myself this time.

As for the lithographs, I have no plan as to how to approach the issue. I will probably rent a car and drive to Pomezia. Perhaps I should go around the same time I did last spring, when Peter was closing up. Was it at four or five o'clock? And what about Omega? Should I meet him before or after I go to the printing house? Should I mention the lithographs directly to him?

I start to jot these thoughts down in my notebook. I decide that if I see that the issue of the lithographs is too delicate, I will let it go. Besides, there are many other things I could ask Omega about, such as his early work (which we had never talked much about), and the triptych which I recently heard he's been working on. This makes me feel better. I close my notebook, as we are asked to board the plane.

I have a window seat. I rejoice in the fact that no one seems to be sitting next to me, which means that I will be able to stretch my legs out and sleep. Five minutes before take-off, a young man rushes down the aisle and the stewardess points to a seat right behind me. I know two elderly Italian women are sitting there, because I saw them when I came on board. One of the women is sitting in the young man's seat. She says something in Italian to her friend, who asks the stewardess in broken English if the man would be so kind as to let them sit there, they really want to be together, and perhaps I would be nice enough to let him sit next to me instead. What can I say? I have no choice. The man plops his jacket on the seat next to me. 'Sorry,' he says, probably responding to the look of disappointment on my face. He opens the overhead compartment above us, where he places both his jacket and a brown leather briefcase.

'That's okay,' I smile. The man is probably in his early thirties. He has blond hair, bleached eyebrows, and wears wire-rimmed glasses. He is dressed casually (a blue cotton shirt, gray and white checkered pants, a black jacket), and wears expensive looking shoes. I wonder what his job could be. I think he's perhaps a professor, but after another quick glance at him decide he either works in advertising or in entertainment law.

I close my eyes and quickly fall asleep. When I wake up, the stewardesses have already begun serving dinner. By the time our trays come, I feel obliged to talk to my unidentified neighbor. I've always found eating to be an intimate activity, and always dreaded meals where one must chew and swallow in front of perfect strangers, a nightmare of self-consciousness, especially during eight-hour flights, where cordiality can occasionally compensate for boredom (notwithstanding the fact that both can sometimes go hand-in-hand).

So as I poke around my beef and string beans, I turn towards my white-eyebrowed neighbor, and say something about the development of airplane food, and how this is actually not bad, although I prefer the little curried things they serve on Pakistan Airlines.

My neighbor barely smiles. 'I wouldn't know,' he says, 'I've never taken Pakistan Airlines.' He speaks hurriedly, as if in a rush to put an end to the conversation.

'Oh. Well, you haven't really missed anything. It's not such a great airline.'

He smiles and digs into his food, focusing his wire-rims on the bottom of his plate. Obviously there is not much point here in making small talk. Well, at least I tried. And frankly, I don't really care about talking to this man either. He seems bland, and devoid of any sense of humor whatsoever. I put my fork and knife down (I'm not hungry), grab one of the magazines I purchased at the busy airport news-stand, and concentrate my attention on an article about a doctor who claims he can create a new smile by bonding and bleaching teeth. As I'm reading, a stewardess comes by, and I hear my neighbor ask her for a scotch on the rocks. She's a young woman with a fresh and rosy face, who is wearing small earrings shaped like leaves. As she pours him his drink, she asks him if by any chance he wasn't on the same flight a couple of weeks ago. He answers that actually yes, he was. He seems surprised that she would recognize him. I close my eyes briefly. I'm still tired. As I can't help but overhear their conversation, I am suddenly struck by the sound of his voice. It is familiar. And what's even more perplexing, is that it takes my closing my eyes to recognize it, because once I open them again, it just seems like any other ordinary nasal voice. I close my eyes again. I try to focus my attention on his voice. Where have I heard it before? Was it recently? Was it a long time ago? Or does it merely sound like another voice I know?

I shrug my shoulders. There is no point in trying to figure it out. I have many more important things to think about, such as Omega, for example. I should be taking down notes, organizing my schedule for the week, but I don't know why I'm so tired, I can feel my eyelids closing, here I go drifting away again, I can hear my neighbor flipping pages of a magazine, the noise is irritating, so incessant, as if he were either nervous or restless and cannot decide what article to focus on.

I'm awakened three hours later. I look at my watch in amazement. I have never slept so well on a plane. I feel refreshed, and stretch my arms out, yawning with content. My neighbor isn't sitting next to me anymore. Perhaps he's changed seats. I don't see any of his belongings on or around his seat. I get up to go to the bathroom. I look around the plane: it seems full. There is a long line for the bathrooms. I wait patiently, behind a mother and her young child. As I get into the bathroom, I fix my hair, and tie it into a pony-tail. I am wearing tight lycra pants and a khaki blouse which is now slightly crumpled; I look surprisingly refreshed, and start to feel excited as I envisage myself tomorrow, walking the streets of Rome, and stopping at a caffé for a cornetto and a caffé latte.

I go back to my seat. My neighbor is not back. He's clearly not sitting next to me anymore. I start planning tomorrow's schedule. After fifteen minutes I get up again and go towards the Business Class section, where there is an enclave reserved for drinks. I ask a steward for a tomato juice. As he is pouring it, I see my ex-neighbor talking to the same stewardess, who is laughing loudly. She has obviously seated him in the Business Class section. Well, good for him. I look at them: they seem to be flirting, although the man doesn't look like the flirtatious type. As the steward hands me over my juice, I see them both walking over towards where I'm standing, and as I hear his voice, this time distinctly, I am again struck by this feeling of familiarity. They approach the steward I am standing next to, and my ex-neighbor barely acknowledges my presence. 'Pietro,' the stewardess says to her colleague, 'this is Ted Shaw, Ted this is Pietro.'

'We've met.' They shake hands and I go back to my seat. I fold my table out and place my tomato juice on it. I start flipping through the pages of my notebook. Ted Shaw. I don't know any Ted Shaw. Did I ever know or meet any Teds in general? No. Yes. Yes. Ted. I start upright and my notebook falls to the ground. Ted was Otto's drug dealer. Ted who I used to have nightmares about, Ted who used to call with the rushed and nasal voice, the Ted I never knew. It's him. I can now place his voice perfectly. I can even recall the way he sounded when he used to call the house. The blond man with the bleached eyebrows who was sitting next to me before, in gray and white checkered pants and wire-rimmed glasses, the man who looks like a lawyer or an advertising executive is nothing less than a drug dealer.

I breathe in deeply. I am suddenly frightened. What is this man doing here? Does he know who I am? Was he following me for some obscure reason? I can see him from the back now, talking to the two stewards. Should I turn him in? It would be so easy. I could just go up to any of them and tell them what I know. This man here is an important drug dealer. He provides drugs to half of New York's entertainment industry, as well as to some other very important people. I know all of this through Otto, who used to boast to me about him, as if having a trendy dealer meant something about his position in life. 'He only likes your money,' I remember remarking to him, 'he doesn't give a shit about you. You're just a rich nothing as far as he's concerned.'

After my comment, Otto refrained from mentioning him anymore. But now, I wish I knew more about him. This is the first time I've ever heard his last name. And for all I know, Ted is not even his real name. The coincidence is frightening. Here I am, sitting on a plane after a whim, and who happens to be my neighbor but the man I consider most responsible for my ex-husband's downfall. On the one hand, I am tempted to go up to him now, to tell him who I am. 'Do you remember Otto Stamballo?' I feel like asking. 'Do you know where he ended up, all thanks to you?' But something is pulling me back, as if turning him in would be acknowledging my old love for Otto. I don't want to think about Otto. He's not part of my life anymore. On the other hand, this man is dangerous, and if caught, could spend many years in jail. I will talk to someone now. I cannot let this man go free.

I get up slowly and feel my heart pounding. I push a strand of hair away from my face and start to walk towards him. I have no control over my legs. I'm afraid my knees are going to bump into each other and I'll collapse. I feel beads of sweat forming on my forehead, which, as his back gets closer and closer to my focal point, erupt into a deluge of sweat, forcing me to return to my seat and pat my forehead dry with an old Kleenex.

I try again. This time, with more bravery. Come on Laura, I mumble to myself, you can do it. At the exact moment in which I am almost at the end of my short though trying journey, Ted swiftly turns around and bumps into me at full force. I find myself on my knees, staring at his shiny shoes, then at his arms as he helps me to get up. 'Are you okay?' he asks me, smiling, as the stewardess looks at me, concerned.

'You're lucky there's carpet on the floor. You could have hurt yourself badly,' she says, frowning a little as if to emphasize the gravity of that possibility. I smile at both of them, hoping that my cheeks are not too red with shame. I still have the propensity to blush, especially in awkward situations like this one when I feel like an utter fool.

After I'm back on my feet and drinking yet another tomato juice, Ted asks me if this is my first time in Italy. I lie and tell him it is. He asks me if I'm heading to Rome. 'Verona,' I tell him, hoping to God that there is a connection from Rome to Verona. 'Lucky you,' he says, in a much more friendly tone of voice than previously, 'it's a great city. Very romantic. Meeting your sweetheart there?'

'Something like that,' I answer with a nervous smile.

'Well, have a nice time. You'll see, Italy's a great place.'

This is the moment to plunge in, I tell myself. Go ahead. But for some reason, something is stopping me from doing it. Maybe it's the way Ted is peering at me scrupulously, or the stewardess's rosy cheeks as she glances at Ted longingly. Something in both their gazes indicates a preoccupation of some sort, prompting me to call off my interference until a more propitious moment, or perhaps, to call it off altogether. Besides, what if Ted is following me, if he does know who I am? What if my paranoia is justified, and for now he's pretending to treat me just the way I'm treating him, as another anodyne passenger?

I thank them for their help, and return to my seat. And what if it's not even the same Ted, I wonder, as I look at the row of cottony white clouds. Perhaps it is wiser for me to keep this to myself. I can think of at least two reasons why: if he is on my trail, it is probably prudent of me to affect ignorance, just in case I need to dupe him and get away. If he isn't on my trail, and this is all pathetic speculation, I have to think of my goal in Rome, and what it could entail. Who knows what could happen to me there; my task may not be devoid of difficulties, and at this stage there's no point in burdening myself with yet another problem. Besides, I perfectly remember Otto's discussion about turning in drug dealers. 'If they see you're on to something, they won't let you get away with it. That is, if they're big time.'

'Is Ted big time?' I remember asking him, finding myself propagating his lame choice of words, which seemed to give such importance to someone who deserved so little.

'Yes, he is,' Otto answered cautiously, 'Why? Do you have any plans to turn him in?'

'Sure,' I retorted, deciding to take advantage of his paranoia. 'I've actually been thinking about it for a long time. If he stops selling to you, you'll be forced to drastically reduce your intake. Am I right, or am I wrong? Oh, I'm sorry. I forgot. There's plenty of other drug dealers around.'

Here Otto's eyes took on a darker color, as I felt him ready to launch into one of his defensive and wasteful tirades, as he always did when I brought up the subject. Except that this time, he knew he was guilty for bringing it up in the first place, so instead of letting it out on me, he chose to maintain a painful silence, and left the room to brood on his own.

Even the memory of those times is enough to make me shudder. We had lost all respect for one another, and spent most of our time snapping at each other, seldom aware, or perhaps consciously avoiding having to face how far we had diverged from our starting point; nostalgia was our enemy.

I take my notebook back out, and try to focus on my 'mission,' as I have now decided to call it. But as I start writing, my eyes get blurry, this time from impending tears. I swallow hard, and try to convince myself that my inability to confront Ted is not weak but logical. I cannot let my emotions run rampant, especially if they could entail danger. This seems to strengthen me in some way. It has been forty-five minutes since my encounter with Ted, and my mind is now in Pomezia, among the rubble of the printing house. I pray that the lithographs are still there, and that I will be able to view them freely.

We are told to fasten our seat-belts in preparation for landing. I breathe deeply, tighten my seat-belt as the plane begins its descent, and as Fiumicino starts to grow in size. The image of my father comes to me, and I can hear his low voice telling me, as he did at the end of his life, 'don't rely on what you know; rely on what you feel.'

These words come back to haunt me as I am standing by the luggage carousel in the airport, waiting for my suitcase. I notice that Ted and Pietro are standing not too far away from me, and are seemingly in the middle of a heated discussion. Obviously, these two have become friends rather quickly. I find Pietro's presence there awkward, since as far as I know, passengers and stewards do not usually collect their luggage at the same time.

As the carousel turns, Pietro suddenly interrupts the discussion and barely manages to retrieve his small black leather suitcase on time. Ted's nearly identical suitcase comes moments later. Their conversation seems to come to a halt as each one of them puts both their suitcases on the ground, and searches their inner jacket pockets; Pietro pulls out a pen, Ted a small paper pad. I cannot keep my gaze from focusing in their direction, as if I were expecting something to happen. At this point, I don't even try to conceal my interest in their interaction. Besides, they barely seem to notice me, or anyone else for that matter, so engrossed are they in each other.

What I see next happens so fast that I later wonder if what I had witnessed was an actual occurrence or a figment of my jet-lagged imagination: both men keep on talking, and write down what I presume to be their phone numbers on the small pad of paper. Then they shake hands, and they reach down for their respective suitcases. I see Ted's arm reaching over for the black suitcase further away from him. At first, I am almost tempted to run over to both men. 'You took your friend's suitcase!' I imagine myself saying to them. But just as quickly I realize that this switch might not be accidental.

This frightening possibility causes me to focus my attention back on to the carousel, where I see my suitcase slowly coming towards me. Curiously enough, what I have just witnessed relieves me in some odd way, because I sense that this surreptitious transaction has nothing to do with me; on the contrary, there is something undeniably dubious about what I may have just observed, although this time I do not have that insatiable urge to explore what it is on my own. I have too many other mysteries to uncover, and frankly I am more interested in Omega than in these two men. By the time I place my weathered suitcase on a cart, both men are gone. I wheel my cart to an exit, hail a taxi, plop my belongings on the back seat and as the driver rolls away, I smile to myself. 'I will win this game,' I say to myself, 'and no one will be able to stop me this time.'

I am standing in a caffé, eating a tomato and mozzarella panino, and drinking a cappuccino. All around me the Via Condotti is bustling with activity. It is a sunny and warm autumn day. I am dressed in a light pale-blue cotton suit, and am wearing the pointy beige moccasins I bought this morning, right after I checked into the Hotel d'Inghilterra which is even more beautiful than I expected: I treated myself to a hearty breakfast early this morning in my living-room, luxuriated in a foam bath (the bathtub being practically the size of my New York kitchen) and could not resist the temptation of going shopping after breakfast, resulting in a spending spree which carried me from the

Via del Corso to the top of the steps of the Piazza di Spagna; there I admired the Roman skyline, the red and yellow brick of its stone houses, the top of the Santa Maria del Popolo church and the Villa Borghese, the blue sky and the deep voice of the man selling 'gelatos' behind me, and this all served to reinforce my love of this twenty-three-hundred-year-old city, where each stone carries more secrets than any of us will ever know.

After walking from the hotel to the Piazza del Popolo (where I stop for another cappuccino at the Caffé Canova), all the way to the Campo dei Fiori, where I stroll by the antique and furniture stores, I decide it is time for me to get ready for my journey. I take a taxi back to the hotel, where I drop off my shopping bags and head towards the train station.

I feel strong and secure enough to face any challenges I may encounter in Pomezia. My hair is loose, and I am wearing more make-up and jewelry than usual, in an attempt to look older (I am often told I look younger than thirty), and more professional. It is now three-thirty, and I figure that by the time I arrive in Pomezia it will be near closing time; the fewer people there are, the better off I'll be. I know that Omega is not there today, because I called up this morning with a fake French accent, and was told by an Italian that Mr Omega wouldn't be there until tomorrow. The voice was definitely not Peter's (the person didn't speak English), which made me hope that Peter was still working there, mostly because he struck me as particularly stupid last time, something that could be used to my advantage. I am hoping he will be cooperative, and not stubborn.

I have decided to take the train instead of renting a car. I am not familiar enough with Rome, and am anxious about arriving at my destination on time.

I board the train at the Stazione Termini. I take my tape-recorder out of my bag for the fifth time, and check again to be sure it works. I have decided to keep it in my bag the whole time, and to tape whoever is there discreetly. I notice furtive glances in my direction, and start to feel self-conscious, especially when I get out at Pomezia, and find myself once again in this wasteland of factories and warehouses, where I seem to be the only visitor. My discomfort increases, so in order to quell my fear, I pretend that I am an actress in an Antonioni film. This association soothes me immediately. My surroundings were a great source of inspiration to Antonioni (*The Eclipse*, *Red Desert*), therefore nothing bad could possibly happen to me (I am not going to dwell on the absurdity of this thought, since for now it is serving its purpose.)

I relax and slow down my pace. I spot the caffé by the printing house. As I approach it, I notice it is empty. There is music playing loudly, and the waiter, a different one than last time, winks at me as I pass by. 'Ciao bellina,' he says. He has a boorish face, and wears a thick gold chain with a cross around his neck.

I pull the heavy door towards me. It won't budge. To my horror, I realize that it is locked. 'Shit,' I mutter. I turn towards the waiter and ask him if he knows Mr Omega's telephone number upstairs. I point towards the window, where I distinguish a tall shadow, probably that of Peter. The waiter shakes his head. No, he doesn't know the number, and besides, why would I want to see Mr Omega?

I tell him I have an appointment with him, and the waiter smiles. 'Non è qui oggi.' He's not here today, he tells me. 'Well then, I'll have to talk to Peter,' I say resolutely. 'I'm a journalist from America, and I'm writing a book on Mr Omega.'

He scrutinizes me, his hands resting on the counter. 'Va be,' he then says, and turns his body towards the window where he whistles so loudly I have to cover my ears.

A window opens on the first floor and a face leans out. 'Si?' I recognize Peter, and right away I shout, 'Hi Peter! It's me! Laura Miller! I'm the one who's writing the book about Dante, do you remember me?'

'What do you want?' Peter shouts back, 'Dante's not here!'

'I know! He must have forgotten we had an appointment, as usual! Can I talk to you instead? Will you let me come up?'

Peter buzzes me in. I thank the waiter and push the heavy door open. I walk up the stairs quickly, and press on the record button of my old tape-recorder before I reach the top floor. When I get to the studio, I notice that Peter is not alone. An older man is in the back room, apparently involved in paperwork.

'How are you, Peter?' I ask, cheerfully.

'I'm fine. What do you want?' He seems worried, or confused about my presence.

'I wanted to see Omega, to talk to him about some of his early work which we began to discuss last time, also find out more about a few of his recent paintings. Since he's not here, I wondered if you could help me. You see,

I'm writing the conclusion of my book, and I feel that I don't have enough information on him. Maybe you could help me out on this one?'

'Why don't you come back tomorrow and interview him? He'll be here tomorrow.'

'I'm going back to New York tomorrow morning,' I press on, 'I'm only here for one day.'

'Oh. Well, I don't know what to tell you,' he replies coldly.

'It's as simple as this Peter,' I explain, softening my tone of voice, 'I need to know more about his childhood, his early works, you know, things like that.'

The word 'childhood' has a magical impact on Peter, whose stiff muscles suddenly slacken, and he smiles at me, revealing crooked teeth.

'Yeah,' he says, 'they say he had a tough childhood.'

'Tell me more about it Peter, I'd be interested in finding out what you have to say about the topic.'

Peter looks at me dumbfounded, as if this is the first time anyone has ever asked him his opinion about something. I pull out my notebook and pen, push my hair back, sit on a stool and cross my legs. I am right on target.

Peter has, as I expected, very little to say about the topic of Omega's childhood. He starts to divert the conversation to his own youth and his father who was a drunk, while I take notes diligently, smiling every so often, encouraging him to such an extent that I realize half an hour has gone by, my tape will run out in a minute and we haven't gotten anywhere. I must interrupt his monologue, which is now strictly about his family, and his sister Germaine who has six kids and who lives on a farm in Nebraska, he's thinking about going to visit them, maybe bringing Patricia with him, his girlfriend, she's been acting strange with him lately, he can't figure out why, it's causing him torment, like he can't sleep at night kind of thing, he really likes her, he doesn't know what to do, maybe I could give him some advice.

'I don't know Peter, let me think about it. For now, let us concentrate on Omega.'

'Will you put my name in your book?' he asks me, grinning.

'Of course I will Peter,' I answer sweetly, 'you're being very cooperative.'

'Hey, you're cute. Real cute. Maybe we can go out for a drink or somethin' once we're done, you know, like just a drink . . .'

'Sure.' I suddenly hear the loud click of my tape-recorder. I freeze. No. He doesn't seem to have heard it. I sigh with relief. His thoughts are somewhere else, probably with Patricia. Could she be the same woman with the straw hat, who was seated in the caffé last time I was here? Should I ask him more about her? No. Time is running out. I must hurry.

'So Peter,' I resumed, 'can you tell me more about Omega's current work?'

He shrugs his shoulders and takes a pack of cigarettes out of his shirt pocket. 'Sure,' he answers, lighting a cigarette. 'What do you want to know?'

'Well, hmmm.' I pretend to be absorbed in thought. 'What about his recent paintings?' What's the most recent he's done? Can you show it to me?'

'Sure. It's right here.'

I follow him to the back room, where we pass the older man, who acknowledges our presence with a quick nod of the head. I notice he is practically bald, and the skin on his face is covered with visible red bumps, as if he has measles.

'Who's that?' I ask Peter.

'Oh. That's Giorgio, the bookkeeper.'

We enter Omega's main studio. It is a light and messy room, with tall windows, and a view on the nearby factories. On an easel stands an unfinished painting of a man with two faces, each one looking in an opposite direction. The man, who is fully dressed and stands by a tall black iron gate, bears a strong resemblance to Dante himself. With my rudimentary grasp of mythology, I am able to identify the man (or the god), as Janus. A Roman, and not a Greek god. A god of beginnings and gateways (looking before and beyond in time), who rarely figures in myth and has a paradoxical nature, possibly because of the schizoid aspect of his personality. Omega's choice is intriguing. The invocation of a parable between the god and himself seems too obvious, although conceivable. As I am reflecting upon the work, I notice, right against the wall and tucked under some paper, the face of the girl who was portrayed in the erotic lithograph I saw six months ago. My heart skips a beat as I bend down to look at it. As I am about to uncover it, and probably a number of them, Peter sets a steady hand on my shoulder. 'You can't look at these,' he says sternly, 'these are private.'

'Why?' I exclaim, 'I think they're great! I think they should be shown to the public!'

'How would you know?' he asks, frowning.

'I saw them last time. They're called "Muse". I think they're beautiful.'

Here, Peter seems disconcerted. 'I can't. I've got orders,' he blurts out, scratching his neck nervously.

I stand up. 'Come on, I'm writing about the guy, I need to know as much as I can about his work.'

'Not this stuff. It's pretty ugly shit,' he says, lighting another cigarette.

'No it's not. I think it's wild and daring and beautiful in its crudity.' I cannot believe the words I am uttering, and I don't seem to be the only one.

'Jesus man, I mean don't you have any morals? This shit is heavy-duty!' He looks at me appalled and shakes his head in dismay.

'All right. So let me see how heavy-duty it is.'

'I got to call Mr Omega first. I can't do this stuff without his approval.'

I'm in trouble. I'm not sure what to say. I hear footsteps and a door slamming. 'What was that?' I ask him, suddenly worried.

'It's Giorgio. He just left.'

'Oh. So does that mean we're all alone?' I ask Peter, who's acting more obstinately than I had predicted.

'Yeah, we're alone, so what?' he answers, eyeing me cautiously, his tall and sturdy body leaning against a table.

'So nothing,' I answer, trying to think of a last maneuver I could use before deploying the most degrading one, flirting with him.

'Peter,' I now say in a much more firm and cold voice, 'I think this game has gone far enough. I'm here to do my work. I've come all the way from New York, I'm tired, I'm hot, I'd like to get this over with as fast as possible.'

'All right,' he retorts, 'so let me call Mr Omega.'

'Fine,' I answer quickly. 'But do you really think it will make a difference? I mean he'll probably say yes, so you might as well save yourself an embarrassing phone call.'

'And what if he says no?' Peter asks, obviously pondering on my last helpless argument.

'Well, if he says no, then it's no,' I answer firmly. 'I wouldn't want to go against his wishes.'

Peter is silent. 'And I'll tell you something else,' I venture. 'If you tell me that these lithographs are immoral, then I have to take your word for it, meaning that I don't have to tell anybody that you let me see them. Not a soul. This can stay between you and me.'

'I didn't say immoral. I said heavy-duty—'

'Fine,' I say impatiently, 'you're right. You didn't say immoral. I'm just interpreting what you told me.'

'Oh yeah?' His eyes light up again. Perhaps this is not a lost cause after all. This man's self-esteem is so low, that flattery may be my only resort. I kneel back down on the floor, and pull out the lithograph from under the Japanese paper. It is the same girl all right.

'Hey!' Peter cries out, 'What the fuck are you doing? I never said you could do that!'

'Come on Peter, we're alone, no one can see us now. Everything will be okay.' I place my hand on his, and smile at him. 'We'll go out for a drink later, and you'll tell me more about yourself. In the meantime, let me look at these.'

I purposefully avoid his glance, and start pulling out

the lithographs one by one. There must be at least twenty of them, some of them reproduced several times. I feel Peter's body close to mine, and when I look up, I notice him looking at me. What's the matter?' I ask him nervously.

'Nothing,' he mutters. 'At this point it's too late. You saw them. You owe me a favor.'

'Don't worry Peter. You helped me out, you're right. I owe you a favor. I'll repeat what I said before. I won't say a word to anyone about this. Not a word.'

'That's not the kind of favor I'm talking about,' he answers, sucking hard on his cigarette.

'Oh,' I respond, feeling a sudden shudder rip through my spine, as I try to convince myself that his words are more innocuous than they sound, and that I have nothing to worry about. Most important of all, I reason quickly, I must appear calm about the situation I've put myself into. I've traveled far enough to see these lithographs, this is not the moment to let panic get in the way of my ambition.

'Well Peter,' I say softly, 'why don't you give me five minutes to look at these alone, and then we can talk about your favor?'

'Fine. Five minutes.'

He gets up quickly and leaves me alone with the lithographs. I go back to the first one I pulled out. The girl is sitting up, her legs crossed in the lotus position. She looks as if she's wearing a wig. Her hair is blond and curly, whereas in the other lithographs it was dark and straight. Well, perhaps she dyed it. She is smiling. Her eyes dreamy, her skin dark, her lips red. She seems serene and beautiful, and once again I am overcome by the feeling that not only does she seemingly share a special intimacy with the artist, but that this intimacy was indulged in just moments before the lithograph was executed.

The girl's hands are resting on a blue floor. There is nothing erotic about this lithograph. It is merely unusual and powerful. But as I am about to put it back in its place, I suddenly notice something I missed before. As I bring the sheet to my eye, I shiver: there is a sharp knife on the floor, right beside the girl's feet. Why is it there? Whom does she wish to hurt? Or does someone wish to hurt her? What is she smiling about? I quickly put the lithograph away and take another one out. And another one.

They all portray what seems to be the same girl (her hair is back to being dark and straight), in different positions. The presence of a man is implied, but not seen. On this one, *Muse XXXVII*, there is a close-up of her vagina, with a white rose inserted in it. On another one, *Muse XXVIII*, she is wearing a mini-skirt which reveals her pubic hair; her face is hidden by her long mane, and she bends forward thrusting her breasts out towards the viewer. The last one I look at, *Muse XXXII*, is the most disturbing: she is on all fours, her back arched, her feet pointing upwards, her tongue sticking out, as she shows off her rear crevice and its open orifice.

I am dumbfounded. I stack the lithographs the same way I found them, taking quick notes in my mind. They are titled *Muse XXVI* through *Muse XXXX*, all signed with the same symbol: α There are obviously some I've missed. But at this point, I'm not sure I really want to see them.

I get up slowly. I feel as if I've just come out of a sophisticated horror movie; the work is powerful, but unbearable to look at. I feel nauseous and disturbed. There is no point in denying the truth: these lithographs are pornographic, and show a side of Omega I don't like. I no longer feel comfortable in dismissing it as 'none of my business', as I had told myself upon my first seeing them. It is my business. If he wants to produce these works, then I want to write about them.

'So,' Peter asks me, showing his crooked teeth again, 'how do you like it?'

'It's . . . It's quite powerful,' I answer. 'I wonder if we'll be seeing these in our New York show.'

'I don't know, I kind of doubt it,' he responds. 'I mean like it's not the kind of stuff you want to show folks, you know . . .'

'I suppose you're right, Peter. Well, I guess I'll be going. Thanks so much for your help.'

'You're welcome.' He reaches his hand out towards me, and as I shake it, he suddenly thrusts me against him and starts to kiss me furiously, his lips covered with saliva, his arms grabbing me forcefully. I start to shout and attempt to free myself from his grasp.

'You said you'd return the favor,' he whispers as I feel his saliva drip down my neck, and suddenly feel so nauseous I'm about to throw up.

'I didn't think this was going to be it,' I shout, trying once again to push him away. 'Come on Peter, let me go, let's be friends—'

'Sure.' He's holding on to me so tightly I can barely breathe, and I start to feel frightened. This man could do anything to me, and no one would know. He is about to rape me, all because of these stupid lithographs. My life is in danger, I must act quickly. I feel his hand gripping my breasts, and ripping my shirt in the process. I scream again but he muffles my mouth with his hand. 'Shut up,' he says, 'I'm not going to hurt you.'

The front door opens brusquely, and a woman's voice can be heard. 'Peter? Are you there?'

Peter mutters 'goddammit' and quickly lets go of me. I hear the woman's footsteps heading in our direction. 'Peter?' she calls out again.

'I'm here Tricia, I'm here,' he replies, adjusting his hair nervously. She stops short at the sight of us. 'What the hell is going on here?'

It is the same woman I met briefly in the caffé five months ago. She looks the same, except that she's not wearing a hat, and her dyed blonde hair is shorter than I expected. She is wearing tight yellow pants, a low-cut matching shirt, golden shoes and heavy make-up.

'You asshole!' she snaps loudly at Peter, 'You fucking asshole!'

'It's not what you think,' I quickly retort, 'it's not at all what you think—'

'Sure,' she scoffs, 'that's why your make-up is running and your shirt is torn, right?'

I look down. There is an undignified hole smack in the middle of my clean white lace shirt. Peter takes her by the shoulder and says something like 'Oh honey,' but she pushes him away and starts running out the door, so I grab my bag and run after her.

'Hey!' Peter yells at me, 'leave her alone, it's none of your goddamn business!'

I slam the door and run down the stairs, relieved that

he hasn't chosen to do so as well. I catch up with her on the street. She is walking rapidly, her high-heels clicking on the sidewalk. 'Get out of my face,' she threatens me.

'Please let me explain,' I plead, 'believe me, it's so far from what you think.'

'Sure,' she laughs nastily, 'go on. Tell me more. I know who you are, you're that interviewer that showed up last summer. I knew you were trouble when I saw you. I just knew it.'

'Patricia,' I implore, 'I'm here because of the lithographs. Your boyfriend attempted to rape me in there because he wanted a favor returned for letting me see those salacious works.'

'Speak English to me,' she mumbles, 'I don't need your fancy words.'

'All right, I'll say it again. I'm a journalist who happened to see something I wasn't supposed to see, and your boyfriend pounced on me like a wild animal.'

'Well, who told you to look at something you weren't supposed to?' She says dryly.

'Please, Patricia,' I say forcefully, 'you must listen to me. I need to talk to somebody, I really do.'

My desperate tone of voice must have softened her somewhat, for she looks at me with a mixture of disdain and pity.

'Well, I guess I might as well tell you that you're lucky Peter didn't really hurt you. When he gets mad, the guy's a fucking maniac. Take my word for it. Unless of course you're all bullshitting me, and I'm just a sucker and you and him were just—'

'Believe me, Patricia. He was pretty rough on me. He

scared me.' I suppose she must believe me since she remains silent. The quiver in my voice confirms my condition, and in truth I am still in shock. This woman's boyfriend is a brute, and I count my blessings that she arrived when she did. I prefer not to imagine what would have happened to me otherwise, and I don't see any purpose in lingering on the alternative. I should tell her about everything that's happened, and try to get some useful information out of her.

'If you don't mind, I'll start from the beginning,' I tell her. 'It's a long story.'

'Go ahead, I've got plenty of time,' she says sarcastically, 'like I've got nothing better to do than to listen to some chick's life story.'

I decide to adopt a firmer tone of voice with her. Obviously my cautious way of approaching the situation isn't getting me anywhere. I will be blunt. Like her.

'Patricia,' I say, 'I know this is an awkward situation, but the truth of the matter is that I need advice.'

'Why don't you see a shrink? I don't give advice. Ever.'

I'm starting to lose my patience, and decide that the best way to deal with her is to start talking and to disregard her snide remarks; from my first day in Pomezia to my numerous arguments with Jaurel, I spare no details. By the time we arrive at the train station, I'm convinced that she knows what I need to know; her knowing glances betray her, as well as the way in which she purses her lips whenever I mention the woman in the lithograph. I ask her if she'll come to Rome with me. I promise to take her out for a nice dinner, where we could talk quietly.

'Who says I want to talk to you?' she replies, 'and who

says I have anything to talk to you about? And anyway, what's in it for me?'

'You have plenty to talk to me about, and I can make it worth your while,' I blurt out. Too late. There's no going back now. I suppose I have no other choice anyway. I'll have to give her a nice chunk of what I brought with me. Or, if she wants more than what I have at the hotel, I could always go to American Express in Piazza di Spagna and get a cash advance. But that's closed at night. She'll have to be patient and wait until tomorrow morning. That's all there is to it.

'How much?' she asks, staring at the train which is coming into the station.

'Three hundred dollars.'

'You gotta be kidding me.' She laughs raucously. 'Here's your train, I'll see you . . .'

'Five hundred dollars. I'll give you five hundred dollars and that's my last offer.' I take hold of her arm, and lower my voice in a threatening way. 'You get on the train with me now, or else forget it.'

'Babe, my information is worth thousands of dollars. I could get killed for telling you what I know. You've got to *really* make it worth my while. Capito?'

She's obviously not intimidated by me.

'All right,' I answer, defeated. 'How much do you want?'

'Fifteen hundred.'

The train conductor whistles, announcing the train's imminent departure.

'I'll give you a thousand. Take it or leave it.'

She steps on the train with me. 'All right, fine. Let's

see the color of your money. 'Cause I'm telling you right now. If you don't have it I'll get pissed.'

'I have it. You'll come with me to my hotel, we'll have dinner around the area and after you've told me what I need to know, I'll give you your money.'

'No way. I want it all up front.' She is speaking in a louder voice, and the passengers on the train are looking at us. I'm exhausted. I have a massive rip in my shirt, my jet lag is catching up with me, this woman is driving me crazy, and I'm wondering if this is going to be worth my losing one thousand dollars. 'I'll tell you what,' I tell her firmly. 'I'll give you half now, half later. After you've told me everything.'

'Let me see it,' she snarls, staring at my bag.

'I don't have it with me, all right? It's in the safe at the hotel. What do you think, that I'm going to walk around Rome with hundreds of dollars in my pocket?' At this point I've lost all countenance. I want to get back to my room, perhaps take two or three showers in order to wash off Peter's disgusting saliva which seems to have immunized itself on my neck.

'Fine.' She shrugs her shoulders. I lay back in my seat and look at her. I wonder how old she is. She could be in her late thirties, or, who knows, perhaps in her mid-forties. I'll find out later.

We hardly talk during the ride. She is fidgety, playing with her imposing bracelet, from which hang various pendants, notably a cross and a shimmery heart. She taps her high-heels against the ground, takes a chewing-gum out of her bag and chews on it loudly. I am worried about this money situation. I have exactly seven hundred dollars in cash, and am apprehensive about telling her, in the event that she leaps off the train at the next station. I will have to give her five hundred now, and tell her she'll have to wait until tomorrow morning before I give her the rest.

'What hotel are you staying at?' she asks me, popping a large bubble at the end of her sentence.

'The Hotel d'Inghilterra.'

Her face takes on an impressed look, as she tilts her head back and forth and mutters 'not bad not bad', this information prompting her to become garrulous. By the time we arrive in Rome, she has told me everything I need to know about Peter, who's so sweet but who can also get violent and possessive, and whom she knows she doesn't treat right, but that's only because he can get so mean and nasty. But when he's sweet and tender with her, he says he wants to get married and settle down, and she's not ready, she wants to live with him first, but he's kind of conservative that way like he doesn't want to live with her until they get married, so she has to figure out what to do, and be sure he's the right guy, because sometimes she wonders, even though when she met him here she really did think he was the right guy, until he started acting weird and crazy, like when he breaks things and talks to himself, even though it doesn't happen often except that when it does it's scary because he acts like a real nut case. Also, now that she's met other people and she's kind of gotten accustomed to Italian men, she's thinking twice about Peter although she has many feelings for him. She likes Italian men. They know how to make a woman feel like a lady. Even the creepy ones. Of course she knows it's all to get you into the sack with them but she doesn't mind. 'I like macho men,' she tells me.

I ask her how she got to Rome in the first place. She answers evasively, saying that she came here to work as a maid in someone's house. I ask her who and she tells me I wouldn't know them, and besides it didn't last long. We step off the train and jump into a cab. The minute I enter my hotel room she whistles in awe and settles herself on the couch, where I hand her something to drink and excuse myself as I run into the shower and scrub myself so hard it leaves red blotches on my neck.

I change quickly, opting for a light dress and high-heels. I dab some perfume on, reapply some make-up, and by the time I step out of my room, she is starting on her second drink, and singing to herself as she flips through a magazine. Fine with me. The more she drinks, the more she'll talk.

'How are we doing here?' I ask her, 'Are you hungry?'

'I'm always hungry,' she replies, her eyes focused on the photograph of a model wearing an atrocious electric-blue leather jacket. 'Cool jacket,' she remarks.

'Do you have any idea of where you want to eat?' I ask her, unable to keep myself from smiling. Despite her vulgarity and crude manners, there is something redeeming about this woman. Something I like.

'Any expensive place will be fine with me,' she says casually, licking her finger before turning the page of the magazine.

'Any expensive place . . . Hmmm. Let's see, let me get my guide book out.'

'Oh I can think of a couple. There's Il Passetto,' she

says. 'Then there's another one that's supposed to be great food and really nice. I don't remember its name, but I know exactly where it is.'

'Fine. But we should try and find the name, just so we can call and make a reservation.'

'Forget that, we can just go there. It's not even eight o'clock. That's damn early by Roman standards. Here, people don't eat dinner until around ten o'clock.'

I don't dare ask her how expensive the restaurant is. I prefer not to know, and not to imagine what it will feel like to walk into an elegant restaurant with her dressed this way. Should I lend her some clothes? She's much bigger than me, they wouldn't fit her. Should I mention something about her appearance? Yes, I think I must.

'Patricia,' I say quickly, 'are you sure you want to go somewhere really elegant? I mean don't you think there's a dress code in those restaurants?'

'What do you mean?' she frowns.

'I mean, don't you think you might not be dressed up enough to go to one of these places?'

'I'm wearing gold. That's good enough. These shoes cost me a fucking fortune, excuse my French.'

What can I say? I glance at her high-heeled sandals, smile at her and tell her we should get going.

'Hey,' she says.

'Yes?'

She rubs her index and middle finger against her thumb. 'The dough. Where's the dough?'

'The dough. Right. Hold on one second.'

I open the safe in my bedroom closet, and remove five hundred dollars. I slide one extra hundred in my pocket just in case. I will tell her about the remainder after dinner. 'Here you go,' I tell her, placing it in her open palm.

She counts it, stuffs it immediately in her pocket and heads towards the door. 'When do I get the other half?' she suddenly stops by the door, and looks at me suspiciously.

'You'll get the other half after dinner,' I lie, not knowing what to do otherwise.

'Let's get out of here, I'm starving,' she says.

'Hold on,' I say, 'I need my handbag.'

I run back to the bedroom, where I stick my wallet in my bag, along with my tape-recorder, an action which, however unethical it might be, I cannot resist: I push the record button before I leave the room, hoping that the click of the stop button won't give me away, as it almost did with Peter.

The doorman of the hotel hails us a cab. The restaurant isn't too far from the hotel, at the top of a long flight of stairs. It is dimly lit, and nicely decorated with large baskets of flowers and copies of Renaissance paintings around the walls. I am surprised and relieved not only by the décor but by the few, though casual looking, sets of people that occupy the round tables. (I was worried she had chosen some kind of lavish place where we would have to more or less walk up the aisle and pass by a hundred pairs of eyes in order to reach our table.)

'How did you hear about this place?' I ask her.

'Peter heard about it from this cool French guy, Jean-Pierre, this guy who sometimes works for Omega, and who told him about it after he had eaten here with some hot chick. That guy knows all the cool places in town, I swear. He took me to this awesome transsexual bar once. Italian transsexuals. Wild things.'

'I met Jean-Pierre Malat' I tell her, 'the day I went over to the printing house for the first time, he was there.'

We follow the maître d'hôtel as he brings us towards our table. I smile at Patricia gently through the flicker of the candle which stands on the white linen tablecloth. I open the menu. The prices are high, though not out-rageous. I let her order as many dishes as she wants though I insist on ordering the wine myself. After the waiter has come and poured us our first glass of wine, I slowly direct the conversation towards Omega. She remains silent, a troubled look on her face.

'What's the matter?' I ask her, terrified that she has decided not to speak.

'Nothing. It's just that this is heavy-duty stuff. If anyone knows I've told you all of this I could get into serious trouble. And I ain't kidding when I say serious.'

She looks older now, and I notice dark bags under her eyes.

'Patricia,' I say, grabbing her hand, 'I can swear to you that whatever you tell me will remain between you and me. I swear.'

'So why do you need the information then?'

'I need it for several reasons which I can promise you are good ones. But I'm paying you to talk to me, not to give you explanations. You're safe with me, that's all you need to know.'

My firmer tone of voice seems to reassure Patricia. She looks at me, breathes very heavily in and out as if trying to control stage fright before facing an audience, lights a cigarette, and starts talking in a low and slightly dramatic voice. 'All right. Here it is. Omega has a daughter. Her name is Maria, and she's blind. Her parents never talk about her. In fact, they told everybody that she died of meningitis when she was four months old. They couldn't deal with the fact that she had gone blind. It freaked them out. Especially Omega. So for years, if anybody accidentally bumped into her, they would pass her off as the neighbor's daughter. I guess she didn't mind it when she was young, but when she became a teenager, she decided that she was sick and tired of always being alone, never going out, always pretending to be someone else. I don't blame the girl, Jesus . . .'

She clears her throat, and continues. 'This made Omega very nervous, and two years ago, he decided to send her to a home for the blind. She told her parents she wouldn't go. Omega got mad. He didn't want her around. She threw a tantrum and begged him to let her stay. He had to give in. The thing is, the girl is gorgeous. I mean fucking gorgeous.'

'I think I saw her,' I say, remembering my glimpse of the girl with the messy dark hair. 'She has dark hair, right?'

'Yeah. I guess more people than Omega realizes have seen her. Peter did too. But the thing is, no one who saw her really knew who she was, until later, when she started to sit for Omega. Then, people started to talk.'

'Which people?'

'The people that work for him. The housekeeper, Omega's assistants, you know . . .'

'I thought Omega didn't employ assistants!' I exclaim,

realizing that my whole perception of Omega had been skewed.

'Well, he does. Twice a week. I mean, can you imagine the guy stretching one of his giant canvases alone? He's too klutzy, he could never do it alone.' Patricia lets out a short laugh, and I can't help but join in with her. But this ephemeral relief quickly turns to tension as she continues her story:

'So I was telling you that people started to talk because they quickly realized that what they were witnessing was actually a big deal.'

'What was a big deal?'

'All right. The girl threw a tantrum, the father let her stay, she's gorgeous. He suddenly got the idea that he could paint her. He asked her to sit for him and she did. She was good too. Didn't move or anything. Sat still for hours.'

'Excuse me, but how do you know this?' I ask her, wanting to be sure my source is reliable.

'Trust me,' she retorts.

'I trust you, but we made a deal. I gave you five hundred dollars, remember?'

'I'll tell you later. After you've given me the other five hundred bucks.'

'I want to know now,' I say sternly.

'Later. Just listen to this,' she says, flicking her ashes in the ashtray and ignoring my impatient glare. 'Maria started to sit for him more and more often. One day, he must have asked her to remove some of her clothes, because that same night there was a lithograph of her in a bra lying under the printing-press in his studio. He worked at home then, the Pomezia building didn't exist.'

'How the hell do you know this!' I exclaim, 'You have to tell me!'

'Later,' she answers again, driving me to gulp down my glass of wine in order to calm my nerves. 'Anyway,' she carries on, 'what happened is simple. As I told you before, she started sitting for him regularly, and with less and less clothes on. When the first like hard-core litho was lifted from the stone, we all knew something was going on between him and his model, but at that time we didn't know that the model was his own daughter.'

'What are you trying to say?' I ask, my body stiff as a rock as I await the predictable answer.

'I'm saying, that not only was this model his daughter, but he was fucking her. And for all I know he still is. He used the home for the blind as a ploy. Tried to force her to go, knowing she would refuse, and then told her that she could stay only if she was a good girl and did everything he wanted. His scheme worked, especially because he knew Maria wanted to stay with her mother, a nice woman who probably knows what's going on but who's too scared shitless of her husband to do anything about it.'

'That doesn't make sense,' I shake my head, 'I don't care how scared she is. It's her own daughter for Christ's sake. She couldn't just stand there and watch.'

'Lady, you don't know what the real world is like,' Patricia says, with a touch of contempt in her voice. 'There's a lot of shit going on out there. And it's been going on for ever. It's a man's world babe, just remember that.'

I remain silent. I'm so overwhelmed by these revelations that I'm unable to touch my food, and watch her instead, gobbling down her gnocchi al gorgonzola.

'Go on. Tell me what happened next.'

'Well, Omega realized these lithographs were a little too gross, and a little too radically different from his other work, to show the public. So instead he started a business on the side; you know, limited editions for private collectors. He got involved in the porn business,' she says, her mouth full, 'and started to sell them to this real important dealer in New York City, this guy who supposedly has this mega collection of porn art stored somewhere in a warehouse in New Jersey—'

'What's this dealer's name?' I interrupt.

'I don't know and that's the honest truth,' she answers. 'All I know is he's legit. He's supposed to be a real respectable and powerful guy in the art world, who also happens to collect that stuff. You know, erotic stuff. Through him, Omega started to sell his lithos to all these rich amateurs, collectors, and all sorts of weirdos. Supposedly even to porn magazines. He started to make a shitload of money, but the problem is that in Italy all this shit is illegal.'

'Why?' I ask her, my hands grasping the table in anticipation.

'First, Maria's a fucking minor. She's sixteen, and was even younger when this started. Second, none of this income is declared, so it has to be laundered. More than once I saw piles of cash sitting in a drawer. So did Peter.'

'Jesus Christ,' I falter, 'I can't believe it. I just can't believe it. And to think I loved Omega's painting and defended it for so many years. What a vile and disgusting man.' I try to pour myself another glass of wine but my hands are trembling too much.

'Take it easy babe, chill out.'

I breathe deeply, and try to collect myself. 'And what about Pomezia? How many people know about Pomezia?'

'Pomezia is where the lithos are produced. It was all kept very quiet, until six months ago, when a guy who worked there talked to a few people, and it got back to Omega. That's why he went berserk when you showed up that day. But once he figured out you had no idea what was going on, he decided to play it cool. Since then, he's done a few Greek lithos there, just to make it look more legit, in case someone else shows up unexpected.'

'How do you know he went berserk when he saw me that day?'

'Peter told me. He's no fool, Peter. He might look like one but he ain't. Besides, there were rumors that Omega beat his poor wife up that same evening, all because she told you where he was.'

'God,' I shake my head in disbelief. 'Poor woman . . .'

'You're not kidding,' Patricia says.

'And what about Peter? What's his job?'

'He helps out with a lot of stuff. Mostly small stuff. Moving, deliveries, guarding the place.'

'How did you meet him?' I try again, hoping that the wine and her two previous drinks are taking effect. 'He was moving things from the Omega home to Pomezia,' she mumbles.

'And?' I try to keep my voice steady.

'That's it. I told you. I'll tell you the rest after you give me the other half of the dough.'

'I need to know who this New York City dealer is. It's important. Are you sure you don't know who it is?'

'Yeah I'm sure. I can find out though if it's real important. You give me the other five hundred now, and I'll find out for you.'

'How?'

'What?'

'How will you find out?'

'I got my contacts. We all got our contacts. But I'll tell you this that I do know. I don't think you realize, but nobody knows anything about what we've been talking about. Nobody asks questions about Omega, because no one would ever think of asking questions. He's too respected as an artist. He's kind of like an institution here, which is why he can get away with all his crap.'

The waiter brings our second courses, and Patricia attacks her veal clumsily, spattering gravy on her shirt.

'What's Jean-Pierre Malat's connection to Omega?' I ask her, suddenly wondering what kind of a role he plays in Omega's life.

'I think he collects erotica.'

'And what happened to the guy that talked?'

'He disappeared the next day, just after Omega found out he had talked about Maria. No one knows where he is. All we know is that Omega freaked out about him.'

'What was his name?' I ask, for no good reason. 'The guy's name?'

'Whatever,' Patricia answers, 'it's not important. He's gone.'

'Where did he go?' I ask.

She shrugs her shoulders and gives me another one of

her disdainful glances. 'Why the hell would you want to know where he went? I have no fucking idea where he is.'

'Of course you know where he is, don't you?' I state plainly, because at this point I'm convinced she's lying to me.

'Yes I do,' she answers, lighting another cigarette.

'Where?' I demand, catching my breath.

'He's in another city in another country,' she answers slowly.

'Was he a friend of yours?'

'Yes, he was,' she answers. 'He was a good friend to many of us. It's a shame what happened to him. A real shame.' Her eyes take on a ferocious look. I extend my hand towards her but she shakes her head. 'I'm fine,' she says. 'It was a while ago, and I don't have to worry about him because I know he's safe.'

'How come you're still involved with these people? After what they did?'

Here she remains silent again. 'Your questions are expensive. Give me the money and I'll tell you more.'

I feel as if I've been hit on the head by a hammer; I'm dizzy, but I need to know more.

'I told you. I'll give you the money after dinner.'

'So I'll tell you what you want to know after dinner. It's as simple as that, babe.'

'What if I give you a hundred dollars now? Will you tell me how you got involved with Omega in the first place?'

'Give me the hundred and I'll think about it.'

I take the folded bill out of my pocket. I congratulate

myself for having had the presence of mind to bring it with me.

'I worked for Omega.'

'What did you do for Omega?' I practically shout. 'Hey, don't freak out on me,' she warns me, 'you're raising your voice.'

'I'm sorry,' I say, trying to regain composure. 'What did you do for him?'

'I used to clean Omega's house, all right? I was the fucking cleaning woman.' The way she says this suggests an unsolved bitterness about something else. 'You were his mistress as well.' I deduce out loud.

She looks stunned by my statement. 'Who says?' she asks me, leaning backwards in her chair.

'It's quite easy to figure out,' I tell her. 'And I suppose that it was going on for a while, right?' As the waiter passes by, I wave him for the bill with which he returns a moment later. I hand him my credit card while Patricia looks on approvingly. I haven't eaten a thing and I'm a little drunk.

'I'm not going to answer any more questions. That's it.'

'Fine. But don't expect the rest of your money then.'

'This is personal information lady, it has nothing to do with all the other stuff you want to know about,' she raises her voice sharply.

'You still love him. You loved him then, and you love him now, don't you?'

'I suppose I do, yes,' she answers, lowering her eyes timidly, an uncharacteristic and revealing gesture.

'Patricia, I'm very grateful for what you've done. You've helped me a tremendous amount.' No sooner have I uttered those words, than I hear the indubitable sound of my tape-recorder, as if it were in perfect synchronicity with the conversation. Exactly ninety minutes have passed. It is nine-forty-five. The stop sound is loud and brief, and I feel beads of sweat forming on my forehead. Anything could happen now. Patricia could get up and ask me for the tape, or she could start screaming. Or, yet again, she could, if she wanted to, call Omega and tell him everything.

I desperately try to think up a new subject of conversation, but to my great surprise, there doesn't seem to be any need to. Patricia looks up at me with her glaring eyes, and as I am awaiting eternal damnation to be thrust upon me, she suddenly utters the following words, which sound like sweet music to my ears:

'What about my money?'

'Meet me tomorrow morning at Piazza di Spagna,' I tell her, speaking rapidly, wondering how on earth I got out of this one intact, 'in front of the American Express office at nine o'clock.'

'Bitch. You bitch,' she snaps icily, 'you fucked around with me.'

'I did not, Patricia. All I have to do is go to the machine and get the money out. It's no big deal.' The waiter arrives with the bill and my credit card receipt. I sign it and tell Patricia we can go now. She remains motionless.

'Why did you wait until now to tell me about this?'

'Because I was worried you wouldn't talk if I told you.'

'And why didn't you get your money out before?'

'Because the office closes at five.'

Patricia pushes her chair back loudly. 'You give me no choice. It's a pretty stinking thing to do. All I know is you better the fuck be there tomorrow.'

'I'll be there, Patricia,' I tell her, catching up with her as she rushes down the stairs towards the empty street.

'Patricia!' I shout, running after her, 'Come on! Wait for me! Don't you want a ride home?'

She stops in her tracks and walks back towards me. 'Sure, I'll take the ride,' she answers, 'but I'm real pissed off at you.'

'I know Patricia, and I'm sorry. But you're going to have to trust me. I'll be waiting for you tomorrow morning. At nine o'clock sharp.' I suddenly feel as if I'm talking to a moody child. I wonder if I haven't over-estimated her age.

The weather has gotten cooler, and I shiver in my cotton jacket. We wait for a cab for a long time. I ask her how old she is. 'Twenty-eight,' she answers.

I'm very surprised. 'My hair is not really this color,' she says almost apologetically, as we finally get a cab and climb in quickly.

I drop her off on a dark street, Via di Bravetta. We shake hands and I tell her I'll meet her tomorrow at the American Express office. As she is about to step outside, she suddenly turns around, brings her face close to mine, and in a hoarse and almost threatening voice, says, 'I've been told I sound pretty good on tape. I guess you'll be able to confirm that tomorrow, you goddamn bitch journalist. Lucky for you that I'm a nice lady. Real lucky.'

And with these words she leaps out of the cab, and slams the door so hard the driver starts shouting some long-winded obscenity out of his window. But by then she is gone, and as the cab speeds along the dark and windy streets, I cannot help wondering why she's done me such an unusual favor. Why didn't she ask me for the tape once my sham was revealed? Why has she let me get away with this? As opposed to assuaging my previous fear, it only enhances it, to the point that as soon as I get back to the hotel, I put the tape-recorder in the safe, and ask the concierge to wake me up at eight o'clock, telling him I will be checking out tomorrow. I decide there is no point in my staying here. I know everything there is to know, and at this point I don't see why I should keep it to myself. I won't listen to Jaurel. I'll go to Ensor directly and tell him to print it. All of it. I want the world to know the truth about Omega.

I undress quickly and shiver under the covers as I attempt to fall asleep. I feel betrayed. As if a lover had suddenly and coldly left me.

I have studied and revered Omega's work for so long. I have felt so close to his characters, his limpid and delicate way of painting, the exactitude of his renditions.

I have felt intimate with his world of gods and goddesses, the stories within the symbols, like Vermeer, or Poussin, and all those painters who have never given me reason to question my admiration for them.

It is one thing to discover man's hidden fetishes, such as in Omega's case, a taste for pornography and erotica. After all, both materials have nowadays reached a near mainstream audience, a usually harmless one at that. Until tonight, I deemed Omega's secret pastime to be surprising, mostly because of what he seemingly stood for: the fact that this figurative painter, categorized as being a classicist and a reactionary by his opponents, had revealed such an unpredictable side to his work was disconcerting, as is always the revelation of a new, hitherto unknown facet of a person. But this revelation was quickly followed by a sort of fascination, since it revolutionized my interpretation of his work, and served to confirm my initial excitement about being an art critic, namely that there is always more to learn than what meets the eye, and that what one takes for granted is often laced with unpredictable layers one should never dismiss. I wonder how the world would have reacted if, say, one had suddenly discovered that Degas roamed the Parisian streets at night, dressed as a transvestite; it would no doubt have caused an uproar.

But pornography, or vice, is one thing. Incest is quite another. What I have just learned about Omega is, if accurate, unforgivable. My instinct is to trust Patricia. Although part of me does not want to believe her, I fear that what she has told me this evening is the truth. And that truth is shocking.

Will I ever be able to look at an Omega painting the same way? I wonder, as I feel myself drowsing off to sleep.

I dream I find Patricia's hair on the sidewalk. A wig of blonde hair. I wake up sweating, and fall back asleep. Soon after, the phone rings and a voice tells me it is eight o'clock.

After a quick breakfast and shower, I get dressed and run to Piazza di Spagna. It starts to rain and I have no umbrella. I stand inside the American Express building. I decide to wait for her before I take the money out.

I wait a long time. It is now nine thirty and she isn't

here. Different faces push the glass doors open; children, old people, American tourists, but not Patricia. Could she have misunderstood our meeting place? No. I repeated it several times. Besides, she badly wants this money. She's probably late and that's all there is to it.

I lean against a counter by the door and cross my arms as I wait. There's a middle-aged woman standing by my side, obviously waiting for someone as well. She is reading *Novella 2000*, a popular tabloid, and every now and then she glances up towards the glass door to see who's coming in. I glance at her newspaper. The front page shows two young men being held up by policemen. The caption says something about a Mafia hit. The woman raises her eyes again and we exchange glances. Then she suddenly cries out, 'Donella!' and rushes to kiss an older woman. She leaves her newspaper on the counter, and since at this point I have nothing better to do, I start leafing through it. It is this week's edition, and just came out this morning. On page two, there is a photograph of an Italian actress kissing a man in a car. The caption implies that the truth has finally come out. Page three is devoted to a disfigured murder victim. I'm about to turn the page, when suddenly I freeze. The victim, who is shown lying face up on a street, wears high-heeled sandals. The rest of her body is covered with blood. But around her wrist, which rests above her head, lies a thick bracelet, from which hang various pendants, notably a cross and a shimmery heart. She is said to live on Via di Bravetta. She was last seen yesterday, in Pomezia, a suburb of Rome. Her name is Patricia Kenworth.

I drop the newspaper on the ground and run back to

the hotel, in the soaking rain. By the time I get back to the hotel and pay my bill, it is practically ten-thirty. I must rush in order to catch a plane home. Any plane. I call my mother in Florida. It is four o'clock in the morning over there. I tell her I'm on my way back home, I just wanted her to know. 'Why would you want to let me know this in the middle of the night?' she asks, in a hoarse voice. 'Are you all right? Actually, you've only been there two days, Laura, how come you're coming back so early?' Suddenly her voice sounds more awake. I tell her I have no time to speak right now, but something significant has happened, she'll hear all about it later this evening. Then, for some reason I attribute mainly to fear and the need to say something I wouldn't say to her in normal circumstances, I tell my mother that Otto's ex-drug dealer was sitting next to me on the plane to Rome. 'Why are you telling me this? What does this mean?' I try to laugh my statement off, saying that it probably doesn't mean anything, it was just one of those strange and eerie coincidences that happen in life, but it's too late; my mother's voice is all tied up in knots as she tells me she's very worried about me. I mutter that I'm in a hurry and hang up.

My life is in danger. I am sure of it. I have no time to lose. I throw all my clothes into my suitcase, and as I'm putting my damp coat back on, there's a loud knock on my door. I don't answer. There's another knock. I must call downstairs immediately and alert the front desk that I'm in danger. I should have done that on my way up. I'm so stupid sometimes. As my hand reaches for the phone, the door bursts open, and two men I've never seen before burst into my room. I scream. One of them pulls out a gun and smiles at me. 'Hello, Miss Miller,' he says with a thick Italian accent. 'I see we are here just in time. You will follow us quietly, we have a car waiting downstairs for you. Do not be afraid, we will not hurt you.'

One of them grabs the suitcase out of my hand, and orders me to walk in front of him. 'Miss Miller,' he continues, 'you will walk slowly in front of me, when we get downstairs you will speak to nobody, you will just wave goodbye to the people at the front desk, you understand?' I nod, petrified. 'If you do not do what I'm asking you, Miss Miller, I will have to shoot you and that will be a great pity. A pretty girl like you should not die so young. So walk like this, yes, yes it's good, now here's the elevator.'

He pushes me gently inside. I can feel the muzzle of his gun against my back. My mouth is dry. There is a man in the elevator. He is looking at the ceiling with his hands crossed behind his back. He is my only hope. I step lightly on his foot. He looks at me and frowns. The kidnapper who hasn't spoken yet, eyes me suspiciously. The muzzle of the gun is pushed a little deeper into my back. I'm paralyzed with fear. I stick my hand in my right pocket. There is a piece of crumpled paper in it. I look up. The man seems to have noticed something strange. I look at him with pleading eyes. I clutch the piece of paper in my pocket. I don't know what it is, and I keep my eyes focused on the silent kidnappers. As the elevator stops, I quickly drop the piece of paper on the floor, and walk out slowly. I manage to look back for just one instant. I see the man bending down to pick up my piece of paper.

I'm not sure if he caught on to what has just occurred before his very eyes. After all, this type of incident happens mostly in films, or novels. Seldom does it happen in real life.

Five

Demeter, the earth goddess, loved her daughter, Persephone, whom she conceived with Zeus. One day, Persephone was picking flowers in a field when she noticed a striking looking narcissus. She bent to pick it up, and as she did so the earth opened up and Hades, the god of the underworld, appeared, dragging her with him to the underworld.

When Demeter heard what had happened to her beloved child, she gradually sank into a despair which turned into anger when she learned that Zeus himself had concocted this abduction for the sake of his brother Hades who wanted to be wed. Demeter threw a dark veil over her shoulders, and wandered through the cities of mortals, all the while searching for Persephone. After several adventures, and still mourning the loss of her daughter, Demeter retired to her temple, at Eleusis. There, she sought revenge on mankind, preventing the earth from harvesting its crop. The human race was about to die of starvation, and Zeus sent his messenger Iris to beg Demeter to allow the earth to bear its fruit, but Demeter's stubbornness was implacable. She declared that as long as she wasn't allowed to see her daughter, she would continue to plague the earth. So

Zeus gave in. He made Hades promise that he would return Persephone to her mother. But what Zeus didn't foretell, was that Hades, before sending his young wife back up, tricked her into eating a few pomegranate seeds, which was to render their union indissoluble.

When Persephone was returned to her mother, she confessed to eating the infamous seeds. Demeter was devastated for this meant that she was going to lose her daughter again.

So Zeus brokered a compromise. Persephone was going to live with her husband for one third of the year, and spend the remaining two thirds with her mother.

So Demeter lifted her plague and allowed the earth to blossom again. And this explains why in winter, the soil is cold and barren, and why in spring the earth abounds with blooming flowers, to symbolize Demeter's joy at the return of Persephone.

I am sitting on the edge of a canopy bed which I was told was used by Garibaldi on his way up the Italian peninsula. Next to it stands a marble-topped bedside table, atop of which stands a large bouquet of sunflowers. The rest of the room is decorated with a large eighteenth-century-looking tapestry, an old wooden desk, and a mahogany bookshelf. Looking out the window, I see an exquisite garden, and a sweet smell emanates from the rosemary bushes, which stand next to orange trees and lemon groves.

The early nineteenth-century villa where I am held hostage is situated somewhere between Cosenza and San Giovanni in Fiore, in the Calabrian region of Southern Italy. It is a sumptuous villa, and were it not for the unfortunate – or should I say dramatic – circumstances of my being here, I would probably better appreciate its beauty and grandeur. But in this particular case, all I can feel towards these ominous stone walls, the imposing furniture in the rooms and the near perfection of the garden, is fear. Two days ago, upon my arrival, it was a deep-rooted fear that these walls would hold me prisoner forever, or that I would be buried within them. Today, I was told by one of my abductors that the visit of Mr M. – the man I presume to be responsible for my being kidnapped – will not coincide with my sojourn, words I interpreted optimistically, as they rule out the possibility of my becoming a permanent resident, or at least I hope they do.

Hope carried me through the anguishing car ride to the gilded cage I've been confined to. After my two kidnappers forced their way into my hotel room, and made me wave to the man at the front desk as if everything were perfectly normal, they threw me into the back seat of a black car, stopped in a small dark street where they blindfolded and handcuffed me, and ordered me to maintain a horizontal position or else they would shoot me. They then drove off rapidly, the sound of the radio drowning my loud cries for help, until the cold muzzle of the gun was gently squeezed against my cheek, and one of the abductors (the one who had been doing all the talking until now) informed me in his adequate English that if I didn't stop screaming, he was going to have to resort to more radical measures. He stressed the word radical, with his Italian accent, pushed the muzzle further into my cheek so that I could feel it digging against my jaw, and this sufficed to silence me until some time later on (how long was it?) I felt the car drive on to a dirt road, and my blood shot up like a thermometer: this was going to be it. They were going to riddle my body with bullet holes, just as they had done with Patricia, and dispose of it in a ravine where it would remain unnoticed until some peasant discovered it, resulting in it being plastered on all the front pages the next morning. The thought of Patricia suddenly awoke me to a more hopeful reality: the tape. I had forgotten to pack the tape in my suitcase. It was lying in the safe at the hotel.

This realization calmed me down temporarily. Could my negligence actually save me? Would the police be able to find it in time? After all, these thugs, whoever they were, couldn't do much with me without recovering the recorded proof of their sins. Or could they? Were they even aware of the tape's existence or was I doomed no matter what? I started screaming again. 'Where are you taking me? What are you going to do with me? Why am I here?'

My incessant screams and cries must have had some effect, because they stopped the car, and one of my abductors leaned over and I felt a rough hand on my knee, which I attempted to remove by kicking it away with my leg. 'You relax, Miss Miller,' he said in a stern voice, 'nobody is going to hurt you. We don't want to hurt you.'

'So why am I here then?' I shouted in between tears.

'We don't know why. We have orders. But you will be well taken care of. You are going to stay in a beautiful house.'

'Sure,' I retorted, 'and I suppose it has a swimming pool too, right?'

The fact that I could be sarcastic at this particular moment assuaged me temporarily – maybe my reflex proved that there was hope – and I was taken aback when the abductor answered in an even voice that no, there wasn't any swimming pool, but the house was 'veramente bella' and I was sure to be most comfortable there. Was this a joke, I wondered, or was this a ploy to keep me quiet?

I did not have to wait long to find out. Soon after, one of the thugs said, 'siamo arrivati', the car came to a full stop, and my handcuffs and blindfold were removed. The neo-classical villa that stood before my eyes seemed to be a mirage of some sort, and it was only when a man dressed as a butler removed my coat, said 'Good afternoon, Miss Miller,' and led me into a palatial marble vestibule, that I was able to regain my senses. On the floor lay polychrome painted tiles. The ceilings in the adjacent dining and living rooms were practically as high as those found in churches. There was no doubt in my mind that a true connoisseur was responsible for the dazzling collection of paintings and drawings which lined the walls, as well as the Rococo and Baroque furniture which was dispersed about the living-room. And when the butler (who introduced himself as André) asked me to follow him to my room, up a grand staircase and into the 'right wing' as he called it, I wondered if I hadn't been drugged somewhere in the course of this trip; but then I remembered that I hadn't eaten or drunk anything since we left Rome. It became clear to me that this was indeed the place where

I was to remain hostage, which led me to conclude that if all abductors conduct their business similarly, in the equivalent of a five-star hotel, it is time for us to revise our definition of hell.

My thoughts were interrupted by André who asked me if I liked Vitello Tonnato, since the cook was preparing some for dinner. I must have answered positively, for André put my suitcase down in what was to be my bedroom for an indefinite amount of time, and left me gazing at a canopy bed, strewn with oriental pillows. I had barely finished using the adjoining bathroom when André came back and asked me if I'd be interested in eating now. I shook my head. 'I'm not hungry,' I said. 'Well,' he said in an embarrassed voice, 'Luigi and Gianni are waiting for you downstairs. They say you must come down now.'

I presumed those two names belonged to the thugs who had abducted me, but instead of asking questions about them, I chose to find out more about André, and asked him what nationality he was. 'Welsh,' he answered, almost bashfully.

'How long have you been working here, André?' I asked him, as I followed him downstairs.

'A long time,' he replied, hurrying his pace as if to avoid any further questions.

When we entered the dining-room, I found myself standing over a marble table, large enough to fit twenty people. Around that table, which was set for one person (presumably me), sat Luigi, Gianni, and an old woman dressed in black whom Gianni introduced as Carmela. She was to take care of me, Gianni said, as he motioned me to sit down, and I was to be very nice to her. She hardly spoke any English, therefore I was going to have to speak to her in Italian. 'Va bene?' he asked, and I nodded my head.

André brought in my food, but I was unable to eat a thing. My mouth felt dry like sawdust, and I could feel my heart pounding furiously. 'Why am I here?' I asked Gianni, who had been the one doing all the talking from the beginning.

'You are here because you play detective. We do not like that. In Italy, everybody minds their own business. That is the rule. If you get mixed up in someone else's business, bad things happen to you.'

This time I felt the color draining from my cheeks, and I had to grab my chair so as not to collapse. Sweat was forming on my forehead so rapidly that I didn't even bother to wipe it off.

'So you're going to kill me then,' I said in a quivering voice, 'you're going to kill me.'

Then, suddenly, all went blank. I must have fainted, because next thing I knew I was lying on a bed, and Carmela was pressing a washcloth to my forehead, while Luigi was peering at me curiously. At first their faces were blurred, but soon enough they were in focus again, as clear as the glass of clear liquid Luigi was offering me. I pushed him away. 'Leave me alone, I'm fine.'

'No, you not fine,' Luigi said, and as I looked at his face, I realized that he looked like the prototype of a Sicilian thug. Medium height, broad shoulders, slicked-back greasy hair, dark skin, a large scar at the bottom of his cheek, and deep-set eyes that looked as if they had been punched in several times.

Gianni, on the other hand, wore expensive clothes and a gold ring on his pinkie. He was slightly shorter and less broad than his counterpart, and though his hair was slicked back as well, and his face was tanned and rugged, his eyes had a shrewd and intimidating look. As I was scrutinizing him from a horizontal position, Gianni said he wanted to tell me something. He sat on the edge of the bed I was laying on, and he cleared his throat. 'Signorina Miller,' he began, 'we are not going to hurt you. It is not in our interest. We just want you to give us some information. If you do not, that is another matter. A very different matter.' Here he paused and lit a cigarette, all the while peering at me from underneath his bushy eyebrows.

'Who's we?' I asked him sitting up, relieved that I had regained control of my body and of my senses.

'He is Mr M. That is all. He is our padrone.'

'And why does Mr M. feel the need to kidnap me in order to get information out of me?'

'I do not know. I am not Mr M.'

'What is Mr M.'s real name?'

'Non lo so. I do not know.'

'Does he live here? Where is he? Is this his house?'

'I cannot say.'

'Will I be meeting him?'

'No. I do not believe you will.'

'Why not? Where will I be?' I asked, feeling my previous fear creeping under my skin again.

'Do you want to be here signorina? I don't believe you do. I'm sure you will prefer to be back in your own house,' Gianni answered, a friendly smile on his face, which revealed nicotine stained teeth.

'No, I don't want to be here. But I think I have a right to know who had me kidnapped here in the first place.'

'A right to know!' Gianni laughed, loudly and raucously. 'That is very amusing. Very amusing,' Gianni answered, as Carmela proceeded to apply a new washcloth to my forehead, and as I gently pushed her away and told her I was fine.

'So who is it? Mr M.?' I asked, not sure whether he was telling me the truth.

'It is a possibility.'

'And what does Mr M. have to do with Dante Omega?'

'You are asking too many questions again. You are tired after the long trip.'

'How long was the trip?' I asked, wondering indeed how long I had been blindfolded and handcuffed.

'I will only tell you this: you tell us what we want to know and you can leave this place,' Gianni replied, as he got up, brushing some imaginary dust off his pants.

'What do you want to know?' I asked, feeling my head pounding like a drum. 'I'll tell you everything I know.'

'Where is the tape?'

'What?'

'You heard my question. Where is the tape you made of Patricia? It is not in your suitcase. We looked. Everywhere.'

'I know it's not in my suitcase,' I answered, almost relieved by his question, 'It's in the hotel. In the safe of my hotel room.'

'How do I know you are telling the truth?' Gianni

asked, beckoning Luigi to come to his side, as his silhouette stopped in the doorway.

'I swear that I'm telling the truth,' I replied calmly. 'I forgot the tape-recorder in the safe. 1321 is the combination.'

'You know what will happen to you if this isn't the right number or if the tape is not there?'

I couldn't answer. My throat suddenly clogged up.

'We will kill you, Signorina Miller,' Gianni said calmly, 'do you understand?'

'Yes, I understand,' I answered in a hoarse whisper, 'I understand perfectly.'

'Good,' Gianni answered. 'I will see you in the morning.'

Carmela asked me if I wanted my food brought up to my room, and I answered that I wanted to be left alone. Carmela smiled at me and said, 'A suo servizio. Buona Notte, signorina,' she added, before disappearing into the corridor.

I locked the door, sat on the bed and looked at the sunset through the open window. How did they know I taped Patricia? Had she told them? She must have. They probably tortured her until she talked. I was in total, absolute shock, and the only thing I wanted to do as I watched the sky turn various hues, was to call my mother to my rescue. For the first time in a long while, I longed for her voice, her solid presence, for never in my life had I felt as fragile, as weak, and as helpless as I did that night in Mr M.'s house, as I awaited my fate in anguished silence.

I awoke the next morning to the smell of coffee. As I opened my eyes, I realized I had fallen asleep with all my clothes on. I found myself unable to recall when exactly I had fallen asleep, but the mascara imprint on my pillow confirmed that it had probably been during one of my outbursts of tears, which had left me drained and hungry. At the same moment, I heard a knock on the door and Carmela's voice piped in though the cracks: 'Signorina, volete la prima colazione?'

I answered with a loud 'Si,' jumped out of bed, undid my suitcase hurriedly, and took a quick shower in the adjacent bathroom. When I re-emerged a little while later, freshened up, my hair washed, a new set of clothes on, I felt slightly revived, only until another knock on the door reminded me of my lot; Carmela unlocked the door, and stepped into my room, renewing her breakfast offer. I followed her slow gait down the staircase, where a tempting aroma of toast emanated from the kitchen. My stomach suddenly twisted itself into a multitude of knots, and by the time I was seated at the long table again, I was unable to eat a thing. Although the breakfast platter in front of me was laden with eggs, toast, marmalade and fresh coffee, I was stricken with the deep-seated fear that these people were trying to poison me, and that if I was to eat anything, I would most certainly die. I was like Ingrid Bergman in Hitchcock's *Notorious*, held captive by Claude Rains. Except that in this case, my abductors had about as much in common with Claude Rains as I had with Ingrid Bergman, whose fate, unlike mine, lay in the hands of a man with poise and social standing; I was going to be killed by common thugs, who had probably never even opened a book in their lives. This was my destiny: to die at the hands of ignorance.

This phobia was exacerbated when Gianni entered the room, wished me a cheerful good morning, and urged me to finish up my breakfast on account of the fact that I had 'not much time,' a sentence which enhanced my fear. Why did I not have time? Because they were going to kill me, or because they were going to release me? And how come Gianni was here? Did he drive all the way to Rome and back in one night? Did he have the tape with him? Or did he send someone else out to get it?

I looked at the coffee, the eggs, the toast, and felt as if I was about to vomit. I was going to sit at the table and vomit in front of Gianni, perhaps overdo it in order to have him call a doctor. But given that my stomach had now been empty for over twenty-four hours, there was not much to regurgitate. Therefore I remained seated, staring at the food, my sudden nausea disappearing almost as quickly as it had come. Gianni asked me what was the matter. 'You not hungry?' he asked aggressively.

'No,' I answered, my head looking at the plate, my throat dried up.

'You tell me that you go two days without eating and you not hungry? That's impossible!'

Gianni grabbed the plate of eggs, slammed it down in front of me, and hollered, 'Eat!'

But I couldn't. I looked at him, and told him in a weak voice that I wasn't hungry. He got angrier. 'We already told you we're not going to hurt you! We don't want trouble! I will not repeat this again! You are to do as we say, and everything will be all right. So eat your breakfast, Signorina Miller, and that is an order.'

His threatening tone, and the way he glanced at his watch, as if he had better things to do than sit by my side, served to convince me that Gianni was probably telling the truth, and that indeed, I was wasting my time as much as his.

My phobia vanished as fast as it had appeared, and I gulped down my breakfast with a savage voracity. As I was about to take a last bite of my toast, Luigi came in, and the look both men gave each other – a complicitous and malevolent look – incited me to drop my piece of bread on the floor, push my chair back, and run towards the front door, where I was met by Luigi's fierce grip. He practically carried me back to the dining-room, and sat me down in the same chair I had bolted from. 'Aspetta,' Luigi barked, crossing my two arms behind my back and pushing me brutally, 'ma do' vai?'

Indeed, where was I going? What was I thinking? That I could outwit these two barbarians and escape unharmed?

As I looked up at the men around me, I felt a mixture of shame and anger. There they stood, my two abductors, looking more threatening than ever, talking to two different men, who seemed to have appeared from a different entrance. One of them was an older man with a formidable head of white hair. The other, tall and lanky with blond hair and bleached eyebrows, wire-rimmed glasses and the same checkered pants he had worn on the plane, was none other than Ted Shaw. I wasn't surprised to see him there; in a way, it all made sense. What it meant exactly I wasn't sure, but it did not bother me at that particular moment. What I was more curious about, however, was how long it would take Ted to acknowledge my presence. He seemed very nervous, as Gianni asked him to please follow him into 'the office to discuss certain matters.' As they were about to walk away, Ted turned his head towards me. His gaze was blank and vacuous, although for one infinitely small moment I thought I caught a befuddled look in his eyes. But he quickly turned back towards Gianni, who, as they walked away, I overheard asking Ted if he knew me, to which the latter answered that he didn't. I heard a door slam at the other end of the house. As I was about to get up, Luigi told me to stay just where I was until Gianni returned. I followed his orders, although I wondered why they would want me around their friends, since I could obviously overhear things I wasn't supposed to know. I stared into the distance, and found myself looking distractedly at the orange tree outside.

As I let my thoughts meander, the old man with white hair came back into the room, and started making small talk with Luigi. As he was talking, in a low and raspy voice, I heard him mention the word Alfa-Romeo. I believe he was mentioning this car in regard to some event he had to attend. Nevertheless, for whatever reason, the word 'alfa' gave me an unexpected insight: in Greek, the letter alpha is represented by the symbol: α. This symbol was the one I had discovered at the bottom right-hand corner of Omega's pornographic lithographs. This was it, then! The evidence I had been looking for, which directly implicated Omega, and which Jaurel could not contest. The Alpha and the Omega. How could I not have thought of it beforehand? It was so simple, childish even. The beginning and the end. Strange to think that the artist saw his infamous lithographs as the beginning. The beginning of what? The beginning of the end!

I must have expressed this realization in some way, for Luigi suddenly gave me a threatening look which sufficed to intimidate me at once.

My old spark of curiosity was back in full gear. Why was Ted here? And who was this old man? He looked to be at least seventy years old, too old to be involved in corruption matters – then again, corruption is ageless, especially for people who have been involved in it ever since they can remember – had this man always been involved in it? And finally, were these people who had kidnapped me part of the Mafia, or did they work for someone else? It was hard to tell. These uncertainties added to the tension I could still feel gnawing at my stomach and which suddenly amplified when I heard the distinct sound of two gunshots. They were fired from the other end of the house, from the 'office' Gianni had seemingly brought Ted to. Luigi ordered me to remain still, and I froze in my seat.

Moments later, I overheard a loud shuffle as Gianni hurriedly came into the room and whispered something to Luigi. Carmela was called in, and as she dragged her feet, Gianni shouted at her to move faster, to sit down in front of me, and to point a gun at me to be sure I wouldn't run away. 'Va bene,' Carmela muttered. Both men then hurriedly walked away, leaving me in the old woman's hands.

She pulled a chair up, and sat down, sighing heavily. 'Sono vecchia,' she moaned, as she pulled a small revolver out of her apron pocket and directed it towards me. 'Non ho più la pazienza per tutte queste cose,' I thought I heard her say although I might have been wrong. Why would she tell me she had no patience for these things anymore? Then again, why wouldn't she; she was old, and she didn't care anymore. I couldn't blame her; I probably would have felt the same way if I had been in her unfortunate position of being a septuagenarian bodyguard.

I tried to avoid looking at the gun she was pointing at me with a wobbly hand, and turned my gaze back to the orange tree outside. It was perfect timing, because at that same exact moment, I caught sight of both Gianni and Luigi, dragging a bleeding body outside.

There was no doubt in my mind that the bleeding body was Ted's, and that he was probably dead. I had time, in that fleeting moment, to catch a glimpse of his pants, and to notice that his glasses were no longer on his face. The whole process (both men dragging the body and passing by the orange tree), couldn't have taken more than the fraction of a second. And yet that fraction of a second had an astonishing effect on me. As opposed to frightening me, it actually imbued me with a strange kind of serenity, and this for two reasons: the first one was that I resigned myself to the situation. I realized there was nothing in the world that I could do to change the position I was in. Only the world could do that for me. And until it came to my rescue, I would have to sit still.

The other feeling of serenity was brought about by the fact that the man who had caused me such grief, was now dead. Life was so ironic, I thought. Ted had been murdered by a man who in most likelihood wished me dead, and yet, that didn't deter me from feeling relieved, as if one page of my life history could finally be turned. But this feeling of serenity was promptly replaced by the horrifying realization that I had just witnessed a murder which, in most likelihood, was going to lead to my execution.

I heard the sound of some additional voices outside, followed by the rumble of a car. I am unsure as to how long I let my thoughts and visions of death wander off into the distance. All I know is that when I heard Gianni's voice right next to my ear, I jumped up in fear.

'Signorina Miller, you are dreaming, are you?' Gianni asked me, with a note of malevolence in his voice.

I had not even heard him enter the room. 'Carmela grazie,' he dismissed her quickly, and she shuffled off, her sluggish footsteps dragging behind her like a heavy weight. 'I have two messages for you Signorina Miller,' Gianni said, pulling a chair up and looking at me too closely. 'The first one is this: there is no point in trying to escape this house, because we have very tight security. You cannot go anywhere. The nearest village is very far away, and there are no neighbors around here. You understand? It will be a waste of your time and of my time. But of course if you do decide to disobey me, then . . . then we will have to do something serious about it.' He looked at me gravely, his lips pressed together clumsily, his foot nervously tapping on the ground.

'Did you see that young man that was here before? With the glasses?' He finally asked after an excruciating silence.

'Yes, I did,' I answered.

'Do you know what happened to this man, Signorina Miller?'

I shook my head. 'No, I don't,' I said softly.

'You are lying!' he suddenly shouted, as he brought me close to him, wrapping my shirt collar around my neck and slowly strangling me in the process. 'You are a little liar, aren't you?'

I nodded my head affirmatively, feeling my breath being taken from me, my blood turning cold, my hands numb.

'Good.' He grinned. 'I do not like liars. Actually, I kill liars. That is what I did to the young man with the glasses. One bullet in the heart, the other in the head. Do you understand this, Signorina Miller?'

'Yes,' I attempted to say, the room now blurry, Gianni's voice a distant grind. He abruptly released his grasp from me, and brought his face so close to mine that as he spoke, I could feel the impact of his words almost hitting my face. 'You see, Signorina Miller, I did not only kill this young man who betrayed us. I tied his arms and legs, and put his dirty body in a large bag, and into the trunk of a car. He is not totalmente dead yet, but he will be soon. You see, this young man is now on his way to the Lago Arvo for a very long swim. It is a pity we did not have more time to skin him alive. Oh yes, but we did have time to rip his eyes out. Carefully, with a knife, of course. Luigi is a good carver. A very good carver. You see, my young nephew lost his eyesight at birth, poverino, and the doctor said that only a new pair of eyes could save Rodolfino. Implants, you call them, is that correct?'

'Yes,' I whispered.

'Would you like to see these eyes, Signorina Miller? I have them right here in my pocket.'

'No,' I gasped, 'please no.'

Gianni leaned back in his chair, pulled out a cigarette, then reached his hand back into his pocket and pulled out a little plastic bag. I closed my eyes. This was too much for me to stand. I wanted to faint, to die, anything but see his horrible trophy.

'Open your eyes, Signorina Miller, or I will get angry.'

'I can't,' I said in a voice that didn't seem like it was mine any longer, 'I just can't. If you want to kill me, go ahead.'

But Gianni obviously had other plans in mind. He stuck his two hands on my closed eyes, and forcefully tried to open them. 'If you don't open those pretty eyes of yours, Signorina Miller,' he said in a raucous voice, 'I will have to kill you.'

I started screaming. A loud, strident scream over which I had no control. I grabbed one of Gianni's hands and bit it as hard as I could. He shouted some Italian obscenity, and let his hand drop in pain. I opened my eyes. 'Little American bitch,' he cursed, his facial expression full of a heinous hatred for me.

Luigi's voice abruptly put an end to this torturous episode. 'Il padrone al telefono!' he yelled out from somewhere in the house.

Gianni looked at me, and gripped my chin with his two fingers. 'You are lucky, Signorina Miller; next time you won't be so lucky. And before I forget, the other message I had for you is this: from now on, you will be kept in your bedroom, until further notice. Carmela will be keeping an eye on you. She carries a gun all the time, like all of us, and has orders to shoot in case you try to get away. Now, please follow me upstairs.'

He grabbed my arm, and practically dragged me up the stairs, as I followed him meekly, my body in a state of shock, my feet barely making it up the stairs. I could almost feel a part of myself being left behind downstairs, my only access to freedom, as Gianni threw me on to the bed, slammed the door shut, and locked it twice. I was left desperately alone, cut off from the world, reduced to die incognito in the hands of the Mafia, masters of clean appearances and corrupt souls.

I've been locked up in this room for forty-eight hours. Though much of this sleepless time has involved crying, and wondering if they were able to get hold of the tape (whom have they sent out to find it, if not Gianni or Luigi?) and if I'm ever going to get out of here alive, the remainder has been spent daydreaming, and concentrating on my memories. I think about my childhood, and the day when my mother, my father and I went to Rhode Island to visit my ailing grandfather. As my parents were busy talking to my grandmother, my grandfather beckoned me over from his bed, took my hand in his, put his finger to his lips and said, 'Don't ever tell anyone I gave you this. It's a secret. Our secret. Here, open your hand.'

I opened my hand, and with a shaky movement he placed a small silver key in my palm, closing my fingers around it so that my father, who had just entered the room, wouldn't see it. My grandfather never had the chance to tell me what the key was for, nor what secret lock it opened, because that same night he fell into a coma, and died the next day.

I kept my grandfather's secret, and never told anyone about it. I hid the key in the bottom of my bedroom drawer, and soon forgot about it until my mother and I moved out of Riverside Drive, and as I was piling my old diaries in a box, the key fell to the floor with a loud clink. I picked it up, looked at it, and got up to tell my mother about it, but she wasn't there, and again, I put the key somewhere safe and forgot about it altogether.

As I sit by the old wooden desk in the bedroom, gazing at the garden outside, I try to remember where I could have put the key, and vow to tell my mother about it as soon as I see her again. In a way, the event of the key has suddenly taken on utmost importance, and the desire to tell her about it is becoming an urgency, as if my life depended on it. The image of my father suddenly comes back to me, lying on his deathbed, the color of his eyes washed out like faded ink, my mother gripping his hand, begging him not to die.

My mind wanders to Madame Moher, and my old apartment in Paris, on the Rue Tournefort. It all seems so far away, so distant. I remember the mornings when, before going to work, I would sit at the Café Flore, or in the summer, at the terrace of La Palette, eating croissants and drinking cafés-crème. Baptiste's face comes to my mind, as well as Otto, and the first time he walked into the Moher gallery. Was this me? That image of myself, impressed and infatuated, spoiled and stubborn, seems almost surreal compared to my current situation; I was lucky then, and I didn't realize it. Such is, as Otto had once said, the predicament of the rich: privilege makes one increasingly blind to the realities of the world. This opinion was rather typical of Otto, who loved to come up with such epigrams, probably using them as indirect apologies for his decadent lifestyle. Did this mean that he felt guilty about it, and needed to prove to himself and to the world that he was merely following his peers? It would certainly seem so. When I think about him, the image of Otto merely triggers disdain. How could I have stayed with him for so long? Who was I then?

I think about my life. Is it bound to stop here, or will it evolve into something else? Am I going to live, or am I going to die?

Here I am, a nice Jewish girl, kidnapped by some thugs because I was trying to do a good job, perhaps a little too recklessly, granted, but a good job nevertheless. Suddenly the image of Luca Barzetti, Otto's old friend, comes to my mind. Admittedly I think of him quite often, mostly because I used to feel a strong, albeit platonic attraction towards him. I wonder where he lives, and if I'll ever see him again. It is just a fleeting thought, which manages to occupy my mind for a few seconds, until I start thinking about Omega's painting of Janus, and the smell of turpentine in his studio. Did he, or anyone in his close entourage kill Patricia? Did he intend on having me killed as well? Do I still consider him a great artist even though he is morally repugnant? And does this corrupt his creations?

I think about sidewalks in different cities: Rome, Paris, New York, Madrid. How many feet a day walk on a sidewalk? Hundreds? Thousands? When will I be able to walk on a sidewalk again, bump into perfect strangers? The vision holds lofty notions of freedom.

As Carmela knocks at the door, interrupting my non-sequiturs, I suddenly have the idea of asking her if I can borrow either a pad and pen, or a typewriter. I reason that writing anything will probably assuage my over-wrought state of mind, and will at least give me the opportunity to concentrate on something else besides my uncertain plight.

I can almost feel Carmela's thin and old body leaning against the door, which she unlocks unbearably slowly. I initially doubted Gianni's warning that she carried a gun with her, and briefly pondered the idea of running away during one of Carmela's visits, an idea I quickly abandoned when last night, I saw the muzzle of the same gun she had pointed at me when Ted was killed, sticking out of her apron pocket.

Carmela's ragged face appears through the doorway, and she hands me over the tray of food. 'Pollo con patate e spinaci,' she says with a grin on her face. I forgot to mention this astounding fact, which is that whenever Carmela hands me my food, she describes it in detail, as if she were a waiter in a restaurant, presenting me with the specials of the day. Notwithstanding that the food in this disreputable establishment is on a par with some of the best restaurants I've been to, I haven't ceased to wonder why it is that I am fed so well. I always imagined that most hostages are basically left to starve. And here I am, devouring three sumptuous meals a day! Perhaps it is that, reassuringly enough, they want me alive and healthy. The infamous 'padrone', as Luigi calls him, probably gave his two consorts orders to take good care of me. I suspect that this order was given the day Gianni attempted to show me Ted Shaw's eyes (the recollection sends chills through my body), and was interrupted by the phone call of his superior; it seems that my witnessing Ted's murder doesn't seem to have put my life in further jeopardy than it already is.

As Carmela stands in front of me, I am tempted to ask her about my destiny. But then again, it is probably wiser to keep her out of this. The typewriter is foremost on my mind at this point.

'Carmela,' I say to her, as I place the tray on my desk, 'I would like to ask you something.'

'Si?'

The problem is Carmela doesn't speak English, and I've forgotten how to say 'paper' in Italian. Ah yes I remember, carta. And what about 'typewriter'?

I go and search for my dictionary, which thankfully, my abductors did not bother to remove from my suitcase, although, for some obscure reason they seemingly found the novel I was reading, V.S. Naipaul's *A House for Mr Biswas*, to be of some kind of threat to them, since I found it shredded to pieces in the bathroom wastebasket.

'Aspetta Carmela, aspetta!'

I fumble through the dictionary, practically tear a page off as I hastily leaf through the 'T' section, until I finally find it: macchina da scrivere.

'Carmela! Carmela! Vorrei sapere se posso avere della carta da scrivere o una macchina da scrivere.'

Carmela nods her head, and tells me she will have to

ask Gianni. By the slightly bewildered look in her eyes, I suspect she doesn't know what a typewriter is. But I pray that she will at least ask Gianni, as she said she would, and that he will grant me this small request.

As she closes my door, and the sound of her halting footsteps disappear down the corridor, I am left gazing at my lunch, a tempting piece of chicken with a bed of spinach and roasted potatoes. I have no choice but to eat; besides the fact that they revitalize me in some small way, these meals are my only indirect contact with the outside world (I wonder where the cook lives, if he has a family). My situation is so drastic, I have given up on finding a concrete way of escaping, rendering my wish to write a satisfactory alternative – after studying practically all the nooks and crannies of this room, it has become quite obvious to me that unless I find a sledge hammer or similar object strong enough to break down the bars on my windows, there is no possible way of escaping this room – hence my question: could writing provide a temporary escape?

Five hours have passed, and I am now lying on my bed, gazing at the ceiling. At this point, I could probably draw a map of the room with my eyes closed. Directly in front of the bed, stands a tall and slim dark-mahogany bookshelf, empty except for three books which line the middle shelf. But before I describe these, I must mention the other and most important one, which I found underneath the bed, as I was looking for a sock I had dropped. It was an English tourist guidebook; worn out and very dusty, it seemed as if it had spent much time lying on the floorboards of the villa. I read the entirety of it in less than two hours, and when I finished reading it, I felt a new surge of hope.

The 1963 guidebook deals exclusively with the region of Calabria and Basilicata, sometimes called Lucania. In addition to the dust that clings to it, the guide is in fairly bad shape, with some of its pages missing, others hanging off it like a weeping willow. The chapter concerning Potenza, Rossano and Cosenza (said to be the poorest region in southern Italy) is filled with comments in blue ink, underlined in heavy red when describing the road between Cosenza and San Giovanni in Fiore, a possible indication of my whereabouts, which I found confirmed this morning when I looked out the window and managed to distinguish in the horizon the Byzantine church of San Marco and its five cupolas, described in the guide book as a 'sweeping panorama as seen from the neighboring hills.'

The fact that my otherwise prudent abductors should leave such an important source of information available to me, struck me at first as uncanny. Were they trying to provoke me, leading me on with deceitful dreams (a way of occupying me until they killed me), or had they actually overlooked it? Could it be that the maid (whoever that might be) didn't bother to clean under the beds? This plausible alternative reassured me. Obviously, my abductors were not as meticulous as I believed them to be.

I surmise I am being held captive somewhere near the neighboring hill mentioned in the book (which figures partially on a torn map of the region), because the panorama I can observe is indeed of sweeping beauty, a stark contrast to my present situation; I reflect that beauty, when tainted by the hands of evil, loses its magic, and becomes

Alba Branca

at best banal, an argument which brings me back to
Omega: if he is indeed evil (which I think he is), does
that in any way influence my view of his work? The answer
is unclear to me, and deserves some thought. Nature,
however, is less complex in the sense that it doesn't need
to be interpreted, and its beauty is devoid of any moral
values. The view from my barred windows is indeed
breathtaking, albeit inaccessible. Perhaps out of self-
preservation, I prefer to observe the landscape with the
cool approach of a philistine, oblivious to anything that
doesn't concern his own material life.

The three other books lining the shelf are the following: *The Epistles of St Paul*, Alessandro Manzoni's *I
Promessi Sposi* (one of those classics most Italians have in
their libraries), and finally, a 1985 guide of the best restaurants of Rome.

Needless to say, this small collection is not particularly
enticing; and though I would have gladly read Manzoni in
translation, I gave it up after having spent close to two
hours on the first three pages.

But the book I read with most interest is the English
guide book. Thanks to the previous reader's comments
(who was he or she? Another hostage?) and to the
accompanying photograph, I believe I have been able to
locate my principal surroundings; the view of the cupolas
is so identical to the photograph, I am more or less convinced that this is the area where I am currently being
held hostage. I imagine a full spread in the local newspaper,
describing my harrowing adventure:

214

Muse

Thanks to a 1963 guidebook hidden under the bed of the room in which she was held hostage, art critic Laura Miller was able to identify her surroundings, and, once she managed to escape by sawing the bars of her window off with a nail file, fleeing immediately to the next village where her cries for help were finally heard by a nearby farmer, she was able to retrace her footsteps with the local police, thus enabling them to capture her whole gang of abductors, who were wanted on drug smuggling and murder charges.

Wishful thinking. I have no nail file with me, and there is no nearby village. Or at least so says the guidebook.

My plight is, for the time being, irreversible. But enough self-pity; I must be brave and concentrate on something else.

My favorite piece of furniture in this room is the desk. It is one of those old school desks which were probably ubiquitous for the best part of this century. It is low, its wood abrasive, a deep hole on its right-hand side, obviously meant to house an inkwell. I can almost picture an Italian schoolboy wearing shorts and a clean shirt, writing conscientiously on this desk, his tongue curled on his upper lip, his left arm circling the page, protecting his scribbles from prying eyes.

There are signs of life everywhere on this wooden desk. A name, Isabella, engraved in large letters. Numerous childish doodles. 'Ti amo Ortensia' written clumsily in black ink on the left-hand side of the desk (Ortensia probably sat on the student's left side, saving her admirer from having to display his love for her on the front of his desk, at the expense of becoming the laughing stock of the class.)

The fact that this desk seems to have been used mostly by children fills me with a soothing feeling: I am not alone; I have at least some innocent ghosts by my side, children who probably lived in some village in the vicinity, married their school sweethearts, bore children who grew up together, followed their parents' footsteps, and married each other as well. Sweet normality, the pride of the Italian rural towns. La Famiglia: A tradition never to be broken, always to be carried on.

At first sight, the desk provoked in me the same reaction as the guidebook did: didn't my abductors worry about the fact that I could, upon my unknown date of release, make some kind of correlation between the names featured on the worn-out wood, and the locality of my surroundings? Or was this too much of a far-fetched interpretation on my part? Again, it seemed to me that too much evidence was left at my disposal, a fact which triggered a deep-rooted suspicion that either these were amateur kidnappers (a possibility which prudence led me to disregard), or that they intended to get rid of me anyway, consequently giving validity to the theory that it didn't really matter what I saw or what I heard. But however frequently this gloomy prospect weighed on me, it was often intertwined with the hope for freedom: I decided to overlook the reason for this desk standing in my room, just as I had decided to overlook the presence of the guidebook.

I look down at my feet: sprawled on the bedroom floor is an old red and blue oriental carpet, torn at the edges. It is not particularly beautiful, certainly not half as beautiful as the French-looking tapestry that takes up most of the front wall of the room.

By the bed, stands a white marble table. It holds a splendid Chinese lamp, on which are painted two women holding orange and yellow parasols. As for the ceiling, it is in need of a paint job, as well as the walls, which seem to be rather thick, though not enough for me to hear the occasional distant sound of the telephone.

Another knock on my door. Carmela again. This time she comes straight into my room, carrying a blank notebook, and an old typewriter, the likes of which are probably not made anymore. 'Per lei,' she says, 'un regalo di Gianni.'

A present from Gianni. I'm surprised he even acquiesced. Especially after I practically bit his hand off. Obviously he must have gotten special orders from Mr M.

I sit at the desk, and start writing on the notebook which smells of mildew. Then, I tear off the page and decide to use the machine exclusively. I start to type. The first thing that comes to my mind is the conclusion of my book. I miss writing it (an important link to my past), and decide to play a little game; I will pretend that I am in my New York bedroom, and this is the text I must submit to M. Jaurel by the end of the week. I am pressed for time, eager to complete my work. I will attempt to write the last pages, without any mention of what I have seen or witnessed. As I start to write, I imagine M. Jaurel warning me that my life will be in danger if I tell the truth. I must stick to my original assignment, I can almost hear his voice reminding me to stick to basic facts, and no interpretation. Who knows? This exercise could actually become my printed conclusion, the one which will be incorporated in the book (will I ever see my finished product? Will I pass by bookstores in New York and see my name in print in the front windows?), the one which will become the Omega reference book.

Despite a few diversions that do occasionally infringe upon my concentration (footsteps that stop by my door, then turn away, a loud laugh coming from the garden), I feel eager to put my plight aside, and focus on the twenty-six letters of the alphabet. I pull up the sleeves of my old blue sweater, and start writing.

I analyze Omega's last painting, recount my short meeting with his wife, and describe my last interview with the artist in depth, until several hours and seven pages later (after Carmela has brought in my dinner which I leave untouched, and after the sky has turned a deep gray), I have to stop. For the first time in my life I am suffering strong pangs of artistic conscience. I have underestimated the impact this whole adventure has had on me. Even though this is a game, and even though there is no reason why I cannot tell all, the mere fact of leaving out what I have witnessed and uncovered provokes in me a deep feeling of frustration, and makes me realize how strongly those who have compromised on the truth must feel; I crave to reveal my alpha discovery. I long to reveal Omega's true side, to bring the readers into the labyrinth I had slowly started to uncover, and I realize that the death penalty I am threatened with (or have threatened myself with) if I tell the truth, is almost as tenebrific as the freedom I am guaranteed if I lie.

This stark insight renders me unable to continue writing. For one brief moment, I even contemplate going ahead with the truth at the expense of my life, but quickly attribute this unrealistic thought to my frail and vulnerable mind rather than an actual wish to jeopardize my life for a painter whose work I do admire, but not to the point of dying for it.

This in turn serves to prove to me how small the disparity is between fiction and reality. Here I am, talking about compromises and truth, when all I am doing is testing myself, writing an imaginary conclusion which will probably go down the annals of Mr M.'s garbage. And yet, it all feels real to me, as if someone is really governing my thoughts, dictating my principles.

On the other hand, I know that I am not going to keep this to myself for ever, and this thought gives me some hope, as well as the awareness that at this point I don't have a choice anyhow; whatever I do will not change the fact that for now, I am a missing person; no one knows my whereabouts, the country may or may not be looking for me, and except for the walls that hold me prisoner, and for the sheets that cover me at night, I might as well be dead to the world, because at this point (and this thought stirs me more than any of my previous ones) *my existence can no longer be proven.*

I don't sleep at night, tossing and turning until early morning; I am periodically haunted by the fear that either Luigi or Gianni are going to enter my room in the middle of the night, and attempt to either rape me, or kill me. At every creak or squeak, I can feel adrenaline rushing through my blood. I pray that someone will get hold of the tape before these thugs do. Because it is at night that I understand what these men want: they want me dead. They are only keeping me alive until they find the tape. I am almost certain of it.

I finally fall asleep around dawn, smelling a whiff of the rosemary outside. It reminds me of the smell of my grandfather's country house in Rhode Island.

This morning, I was awakened by a loud knock on the door, as Carmela yelled out, 'sono le nove signorina, la prima colazione è pronta!'

And though I had barely slept four hours, I jumped out of bed, for the sound of her voice and the reminder of my surroundings were enough to trigger in me an acute sense of alertness, which was due to the fact that in this house, my every thought, my every action was governed by fear; anything short of this adrenaline induced reaction was bound to result in some kind of breakdown. So I turned fear to my advantage: it became my guiding light for food, work and conversation (the very little I had), and I was currently in the process of training myself for deep sleep – with the hope that it would enable me to dream, my only escape from reality. After a hearty breakfast of eggs, coffee and toast, I resumed my task.

It has now been three hours since I sat down at the wooden table, and I am ready to take a break. I do not dare look at what I have just written, because I know that it is an unsatisfactory compromise. A few more of these pages, perhaps between five and ten, and I can put this document to rest. As I gaze outside this sumptuous garden,

I wonder for the umpteenth time who the person behind all of this is. Could it be Omega himself? Or Alain Jaurel? And who is this Mr M.? Can I trust that he, or his minions, will let me get out of this house alive? Will anybody ever find me? Have they found the tape? Has my mother called the police? Are they looking for me? What can I do to put this out of my mind?

Nothing, of course. I know too well that these questions will remain unanswered for a while, therefore I must be grateful for the fact that I'm alive, and that I am treated here with relative respect (in the sense that I am neither tortured nor abused, although I am locked up and periodically threatened), fed sumptuously and lodged in a luxurious setting, a paradox which I'm sure most people will have trouble believing when I tell them my story. After all, how many captives has one heard of who are, on a nightly basis, given the choice between eating Vitello Tonnato, Risotto con Funghi, or Arrosto alla Palermitana, followed by a variety of desserts ranging from Mustaccioli cookies, to Cassata Siciliana, or Tiramisu?

Not many I presume. I have gotten over my phobia of the other day, and now eat whatever is given to me. My appreciation of his food has seemingly been duly noted by Fernando, the invisible cook, who seems to have gradually increased the portions of his concoctions.

I start to type what I have been eating for the last few days. Thanks to Carmela's gastronomical introductions and to this rattly old typewriter, I have started to keep a diary of my days here; everything is noted: meals, how many hours I sleep, how I feel, what I crave, what I miss. Then, there are the more important aspects of my life, such as a long list of childhood and adult memories, and a re-evaluation of myself. It seems that being alone and shut off from reality, has infused me with a new awareness of who I am and what is really primordial in my life. It has revealed to me that I am able to face disaster, or at least precarious situations, with a relative amount of coolness and stoicism, something I did not previously believe I was capable of. I think of the people I have deceived and those who have deceived me. I realize my priorities are now different. Things that mattered to me once, seem trivial and pale in comparison to what I am going through now, and to what life seems really to be about: survival, in every shape and color. Everything else seems paltry.

As I type, various events come to my mind, especially those that took place in New York, before my trip to Rome. Suddenly, an evening with Rebecca takes on unprecedented importance, and I feel the urge to write it down:

Two days before I left, I had dinner with Rebecca. We bought homemade ravioli with porcini at Balducci's, a bottle of red wine, and finished it off between the two of us. Rebecca got so drunk she couldn't go home, and fell asleep on my living-room couch. But before she did so, she confessed that she was having an affair with Andrew, Mandy's fiancé. It turned out that the night Sandra called me, complaining about the fact that Mandy was driving her crazy because she didn't know where Andrew was (they had only been living together three weeks at that point), Rebecca was lying in Andrew's arms, in a log cabin some-where in the Catskill mountains. She was, she claimed, desperately in love with him, and was hoping he was going to call off his engagement to Mandy.

I was stunned. Rebecca had never even hinted a word to me about this, and besides Mandy being a friend of mine, I found it unlike Rebecca, who was usually so honest and considerate, to conduct an affair behind someone's back. I couldn't refute Rebecca's argument that Mandy and she barely knew each other. But the news still irked me in some way. I actually found myself feeling sorry for Mandy (who venerated Andrew, and who claimed that the happiest moment in her adult life was when he asked her to marry him) and a little annoyed with Rebecca; then again, the real person to blame here was Andrew, so I quickly shifted my irritation to him, at which point Rebecca went to lie down on the couch, and fell asleep almost immediately. When the next morning I asked her to elaborate on the previous night's confession, she looked at me wide-eyed and asked, 'What confession?'

I decided to drop the whole thing, at least for the time being, and didn't ask any more questions.

Now, I find myself wondering about it, and vow that upon my return I will press her for details.

Another thought I jot down.

Laurence. She is beautiful, vivacious, and intelligent. She has her own gallery in SoHo. I met her in Paris with Otto (I thoroughly suspect they were involved at some point, though both of them deny it with suspicious vehemence). She moved to New York around the same time we did, and got involved with her Swedish analyst.

Lie.

She never got involved with her analyst, and for all I know, she doesn't even see an analyst. But for some odd, perverse reason, I like the idea, and shall develop it. I shall invent a story about her, her life, and her relationship with her analyst. The fact that I don't know her well is actually to my advantage, since it will allow me to embellish freely, without feeling awkward about distorting her actual life.

Laurence's analyst is called Gustav Malström. He has been married for eleven years and has three children. He lives on Fifth Avenue, on the corner of 75th Street, in a sprawling apartment overlooking the park.

Gustav is a serious professional. His reputation is renowned worldwide, and he often travels to give lectures. His main field of study is anxiety.

Gustav's wife, Johanna, is prone to nervous break-downs. She hates living in New York, misses Sweden, and has often threatened to take the children back there with her if Gustav doesn't soon make up his mind about going back to their homeland. The problem is, Gustav is very settled here, in New York. He completed his MD and Ph.D. at Columbia University, and started his own practice soon afterwards. By the time he met Johanna two years later (they were introduced in a restaurant by a mutual friend), he was ensconced in his new job, and quite overwhelmed by the praise and attention he was getting. Johanna was not insensitive to it. She had just arrived in New York, and was enthralled by what she saw and experienced in the city. When Gustav told her that he was planning on staying put for the next two or three years, she didn't seem to mind, and even told him about her plans to go back to school and get a Masters degree in history.

Several months later, Gustav and Johanna got married. The bride's protuberant belly did not seem to bother the audience of mainly elderly Swedish relatives who cried during the ceremony, which was immediately followed by the younger guests drinking substantial amounts of vodka in celebration of both occasions.

Johanna never did go back to school, and several things happened:

Gustav's father died, leaving the young couple a considerable sum of money.

Gustav, after the publication of his book on the study of anxiety, suddenly became a prominent figure in his field, attracting much professional attention, and an outpouring of patients eager to seek treatment with him.

Thomas was born in the spring. Then came Vera. And Axel. The family moved from the Upper West Side to their current Upper East Side apartment. Johanna, charmed by her small children and the high society she was slowly but surely starting to be part of (she had never lived so luxuriously, nor had she ever had the money to afford such beautiful clothes), did not really argue with Gustav when he explained that things were going so well for him, he could not possibly think of moving back, meaning that they would have to wait and see. However, he agreed on a compromise: they would spend every Christmas and every summer in Sweden.

The compromise was respected. On average, they spent approximately two months a year in Sweden. But that wasn't enough for Johanna.

She waited. One year. Two years. Three, four, five, six years.

She had her first nervous breakdown, and Gustav sent her to Sweden in order to recover. She returned weighing more, and looking older. She fired the nanny and decided to bring up her children alone. She denied that this was in order to fill in those long hours of loneliness she had experienced before her trip to Sweden.

Two years later, Johanna had another breakdown. Gustav went to Sweden with her for three months. He hated it, and felt like a foreigner in his own country. Johanna loved it, and implored her husband to move back there. 'You can continue your business here,' she implored. 'Please, do this for me, please.'

'It's not that easy,' Gustav replied, distraught and feeling helpless at the sight of his saddened and unhappy wife. 'But I promise I'll think of something.'

Six months later, Johanna had her third breakdown, and Gustav referred her to a psychiatrist, who urged her to start taking lithium, but she refused adamantly. 'I'm not a sick woman,' she said, 'I refuse to take pills for crazy people.'

This is where Laurence comes into Gustav's life. She was referred to him by someone who praised his work, and who assured her that she wouldn't be disappointed with him. She quickly realized that this was accurate information: the day she met Gustav and started to open herself up to him, she felt as if a door was slowly being unlocked within her, revealing all kinds of rusty memories and bolted sorrows.

Gustav was struck by this young woman's beauty and sensitivity. He gently helped her to unravel her feelings, and the first time she stretched her long legs out on the couch, crisscrossing her feet, he was overcome by a dizzying feeling, which he managed to master as she talked about the boyfriend she was having problems with, some

Italian socialite who sounded like a terrific idiot as well as a pretentious ass. Gustav couldn't help himself asking her how this Otto made her feel, and when she answered, in her purring French accent, 'he makes me feel special and beautiful,' the famous Swedish psychoanalyst decided that perhaps this young woman was on the same intellectual level as her Italian boyfriend, and this time, when she folded her legs again, he clung to the disdain he was starting to feel towards her, and remained impassive, glancing impatiently at his clock, which stood in the center of his imposing desk.

But at the following session, Dr Malström felt that dizzying sensation again, as Laurence irrupted into his office five minutes late, her long hair wet from the rain, a smell of sweet perfume emanating from somewhere along her elongated body.

And when he went home that evening after his last session, he walked down his block in a daydream, as the image of his French patient's blue eyes drifted in and out of his mind. When Johanna and he went out to dinner that night, with some old Swedish friends, Gustav wasn't able to concentrate on what they were saying. And when at one point Johanna smiled at him from behind her glass of wine, Gustav noticed that she had lost all of her youthful beauty.

It was a strikingly painful revelation, and Gustav felt a stir of guilt when he looked at her again. 'Am I the one who's done this to her?' he wondered, 'Is this all because I never went back to Stockholm with her? Have I made her so unhappy?'

But on their way home, as Gustav was about to bring

her most cherished topic up again, Johanna (who seemed drunk by the way she staggered along), suddenly stopped him in the middle of the sidewalk, threw her arms around her husband's neck, and cooed in his ear, 'Gustav, my Gustav, you look so handsome these days!' Then, she proceeded to press her made-up lips against Gustav, raised her right leg towards his crotch, and started to rub her large body against his. This disgusted Gustav, and he pushed her away as gently as he could, saying something to the extent that she should wait until they got home, what was this sudden impulse, so unlike her, these things should not be done on the street but in the bedroom.

As you can well imagine, Johanna was deeply hurt and insulted. She practically ran home, almost got hit by a car on the way, and refused to say a word to Gustav until the next afternoon, at which point our doctor had stopped feeling guilty about his wife, and was back to daydreaming about Laurence.

I'm not sure how Laurence feels physically about Gustav. He is extremely tall, well built, dark blond and blue-eyed, and attractive in a Teutonic kind of way. I suspect that Laurence's taste veers more towards what the French call the 'bruns tenebreux', those sullen dark-haired men with whom she has had her share of problems, Otto being one of them.

But there is one thing I am sure about: Laurence has no idea how Gustav feels about her, mostly because she has her back turned to him during the sessions (thus preventing her from seeing his facial expressions as he pays more attention to her body, the nipple he can decode under her silk shirt, the strand of her chestnut hair that hangs over the couch), and because she is so wrapped up in her emotions, so grateful that she can finally unveil her true self to a perfect stranger, that she does not, understandingly, question Gustav's position in relation to her, except for the fact that she pays him to listen and to help solve her problems.

A week after Gustav and Johanna's fight, and two months after Laurence became Gustav's patient, Johanna announces that she needs a break from everything, and she is taking Axel with her to Stockholm for one month. Whereas a few months ago Gustav might have questioned this abrupt departure, this time he barely reacts to her decision, waving her announcement away with his hand, muttering, 'You do what you want, Johanna.'

This makes her immediately suspicious. 'How can you be so casual about this?' she retorts, 'Don't you care at all?'

Husband and wife start screaming at each other, so loudly that the children start to worry that something terrible is happening and they might lose both of their parents.

So Thomas and Vera barge into the living-room, where they find their parents standing on the couch, their father holding a crystal decanter over his wife's head. 'Stop it papa!' Thomas cries out, 'Leave mama alone!'

Gustav, suddenly aware of the embarrassing situation he's put himself into (especially in front of the children), jumps clumsily off the couch. Both children suddenly burst out laughing. 'Papa can't jump!' they cry out, 'Papa jumps like a frog!' And they proceed to imitate him, jumping on and off the couch, until Gustav, feebly trying to conceal his irritation at being made fun of, tells them to stop their nonsense immediately.

As the children finally calm down, Gustav hears Johanna's voice in the next room, calling Scandinavian Airlines, canceling her flight to Stockholm.

When Gustav is in the presence of Laurence, he not only forgets entirely about his wife, but about his children as well. They are no longer part of his existence. The only things that matter to him, are Laurence's voice, the way she pronounces 'I cannot beelieeve,' and the musky smell of perfume in the air, which insinuates itself around her body.

As the sessions progress, and our doctor nervously awaits his patient's 'transference' period, Laurence starts to wonder about her analyst. She notices that whenever the session is over and she gets up to leave, the doctor looks at her in an awkward way, his cheeks slightly flushed, as if she did something wrong and he had trouble verbalizing it. It is only recently, when, as she turned her head towards the doctor to ask him a question in the middle of the session, that she noticed his eyes were fixated on her legs, and realized that the doctor was not irritated or angry with her (which she had believed at first, eliciting in her a highly insecure reaction), but merely attracted to her, and this is probably what made his cheeks flush.

This discovery greatly excites Laurence, and she decides that at the next session, she will—

'Signorina Laura! La colazione!'

Carmela's voice pipes in through my locked door, and I am once again jerked back into the world of criminals and murderers, far away from my analyst, his couch, and his beautiful patient who lies down, her long legs criss-crossed.

DIARY ENTRY

It is a rainy morning. After Carmela hands me a pot of steaming black coffee, she tells me that at five o'clock this afternoon, I should be ready to expect 'qualcosa,' meaning 'something was going to happen.' Needless to say, these words make me cringe and set off in me a whole array of emotions, ranging from a fear of being killed, to the possibility of my being released.

LATER ON

It is two o'clock in the afternoon. I realize that this five o'clock appointment could have something to do with the missing tape-recorder. Could they have found it? Are they going to get rid of me? No, they couldn't. Something makes me think that they haven't found it, and are getting agitated about it. I was kidnapped because I had seen and heard too much, and all of it was, or probably still is, on tape. And at this point, as long as I can regain my freedom, I am ready to supply them with any additional information they wish to hear, something I am actually surprised they haven't asked me about directly. Don't these people realize that I know even more than what was recorded on tape? Or are they so suspicious that they're only willing to believe my recorded, as opposed to live, words?

I must wait patiently. Everything will be all right. The

sky is an anthracite gray, it hasn't stopped raining since this morning. A violent rain, accompanied by a wrathful wind, that reminds me of the 'mistral,' that terrible wind in southern France, which never ebbs without leaving some kind of dilapidated vestige behind: floods, fallen or wobbly trees, frightened inhabitants.

Time passes slowly in crucial moments. I long for it to be five o'clock, so that my quandary will be resolved.

Will I live, or will I die?

I hear low voices by my door, ominous whispers. Then, a thundering silence. Footsteps walking down the corridor. High-heeled footsteps. A woman. Who is she?

I walk over to the door and press my eye against the crack, where I can barely distinguish the parquet floor and the door across the hallway, behind which I believe is a room. I've never seen that room. Actually, come to think of it, besides the living- and dining-room, I've never seen any other rooms in this grandiose house.

I hear a telephone. No one answers until the sixth ring. Does anyone answer? I hear no voices. An icy quiet reigns about the house.

Mother. Again this feeling of wanting to be near my mother, a feeling I seldom have, perhaps because I have consciously avoided it all these years in order to be able to survive on my own. Now that my survival is at stake, I can no longer ignore my inner wish. I need my mother. It is in this moment of utter distress that I realize how important she is to me, and how impatient I have been with her. Why is it that we have so much trouble getting along? It must change. I must stop being abrupt with her. She's getting older, and I'm no longer a child. Will she be able to save me? Has she found out where I am? Has she called the police? What if she's also been kidnapped? The thought sends shivers down my spine. Mother, don't worry, I whisper, I love you, I'm with you.

If I survive this, I know my life will be different forever. And so will my relationship with you.

I walk towards the window and look outside into the garden. The rain has stopped temporarily, but the sky is still as dark. There is a sweet smell of wet soil, and the air feels purified and clean. It is now ten after two. I must do something else. I will read the guidebook again, with its description of restaurants, pharmacies and market-places. And perhaps after that, I will go back to Laurence and Gustav. I must resolve their story.

From. *Calabria and Basilicata: The Guidebook for the Audacious Traveler.* Canon Press, New York. 1963.

In the center of Rossano, on the Via della Rosa, you will find the Farmacia Tagliese. Mr Tagliese is nearing seventy, and has acquired the most faithful clientele in the Calabria region. Not only will the alert voyager find a vast array of medicinal products ranging from local homeopathic treatments to French aspirin and Indian hand creams, but he will not be able to resist sitting at the much frequented caffé next door, where his wife, Signora Tagliese, will make you a delicious espresso, thus creating a true Italian atmosphere of congeniality.

As for those ladies who can never resist the scent of a good perfume, Mr Tagliese's pharmacy boasts an impressive variety of fragrances, some of them reputed to have been shipped straight from Arabia. It is said that Mr Tagliese's brother Gerardo, has traveled around the world twice, and from each of his voyages has brought home a plethora of exotic products, which have made the Signore Tagliese and his 'farmacia', a national celebrity.

Store hours: Monday to Friday, 9. a.m. to 12.30 p.m., afternoons 3.30 to 7.30 p.m.

Laurence is immensely flattered by her analyst's attraction to her. Not so much for his looks (which are slightly too Teutonic for her), but because for the first time in her life, she really feels under a man's control. Dr Malström dominates her completely. He knows her innermost thoughts, helps her disentangle her web of knotted emotions. He seems to know when she's lying and always seems to find importance in matters which she deems trivial.

In today's session, Laurence is telling Dr Malström about the dream she had last night, after having had a rather unpleasant dinner with her best friend Tiffany. Laurence and Tiffany have been friends since kindergarten. Although they grew up on separate sides of the Atlantic after Laurence left for Paris at the age of eight, they have managed to keep in touch for all these years, writing letters and spending summers together in Maine, where Laurence's parents had a large stone house. Of course the fact that their parents were such close friends (Laurence's mother is Tiffany's godmother), made it easier for them to maintain their friendship, and today they are thankful for that, especially because now that Laurence lives in New York, they spend a lot of time in each other's company.

Tiffany is a lanky young woman with short black hair, and a wide and open face, most striking because of her almond-shaped, deep green eyes. After so many years of Laurence attempting to reform her taste, Tiffany still refuses to listen to her advice when it comes to clothes. The result is /that Tiffany dresses appallingly, always wearing loose, unflattering clothes which hide her figure and make her look much heavier than she really is. When confronted with it, Tiffany usually answers that she doesn't have time to worry about her clothes, since her work takes up most of her time. This is unarguably true, since she is completing her masters degree in International Affairs, and has a job at the United Nations, where she is involved in setting up an educational fund for Third World women. Actually, she is so busy these days, that merely setting up a simple lunch date with her has proven to be quite aggravating, and has resulted in Laurence taking personal offense at the fact that her friend isn't able, or doesn't seem to care, to devote even a minimal amount of time to her.

This is why both friends finally met for dinner the previous night. And when they did, Laurence tells Dr Malström, they ended up fighting, something they had never done before. Laurence accused Tiffany of being selfish, and Tiffany accused Laurence of being jealous, a statement which prompted the latter to laugh, which in turn set Tiffany in a fury, and resulted in her bringing up Laurence's relationship with her brother Eric, an unpleasant event which Laurence had kept out of their lives until now. (At this point, Laurence turns toward her analyst, and asks him how much time they have left, to which he responds ten minutes.) Laurence was once madly in love with Eric, who broke her heart. Today, Eric is married to the great niece of the Queen of Denmark, and has become an alcoholic. At a recent black tie dinner at the Knickerbocker Club, which he was attending with his unassuming wife, he was asked to leave on account of his obtrusive drunkenness which was causing increased discomfort among the guests, particularly a Danish fashion model, who, after Eric attempted to disrobe her in public, complained to the manager who promptly ordered two men to firmly escort the agitator out through the back door, to the horror and utter embarrassment of his wife who was left to go home alone.

The event was written about the following week in 'The Transom' section of *The New York Observer*. The author duly reported that in this particular case, the club had chosen to disregard the fact that the disrupter was, by his marriage, a standing member of the Scandinavian royalty. Furthermore, the club did not anticipate the Queen's reaction which she made public, through her solicitor, in an acrid letter where she stated that if such a prestigious club as the Knickerbocker chose to resolve the problem of inebriated guests by throwing them out on to the street, then she was going to reconsider her membership at the club altogether.

Needless to say, this put the club's President in a most uncomfortable situation, and started a heated debate, the crux of the matter being that if one couldn't apply the same rules to everybody, what was the purpose of having those rules in the first place.

Tiffany, usually quite boisterous and opinionated, surprised everyone, Laurence included, by opting to take a neutral stand in this matter. But when she thought about it afterwards, Laurence decided that Tiffany was probably right, since discretion was probably the wisest stance to adopt in a matter that had been unnecessarily blown out of proportion.

All this to say that after their dinner, Laurence went home and had this dream: she was at a party with Tiffany, and wanted to go home, specifically to get her handbag. The only problem was that Tiffany, for some obscure reason, had Laurence's house keys and refused to give them to her. Laurence kept insisting ('I need my handbag, I want to go home'), and Tiffany kept resisting. Finally, Laurence pounced on her friend, in an attempt to grab her house keys, but Tiffany pushed her away. 'I don't have them on me,' she said, 'and even if I did, I wouldn't give them back to you.'

After telling her dream, Laurence shifts on to an entirely new subject, but Dr Malström stops her. 'I would like to know something. Why do you think you digressed so much before telling me about your dream?'

'I don't know!' Laurence answers, embarrassed. 'I guess I just wanted to. Why? Was it really boring? The digression I mean.'

'Do you know what handbags represent, according to Freud?' Dr Malström asks gently, avoiding her question.

'I have no idea,' Laurence answers.

'Handbags represent the female genitalia. Your dream

237

is quite simple: by denying you access to your handbag, your friend Tiffany was trying to usurp your femininity, keeping you from regaining it. When you were telling me about Tiffany, you mentioned the fact that Tiffany did not take your "feminine" advice into consideration. Think about that. Think about why. And also, it might be interesting to know why you think you needed your handbag so desperately. Did you feel lost without it, weaker without it? Could it be that the handbag defined your femininity, and without it you felt deprived of it?'

'I don't know,' Laurence answers vaguely, 'it could be.'

'The dream,' the doctor continues heatedly, 'also raises the more obvious issue of your relationship with your friend Tiffany. Did she ever hint to feeling any kind of attraction towards you?'

'Why do you ask?' Laurence asks, in a slightly annoyed tone of voice.

'Please answer my question, Miss de Valors,' Dr Malström says, trying to sound authoritative. The doctor knows he has stepped over the boundaries of psychoanalytical ethics. He is talking too much, displaying too much interest in his patient's life. The worst part is that he is unable to feel any qualms about it. The perverse pleasure he is getting out of asking her these questions, delving into her sexuality and her deepest insecurities, is causing him undue excitement; his hands are trembling, his knee jittering uncontrollably. When Laurence changes position on the couch, resulting in her exhibiting a small part of her white bra strap, Dr Malström must close his eyes. This is too much to endure, and he is behaving like a child.

What has come over him? Where is the calm, diplomatic man that he once was?

As he is thinking these thoughts, Laurence, who has been quiet until now, suddenly turns her head towards him and smiles. 'You know doctor,' she says, the warmth of her limpid blue eyes sifting down into his heart, 'you're an intelligent man. You're right about Tiffany, about her attraction to me. Tiffany is a lesbian. We never talk about it, although she knows that I know. I think she feels uncomfortable talking about it. If her family ever found out, they'd have a fit.'

Here, Dr Malström must close his eyes again and breathe deeply. 'Did you ever have any sexual relations with her?' He manages to ask, although he's not quite sure how the words actually make it out of his mouth.

Laurence doesn't answer right away, which causes the doctor to grasp the wooden bars of the chair underneath him with such force, that he could probably break them in one go. The agonizing pause between his question and her answer suddenly causes our distraught doctor to be aroused to such an extent, that he is ready to leap on to her with carnal voracity. Just as he is about to lift himself out of his chair and dive into the silkiness of the body he's dreamt of so many times, his mermaid-like patient answers in her sweet voice, 'No, actually we've never had any sexual relations. You see, I've never been attracted to women.'

Her answer, and the fact that she continues talking, enables Dr Malström to regain his professional composure, although he feels as if he has just come out of a steam room: his body feels sweaty, his head light. He focuses his attention on Laurence's words, making a pact with himself that if he doesn't pull himself together, he will have to retire from the profession altogether. This has the desired effect, and the doctor finally feels his muscles unwinding. He breathes deeply, ready to face his task with the aplomb it requires.

'This is really interesting,' Laurence is saying, seemingly oblivious to the torture she has just put the doctor through. 'Are you trying to tell me that actually Tiffany is in a way jealous of my femininity, and that she feels less threatened when I'm in the same position as she is? Could that be? Is Tiffany actually much more insecure than I realized?'

Dr Malström doesn't answer.

'Yes, I suppose she is,' Laurence continues, disregarding his silence, 'I suppose I never wanted to believe that about her. She's so strong on the surface, so serious. Sometimes it's hard to remember that serious people are also insecure.'

'Why do you say that?' Dr Malström asks.

'I guess because you would think that serious people don't have time to think about their insecurities, or at least choose to ignore them. Actually, maybe serious people are even more insecure than the others, since they seek refuge from their insecurities in their work. Could that be?'

'Do you consider yourself serious?' Dr Malström asks.

'I don't know . . . I guess not. I mean I wouldn't mind being serious. I guess though, that I am serious in my gallery. I take my work seriously, but I don't take myself seriously,' Laurence says, laughing.

'Why not?' Dr Malström asks.

'I don't know. I never did. I take life as it comes. You know, "e la nave va," and the boat, or should I say the beat goes on. Does that sound really stupid?'

'Why did you digress for such a long time, when you were telling me about your friend Tiffany?' Dr Malström asks again.

'I don't know ... Maybe ... well maybe I felt I should give your more details about her life, and also ... Maybe, I don't know, maybe I was trying to ... impress you.'

'Why would you do that?' Dr Malström asks, feeling his heartbeat suddenly increase to a tachycardic level.

'Well, I think it could be that I felt you would be impressed by the fact that I knew someone who was related to Scandinavian royalty, since you're Scandinavian, I mean Swedish not Danish but still ...'

'And why would you want to impress me, Miss de Valors?' Dr Malström manages to ask, though his throat feels as dry as if he were stranded in the Sahara desert.

'I don't think I can answer that question, Dr Malström,' Laurence answers in a lower and firmer voice.

There was nothing which could have made Dr Malström happier than those words. As she finishes uttering them, he feels thick beads of sweat once again forming on his forehead, and as he whispers, 'I think our time is up,' he feels that sudden dizziness take hold of his body again. As Laurence gets up and straightens her skirt, Dr Malström moves towards her like an automaton, unable to really feel what he is doing, as if guided by some external force. As Laurence turns her head towards him, and her perfume enters his endocrine system like a powerful aphrodisiac, he puts his hand on her shoulder, and starts saying something, he isn't quite sure what, and Laurence takes hold of his hand, pressing it tightly against hers. He shivers, and brings his face closer to hers. He watches as her luscious lips come dangerously close to his, and he closes his eyes because the emotion is too powerful for him to bear with his eyes open. Her lips press themselves tentatively against his, a warm and silky feeling, and at that same moment, the telephone rings, an unpleasant and shrill sound. How could that be? He usually turns his phone off during sessions. He must have forgotten to do so today. Of all days. Dr Malström opens his eyes and walks towards his telephone. It is Johanna, who wants to know if he wants to have dinner with Abel Schwartz that evening. 'Of course darling,' Dr Malström says, in a perfectly composed voice. 'It's always nice to see Abel.'

But when he turns around to face the object of his desire, she is gone, evaporated, and only the smell of her perfume is a reminder of her sensuous presence. And as he lets the residue of her smell fill his senses with its sweetness, Dr Malström knows that from now on, his life is heading towards disaster.

I stop typing, and stretch out my arms. I look at my watch: four-thirty. The story of Laurence and Dr Malström has enabled me to escape into the kingdom of imagination, a soothing palliative to my present condition. I thank this uncanny stroke of creativity (dormant until today), and decide that if this spark of inspiration remains, I will elaborate on this story once I'm free. One more thing to look forward to.

I look out of the window. It is still raining and I can

hear the looming sounds of thunder. As I watch the branches of the cypress tree outside, dangerously flailing in the wind, I suddenly distinguish, in the vicinity of the tree and the iron gate, a dark shadow. At first, I think it's an animal. But then, I freeze: the shadow moves quickly, furtively, to the other side of the tree and now there is no doubt in my mind that this is a man. He is crouching, his knees are bent, and as far as I can tell, he is holding a gun. Who is he? Has he come to rescue me, or is he merely one of the house guards? Although he appears to be hiding, the latter seems more probable, or at least seems to be a more prudent theory; I do not want to harbor false hopes. At least not for the next half hour.

I go to the bathroom. I stand by the mirror and look at the image it is reflecting of me. I look pale and thin, my eyes look small, lined with dark shadows. Despite the fact that I am properly fed, my imprisonment is wearing on me. I hardly sleep at night, because I am too nervous, and my physical appearance shows it: My hair is greasy, my clothes are baggy and dirty. I have been wearing the same jeans every day since I've been here, and haven't been wearing any make-up. I suppose one of the reasons (besides the obvious one that there is no reason for me to do so), is that I instinctively want to look as unattractive as possible, in order to dissuade my abductors from feeling any sexual inclination towards me. Indeed, I am still so terrified of being raped by one of them, that I have come to sleep at night with the clothes I wear by day.

As I come out of the bathroom, there is a knock on my door, and before I have time to reach it, it opens abruptly, and Gianni stands in the doorway, smirking, a cigarette dangling from his lips. 'Signorina Miller, you are wanted downstairs,' he says, blowing smoke into my face. His overall tone and demeanor suggest the worst and I panic. 'What are you going to do to me?' I ask him, trying to keep my voice firm.

'We are just going to ask you a few questions. Follow me.'

He grabs my arm and practically pushes me down the stairs where he leaves me in a study, filled with encyclopedias and old maps lining the walls. Standing by the window is Luigi, who looks at me with his usual vacuous expression. Behind an opulent desk, sits a man I've never seen before, who must be in his mid-fifties. He has a rather pleasant face, but for a pouting lower lip, as if he were sulking about something. He has salt and pepper thinning hair, wears wire-rimmed glasses and is wearing a suit and tie. He reminds me of an older version of Ted Shaw. As the man starts talking, in slow and perfect English, asking me if my stay at the villa has been comfortable, and what neighborhood I live in in New York, a city he likes very much (an addendum I could do without), I realize that his resemblance to Ted is related to the fact that they are both criminals with a blatant air of normality. Could this man be Mr M.? I thought he was away. Is his presence here a confirmation of my death sentence? Then again, how can I be sure this is him?

The hypothetical Mr M. looks at me, his eyes fixed upon my face, his lips seemingly ready to embark on a confirmation of my death sentence. But suddenly he looks away, as if I do not exist anymore. His impending question is interrupted by a series of annoyed sighs, as if he were distracted about something, as illustrated by the way he keeps moving papers around his large desk, seemingly looking for an important piece of information. Then, he turns around again to face me:

'Miss Miller,' he begins in a more serious tone of voice, plumping a stack of papers on the floor and asking Luigi to carry them to 'il Signore Cappelli's' room, 'I am sorry we had to put you in this uncomfortable situation. I hope you have been treated well, and have enjoyed Fernando's cooking. You must admit, his cassata Siciliana is remarkable. The best in the region. And I suppose you tried his canelloni as well, didn't you?'

'Yes, I did. They're very good,' I answer, wondering what he's trying to get to, if he got hold of the tape, and who Signore Cappelli is.

'I'm glad you liked Fernando's cooking, Miss Miller. You see, we wanted to treat you well. After all, you are a very attractive young girl, and you are an American. We have great respect for the Americans. Great respect.'

'Who are you? Are you Mr M.?' I ask him bluntly, focusing my gaze on a fly which is stubbornly striking the window pane, furiously looking for a way out.

'Yes, I was told you ask many questions. And I will take the liberty to inform you that your search for too many answers is what got you here.'

'Did you find the tape?' I ask him haltingly, unable to keep the question to myself.

'I see that I must repeat myself again, Miss Miller. You ask too many questions.'

'I'm . . . sorry,' I answer, feeling a wave of nausea overtake me. 'What will you do with me now?' I whisper, ready to fall down and faint in front of him.

'I will release you. But you must promise to leave the country now and never return. Luigi here will be escorting you to the airplane. If we have even a shadow of a doubt that you have disclosed what you witnessed in this house, we will have to take some unfortunate action. I believe you will follow this order, because I don't think you want to end up like Patricia. I suppose this is a correct assumption?'

'Yes,' I answer, realizing my whole body is trembling with fear and apprehension, 'yes it is.'

'All right Miss Miller,' he says extending his hand towards me, 'I will now wish you farewell. I do not believe we will meet again. Go to your room and get your belongings. There will be a car outside to bring you back to Rome, or, to be precise, the airport. Goodbye Miss Miller and have a nice journey home.'

He smiles at me, his lower lip curves up into a warm and sympathetic smile, and I start to feel those aching stomach muscles unwinding cautiously. This probably means that they have recovered the tape from the safe. If not, why else would they let me go? And after all, my knowledge of abductions is strictly based on movies. What do I really know about the internal dynamics of kidnapping?

I leave the study at the same time as the fly finally finds its longed-for exit. The guard at the front door motions me to go upstairs. And as he does that, a simple gesture of the hand, it suddenly dawns on me that I am now a free woman. I run up the stairs, and open the door to my bedroom. I am surprised to see the curtains are closed and it is dark. I search for the switch on the wall, and at that same moment, a hand grabs me and throws me on to the bed. I scream and try to push the hand away. 'There is no use, Signorina Miller, nobody will hear you, especially because in a few moments you will be dead,' Gianni's voice echoes in the room, 'I hope you understand that there was no possible way we were going to let you go, now be a good little girl Signorina Miller—' I feel him tearing my clothes off in the process and my ears are deafened by the sound of my shrill screams. He twists my arms backwards. 'Don't kill me!' I plead, 'Please don't kill me, I'll do anything!'

But Luigi's body appears in the doorway, and before I know it, he points a gun towards me, I hear the sound of an explosion followed by a scream. Suddenly my vision is blurred, and I feel myself entering a dark tunnel.

Six

Clytemnestra was the sister of the beautiful Helen and the wife of Agamemnon. Helen was the wife of Menelaus, Agamemnon's brother. According to the legend, whoever won Helen over was entitled to special rights and protection. So when Helen was abducted by Paris of Troy, her former suitors and her family (Agamemnon) sought to free her and bring her back to the humiliated Menelaus.

To Agamemnon, family honor was paramount. As he needed Artemis' favors to get auspicious winds in order to sail to Troy, Agamemnon had to reluctantly agree to Artemis' wish that he sacrifice the favorite of his four children, his daughter Iphigenia.

So Agamemnon tricked Clytemnestra and her daughter into believing that he was sending Iphigenia to the altar to marry her to Achilles. When she approached the altar, Iphigenia was killed by two priests. After hearing that her husband had duped her and had killed their daughter, Clytemnestra killed him while he was in the bath, with the help of her lover Aegisthus.

Faces float above my head like balloons. I would like to reach out and grab one of them, but they are out of my reach, and it requires too much of an effort to raise my arms towards the dark and mysterious galaxy above my head, dark and glittering with unbearably shiny stars which burn my eyes with their rays.

The balloons suddenly disappear. I am left alone in this unknown galaxy of blinding stars and strange sounds, cottony bubbles of air which burst open every time a star passes by.

Then, suddenly, the dark galaxy breaks open. The sounds become voices, the stars become eyes and noses, mouths that move and talk a strange language. The lights though are even more unbearable. They pierce my eyes like a sharp needle and then, all of a sudden, the brightness gives way to a soothing and gentle blue, like the color of the sea at dusk. The sensation rocks me to and fro, until I hear a blurry murmur. At first it is low and monotonous. Then, as it becomes louder and more persistent, it disrupts the rocking sensation and lifts me higher and higher, back to the glaring lights which this time I cannot fight against.

They are hanging above my head, surrounding me as the loud murmur becomes the sound of a voice. The voice is talking to me. It is calling my name, and the mere sound of it is the most beautiful I have ever heard. It is a familiar and pacifying voice, there is nothing sweeter to my ear, irrefutable proof of my existence, and the fact that I am alive.

I open my eyes. 'Laura!' My mother throws her arms around me, and as I feel her familiar warmth against me, I start to smile and cry at the same time, because there is no person I love more than my mother, no soul that knows me better than she who has created me.

*

As far as I am concerned, there is no experience as para-doxical in life as that of escaping death. On the one hand, the experience has left me feeling weak and humble, drained of any energy whatsoever. On the other hand, it has imbued me with a renewed emotional strength, a direct consequence of the life lesson I have just learned: although none of us are invincible, it isn't that easy to die. Or at least not as easy as my neurotic self previously thought it was.

I have spent nearly two days in this cheerful hospital room on the outskirts of Rossano, recovering from the shock of my abduction, and am now preparing to go back to Rome, where I am to be the prime witness in what is now called 'The Omega case.' My mother is helping me pack my suitcase, and is busy stuffing my toiletry kit with a remarkable variety of perfume and cream samples, and vitamin and mineral pills.

I first reacted to my survival, to the fact that I hadn't been shot dead but that a bullet had merely grazed my head, and to my mother's presence, with dramatic fanfare: I greeted my mother with an unending flow of grateful tears and declarations of love, those I had mournfully bestowed upon her during my imprisonment. This flow has unfortunately deviated to a drier stream of impatience and the firm decision to stay with her for only three days, after which I will spend the remaining week at Luca Barzetti's place. Indeed, my premonition about seeing Otto's childhood friend again was correct: my mother con-fessed to having called him during those frantic three days ('I called the whole world looking for you,' she admitted, 'and was willing to give away all my money in order to

find you.') Luca's response was, according to her, 'as concerned as if he had been your own husband. The boy was
devastated, and said he would do everything to help out.
Which, as you know, he did. Not like that ex-husband of
yours who didn't seem to give two cents about the whole
damn thing.'

Luca's father is Antonio Barzetti, the 'Procuratore della
Republica,' or public prosecutor of Rome, and an
important figure in the judicial world and Italian politics.
After hearing what had happened to me, Luca instantly
informed his father of the matter, who in turn called up
the chief of the Carabinieri (who had already heard
about the case through a lower-ranking commissioner my
mother had contacted), demanded prompt action and to
be kept abreast of the situation, an order that was swiftly
obeyed, and which bore its fruits faster than anyone could
have anticipated.

The efficiency and swiftness of the procedures involved
in my rescue impressed my mother no end. During my
twenty-four hours in this hospital, she didn't stop praising
Barzetti and 'the people who work under him,' thanking
God that I knew his son – who by the way is the most
charming young man she's ever met and so handsome,
although too bad he's not Jewish – because had I been a
nobody, I could have ended up like that poor girl who
was found dead outside a Palermo restaurant, and whose
face was so disfigured, her identity remained unknown for
three days, all this while her parents were enjoying a
vacation on the Amalfi coast, utterly unaware of what had
happened to their poor daughter, who, it finally transpired,
was the unfortunate victim of mistaken identity.

I felt very grateful towards Procuratore Barzetti, and once I had regained strength, I called him. Barzetti was brief and cold, his perfect English punctuated by two brief Italian reprimands seemingly directed towards his secretary. He obviously was not interested, nor did he have the time, to hear my ceaseless flow of gratitude and thank you's which I poured out over the phone breathlessly. What did preoccupy him, he said, was to know whether I would be willing to testify at the trial, if there was to be one, a question he told me to think over. He reassured me about the status of my abductors, 'they've all been arrested,' and quelled my fear about any possible retaliation on their part. 'This isn't the Sicilian Mafia, although we believe these men belong to an organized clan which we are investigating,' Barzetti answered. 'Although we do not believe this to be necessary, we will provide you with some protection if you feel the need for it,' he added, before hanging up and telling me to call him again in two days. I declined his offer for protection. It would infringe upon my new found freedom, I reasoned, and from what he had just told me there didn't seem to be a real need for it. No sooner had I hung up than the phone rang again, and this time it was Luca, inquiring about my health. His voice was deeper than I remembered it being, and I felt myself blushing slightly at the sound of it. 'Come stay with me in Rome,' Luca offered, 'you can have your own bedroom and bathroom with a view on the "Ara Pacis". The Roman altar of peace. It's a nice thing to wake up to in the morning. You'll be a most welcome guest.'

I accepted immediately. The prospect of seeing Luca again filled me with joy, and the idea of staying seven days with my mother at the Hotel Excelsior filled me with dread, a reaction which caused an immediate outpouring of grief.

'Thanks a lot,' she said in a quivering voice, 'I see that you prefer to stay with Luca rather than with me. I who, after all, only turned the world over a few times in order to find you, and, if I hadn't done so, would have probably lost you at the hands of those thugs who nearly killed you. I mean of course you don't realize what it means for a mother to lose a daughter, how could you, after all?'

'Stop!' I ordered her firmly. 'Stop it. You didn't lose me. I told you I was going to stay with you until Oscar shows up. Once he arrives, I'll go stay with Luca. There's nothing wrong with that.'

'No, I suppose there isn't as far as you're concerned,' she answered, sitting on the edge of my bed, 'and I suppose that's all you care about right now?'

'Yes it is,' I answered her, throwing off the covers and getting out of the bed I had lain in for the last twenty-four hours. 'I almost died. I think I have a good excuse. I don't need to tell you I'm very happy to see you, that goes without saying. I don't think there's any harm in my staying with Luca. I'll be seeing you every day anyway, so I don't think you should get upset about it. And frankly, if you hadn't asked Oscar to come here, I would have spent the whole time with you.'

'Yes, we know what you think of my husband. We know,' she replied icily, getting up and fetching her handbag which she nervously dug into, retrieving a lipstick which she held in her hand as she talked to me. 'And if I were you,' she added, in a snappy voice, 'I would take a shower since we're leaving soon.'

I declined to comment and followed her order. The idea of taking a shower appealed to me, and I stayed a long time under the pouring water, scrubbing myself so many times, my body and hair squeaked with cleanliness.

After my shower I changed into a white and blue polka dot shirt and a short beige skirt. I sat on the bed, and combed through my entangled hair until it became smooth. I watched my mother as she held her compact firmly, carefully reapplied bright red lipstick to her already colored lips, and powdered her nose and chin. After she was done, and had placed her make-up back in her handbag, she returned to fussing about my suitcase; a wave of tenderness overtook me. I got up, walked towards her, and hugged her tightly. She felt small and thin. 'I love you mother,' I said to her, as she suddenly started crying, and I held her for a long time until the nurse came in with some tea.

We are leaving the hospital. We are told a car is waiting for us downstairs. I wonder if Barzetti sent it. I apply some lipstick to my lips, some mascara around my eyes. The mere gesture of putting on make-up seems new to me. For the first time in what seems to be a long time, I have someone to please. As I wonder whom that might be, I realize that it is none other than myself, a thought which makes me smile.

'What's so funny?' my grindingly attentive mother asks.

'Nothing. It feels good to be free, that's all.'

She squeezes my hand. 'It will be so much fun to

spend time with you alone,' she says. 'We can go shopping, we can go out to nice restaurants, we can do all kinds of nice things.'

'Whatever you want,' I tell her, obviously the wrong response.

'What do you mean by "whatever you want?" Do you always have to respond to me like that? As if every question I ask you bothers you, as if spending leisure time with me is such a burden to you! Is it? Do you really hate being with me so much? Do you? Do you realize how difficult, how inconsiderate you've been towards me? Do you?'

My mother is wearing a bright pink suit, her skin is tanned and her hair is too blond. As she starts lashing out at me I cannot help but ignore her reprimands. The fact of the matter is that I do indeed feel selfish and egotistic, though for reasons that have nothing to do with her. But how to explain that to her? She's right. I have been inconsiderate towards her. But she herself is so demanding, it's hard to comply with her every wish, precisely because she has so many of them, and because she seems to feel (or at least this is the impression she gives me), that she suffered more during my abduction than I did, therefore she needs some kind of emotional compensation. This in turn raises the question of who is more guilty of selfishness: she, or I? I decide to bring it out in the open, for better or for worse.

'Mother,' I venture, with a deep sigh, 'I don't know how to convey this to you, but I feel selfish for reasons that have nothing to do with you. I didn't know if I was going to live or die for four days. I'm worried about my work, about my book. It's the only thing that I can think of. Omega, the girl, the book, getting my life back on track.'

'Dear child,' she whispers faintly, 'You really did inherit your father's neurotic side, didn't you; work before everything, family comes later . . .'

'Come on mother, relax. I just can't think about shopping and dinners now. I just want to take it easy, and do whatever I want to do, and not what you want me to do. Stop taking everything so personally for Christ's sake.'

This remark seems to have an undeniable effect on my mother, whose face suddenly brightens up. 'Fine. In that case, please promise me only one dinner. Tonight, in Rome. I'll bring you to a great restaurant. After that, you can do whatever you want.'

'It's a deal,' I smile at her.

'And the zipper in the back of your skirt is halfway open.'

I feel her long nails against my back, her perfume floats around the room heavily. I realize that even though she drives me crazy and my relationship with her is far from easy, I am happy to have my mother by my side; she makes me feel protected.

As I convey those thoughts to her, she clears her throat, clumsily tries to hide a smile, and orders me to hurry up.

'Let's leave this goddamn town and get to Rome quickly,' she declares steadily.

'Good idea; this whole area gives me the creeps.'

I grab my white summer jacket and put it on, relishing the smoothness of the silk against my skin. 'Let's go,' I say, 'I've had it with this hospital room.'

'You know,' my mother says looking at me and

brushing an eyelash away from my cheek, 'I think you get this insatiable sense of adventure from your father. He was like you.'

'Was he really? How was he like me?'

'Nothing could stop him. But we'll talk about that another day. Let's get out of here. I've paid the bill, and someone is waiting for us downstairs.'

We collect our suitcases, and as I walk down the stairs towards the car, I see Luca is waiting for my mother and me with a massive bouquet of flowers. I feel suddenly swept away by an intense feeling of happiness: I am alive, I am free, and everything around me seems beautiful and new, as if this were the first time that I was noticing the world around me.

The story of how I was released, and who was involved in my rescue, reads like some kind of detective story. I found it out yesterday, during a late lunch with Luca and his father, in the latter's comfortable apartment in the Parioli district in Rome. It is a story which, like most detective stories, involves punctiliousness and perseverance, pay-offs and perjury, one dead body and several lies.

It all started on the very day of my disappearance, when the stranger I shared the elevator with, picked up the piece of paper I managed to throw in his direction, unbeknownst to my abductors.

The piece of paper I happened to throw turned out to be a fifty-dollar note. This man, his suspicions by then aroused, immediately alerted the hotel's security manager, saying that although he was checking out of the hotel that same day, he felt compelled to recount a strange event he had just witnessed and which he felt, according to the written report presented later on to the police commissioner, was 'just not right'. The man, a Swiss banker named Matthias Danzig, showed the fifty-dollar note to the manager, and described the abductors and myself in astonishing detail, even down to the exact shoes Gianni was wearing, and the color of the coat I had on.

The manager, who was distracted that day because he had found out his fiancée was seeing another man, somewhat rudely dismissed Danzig's soliloquy, thanked him for taking the time to come to him, wished him farewell and, once assured Danzig had closed the door behind him (a false assurance as he was later to find out), surreptitiously slipped the bill into his pocket, and forgot about the whole incident.

Several hours later, that same manager was in a panic, and had promised one of his employees a one week vacation in Capri if he managed to track down that same man he had so rudely dismissed. The employee, a swift and ambitious young man, managed to track Danzig down within a few hours, to the Hong-Kong Peninsula Hotel, where he was expected to arrive later that evening.

The time difference being quite substantial between both countries, they did not hear from Danzig until the next day, at which point our manager, Edoardo Fez, was so nervous he had to send that same employee out to get him a box of tranquilizers.

Fez had reason to be nervous. Right after Danzig's visit to him, and after he had had a long and arduous lunch with his fiancée who had confessed to sleeping with the other man (the commissioner's assistant took pride in transcribing every word that was said, down to the minutest details), he returned to the hotel to find it invaded with police cars and the commissario della polizia of Rome, who had been appointed by Barzetti on this particular case. The matter was important, he was told, and a lot depended on his collaboration. As a child, Fez had had dreams of becoming a bellboy in the hotel d'Inghilterra (a job one of his schoolmates held). As a teenager, Fez had had dreams of becoming a police officer. But because of a slight vision problem (he turned out to have a severe case of presbyopia which was eventually corrected with glasses), he had not passed the required test, a disappointment which instilled some bitterness in his young heart, until, at the age of twenty-one, he was granted the opportunity to prove himself as a security guard at the Banco di Roma, a task he dutifully accomplished for the next five years, until he was laid off upon being accused of accepting a bribe from one of the bank clerks (who was arrested for trying to break into the safe), an accusation which was never corroborated, and which Fez always denied.

But Fez wasn't unemployed for long. It turned out that his uncle, a rather intimidating man over six foot tall named Marcello Spontini, moved from Turin to Rome, where he decided to open up a modest hotel of his own, off the Via Nomentana. Fez was given, once again, the job of security guard, in which capacity he displayed such good faith and obsequiousness towards his uncle, that the following year he was promoted to the position of assistant to the security manager, until he became the manager himself, a job he maintained until Spontini's death and the hotel's bankruptcy.

Many other jobs followed, until he moved on to the glamorous post he how held in the hotel of his childhood dreams. Crime was therefore not out of his league, although in his last twenty-five years in the hotel business he hadn't had to deal with more than minor misdemeanors, resulting in his being slightly at a loss when it came to larger issues. So when Commissioner Razzi explained that a young American woman had disappeared and was last seen in his hotel, Fez got nervous. He confessed to having dismissed Danzig's allegations as nonsensical, at which point the Commissioner looked at Fez, cleared his throat, and said, seemingly trying to keep his voice from rising to a high shriek, 'Find the man. Now. And find any other person who might have seen those two men. Who let them up to the girl's room? Who gave them the room number?'

No sooner had he pronounced those words than the phone rang with a special message for Fez, from one of the aides at the American Embassy, who, in a similar tone of voice, informed the manager that this matter might have international repercussions if the girl was not found immediately, something which the embassy would much rather avoid, therefore his cooperation in the matter would be greatly appreciated.

'Of course!' Fez exclaimed, 'but what does everybody want from me? Who is this girl and what is this about?'

The aide proceeded to explain that I was a friend of the son of Barzetti, 'il Procuratore della Republica di Roma,' and that I had been in Rome to sum up the conclusion of a book I was writing on Dante Omega. I had been kidnapped by some men who could be part of the Mafia although it wasn't certain, and the Procuratore seemed adamant on getting this case settled as rapidly as possible.

These two names seem to have had an instant effect on Fez (Barzetti is as well-known a figure as Omega), who immediately summoned his assistant to his office, introduced him to the Commissioner who was on his way out, and promised him he would have information ready for him the following morning, which, thankfully for him, he did. When they were finally able to reach Danzig the following morning, Fez sighed with relief: at least one part of the job was done. But when it came to finding out who had seen the two men and let them up to my room, matters became more difficult. No one seemed to remember anything. The old man behind the front desk, to whom I had been forced to wave goodbye, claimed the men must have gone upstairs directly without checking in with him, and yes he remembered them leaving with me, but he couldn't really pay attention because he was having an argument with Signorina Mastrilla from room 242, who was complaining that the springs on her bed were loose.

The chambermaid however, did remember the men, notably Luigi, whom she blushingly admitted to having found 'bello', an inconsequential revelation, since all she seemed to recall was the 'soft look in his eyes'.

Danzig was by far the most helpful. When Fez was finally able to reach him, the banker laughed and said, 'I knew I might hear from you again. What happened? Did I witness something important?'

'Maybe,' Fez answered, wondering which diplomatic tactics were most efficient when it came to retrieving important information and appearing anodyne in the process.

But such tactics were obviously a waste of time on Danzig. He volunteered all the information he knew, including the most important: as I was being taken away, he had followed me out to the street, where he had seen the two men 'rather brusquely,' as he put it, shove me into the back seat of a black Fiat. He had then had the presence of mind to jot down the license-plate number of the car which drove me to my near death. 'At that point,' he told Fez, 'it was quite clear to me that this wasn't a lover's quarrel; it was something more serious than that. So I wrote the license-plate number down, just in case.'

Needless to say, this valuable information was one of the most important contributions to my rescue, which, had it not been for Danzig, would not only have taken much longer, but might have never happened.

Danzig was promised a lifelong room upgrade at the hotel, and when Fez called the commissioner back, he failed to admit that the license-plate number had been jotted down by Danzig, instead attributing this new piece of information to 'a little research' he claimed to have done, thus granting himself the pleasure of hearing Razzi compliment him on his good work, a remark which gave him great pride and no scruples whatsoever. (The truth was discovered later on when Fez's assistant, who had witnessed his boss pocket my fifty dollars, an incident which confirmed his suspicions that Fez was a dishonest man, got in touch with Danzig himself.)

Half an hour after Fez revealed this new information, the car had been tracked down and identified: it belonged to a certain Giulio Bennato, who lived in the outskirts of Taranto in the Puglia region.

Razzi sent out ten of his men to Taranto. Then he called Martini, the local police commissioner, to whom he quickly explained the situation. Martini in turn deployed a few of his men, who did not waste any time: in less than half an hour, they were knocking at Bennato's door, where his wife, an old woman who was obviously deaf, told them that she didn't know what in the world they were talking about. 'Mio marito non è qui,' she kept repeating, 'è al bar'.

Martini's men found Bennato indeed in the back room of a caffè, where he was playing cards with four other men. They immediately handcuffed him and brought him to Martini's office. Bennato, a short and stocky man about seventy years old, echoed his wife's statement that he had no idea what they were talking about, until Martini asked him if he wanted to spend the night in jail, at which point Bennato started to lose the color in his ruddy face, and confessed to having lent the car to his cousin, a certain Gianni, a good-for-nothing he was quick to add, whose whereabouts were unknown to him because he moved around a lot.

'Why did you lend him your car then, if he's a good-for-nothing?' Martini asked him.

Bennato didn't answer; the color of his face was now a deep red. 'I cannot say,' he faltered, lowering his eyelids towards the dark gray floor of the police station.

'Answer me!' Martini shouted, so loudly Bennato

almost jumped out of his chair. 'We don't have time for this! Answer me now! What did he promise you in return for lending him the car?'

Martini's direct question seemed to have caught Bennato off guard, since he answered promptly, 'Pictures. But my wife doesn't know. Don't tell my wife.'

'What pictures?' Martini shouted again, inadvertently sputtering on Bennato's face.

'Women. Naked. Pornography.'

'And where does your good-for-nothing cousin get these lovely pictures?'

Here, Bennato started shaking again. 'I can't say,' he mumbled.

'Fine,' Martini said, standing up and crossing his hands behind his back. 'Angelo,' he called to one of the officers who was posted by the door, 'book him. Cell twenty-three.'

'No!' Bennato started shouting, 'no don't do that. I'm an old man, I have a wife, I—'

'Speak!' Martini hollered.

'Gianni gets the pictures from a man who collects them and who's very rich. I don't know his name, but I know that he lives in a villa on a road near San Giovanni in Fiore. They have a cook in the villa who makes good cassata Siciliana. Sometimes when Gianni is in a good mood he brings me some.'

I cannot transcribe every bit of the conversation that ensued between Martini and Bennato, although I took great pleasure in hearing all that was relayed to me. The outcome of the session, however, was that Martini let Bennato go, called up Commissioner Razzi in Rome and told him of his dilemma. 'These people must be stupid amateurs,' he told Razzi, 'otherwise they wouldn't use a relative's car to kidnap someone. They would use a stolen car. Something's strange. In the meantime, let's send our men to San Giovanni in Fiore.'

Martini's suspicions were right. There was something wrong, which was clarified three days later, when all three men were arrested, and each was interrogated separately, by Razzi himself. Luigi was the one who elucidated the mystery of Bennato's car, and his confession triggered more than a few laughs in the Italian police stations.

'Gianni had a dream before we kidnapped the girl,' he explained, chain-smoking cigarettes. 'He had a dream we got caught stealing a car. He said his dream was so vivid that he didn't want to take a chance, especially because he had gotten caught four months before for stealing a car. So we decided to borrow Gianni's cousin's car. I knew it wasn't a good idea but Gianni wouldn't hear of anything else. He convinced me that it would be fine. We didn't tell the boss because he would have gotten angry. We didn't think we'd get caught, so we didn't think it would matter. You see, Gianni is very superstitious,' he added, crushing his cigarette with all his might into a filled ashtray.

'Superstition brings bad luck,' Razzi responded, before ordering him to be locked up.

It took both the Calabrian and the Roman police two days to find the house. Information on the villa was scarce. Nobody seemed to know anything about any beautiful villa on the top of a hill, which led Barzetti to conclude that either these people were indeed amateurs, or they were powerful and feared by the local inhabitants, in which instance the case was going to be trickier to handle.

It seemed that the connection between my disappearance and my abductors lay elsewhere than on the top of a Calabrian hill. There was a crucial lead that needed to be followed. And the core of that lead lay, as it always does, as Barzetti explained over lunch, in the most obvious place.

The Mafia was quickly ruled out. The ways and means of that notorious organization were well-known amongst the whole population, let alone the judicial system. The Mafia was not, if anything, clumsy; these operators seemingly were.

What led Barzetti to the Omega lead was the following chain of events: after finding Patricia's body, the police closed down the Pomezia factory. They issued a warrant for Peter's and, to everyone's shock and dismay, for Dante Omega's arrest. Peter however, when he was finally found at the Fiumicino airport ten minutes before boarding a plane to Denver with a fake passport, told the police a different story than they had expected, which was quickly corroborated when one hundred thousand dollars in cash were found sewn into the lining of his leather jacket.

Peter had been paid to commit that heinous crime, and he didn't seem to have much trouble in confessing who had supplied him with such a quantity of cash. 'The bitch needed to be punished and I don't give a shit what happens to me,' he told the police officers as they drove him to the police station, 'as long as you let me go back to Nebraska. I don't wanna stay in this goddam wop country anymore. Bunch of retard child molesters.'

Needless to say, Peter didn't make it back to Nebraska. Instead, he ended up sitting at Barzetti's desk, spitting out all the information that was required of him, interspersing it with 'a remarkable variety of filthy words', according to Barzetti, who added that Peter's rage at everyone was such that after having been seated for no more than five minutes, he started to pound his heavy fist against the desk, harder and harder, at which point three police officers came to drag him out of the room, where he began 'kicking and screaming like a baby'.

The information which Peter supplied Barzetti with, left the latter baffled. He told the Procuratore everything: who had ordered him to kill his 'bitchy—', (Barzetti apologized and said that Peter's definition of Patricia was too terrible to quote), who had ordered the 'Manhattan babe' to be kidnapped, and finally, why it was that he had agreed to get involved in all of this in the first place. There was no reason to doubt the veracity of his words, as Barzetti soon found out, and once all parts of the statement were verified, the Procuratore was again reminded of why he loved his job so much, and why he had stuck with it for close to thirty years. 'You see,' he told Luca and me, as his maid passed some salad around the table, 'it is always like this in murder cases; it is almost always the person who seems to be the most innocent, the person no one ever thinks of, who ends up being guilty.'

It turned out that in this case, the person responsible for Patricia's death and for my abduction was none other than Isabella Omega, the faithful and frightened wife of Dante Omega, who had come to view her plight as a curse from God.

This information sent shivers down my spine and left me speechless. Isabella Omega? But why?

My question was easily answered.

It was no secret to anyone that Isabella was madly in love with her feared husband. Yes, she lived in his shadow, she had few friends, she seldom went out, but this was the choice, or the compromise she had come to accept in her life: her husband came first.

As for Maria, whom Isabella loved as much as she loved her husband, her relationship with her was different in that she had a certain power over her daughter; not a conscious power which she could abuse (such as her husband did), but a power which was brought about by the consequences of her condition, namely her blindness, and her total ignorance of the outside world. Isabella knew that Maria was unalterably attached to her parents, without whom she couldn't possibly function, and in a way, one could say that she thrived on Maria's weakness: the less her daughter knew, the more she relied on her mother. This created an unhealthy interdependency between them which, as Luca remarked, was bound to eventually cause a crisis. 'There's always a climax in these kinds of situations. A culmination point.' He nibbled on a piece of cacciota cheese to which he had generously helped himself, and winked at me as he caught me staring at him.

I welcomed Luca's interruption. The information I had just heard was overwhelming. A pause was needed here, some kind of diversion; I let my thoughts float away from the horror of these revelations, and let them drift to Luca himself. It felt comfortable, almost natural to be in his presence, and I wondered why it was that we had allowed ourselves to lose touch with one another for so many years. I focused my gaze back on to the Procuratore, his balding scalp, his thick glasses which enhanced pigmented hazel eyes, a trait which his son seemed to have inherited, although the latter boasted a full head of light brown hair, and his tall and robust figure dwarfed his short and slightly hunched father who seemingly had spent too much time reading small print documents, as was illustrated at one point before dinner, when he virtually pasted the newspaper against his glasses. 'Does he have really bad eyesight?' I whispered to Luca, as he was pouring me a drink at the bar.

'Only when he's very tired,' Luca answered, 'and usually this is where my mother comes in; she tends to spend a lot of time worrying about him, telling him he works too hard and he should take a vacation, something he does for two weeks out of the whole year. And when he's on vacation he can never relax because he's worrying about his work!'

My thoughts reverted quickly back to the present, as the maid brought in a large strawberry tart, and Luca clapped loudly, 'Brava Angela, brava! Come sei gentile!'

'She knows I love strawberry tart,' Luca said. 'Angela's worked here for seventeen years. She knows all our family's culinary preferences: my father loves risotto, my brother straccetti, my—'

'Luca,' Barzetti senior reproached him, 'I'm not sure Laura is interested in our culinary preferences, after all we have many more important things to discuss.'

'Please, it's so nice to be here,' I said in all sincerity.

'I'm glad you like it. But let's get back to business,'

Barzetti replied severely, 'I don't have all the time in the world like you young people.'

Luca and I smiled at each other as Barzetti continued the story, which I suddenly dreaded to hear. Now that I had discovered who the guilty party was, I felt that I needn't know more. Perhaps it was my still fragile state of mind, or perhaps the ugly truth was too much for me to bear, but I had the urge to cover my ears and leave the room. This was one deception too many.

Until I had met Otto, I had never had any reason to doubt what was in front of me. Since then, I felt as if I was going to doubt everything. Would I ever be able to trust anybody, I wondered, as I gazed at the slice of strawberry tart on my plate. If a face such as Isabella Omega's, whose innocent brown eyes, sallow skin, and gentle smile exuded sadness and provoked pity, if that face was one of a criminal, then perhaps Nietzsche wasn't wrong in saying: 'The great epochs in our life come when we gain the courage to rechristen our evil as what is best in us.'

But if Nietzsche's interpretation of evil cast a more positive light on it, such as the idea of an emotional release or liberation of the soul, the evil that had settled into Dante and Isabella's hearts was far more nefarious:

Once he had committed his abhorrent act, Dante, as a way of justifying himself (every dubious action requires some kind of self-justification), probably led himself to believe that creativity comes above all, including incest. He probably convinced himself that this display of crude eroticism would only raise his reputation to higher spheres, ranking him alongside those other powerful and untouchable entities: geniuses, those whose defiance knew no boundaries, and whose imprudence was always forgiven (national pride being a near-guarantee against the loss of a country's glories).

And the irony of it all, was that Dante did not, in fact, have much to lose. He was part of the country's national pride. He still is. Whether his compatriots will eventually forgive him depends on two important conditions: that the artist has maintained artistic consistency, and, this one being the one which will determine whether the name Dante Omega is removed or stays on the artistic map, the public's willingness to view the artist's work irrespective of the evil deed performed in order to achieve greatness.

The issue of forgiveness might be less intricate in the case of Isabella, who, as the prototypical victimized woman, stands much more of a chance of generating pity, as opposed to wrath. She committed a crime because she wanted to protect her husband, who, besides her daughter, was the only reason for her existence. She also committed a crime because she was led to it by her unscrupulous husband, who had discovered in himself a sudden thirst for power; ambition had now replaced virtue. Isabella sought to expiate the guilt she felt after she committed her act, by confessing to Barzetti and Commissioner Razzi. And I wouldn't be surprised if she equally sought to justify her act of contrition by exposing her life story, in an attempt to win sympathy and pity. She was a victimized woman, and we were not to forget that.

Isabella saw Patricia as a threat (not only had she had an affair with her husband, but she had witnessed his infidelities with her daughter), and therefore needed to get rid of her. Though she didn't feel capable of doing it herself, she seemingly had no qualms about having some-body do it for her. Crimes of passion are certainly common in Italy, a country where the woman still plays a predomi-nant role as a housewife and a procreator; the family comes before anything, and if endangered, all must be done to save it.

Isabella Omega's act was certainly a desperate one. Luca's use of the word 'culmination point' was quite accu-rate. From what the Procuratore told us, as we moved from the dining-room to the living-room where we were served coffee in gold-rimmed espresso cups, Isabella's con-fession, the day after her husband and Peter's arrest, when she barged into the police station and asked to talk to 'the highest authority because she wanted to tell all even though she knew God would never forgive her,' was the expression of a tormented soul, whose self-esteem was so low that, as Barzetti put it, 'she seemed to be one of those women who, when asked to describe themselves physically, would be at a complete loss as to what to say, probably believing that the image they see of themselves in the mirror is fallacious.'

Isabella needed courage to accomplish such an act, and she found that courage, after months and years of trying to keep it from rising to the surface, somewhere in the bottom of her ailing soul, where she retrieved it like a bad tooth: 'See how rotten this tooth was?' she probably said to herself, just as a dentist would say to a patient, holding the extracted tooth, 'It really needed to come out.'

And, just as the patient does after leaving the dentist's office, Isabella probably felt a combination of pain and relief once the operation was over.

What finally led Isabella to accomplish her deed happened one rainy morning two years previous to the incident, the day she found a lithograph of her husband's which was unlike any she had seen before. Her discovery of the lithograph was purely accidental, since she seldom entered Dante's studio, a much smaller version of the Pomezia factory, which occupied the second floor of their apartment. That morning, as she told Barzetti in a trembling voice, she entered the studio because she needed some glue to paste a frame back together. Unable to find the glue downstairs, she climbed the stairs to the studio, where she found it lying on the floor. As she bent down slowly to pick it up (she had had back problems for as long as she could remember), she caught sight of a lithograph, underneath the printing press. Wondering how Dante could have been so careless, she picked it up and there, as she expressed it to Barzetti, her heart fell to pieces, and has not been the same ever since.

The lithograph was undeniably one of Maria, a white rose inserted between her open legs. If Isabella wanted to doubt the identity of the sitter, she couldn't. 'You know your own children,' she said.

She confronted Dante with her discovery, and the latter at first rebuffed her, then, seeing that there was no use in pretending, admitted to having drawn her, but 'certainly not anything else'.

But however weak and naive Isabella Omega was, her instincts had never deceived her. She knew, and nothing was going to make her believe the contrary. When she asked her daughter how the sessions were going with her father, the latter shrugged her shoulders and said fine.

When Isabella asked her if Dante had touched her in any way, Maria answered that yes he had. When her mother asked her for more details, the daughter refused to contribute any more information, claiming that she didn't really know anything.

The fact that her husband had touched their own daughter made Isabella want to kill him, she told Barzetti. It was beyond anything she had ever expected of life, which was difficult enough. Had she done anything to deserve this? She tried to put the affair in the back of her mind, but at that point it was too late; the family thread was broken beyond repair. She stopped spending time with her daughter. She became impatient with her, threatening to kick her out of the house numerous times. 'She wasn't my daughter anymore but my enemy,' she told Barzetti in a hoarse voice. 'I hated her, and she started to hate me. After a while, she wouldn't talk to me anymore. The only person she would talk to was Dante and Giovanna, the housekeeper (who was also asked to be a witness for the prosecution). The family had reached a dead end. One evening, Dante came into the kitchen where his wife was having a cup of tea. He told her that she should stop behaving this way with Maria, it wasn't her fault, it was his, Dante's, he was the bad man, not her, and he felt sorry about it. Then, he bent his head down and gave his tormented wife a long kiss on the lips, something he hadn't done for as long as she could remember. He followed up with a long declaration of love, a passionate outburst whose earliest equivalent she traced back to their wedding night. 'His lips were always hard, so no soft words ever came out of him.' All these tender gestures seemed to be sufficiently convincing for Isabella Omega to adopt a new attitude: she decided to overlook the incident. It was easier that way. When she found out that Patricia the cleaning woman was having an affair with her husband, she decided to overlook it as well. After all, Dante did not deny any of his wrongdoings, he really felt sorry about them, and he was becoming more and more 'tender with her', as she confessed to Barzetti, bashfully.

As the 'incidents' persisted, so did Dante's tenderness. At night, when they were in bed together, Dante did not content himself with merely kissing his wife on the forehead good night and turning the light off, as he had done all these previous years. Now, when he turned the lights off, it wasn't in order to sleep. He seemed to have found a new and sudden interest in his wife's body ('me a plump mass,' she told Barzetti), and his interest did not go unreciprocated. Isabella reveled in this new sensuality, and it made her feel 'like a real woman'. She found herself paying more attention to the way she looked, the clothes she wore. One day, she was surprised to catch sight of herself in the mirror and noticed that her cheeks were pink, like a schoolgirl. She asked the neighbor, Carla, for advice on perfume, and when the latter suggested an expensive French perfume, Isabella ran to the Corso Vittorio Emmanuele and bought a large bottle, which she dabbed all over her neck and ears that same evening: when her husband rolled his body towards hers, he was seized by an uncontrollable paroxysm of coughs and sneezes, which consequently resulted in Isabella giving the precious bottle to Carla, who probably made very good use of it.

Isabella Omega found herself looking forward to those

nights and now, when the image of her husband came to haunt her long and lonely days, it was no longer with detachment that she thought of him, but with a strong feeling of unconditional love and admiration; for him, she would do anything, forgive all.

This blissful period lasted approximately two years, during which time she started a friendship with Peter, who worked at the Pomezia factory, and who often came around to do odd jobs at the house. Peter was Patricia's boyfriend, and, as he told Isabella numerous times, he planned on marrying her some day. Peter didn't know about Patricia's affair with Omega; Dante (who claimed to have terminated the affair months before) had advised his wife on keeping all this quiet, for fear that Peter 'goes crazy and kills everybody'. Peter had the reputation of being 'pazzo', which besides meaning crazy, led Barzetti to believe (especially after I had told him about my near rape experience with him) that the man might also be disturbed.

So Isabella followed her husband's orders, and kept the affair quiet. She made lunch for Peter whenever he came over, and she listened to his 'affairs of the heart'. One afternoon he inadvertently bumped into Maria who was coming out of the bathroom, and Isabella began explaining who she was, but was quickly interrupted by Peter who said that he 'already knew everything from Patricia'.

The seasons changed, one year went by and then came the Fall. The leaves started changing colors in the streets of Rome, and the temperature dropped. One night, at around ten-fifteen, the phone rang. Dante picked it up, and asked Isabella to leave the room. Several minutes later, he came out in his pajamas and asked his wife to come back in; he needed to talk to her. From the look on his face, she knew that something terrible had happened.

Dante told her the following: Peter had just called with disturbing news; he was on his way to see Patricia who had just confessed to a young reporter all there was to know about Dante's wrongdoings. The reporter had taped everything, and Patricia was worried that she had talked too much. She was full of remorse, and didn't know what to do. Peter felt that he had to communicate this piece of information to Dante, and added that he too was sorry about something: he had allowed that same girl to see the 'dirty' lithographs. The girl was Laura Miller, who had been sent over by Alain Jaurel in New York.

The Omegas acted quickly. Isabella, not forgetting where her roots lay, suggested she call her uncle Manfredi Dell' Aquila, a rich and shady entrepreneur who lived high up in the Calabrian mountains, and ask him for advice. The house he lived in had been Isabella's father's house. She had grown up there, attended school in the next village, and married Dante in the garden which I had observed from my barred windows. She had played childhood games with her cousins Gianni and Luigi, and liked to have her palm read by her aunt Carmela. As the Procuratore spoke, my heart suddenly skipped a beat. So my abductors were related! And Isabella had gone to school in the next village... Could it be then, that the old school desk that stood in my locked room had been hers? That the engraved name Isabella belonged to her and no one else but her? Had I been facing her memory during those fatal three days?

I kept those wrenching thoughts to myself, with the image of young Isabella occupying my mind for a few moments.

Evidently, it took Dante much coaxing before he agreed to have Isabella's family meddle in their affairs: having once been 'driven' to use Dell' Aquila's favors for a 'little problem he was having with one of his assistants', he was all too familiar with Isabella's family's way of 'giving advice', which usually comprised torturous admonitions and eventual body disposal. Dante couldn't deny that he had been forewarned by his future father-in-law before the wedding: 'You marry my daughter, you marry the family,' he had told the frightened painter. 'And I don't know about your family, but in this one, we don't mess around. In this part of the boot, anybody who misbehaves is severely punished.'

Interestingly enough, Omega had revealed this to me during our last interview. He had obviously come to terms with the fact that he had married into a corrupt family, and if he was bothered by it, he was careful not to display it publicly; I remember him telling me that his father-in-law's warning, which would obviously have dissuaded many from entering into marriage, did not do so for him, who by his own admission, 'was not interested in misbehaving. Childish word, futile pastime'.

But let us get back to the husband and wife who, one daughter and many years later, overlooked the deceased man's advice. Dante went to the bedroom at around ten-forty, and as he kissed his wife good-night, she saw that he had tears in his eyes. This stirred her so much, she decided that she would do everything she could to save her husband from scandal. She had to find Patricia, and find that reporter.

Isabella called up her uncle Manfredi, whose answer was prompt and to the point. 'Tell your husband to give me five lithographs and I'll take care of it all.'

This little exchange had actually been taking place for a while. Barzetti had already opened a separate dossier about the matter, which he had nicknamed 'the erotica network'. It was believed that this illegal network had been operating ever since Omega had started to draw his daughter. What first started as a minor trade between Omega and Dell' Aquila, had grown into a fully fledged business. At first, Dell' Aquila bought the lithographs from the artist for a nominal fee, then sold them to various erotica collectors for a higher price. Once the name of the artist was revealed and the interest turned into a near frenzy which expanded beyond the boundaries of petty criminals and erotica dealers, these lithographs were labeled as collector's items, enriching both men very quickly.

Hence, the 'Muse' series was born. Among those men who were aware of its existence was one collector, who had no criminal history and whose business was taken quite seriously. That man was Alain Jaurel, who boasted an important erotica collection which he kept in a New Jersey warehouse, out of shame and the fear that it be discovered. When he first got word that some 'very special' lithographs were circulating, he called up his main supplier, a certain Roger Coleman (who was traced by Razzi's team), and asked him to look into the matter. When

Coleman called back the next day, he sounded enthusiastic. 'They're supposed to be fantastic,' he is said to have told Jaurel.

Jaurel agreed to pay for three lithographs without even bothering to see transparencies beforehand, a highly unlikely procedure for a man who was renowned for his punctiliousness.

According to Coleman, Jaurel probably had an idea that this was indeed an exceptional venture. 'The man has a sixth sense,' Coleman reportedly told Razzi. 'I guess that's why he's such a good art dealer.'

But Jaurel's sixth sense obviously didn't prepare him for what he saw. After he had received the lithographs, he called Coleman up and told him point blank that he couldn't accept them, without offering any explanation. At this point, only a very small circle of people were aware of the true identity of the artist, therefore Jaurel's unusual rebuttal was a surprise to Coleman who chose to interpret it, wisely enough, quite seriously. He decided to do some research on his own. After a few phone calls, notably one to a certain Ted Shaw whom he knew was supplying drugs to his most important client (a notorious erotica dealer who happened to be a media mogul), and whom he had met twice at that client's Bel Air home, in strictly professional circumstances, Coleman found out exactly what he wanted. In fact, he found out what he could know pending, of course, the payment of a certain astronomical sum to the drug dealer, which put him in a most delicate situation in relation to his client. 'Only mucho money will make me talk,' Ted Shaw is claimed to have told him. And as for the subject of the drug dealer himself and his gruesome death, Barzetti told me that he would get to that later.

Despite this controversy, the fact of the matter is that for some reason which Barzetti is still investigating, Coleman himself ended up with the lithographs and with the truth. He is said to have called Jaurel up and told him that he had solved the 'signature mystery at the bottom of the lithograph', to which Jaurel answered that he had had a strong inkling about it all along.

What has now put Jaurel in trouble with the law seems to be the fact that according to Barzetti, it appears more and more likely that he is the one who agreed to pay Ted the required sum, via Coleman; evidently, he also wanted to find out the truth, and this is his defense, but without getting his hands dirty, a feat he may have managed to accomplish.

Needless to say, the discovery that Jaurel was also involved in this came as a surprise to me, although not as much as I would have thought it to be, perhaps a sign that I was becoming street smart, so to speak. I was ready to believe anything.

I also knew, and still know, that despite his bouts of fury, his threats and misogynistic remarks, and although I would never have suspected him of being an erotica dealer (then again who does fit the mold?) I do not believe Alain Jaurel to be a bad man. Seemingly Patricia got her information wrong when she believed him to be one of the main Omega dealers. He is, but not of that expertise. 'Lucky for him that he gave back those lithographs,' Barzetti told me, 'that was a smart move. It will make things much easier for him.'

'He gave them back at exactly the same time as I told him about my discovery,' I said out loud. 'I first told him about the lithographs in the springtime, and it must have been around the same time that he heard about them! This means, without wanting to sound too self-congratulatory, that without my tip which he so vehemently refused to believe, or pretended not to because he already suspected it, Jaurel could have been in jail at this exact moment.'

Luca and his father looked at me with a grin on their faces. 'You are a genius Laura, there's no doubt about it,' Luca told me with a twinkle in his eye.

'I know, I know, what can I do . . . It's one of those injustices of nature.'

We both started laughing until the Procuratore announced in a solemn voice that he had only a few minutes left, so I urged him to finish up the story.

'Well,' he continued, lighting a pipe and sucking on its tip pensively, 'what happened next is simple.' Apparently, the advice Manfredi Dell' Aquila gave his niece, after she had tearfully told him of her and her husband's plight, is the following: he told her that she needed to divide her plans in two, cut them in half like an apple: plan A, plan B. Plan A was that she needed to get rid of Patricia. To do so she would have to make Peter furious, or jealous, and promise him lots of money if he killed her. She needed to do it now. Manfredi seemed to feel confident about the outcome of the situation. Peter's dubious past was no secret to him, and as Isabella recounted how Dante had made her swear never to tell Peter anything, for fear that he might 'lose it again and go on a murderous rampage', what Manfredi said supported Omega's prediction:

'Dante's fear is probably justified,' he said. 'The man is pazzo, crazy, there's no question about it. Which is why this plan will work. Do this, Isabella: promise him sixty thousand dollars, then, if he bargains with you (good sign), go up to one hundred thousand, but no more. If he becomes difficult, remind him that Dante got him out of jail. It is a matter of family honor that he do this for us. Besides, it's not the first time he's killed somebody as we all know. I'll send Gianni over right now, he's in Rome doing some other business for me. In the meantime, you go ask your husband for the lithographs.'

Plan B consisted of Isabella getting rid of me immediately, along with my taped conversation of Patricia. When Isabella told Manfredi that she didn't feel capable of doing this herself, her uncle suggested that he have me kidnapped, and killed if necessary. 'No, don't do that,' Isabella is said to have pleaded, 'don't kill her, she's an American, and she's not like Patricia who was a poor girl with nobody in the world. This one is a rich girl, and she knows people. Dante told me that. It could get us into a lot of trouble. I don't think Dante wants to have her killed. And she's not a bad girl; she's just curious.'

'You know what the family, especially your father, thought about curious people,' Manfredi told her. Isabella told Barzetti that at this point she felt nervous, and implored God's rescue, a plea that did not go unnoticed; Manfredi promised her he wouldn't kill me, but advised her to ask her husband what he thought about both plans.

She went to tell Dante, who was lying in bed with his

eyes open, about the options. 'You can give Manfredi the lithographs,' he said. 'But I don't want to know anything more than I have to.'

'What about that reporter?' Isabella asked.

'I like Manfredi's plan,' Dante declared. 'I don't like that girl. She's trouble. Manfredi can do whatever he wants with her. Get the tape, lock her up, whatever. He should only kill her if he feels he has no other choice. But it would be better if he didn't. I'll be in trouble if he does.'

'And what about Patricia?' Isabella asked her agitated husband.

'You do whatever you think is best,' he told his wife, who recounted this incident to Barzetti with such verve and pride, the Procuratore understood she was exulting in the knowledge that her husband was entrusting her with the family affairs, something he had obviously never done before. 'She was like a child who's just been handed over the keys to the locked cabinet; instead of handling its contents with care, she went too far and dug too deep inside, causing the contents to come tumbling down.'

She called Peter up at Patricia's. The phone rang a long time before anyone picked up. Then, she heard a faint 'hello'. It was Peter. She asked him if she was waking them up and he said no, how could they be sleeping at a time like this. She told him she had bad news for him, which might make him very angry, but however angry it made him he musn't hang up.

She told him that Patricia had been having an affair with her husband for over a year. She told him that if he got rid of her, she would pay him sixty thousand dollars. It was a matter of honor that he do this for the family, who had, after all, gotten him out of jail. If he didn't do it, he would be killed. Her uncle was going to take care of it. The line went dead.

Her nerves were frayed, she told Barzetti, and she didn't recognize herself anymore. She had turned into a monster.

'So the bloke did go ahead with it,' Luca interjected.

'Yes, and actually I was surprised,' Barzetti admitted. 'Death threats never seemed to deter him from doing anything before, but obviously this time, it worked. I suppose he did believe he was indebted towards the family, and he was. Besides the fact that he is a madman.'

'Why was he in jail before?' I asked Barzetti.

'He killed a prostitute in Naples. But Dante got him out of jail on the grounds that there was not enough evidence to convict him. He hired a very good lawyer for him. Of course we all know he did kill the poor woman. But thanks to Dante and his money, the law, as opposed to justice, was on his side.'

'So he killed again?' I asked, haltingly.

'Yes.'

Peter called Isabella back twenty minutes later, at eleven-twenty-five. He was breathing rapidly, and his voice was a mere whisper. 'I killed the bitch outside. She wouldn't let me do it in the apartment. I had a knife, and she started screaming. I put my hand over her mouth, she bit it, and managed to run away. I caught up with her downstairs outside her building. She's lying there now. I'm coming over to get the money. And make that one hundred and twenty thousand. You don't give it to me I go to the police and tell them that your fucking husband is fucking your goddamn daughter, and that you made me kill Patricia to save your honor and that you threatened to have me killed.'

'One hundred thousand,' Isabella answered, as the doorbell rang and she went to open it; Gianni was standing in the doorway, holding a thick envelope. 'Pacchetto for you,' he said, grinning. 'And now I need the pacchetto from you.'

Isabella handed the lithographs over to Gianni, her hands trembling in anticipation. Peter arrived fifteen minutes later, 'his shirt stained with blood, his eyes looking as if they were going to fall on the floor like egg yolks'. Omega was in the bedroom, the house was quiet. Peter was obviously in an utter state of panic, and was speaking so breathlessly that Isabella could barely understand what he was saying. 'I need a passport and a clean shirt to get out of here,' she finally understood.

She gave him one of her husband's old shirts (which was much too small for him) and called Manfredi back. He promised a false passport in the next two days. 'But where am I going to go until it's ready?' Peter asked, in a state of near hysteria.

Isabella thought quickly. 'Go to a hotel,' was all she could think of.

That advice proved to be sensible. Peter checked into a dismal hotel on the outskirts of Rome, and stayed there for a day and a half, until he attempted to board his plane. Unluckily for him, Patricia's body was found barely five minutes after he had killed her, by one of the tenants of the building she lived in. This tenant, Paolo Fresco, an unsuccessful photographer who had until recently made his living as a salesman in a hardware store, made one stop before calling the police. He ran up to his apartment, snatched his camera and ran back down to photograph the disfigured victim. He then proceeded to call the police, as well as information, where he requested the address of the magazine *Novella 2000*. He jumped into a cab straight to the office, clutching the film in his left hand. Here was the opportunity of his lifetime, and he was not about to let it go. He was in real financial straits, and he was not going to let ethics get in the way of money. He would gladly contribute any gruesome piece of information or photograph to a magazine which was notorious for paying its reporters handsomely.

By the time he had spoken to someone in the almost deserted offices, and presented them with the film, it was near the magazine's deadline. But his insistence on having someone run over there to cover the story was such that they proceeded to dispatch a reporter to Via di Bravetta. 'I'm telling you it's big news,' Fresco said, 'it's an ugly murder, and we'll be hearing about it for days.'

Paolo Fresco's intuition certainly proved to be right on target. Not only was the story covered, but since he did not sign an exclusive with *Novella 2000*, his photographs were picked up by different magazines and used repeatedly during the month that followed the event. Paolo Fresco quickly moved out of his shabby apartment on the Via di Bravetta, and found himself a cozy niche in a nicer part of town.

In the meantime, Manfredi, acting quickly, found out where I was staying. He ordered Gianni and Luigi to abduct me as fast as possible, and in the meantime decided to spend the following night at his mistress's house. He did not want me to see him, probably thinking that I might make a link between him and his niece, a highly improbable conjecture which he obviously did not want to risk. Since the house was a good six hours away, it took Luigi (who was with Manfredi at that point) some time before he was able to meet Gianni in Rome, picking up Bennato's car on the way. All took place exactly as it was supposed to, except for one minute detail: not quite familiar with abduction tactics, since after all they had never performed anything quite so drastic before, and flustered by the short span of time they had to bring me safely out of the hotel, they omitted to check on whether the tape was indeed in my possession, an omission which cost them dearly; upon hearing that it was not in his deceased brother's sumptuous abode, Manfredi almost had 'un piccolo attacco', according to Luigi, and sent another one of his men, Rocco, back to the hotel to get it.

But an unforeseen event had happened in the meantime: the police were following my tracks, having been alerted by Razzi. This made matters a little more complicated for Rocco. When he arrived in front of the hotel the following morning, he noticed that four police cars were stationed in front of the building, and there seemed to be an unusual amount of activity going on; people were running around right and left, and when he saw the face of the police commissioner coming out of the front door, Rocco immediately stepped back, and hurriedly walked to the nearest phone booth where he called Manfredi. 'Stay in Rome and go back later on this afternoon. With some luck the tape will still be there.'

What could have led Dell' Aquila to believe such a

ludicrous thing? This at least confirmed one of my previous suspicions: these men were indeed amateurs, although Barzetti added another interesting element to this conclusion. According to Manfredi's mistress, who was with him at the time, it seems that at the point when Rocco called his capo, the latter was in a delusional state of mind, having just absorbed a large quantity of cocaine. 'One could say his judgment on this matter was a little clouded,' Barzetti added, with a faint smirk.

'Does Ted Shaw have anything to do with all of this?' I asked, out of sheer curiosity.

'In a way,' Barzetti answered curtly.

Ever since I had seen him at 'the hostage house' as I had come to call it, I couldn't help but wonder what would have happened had I indeed denounced Ted. Would I have been spared the unfortunate experience of being abducted? Or would I have been ruthlessly killed at arrival time, by one of his accomplices?

Whichever theory is more likely, one thing is clear: my past has been invariably linked to my present life; had I been religious, like Isabella, I would have believed that destiny or God's will had made it so: the past was here to haunt me, and however far I fled, it would always catch up with me. Being a skeptic, I attributed this latest turn of events purely and simply to a coincidence; yes, my past was catching up with my present life; but this could be explained by the fact that I hadn't fully moved out of Otto's circle of acquaintances and contacts. This was perhaps one of the only positive factors left over from our relationship, since my ex-husband had unknowingly been a stepping stone, a catalyst who had transformed my life, arguably, for the better; through him I had been introduced to those men and women responsible for making the world go round. Those with the money, the power, the ambition, the ideas; those who created what we took for granted; machines, networks, businesses. Their achievements had inspired in me a strong will to fulfill my own ambitions: if they could do it, so could I.

And since I quickly learned that not all of these successful men and women were virtuous or honest, it was becoming less and less of a surprise to discover that some of them relied on various substances to allay their daily frustrations.

I had told the Procuratore about Ted's role in Otto's life, and about our flight across the Atlantic ocean, where I had recognized Ted's nasal voice with my eyes closed, how I had witnessed an exchange of briefcases at the Fiumicino airport, and about our quick exchange of glances at the Manfredi house.

'I don't think he knew who I was,' I added. 'I especially don't think he had any idea how much I knew about him, like the sound of his voice for example. Those things don't go away,' I told him in all earnestness. 'Once you hear them, or smell them, they remain indelibly in your mind. Especially if they're linked to trouble.'

'I know,' Barzetti answered solemnly.

At this moment, all three of us paused in the conversation; whether it was a reverential silence in honor of the dead, or a complicitous wish to establish a concrete break between the past and the present, it brought the image of my father to my mind, and I started to miss him terribly, more than I ever had. A knock on the door interrupted

our thoughts. It was Angela, with an important phone call
for Barzetti, who got up and excused himself. Luca followed suit, running downstairs to get a pack of cigarettes.

I was left alone in the room, gazing at the top of the
yellow stone building in front of me. I felt very vulnerable
suddenly; it was as if I was finally experiencing the full
impact of my father's death. I needed to talk to him, to
share my latest adventures with him, to ask him for advice;
I was feeling lost, confused, overwhelmed. I remembered
a discussion we had had a few weeks before his death.

As he lay on his death bed, my father told me he had
been wondering all day about the concept of the full circle
of life. When I asked him to elaborate on his comment,
he told me the following story:

'When my father, your grandfather, turned seventy-
two, one week before he died, he called me into his
bedroom, the same way I called you in—'

'Father, don't say that,' I implored, squeezing his hand
tightly, feeling the palm of his hand against mine, praying
for this sensation to last for as long as possible.

'As I said, my father called me in,' he continued, ignoring my emotional interruption, 'and told me the
following: "Son," he said, grabbing my hand just as you're
grabbing mine, "I will now die a happy man. Do you
know why?"

' "Why?" I asked him, sitting on the edge of his bed.

' "Because I have accomplished the full circle of life. The
loop of life, as I like to call it. I've done and experienced
everything I've ever wanted to do; I've read the books I
wanted to read. I visited the countries I wanted to visit.
I married the woman I loved, and produced the children I

wanted. I created the business I dreamt of as a young boy, and I went out of my way to satisfy my curiosity. Now I am tired, I am old, and I'm not interested in anything anymore. I'm not interested in what once was, because I immersed myself in so much of it, in fiction or in reality; I'm not interested in what will be, because in any case the attraction of newness eventually wanes. So you see, it is good that I am dying now. If I live longer, I will become bitter. You know why? Because I will be like a shriveled up leaf that believes it still hangs on the proudest and tallest tree. So this is why I prefer to die now, happy; rather than later, a bitter man." '

Here my father paused and cleared his throat.

'What about you, father?' I asked him, steadying my voice, 'do you feel as if you've accomplished the full circle of life?'

'No, I don't,' he answered gravely, turning his gray face towards the window where one could hear children playing in the next door kindergarten. 'I don't, and I regret it. I still have an appetite for life. There are many books left to read, many countries left to discover.'

'But the doctor said there's a big chance that you'll get better!' I exclaimed, breaking down into uncontrollable sobs, 'You will be able to read those books, and you will be able to visit those countries!'

I buried my face in my hands and went on sobbing as he remained silent. Finally, as I managed to calm myself down, he started to speak again.

'You know as well as I do that there is no hope. But you should also remember, Laura, that you're a grown-up, not a child. You cannot break down like this. You'll get over this, just as most healthy people get over things in life. It's the secret of survival; we're like boats. We float, sometimes serenely, sometimes on stormy waters, but we always manage to bring ourselves back into port again. When we don't, we only have ourselves, or the circumstances surrounding our failure, to blame. It's as simple as that. You must endure. Be tough. Don't lose control, don't be weak, or the merciless waters will sink you right down to the bottom. If you're lucky, you will go through the circle of life, as my father called it, and like him, when you grow old and you've accomplished what you've always wanted to do, you'll reach a point of indifference. That is, there is a strong chance that nothing will titillate your curiosity anymore.'

'What if I reach that point before I grow old and before I accomplish what I want to do?' I asked him, wiping my eyes with an old Kleenex.

'If you do, which I doubt, it will mean that you've become selfish.'

'And what if I never accomplish what I want to do?'

'Then you'll have to deal with it without becoming bitter about it.'

'Except that I might become bitter before I become indifferent,' I ventured.

'True.' He paused and raised his eyes towards me. His gaze was tender and tired, and I squeezed his hand as he smiled at me: 'If you do become bitter, which I hope you don't, try at least to do so gracefully. Keep it to yourself. Don't blame the world for it.'

And with those last words, my father asked me, as he

had gotten used to doing, to pull the shades down and to leave the room.

Have I gone, in these past three weeks, through the full circle of life? A half-circle is what my father would have probably said. Or would he?

These cogitations only served to frustrate me more, so I concentrated my thoughts back on Barzetti and Luca who had just entered the living-room, and who took up their previous seats. Barzetti removed his pipe from the corner of his mouth, and resumed talking about Ted Shaw, 'a small boat bobbing in this big sea of trouble,' as he nicely put it. 'This Ted Shaw you see,' he added, used to be a nice college student who turned rotten like an apple. At the age of twenty he quit university and became a drug dealer. Ten years later, he was still doing the same thing, and making a handsome profit in the process. What you witnessed at the airport Laura, was not a hallucination as you first thought. What you saw is what got Ted killed.'

Barzetti puffed on his pipe pensively.

'What happened?' I asked, perhaps a little too eagerly, 'What did I witness?'

'Well, it's quite simple. Ted Shaw's suitcase contained a serious amount of cocaine, and that steward's suitcase contained money. Lots of money. The clean-shaven steward, Pietro, later sold the cocaine to his clients, who happened to be (an unfortunate coincidence for Pietro and Ted) Dell' Aquila's "clients" as well. You see, Dell' Aquila had only recently gotten involved in the drug trade, so he took this matter much to heart. These were his buyers, and here was some unknown airplane steward and some rough American trespassing on his territory. His pride was at stake here. And since this deal was no ordinary deal, and it involved lots of money, Dell' Aquila got angry. Very angry. He decided to set an example once and for all.'

'How did they figure out that Ted was the main connection?' I asked, dismayed by all this new information.

'My sources tell me Dell' Aquila's men found out through Pietro who has since disappeared.'

'So my being on the plane with Ted was only a coincidence—'

'Yes, it was,' Barzetti answered.

'Who are Manfredi's buyers?' Lucas asked.

'We are not sure,' Barzetti answered firmly.

'It's not hard to figure out,' Luca conjectured. 'He was probably planning to get involved in local politics, and was setting up shop, as they say, with some minor politician.'

'Perhaps,' the Procuratore answered evasively, 'but let me get to the main point here because we are running out of time.'

'Yes, I'd like to know how they all finally got caught!' I said.

'Well, when Manfredi was alerted that Peter and Dante were arrested, our Mr M. realized that he had everything to lose and very little to gain. But he was determined to get the tape which was still in your hotel room. He knew that sending Rocco back to the hotel was crazy, but he had to take the chance. Rocco of course had to wait two days before returning to the hotel, at which time Manfredi reappeared at the house, with the intention, I'm sorry to say, of, well . . . getting rid of you. Between his drug dealing gone sour and your kidnapping, he was starting to feel very nervous. He was getting worried, and you were more of an encumbrance than anything else. We had taken note of this because my men had been guarding the house for twenty-four hours, ready to snatch our prey when he appeared, which he did the morning he summoned you to the office, using the excuse that he was going to let you go free.'

'How did you hear him say that? And why did he even bother to summon me to his office if he knew that he was going to kill me?'

'He was waiting until the very last moment to see if the tape had been found. Also, he had heard that you were a very pretty young woman.' Barzetti looked embarrassed here, so I understood that he was probably keeping the whole truth from me, which, given the way he faltered on his last words, made me believe that it was most likely something I was better off not knowing.

'And as for how we were able to hear all the activity inside the house,' Barzetti continued, 'we had wires planted everywhere, which were connected directly to my men, five of whom were parked in a car nearby, where they were intercepting all the conversations that were taking place in the house, and relaying them to the other three men in the garden.'

'How where you able to plant wires all over the house?' I asked, incredulous.

'It was difficult,' Barzetti conceded, with false modesty, 'and we're glad the operation was successful.'

'And what happened? Did Rocco go back for the tape?'

'Yes, quite stupidly, he did. Of course by that time our men had gotten hold of it (actually we got hold of it the day we found out what had happened to you), and were just waiting around the hotel, hoping that someone might show up, although the possibility was quite small. It seemed almost too good to be true when they saw Rocco sneak into your hotel room and open the safe. As he was stepping out of the room, his hands empty, they picked him up like a fresh fish and threw him right where he belonged: first into Razzi's office, where he gave us precise instructions as to how to get to the villa and what was going on there, then into jail, where he got beaten up by some inmates because he wouldn't give away his last cigarette.'

'So Mr Barzetti, how come it was that you waited right until the last moment to save me? I mean it was pretty close, you know . . . If you had barged in one second after Luigi pulled the trigger I would have been dead. It's almost a miracle that he missed his target.' That thought made me shudder, and I put my cup of coffee back on the table with a trembling hand.

'Well Miss Miller,' Barzetti answered nervously, 'to tell you the perfect truth, Luigi didn't have time to pull the trigger.'

'What do you mean? So who pulled it then?'

'One of my marksman did. As soon as he saw Gianni throw you on the bed like that, and Luigi pointing the gun towards you, he shot the weapon out of Luigi's hand, and the bullet ricocheted, grazing your temple.'

'But how could your marksman see anything?' I asked, bewildered by this new information.

'He was hiding right behind the curtains.'

'How did he get there?'

'Five of my men entered the house while you were in Dell' Aquila's office.'

'But how did they get in there?' I asked, feeling a surge of admiration for the Italian task force, 'That place is like a bunker!'

'We have our ways,' Barzetti answered, not without a note of pride in his voice.

'So if Luigi got shot in the hand, what about Gianni?'

'He tried to run away but we got him on the staircase. And as for your charming host, he never had time to make it out of his office. But don't you worry. All these bandits will lie in their prison cells for a long time. A long time. And to answer your question about why we waited so long to do anything, the reason is the following: you see, we wanted to get hold of Dell' Aquila. We waited three days for him to show up, and he only did so the last day. We had been wanting to arrest that scoundrel for quite a while now, but we had to catch him in delitto flagrante. Catch him in the act, I think you Americans say. That is why the whole procedure took so long. I realize how unpleasant this whole affair must have been for you. You are a cour-ageous girl, and I'm happy it all ended up well. And now if you excuse me, I really must go. I will see you tomorrow, Laura.'

I got up to shake the Procuratore's hand. 'I don't know how to thank you Mr Barzetti,' I said, somewhat fumbling for words, because at that point I truly was at a loss as to how to express the gratitude I felt towards him.

'Va be, va be,' he grumbled, before dashing out of the door.

I went to fetch my jacket. 'You know, I must go too,' I told Luca hurriedly, 'there's so much I have to do.'

'What do you have to do? Sit down, relax!'

'Luca, I have to call Alain Jaurel. I have to meet my mother in half an hour, I—'

'Call Jaurel from here,' he ordered sternly, 'and don't argue with me. You can use my father's phone.'

'Are you sure?'

'Yes. I'm positive.'

As he pronounced those words, it dawned on me that Luca had, just like his father, acquired a slight English accent. He had barely returned from four years living in London, where, just as his father had many years before, he had worked for the Italian consulate. He had successfully passed the exam required to become a diplomat, and had recently qualified for a job at the Embassy in Lisbon, as a cultural affairs attaché. He was serious and ambitious about his work, to his father's great satisfaction, he admitted to me. 'I'm a real papa's boy,' he told me laughing, as we had dinner together on my first night at his large and airy apartment on the Via della Frezza, off the Via di Ripetta. 'I went to the same university as he did, I completed the diplomat's course he so wanted me to complete, and I'm on my way to becoming a diplomat. The worst part is, I don't mind any of this. I love what I'm doing. I love traveling, I love speaking different languages, I love meeting people. It's a perfect job for me. Besides, I always knew I would eventually be doing this. Rather pathetic I must say . . .'

'What's so pathetic about it? At least you always knew

what you wanted to do. That's something I can't really say about myself. It took me a while, that's for sure.'

'Well, you've done quite well with it.'

'No kidding. Look where's it led me. To the bowels of the underworld and into the hands of death.'

'Only its fingers, shall I say. It wasn't quite able to get full hold of you. Thank goodness for that.'

We both looked at each other and smiled. He was one of the most pleasant people I had been with in a long time, someone I actually felt attracted to. Then again, the notion of being with someone seemed to be somehow foreign to me, possibly because I was still recovering from my latest trials and tribulations, or merely because I was frightened of being beguiled once again. So as I watched Luca tell me about his work ventures, his eyes shining in the process, I decided that at this point in my life, I liked the idea of being platonically attracted to someone more than being seduced. It was more exciting, and far less dangerous. This was no doubt a rather dastardly decision on my part, but one which felt safer and sounder for the time being.

Luca and I resumed our conversation about his new-found profession, and how, after several diversions, he had come to the conclusion that this was indeed what he wanted to do.

'What about the publishing company you were involved in while we were in Paris?' I asked him, remembering the small one-bedroom flat he then occupied in the Marais, and the overcrowded parties he frequently held there.

'It didn't do well. Art publications are a hard sell. I

quite liked doing it actually, but we kept losing money. So after three years we closed it down.'

My thoughts were interrupted by the strident sound of a telephone. As Luca was about to pick up the receiver, he told me his father had a separate line so there was no problem in my making a call at this time. I wandered into the hallway and his father's office, a tidy room filled with rows of books, many of them bound in leather. The room had a musty smell which wasn't disagreeable. His desk was overflowing with papers. On one of the only empty shelves in the room, stood an imposing collection of pipes, the likes of which I had never seen before. As I turned around to reach the telephone, I noticed a large black and white photograph on the wall. It was no doubt an old photo-graph of Luca and another little boy, probably taken when they were about seven or eight years old. Luca was immedi-ately recognizable; the expression, the eyes were the same as today. As for the other little boy, upon closer inspection I realized that it was none other than Otto. He was blond, standing on a pile of sand and laughing, while Luca was busy looking self-consciously at the camera. A man was kneeling beside both boys, his arms outstretched as if to hold them. I wondered if it was Otto's father. This was one of the few photographs I had ever seen of Otto as a child, and it stirred various emotions in me which spanned from tenderness to impartiality.

The photograph brought me back to an evening I had spent with Luca and Otto, many years ago it seemed, sitting at the terrace of a restaurant in Tribeca during one of those muggy New York summer nights. Luca was going through a hard time with his then girlfriend, a pretty and boisterous woman called Lucrezia, who, being significantly older than him, was eager to marry him and had no qualms about informing their circle of friends of her desire, which, as those things usually do, eventually backfired against her. 'I wish she weren't so eager,' I remember Luca telling us, 'because I actually really like her. But she doesn't give me the time to like her; she's always one step ahead of me. By the time I've finished rolling the dough, she's already taken the cake out of the oven. That kind of thing.'

Shortly after that conversation, Luca and Lucrezia split up. It was a noisy, rather bitter separation. Luca spent a lot of time at our Mercer Street loft, seeking comfort from Otto who wasn't able to dispense it, since he was immersing himself deeper and deeper into his drug habit, and desperately trying to prove to his friend the contrary, which made matters worse. 'You'd better start dealing with this as a problem and get treated,' I once overheard Luca tell him in Italian, to which Otto responded with a laugh, 'I don't have a problem,' a reply which filled me with utter disdain and near hatred for him. I obviously wasn't the only one to disapprove of Otto's behavior. Luca seemingly wasn't able to cope with it either. We ended up spending many hours alone (Otto would usually fall asleep at dawn, sleeping until three or four in the afternoon), and I remember wondering why it was that I had met Otto before Luca, who was slowly detaching himself from his childhood friend. 'Stop this shit,' he shouted at Otto one afternoon, 'you're screwing your whole life up.'

In October of that same year, Otto and Luca had a fight. Otto woke me up one morning and told me that Luca was not to be allowed back into the loft under any circumstances. It was over between them, he said, and he never wanted to see him again, and that went for me as well. 'I don't want you to see him alone,' he ordered me, as if he were afraid of something happening between us.

His wish was satisfied. I did not see Luca again. And as far as I know, neither did Otto. And now, here I was with him on this day, alone, and the same feelings I had about him all those years were reawakened, although in a more mature and cautious way. I hadn't been in a man's arms in so long, and yet, I didn't feel the need to remedy that situation. No, I told myself again as I picked up the phone. I wasn't ready for Luca. Not yet.

I dialed New York and the Jaurel Gallery. Alain Jaurel's voice came on the phone and I didn't recognize him. He sounded drained and feeble, as though all his formidable energy had been sucked out of him. He asked me to come back to New York as quickly as I could, with or without my conclusion. I promised him I would be there the fol-lowing week, with a conclusion that would make him happy. 'You can write whatever you want Mademoiselle Miller,' he said, 'whatever in the world you want. After all, you practically ruined my life. I don't have much more to lose after all this. I warned you several times and this is what you do to me.'

'I'm very sorry M. Jaurel,' I told him, feeling guilty and worried about him, 'I didn't mean to make your life so difficult. I just wanted to uncover the truth, I didn't realize it was going to be so gloomy.'

'Bon bon d'accord ça va, I'll see you in New York. We'll talk about it then. Goodbye.'

I hung up and went into the living-room. Luca turned

his green eyes towards me, warmly, and enigmatically. 'Is everything all right?'

'Not really but never mind. There's nothing I can do about it right now. I just have to get back to New York, that's all. By the way, is that you and Otto in your father's office? You know, the large photograph.'

'I know. Yes, it is.'

'It's a nice photograph.'

'Thank you.'

An uneasy silence crept up between us. I desperately searched for words, while hoping he'd break this moment in some way.

'Have you heard from him?' he finally asked, lighting a cigarette.

'No. I mean not since our divorce. How about you?'

Luca nodded, and I detected a slight discomfort in his expression. 'Yes, I've heard from him. He's living in Caracas with a woman. An older woman. He's given up photography and works full time in a gallery, believe it or not.'

'Otto Stamballo has a full-time job. I see. Indeed hard to believe but why not . . . And what about, you know . . . is he clean?'

'So he says.'

'How come he's in Caracas, of all places? ' I asked, wondering if this was the same woman he had told me about years ago.

'I think he knew this woman there, and I don't know . . . Let's not talk about it. It's an unpleasant subject for both of us. Otto's not part of either our lives anymore.'

'That's true. Although he did bring us together in the first place.'

'That doesn't mean anything. We don't owe him anything,' Luca snapped.

'No, we don't. I never said we did. And you're right, let's forget about it,' I added, feeling that this could escalate into something truly disagreeable. Obviously Luca did not like to be reminded of Otto, and that was fine with me. I felt the same way.

'By the way,' he said in a lighter tone of voice, 'I've planned a small dinner party tonight, I hope you're not busy.'

'Well, I have to spend some time with my mother but I can do that before your dinner. What time?'

'Nine-thirty, my house. I can leave you a key if you'd like,' he smiled again, 'you should be able to come and go as you please.'

'Actually Luca, I wanted to talk to you about that,' I said mechanically, as if I had indeed given this some thought although this was evidently coming from somewhere else.

'Laura, don't worry about it. You should do whatever makes you feel comfortable. You should probably stay with your mother anyway, I'm sure she wants to be near you.'

'I guess she does. Well, thank you for everything,' I said a little awkwardly.

Luca gave me a warm and lasting kiss on each cheek. 'I'll see you tonight,' he said.

I dashed off into those ebullient streets of Rome, where the sun was shining so brightly it burnt my eyes. Here was the true sign of a gentleman, I said to myself, as I thought of how gracefully Luca had dismissed any feeling of rejection he may have had pertaining to my staying with my mother. After all, I had only stayed at his place one night, where I had barely seen him since I had fallen fast asleep, so he couldn't be that offended by it. But something told me that it was indeed better to stay with my mother. Perhaps she was right after all. Perhaps I still was a little shaken up about everything.

I walked a while until I got tired and hailed a taxi, my thoughts a clutter of non-sequiturs as I reached the Hotel Excelsior. I entered my mother's suite, where I found her embracing Oscar, who had just arrived from Palm Beach, as was demonstrated by his unopened suitcase which lay on the bed.

'Laura darling!' My mother squealed as she saw me. 'Look who just arrived! And two days early at that! Isn't that the sweetest most adorable surprise?' She kissed him loudly on the cheek and I couldn't help but roll my eyes at the sight of both of them.

'Hi Oscar,' I said, trying to sound mildly excited, obviously a useless attempt, since he looked at me and said, 'You're lucky you're alive girl. Could have been worse. Much worse.'

'She knows Oscar, she knows,' my mother told him, as she pointed towards the living-room, a request I was more than glad to accommodate.

As I made myself comfortable on the couch, I felt myself drowse off to sleep. Next thing I knew there was a torrential downpour of rain which threw the window open, knocking over the end table, and my mother was scurrying about the room in her silk bathrobe. 'Wake up honey, it's seven o'clock,' she said, as she noticed my half-opened eyes.

We had a cup of tea in the kitchen. I told her I would be staying with her. 'What's the matter, you don't like Luca anymore?' she asked, eyeing me intently. 'Oh yes I do,' I replied, perhaps a little too enthusiastically.

'You like him too much, that's the problem isn't it?' she asked me directly, a mischievous grin on her face. 'Well that's fine with me,' she added, before I could answer anything, 'I like that young man. Very much actually. This is a relationship I could approve of.'

'Like I need your approval,' I hissed.

'Oh come on Laura, let's not get so touchy. I think we're beyond that, aren't we?'

I drank my tea in silence. So here I was, at thirty years old; I'd written a book, I got divorced, I'd been kidnapped and I survived, and yet, as far as my mother and I are concerned, nothing's changed. Our relationship is the same as it always was. If I have indeed gone through the full circle of life, to quote my grandfather, well, I ended up exactly where I began: rebelling against my family, and finding myself wanting to honor its traditions at the same time; the dilemma of every generation.

My mother went to get changed, and I could hear her humming in the next room. I closed my eyes, and for a short moment, I was brought back to our apartment on Riverside Drive. I expected my father to come into the kitchen and ask my mother if dinner was ready. But when I opened my eyes again it was to see one of the hotel bell-boys deliver some champagne and canapés which Oscar had ordered. 'Buona sera signorina,' he said timidly, as he caught me staring at him.

I still have a long way to go. The past is too present in my life. And until I am able to coolly distance myself from it (as if I were reminiscing about a friend or relative) until then, I will not allow myself the luxury of becoming indifferent.

Seven

Daedalus was said to be the best painter and sculptor in Athens. He was given an apprentice, Perdix, but when the latter surpassed his teacher by inventing the saw, Daedalus killed him in a fit of jealousy by throwing him off a cliff. Athena, who loved Perdix and who witnessed his fall, turned him into a partridge.

Daedalus was put on trial for his crime, and went into exile in Crete, where he was received by King Minos, for whom he created many feats of engineering. When the King's wife, Pasiphae, with whom he had several children, gave birth to a Minotaur, half-man half-bull, the King was outraged and ashamed. He had to find a way to hide the existence of this monster. So he commissioned Daedalus to build a labyrinth from which no one could escape, and where he imprisoned the Minotaur.

When some years later Theseus came to Crete in order to kill the Minotaur, Ariadne gave him the ball of thread which Daedalus had made, and which would enable Theseus to escape from the labyrinth after he had committed his deed.

When the King found out about Daedalus' disloyalty, he ordered him to be locked up in the labyrinth with his young son, Icarus. Realizing that there were no means of escape, Daedalus devised a pair of wings for his son and himself. But as they were flying above a stretch of sea, Icarus flew too high, and as he approached the sun, the heat melted the wax by which his wings were attached, and he plummeted into the sea that was then named after him, the Icarian sea.

Daedalus sought refuge in Sicily, at the court of King Cocalus, where he gained his favors by building him an impregnable city, as well as various constructions, among which were a reservoir, a steam bath and the terrace of Aphrodite's temple at Eryx. He also invented tools, such as sails, the plumb line, glue, and many tools used in carpentry today.

King Minos pursued Daedalus after his lofty escape, seeking to kill him, but the latter was protected by King Cocalus who got rid of the intruder by drowning him in a torrent of boiling water.

Daedalus lived on to build many more things.

Maria Omega is being sent to a special home for the blind. In the meantime, she has publicly denied being abused or raped by her father. She is quoted as having said, in this morning's paper which I am reading while drinking my cappuccino, that she doesn't know anything, and doesn't understand what all these questions are about.

'Did your father ever touch you anywhere?' a renowned psychotherapist asked her.

'Yes,' she is said to have answered.

'Where did he touch you?'

'I don't remember.'

'Did he touch you between your legs?' the therapist asked her.

'No,' she answered, causing the press to widely conjecture over the probity of her comments, and whether or not she actually would be able to differentiate sex from any innocuous gesture, considering that the girl has never been outside her immediate family, and has never been subjected to the wonders and mysteries of the world.

Dante and Isabella Omega are being interrogated by the police, and this is the third morning that their faces have made the front page of the newspapers. On today's photograph they are holding hands. Dante's gaze is directed defiantly towards the camera. Isabella is looking downwards, her hand is covering her face, in an attempt to avoid the paparazzi. She is quoted as having said, before entering the pre-trial courtroom, 'I will do anything for my husband. My husband is not guilty of anything. He's a good man.'

'What about you? Are you a good woman?' A journalist asked her. 'You tell me,' she is said to have answered, with the same defiance her husband projected in front of the camera.

Manfredi Dell' Aquila has been arrested in connection with my abduction, his primordial role in the lucrative erotica business, and his possible involvement in drug trafficking. As for his loyal nephews, they have been arrested as well, including his sister Carmela, although rumors are the court will be lenient towards her because of her age (she is seventy-nine). Peter is being extradited back to the United States. Edoardo Fez has declared himself a hero, whereas Matthias Danzig is nowhere to be found, even though I have told Barzetti that I'd like to talk to him personally and thank him for what he did. Alain Jaurel's name is also mentioned in today's paper, except that he seems to have been cleared of any wrongdoing. 'The artist's New York dealer,' it is quoted, 'is preparing his client's show in conjunction with a book on the artist, written by the American critic Laura Miller, who was abducted because of information she had regarding Dante Omega's life, and which she was about to divulge publicly, namely that the artist had been committing incest with his sixteen-year-old daughter, whom he drew and sketched extensively in various compromising positions. Miller, after being released by the Carabinieri, spent two days in a Rossano hospital where she was described by one source as being "in good health". Laura Miller is now back in Rome, where she is to be a prime witness in the Omega case.'

I am flying back today. My apartment is in good condition, according to Rebecca who's been watering my plants. Alain Jaurel is anxiously awaiting my arrival. He'd like to send the book off to the printer and concentrate on his next show, that of the ninety-year-old Japanese artist, Nekuso. The charges against Jaurel, complicity in child pornography, are still pending, though his lawyer has categorically stated that his client never owned any of those lithographs, except for that twenty-four-hour period, when he was evaluating whether or not those lithographs were indeed the work of his client, Dante Omega. Those fatal twenty-four hours are the ones that are now causing Jaurel much anxiety, but, as he told me over the phone, he's trying not to worry too much about it, an understatement, as illustrated by the high-strung tone of his voice. As for his erotica collection, Jaurel told me over the phone that he intended to sell all of it and never have anything to do with it anymore. I don't blame him, especially since his wife is now asking for a divorce, on the grounds that his erotica fetish is clearly indicative of a latent illness, one I would only characterize as a harmless perversion or simple loneliness, but which she seems to have branded as pedophilia, an accusation I find rather far-fetched, and most likely a cover for something else which she is not telling her husband or us about.

It is still unclear whether there will be a trial, because of the lack of evidence involved in this case: the authorities are not convinced by the widely held belief that a minor was depicted in these pornographic lithographs. In yesterday's *La Repubblica*, one of them was quoted as saying, 'Never, in the history of Italy, have we conducted our arrests on the basis of assumptions.'

Maria has repeatedly claimed that she loves her father and doesn't know anything, and Omega has repeatedly said that he is innocent of any wrongdoing and the only reason why everyone is making such a fuss about this, is because the Italians are bored and have nothing better to think about.

I hope there will be no trial. I would like to move ahead, to put this whole affair to the back of my mind, put a final ending to it, as opposed to making it a lingering misfortune.

I said my final goodbyes to Luca last night. They were tender goodbyes, I must admit, which started after his dinner party, a lively and crowded occasion. There must have been approximately twenty people there, a larger number than I had expected. Most were elegantly dressed, with the poise and style which can be seen in countries on this side of the Atlantic. I was rather glad to see how well attended this event was, considering that I had agonized perhaps too long on what attire to wear, a quandary which was resolved thanks to my mother's surprisingly ungarish intervention: 'Wear a black dress. You can get away with anything in a little black dress.'

Pondering over whether she had dug this quote up from one of the innumerable fashion magazines she read, or whether this was a statement she ardently believed in, I finally decided that she was probably right, especially since I had recently purchased that infamous little black dress which, once I tried it on, only served to validate her sartorial suggestion. It did look good, and once I had topped it off with high-heeled black shoes, my mother's black and white pearl earrings, my hair floating around my shoulders, I took my much remarked exit from the hotel as a sign that my outfit was appreciated, a fact which did not leave me indifferent.

When I arrived at Luca's, classical music was playing, and a buffet table covered with a white tablecloth was dressed in the far corner of the room. A bartender and a waiter were passing around drinks and canapés, and the whole event was so civilized, I wondered whether I was not predestined to spend the rest of my life in this company. 'What's Morton Street next to this?' I thought as I helped myself to a glass of white wine and walked over to Luca, who was dressed in a cool white shirt and dark linen pants. His hair looked shorter, revealing a high forehead and making his eyes look bigger, and when he smiled and kissed my hand, I felt a familiar tremor pass through my body.

That evening I ended up chatting with various people; a lawyer, his wife, an American expatriate whom I found out knew my old friend Sarah (the one I had had that rather disheartening dinner with last year) who informed me that our friend had given birth to a baby boy named James. Sarah was still living in Rome, she said, raising the child on her own. As for the father, the con-man, it appeared that she had changed her mind about him. She was now adamant about finding him, convinced that when he saw the child he would fall in love with him. I decided that the following morning I would call Sarah, and try to see her and her baby.

Among the other people I talked to were an actress, and several of her friends, one of whom was a rather attractive painter whose name I had heard mentioned, and who flirted with me unabashedly.

The food was delicious, the atmosphere was one of pleasure and farniente, and, perhaps due to my three glasses of wine, I spoke freely, with no inhibitions whatso-ever, even though most of my conversation had to do with my abduction. Everyone had seen my picture in the paper, had heard about it on television, and all wanted to hear more about it, even though they tried to appear discreet.

So I ended up telling them all, as the evening progressed. I found myself speaking alone to a crowd of people, almost as if I were giving an informal lecture. It was the first time I had actually spoken about it in such detail, and I felt I held my audience spellbound, especially when midway I had to switch to English since I was getting tired, which required my listeners to pay even more attention since a few of them weren't quite so fluent in the language.

I told them about everything, except for my story about Laurence and Dr Malström. I kept that to myself, because it was becoming clear to me that this story had indeed been my sole refuge during my stay in the villa, and had actually helped me stay calm and relatively composed. It was a new concept for me, namely that my fictive world had helped me overcome the burden of my reality. I had immersed myself in that story with all my might. My imagination had been my hidden strength, which I suddenly envisioned as the bulb of a flower: until I had uncovered the first layer of earth, I hadn't been aware of its existence. Now, if I took proper care of it, it was going to grow stronger and bolder. This drunken analogy stopped me in my tracks and I found myself laughing alone. Luca's guests looked at me inquisitively. 'Non è niente,' I said, fumbling for words. 'E la fine della mia storia.' The end of the story. For me perhaps, but not for them. 'How did she get released?' A tall and sultry looking man asked Luca, as if I didn't exist and he needed to know the ending of a movie. 'Ask her, not me,' Luca answered evasively.

The tall man didn't ask me. He preferred to grab his coat and leave. A few other guests followed. It was getting late, and I felt very drunk, a condition that had apparently extended to other guests of the party: Sarah's actress friend walked right into a mirror, and the lawyer showered me with his alcoholic breath when he kissed me goodbye.

I was the last one to leave Luca's apartment that evening. Not because I was expecting anything from him, but because I enjoyed talking to him so much. We gossiped about the guests, we reminisced about Paris and New York, and we both agreed that we had wasted many years apart from each other. 'You know, I thought about you very often,' Luca said matter-of-factly, and I answered that I had too, in the same tone of voice because any other way would have sounded sentimental.

We discussed our relationships. Luca told me about his last girlfriend, a certain Donella, whom he'd been seeing on and off for the past two years.

'Are you in love?' I asked, following his gesture to sit on the floor, and taking my shoes off in the process.

'I was. I'm not anymore.'

As if to demonstrate the sincerity of that comment, Luca suddenly grabbed my hand, turned my head towards his, and kissed me. At first tentatively, then, as he saw that I was reciprocating his gesture, it became a passionate embrace which eventually took on a more horizontal position. Luca caressed my body, his hands gliding over my breasts, my thighs, my face, but not venturing anywhere underneath my dress. He whispered in my ear that everything about me was perfect, he had waited for me all these years, and finally I was here. Even in my drunkenness, which was thankfully starting to wear off, I found his declaration to be a tad too dramatic, a reaction which caused me to wonder whether I was becoming a cynic, an ephemeral reflection considering the speed in which I yielded back to his arms and warm lips. We remained clasped together until dawn, when I heard the bells in the nearby church ring five times. 'I've got to go,' I told Luca, sitting up and feeling sick in the process.

'I'll drive you back.'

We both stood up and, slightly embarrassed, looked at each other; Luca proceeded to tuck his shirt back in his pants, I combed through my hair with my fingers. We left his apartment abruptly and drove in silence to the hotel. I felt very tired, and was happy to watch Rome stream past the windows in all its splendor, without needing to talk. It was actually a nice feeling to know that Luca didn't mind silence. It made him all the more attractive in my eyes.

Luca stopped the car in front of the hotel, and kissed me. As I closed my eyes and felt the warmth of his lips against mine, I decided that I really did like this, there was nothing wrong with it in the least; actually at that particular moment I could think of nothing more sweet, sensual, and divinely seductive.

This feeling was intensified two days later, when we made love on the floor of his bedroom, and fell asleep on his rug, a sheet covering our naked bodies.

Since I had told Luca about my old floor fantasy (quite an innocent one, I admit, but a fantasy nevertheless), we ended up experimenting on every floor of his apartment, including the bathroom and the kitchen, where I knocked my head sharply against his table, which put an abrupt end to my fantasies.

Luca has already decided that he's coming to see me in a month, and has implied that he is not willing to let this romance become a memory. Because of his work, it may be hard for him to come often to New York, he has told me, and he knows that it may be hard for me to come often to Rome. But he doesn't believe geography will influence us, because he's certain that if we really want to be together, we will find a solution. 'I'm not going to let go of you so fast,' he said to me last night, as we had a candlelit dinner in one of Rome's best restaurants. 'I would like to be with you.'

The fact that a man so unlike Otto, so much more serious, interesting and intelligent could tell me such things filled me with a childish pride. And yet, I did not feel ready to encourage him, to support his idea that we needed to be together. All I kept repeating was something to the extent that we should start things slowly and see where they led.

My response did not deter him in any way. He admitted to feeling foolish about his declarations, yet he couldn't control them. 'I just feel very close to you,' he concluded at the end of the meal. I didn't answer him, but kissed him tenderly. Finally we got up, walked slowly towards the car, and as he took me in his arms for an embrace, I burst out crying, totally unexpectedly. He held me tightly and let me cry. It was as if the events of these last two weeks were being projected before my eyes and I was witnessing them in all their horror, as well as their beauty. The image of Gianni came to my eyes, as he tore my shirt off and nearly raped me. The vision of myself in that sad room, looking out of the barred window and depending upon my imagination to free myself from the terror of it all. The sight of my mother as I woke up from my unconscious state, and the sound of her voice as she pronounced my name. And finally the idea that a man wanted me so much, a realization which frightened me and overwhelmed me at the same time, because I couldn't understand why I was having trouble opening up to him, and mostly because for the first time in a long while I found myself trusting somebody. I knew Luca was telling me the truth. He was willing to accept me as I was, without the need to dress me, to manipulate me, and to test my patience. He did not need to be taken care of, like Otto. On the contrary. He was one of the most self-sufficient men I had ever met. He did not promise me the moon, nor did he hint at being financially able to offer me a slice of the good life, such as Otto had done. He encouraged me to write more, to find a job that would occupy me, to keep my mind busy. The only thing he seemed to be offering me was himself, not his possessions.

Luca held me tight as I attempted to describe to him what I was thinking, leaving out the part about my feelings for him. He stepped back a little, grabbed my hands and held them firmly. 'You're feeling sorry for yourself is what's happening to you,' he told me simply. 'You were too afraid of feeling sorry for yourself before, mainly because you had no choice, so you're doing it now. It's understandable and you'll get over it. If you need some time alone, please tell me. I'll understand perfectly. And if you need company, I'll be more than happy to be by your side. But I've said that already. I'm going to start sounding like a soap opera if I continue.'

His words had such an effect on me that I stopped crying immediately, and as I gazed at him, standing self-consciously in front of me, his foot playing with a pebble, I couldn't help but smile.

We said goodbye in the car, in the driveway of the hotel. A short and meaningful kiss, various words of com-

mitment were bounced around, until we decided that it
was time for me to leave. Luca stepped around the car to
let me out, and kissed me again, in full view of the hotel
concierge. Then he stepped back into his car, and quickly
drove away.

He called me this morning and told me he hated
goodbyes. I admitted to feeling the same way. We hung up
quickly because there was nothing more to say. My mother,
Oscar and I left for the airport and now here I am, coaxed
by my mother to travel with her first class, flying in the
Italian sky, overlooking its cities which soon become an
intricate variety of dots.

'Would you like something to drink, Miss?' a feminine
voice asks me. I turn around. The stewardess is the one I
had seen with Ted Shaw, the one with the rosy cheeks and
earrings shaped like leaves. She does not seem to recognize
me, and as she pours me a tomato juice, I wonder whether
I should refresh her memory. Not only that, but what if
she knows where her colleague Pietro is? Then again, not
only is he probably dead as well, but she wouldn't tell me
where he was even if she knew. And after all, do I really
want to know, and do I really care? No, not really.

My mother taps my hand. 'It's so nice to be traveling
with you sweetie,' she says, 'we haven't done this in so
long.'

'I know, it's been a while hasn't it?' I tell her, wondering
when indeed was the last time I flew anywhere with her.

'When we get to New York,' my mother tells me, 'I
will buy you a whole day's worth of beauty treatment at
Elizabeth Arden. You'll get a great facial, manicure and
pedicure. You'll get a massage, lie in the sauna and take a

mud bath. You'll feel great. You could really use it you know; your skin doesn't look so good, you need to get your pores opened up and purified. I mean no wonder with everything that's happened to you. It's a miracle you didn't come out of there with acne. I mean can you imagine.'

'I know, really, thank God...' I answer her sighing deeply, and wondering whether this comment of hers is actually serious, something I wouldn't put past her. Then again, I have come to acknowledge my mother's comments for what they are: part of a blend of things, a small imperfection in a sea of magnificent treasures.

I suddenly think about Sarah and her baby: I have forgotten to call her. I vow that upon my return to New York, I will write her a letter. I wonder if the baby looks like his mother or like his father. I wonder if Sarah will ever find the man whose child she bore.

The stewardess with the rosy cheeks comes out with a bottle of Veuve Cliquot champagne. 'With compliments,' she tells me smiling, as she pours each of us a glass in tall flutes.

The pilot comes out of his cabin. 'Welcome aboard,' he tells me shaking my hand. 'I hope your trip back won't be as dramatic as your trip to Rome was...' He laughs, a tanned and dimpled laugh, and all three of us raise our glasses. 'To Italy!' I exclaim before swallowing the first sip of champagne.

My mother and Oscar look at me as if I have lost my mind. 'To Italy! What are you nuts?' Oscar asks me, sending a strong whiff of cologne in my direction. 'I'm not making no toast to Italy.'

'Are you sure you want to toast to Italy darling, with all that's happened to you there?' My mother asks carefully.

'Of course I'm sure! Why wouldn't I? Italy saved my life! I'm in love with Italy!'

'Oy vey zmir,' Oscar grumbles in Yiddish, 'there she goes. In love one more time . . .'

'Come on Oscar,' my mother says, giving him a gentle nudge. 'Just do it. Toast with us. Don't ask questions.'

'Like I'm ever allowed to ask questions . . . what a family. What a family I married into,' he says, before loudly gulping down his first sip.

'I wish I could toast with you too,' the pilot says, 'so instead I'll just do this.' He bends down and gives me a loud kiss on the cheek. 'A l'Italia!' he says, and as he does so I know that I have now become part of that country, and that however long I stay away from it, I will always be accepted there, and its memory will forever be imprinted on my mind.

Epilogue

Ten Months Later

I have just received a letter from Madame Moher. A note written in her elegant handwriting, where she says that she was sorry to hear about my troubles in Italy, and that she wished me luck with my book which she'd love to read. The note, which touched me unexpectedly, was sent to the Jaurel Gallery where I picked it up last week. Upon returning home that day (I have since moved to a substantially larger apartment in Gramercy Park, windows facing the park, and a doorman who keeps at bay those few intruders who still seem to want to barge into my private life), I wrote Madame Moher a letter, in which I told her a little about my trip to Italy, my meeting Luca, and my divorce with Otto. I was probably more forthcoming in that letter with her than I'd ever been while working with her, mostly because I was so happy to hear from her. We had parted on such bad terms, it would have been a shame to let that memory represent the sum total of a relationship which did have many pleasant and intimate moments.

Madame Moher said the gallery was not doing well in this period of crisis, and that she was seriously considering closing it down. Paris was tired, she wrote, and it was going to be a long time before it woke up. In the meantime, if

Muse

I ever came to Paris I should stop by the Moher Gallery and we could have lunch at the brasserie Lipp together. This somewhat nostalgic recollection, an uncharacteristic trait as far as I could remember, made me wonder whether she was feeling lonely. Three days later, I found out from Alain Jaurel himself, who knew Madame Moher from the old days when her husband was still alive, that she had lost all of her money. She had sold her large apartment on the Avenue de Breteuil, and had moved into a small apartment on the Boulevard de Port-Royal. She only kept her gallery open because she did not want to admit defeat.

Today is the Omega opening. I have bought myself a long, tight-fitting white dress which is open at the back, and a pair of gold pumps. I had my hair trimmed and put up in a sophisticated bun, all this in preparation for the elegant dinner which is to take place after the opening.

As I walk down Fifth Avenue with Luca, holding his arm tightly against my side, my heart starts to pound in apprehension of the event. My book will be on display in the gallery, and I imagine that the crowds will be phenomenal. There are even some rumors about the artist himself showing up, a rumor I consider (and pray to be) most unlikely. At this point, there is nothing I dread more than the idea of facing Omega.

It is no secret that the artist committed an abhorrent crime against his daughter. The scandal was widely reported in the press, filled with details about the lithographs (which have become more than ever a collector's item), about Dante's childhood (some journalist even suggested that his father was still alive) and about all the abominable things the painter had supposedly done to his daughter. As for myself, where my name was brandished across the paper when the incident was first revealed ('imprisoned in a Calabrian castle and starved for three days' was one of the more memorable quotes), my presence seems to have thankfully faded away for those tenacious journalists, enabling me to resume my life more or less normally.

But neither the knowledge that he had supposedly committed an abhorrent crime against his daughter, nor my overplayed tape of Patricia's indictment of him were enough to convince the judges to sentence him to jail. The charges against Dante Omega have been dropped, for lack of sufficient evidence that a crime had indeed been committed. His daughter's refusal to cooperate, and the impossibility of proving that the girl on the lithographs was really his daughter, made the case too flimsy. As for Isabella, her case is still pending, although it looks as if she might be able to avoid jail, but not probation.

One trial that did occur though, with plenty of evidence to back it up, was the one against Manfredi Dell' Aquila, another media event which sent the Italian public into a near frenzy, especially because Dell' Aquila did turn out to have, as Luca had predicted, connections with two rather important politicians.

I was asked to testify at this trial. I had to sit and testify against Dell' Aquila, Gianni, Luigi. No questions were asked about Omega, and whenever I brought his name up, I was told that it didn't belong in this courtroom.

I had underestimated the consequences of my testimony against Dell' Aquila. That same afternoon and the following two days, I received threatening letters at Luca's address, which said things like 'You will not get away with this alive,' and 'the eagle will seek revenge'. When on the final day of the trial my eyes met Omega's who was sitting in the audience, the glance he gave me was similar to being sliced open by a sharp knife: it was unbearably painful and ruthless and made me all the more terrified about ever finding myself alone with him.

And yet all of this media hype, instead of keeping the public away in shock and dismay, has created a kind of collective hysteria. The Omega scandal has tripled the value of his work, and Jaurel told me that practically all of the paintings had already been sold, even though the show hadn't even opened yet.

Jaurel's explanation, as Luca and I have to literally force our way into the gallery which is remarkably crowded, is that 'these people are all voyeurs. Yes, they like Omega's work. But they also like to see people suffer, and love gossip. Basically, they're all marchands de poisson, Mademoiselle Miller, and you know what? Tant mieux. My fish is selling well. Very well. It's the best there is around right now. Here is Mr Tillcastle. And Mrs Dabenson. Come, come, let me introduce you. And by the way, Mademoiselle Miller, you look very nice. Very nice. She's a beautiful girl, you know,' he tells Luca with a large grin, 'and she's also a good worker. Obedient, patient, discreet, not at all curious and aventureuse, not at all. A nice and simple girl just as I like them. Ah si vous saviez . . . Qu'est ce qu'elle m'en a fait voir celle-là alors . . .'

But his reprimands are quickly engulfed by a loud swell of admiration about the show, as a crowd of well dressed men and women, prospective clients with thick pocketbooks, gather around Jaurel who seems to be sitting on a cloud of ecstasy.

I motion Luca to follow me to the end of the gallery, where stacks of my book are displayed: the edition which comprises the original reproduction lies open in a glass showcase. All the other editions are grossly piled one on top of the other. I pick a copy up and proudly show it to Luca. My name is printed in thick black print on the cover, which is a reproduction of the Janus painting. We both skip to the conclusion. It is, as we knew it would be, the new and revised edition. 'So sorry you went through all this trouble Laura,' a voice says near me. It is Ensor Mason. His wire-rimmed glasses have visible spots on the glass. He is dressed in a plaid suit and bow tie. He reaches his hand out towards me. 'You did good work Laura, it's a good book. I'm sorry if we had our difficulties. You know how it is . . .'

'Oh please Ensor, that's fine!' I shake his hand warmly, full of gratitude. He has indeed been severe with me, but probably for the best. The truth of the matter is, he's a very good editor and I tell him so. He blushes like a schoolboy and walks away.

Luca and I both smile at each other and kiss quickly. 'I'm so glad he came up to me,' I tell Luca, 'because you don't know how miserable he made me with all his corrections and "words of advice". But I guess I wasn't too nice to him either. He's actually a very sweet man.'

'And you're actually a very sweet woman.'

He grabs my waist and we walk towards the sea of

people and clouds of smoke. As we stop briefly to chat with Rebecca and Sandra, Luca tells me he's going to get us some wine. As he turns away, I suddenly find myself face to face with Otto. Actually, our faces are almost thrust together because so many people are pushing all of us to and fro. 'Laura! Look at you!' He exclaims, letting go of a hand I trace amidst the crowd to a dark-haired woman he introduces to me as Margarita, and giving me a hasty hug. 'What are you doing here?' I ask him, annoyed by his presence, and relieved to be feeling this way; was this the man I had been so in love with, not so many years ago?

'I'm here for a few days. I live in Caracas now, with Margarita, but she had some business to do in the city. By the way, I heard about what happened to you in Italy, that's pretty terrible. Alessandra saw a picture of you in the paper and called me up.'

'How is she? How's your family?' I demand out of courtesy more than curiosity.

'They're fine. Alessandra got married last year, and she just had twins. What about your mother?'

'Fine. She's fine.'

'Oh by the way, congratulations on your book. It looks good.'

'Thank you.' I cannot wait for this conversation to end, and look around anxiously for Luca, hoping he'll hurry back.

Margarita smiles at me. She has puffy lips, jet-black hair and thick gold hoops in her ears. She has a beautiful face, although her skin bears the scars of severe acne. She looks like she could be either Indian or Mexican, or perhaps both. As I look at her, I wonder if she is indeed the same woman Otto had told me about when we had first met, the woman he was supposed to visit in Caracas, a visit he canceled when we started our affair. She remains silent as I distractedly talk to Otto, who looks basically the same. Perhaps a little thinner, and he now wears his hair in a pony-tail.

'So what are you doing in Caracas?' I ask him, making an effort to sound interested. 'Luca told me you were living there. Actually, I'm here with Luca,' I add nervously.

'That's interesting,' he says, as Luca appears, holding two glasses of white wine above his head, 'how long have you been together?'

'Almost a year,' I answer, irritated by his use of the word 'interesting'.

He shakes hands with Luca, who, as he hands me my glass of wine, makes no particular effort to hide his lack of enthusiasm upon seeing him, an attitude Otto seems to ignore. 'Come stai Luca? Che fai qui?' His voice is cheerful and friendly, and he seems genuinely happy to see his old friend, who warms up slightly when Otto tells him about an old high-school friend of theirs he's just had lunch with the other day.

As he goes on talking to him, I realize that Otto's voice sounds different. He seems to drag on his words as if they were difficult to pronounce.

As they continue their conversation in Italian, I am left talking to Margarita. I'm not quite sure exactly what I'm telling her; all I know is that they are mundane things such as the weather and no I've never been to Caracas. Luca quickly comes to my rescue. 'We must go and talk to Jaurel,' he tells me. Otto and I look at each other briefly, and he wishes me luck on my book again. 'If ever either of you want to take a little vacation in the sun, you should come see us in Caracas!' he says, before walking away with Margarita.

'This guy is a stronzo,' Luca says to me immediately, pointing a finger in the direction of Otto's back. 'I don't trust him. He's a jerk. A real loser. A stupid one too. I never realized that before, but it's true. He's stupid. And this wine is disgusting. I'm putting it down.'

Unable to disagree on that point, I follow suit and leave my glass on the bar, where I see Jaurel lighting the cigarette of a very tall woman who wears a black feathered hat and a gold lamé dress.

We walk around the gallery, looking at Omega's latest paintings, a succession of portraits, views of Rome, and his last three mythological paintings, Janus, and a large triptych entitled *Helen and Paris*, which depicts the plight of the two forbidden lovers, alone on a small boat, their bodies clasped together, Helen's face raised upwards, her dark hair blending in with the purple and blue colors of the sea.

'Look at this painting,' I tell Luca, hoping to distract him (and myself for that matter), from what has just happened. 'It's really great, don't you think so?'

Luca pulls on the sleeves of his beige suit. 'I think these sleeves are too short. The tailor wasn't a good one. He made my sleeves too short. I've got to find a better tailor. But you're right. This is a beautiful painting.'

'Come on Luca!' I wrap my arms around his waist and kiss his cheek. 'If this can make you feel better, seeing

Otto left me absolutely and totally cold. It did nothing to me, except for making me wonder why the hell he had to show up on a special night like this one.' I am conscious of my lie as I utter these words, yet I feel it to be a necessity to express them. However much seeing Otto did trigger in me a whole amalgam of emotions, I could never imagine myself by his side again. And this is what, in my own way, I am trying to let Luca know: there will be no going back.

Luca smiles as if relieved. 'He probably came here to see you, since I can't think of any other reason why he would be here. I suppose it felt a little strange for me too to see him after all these years. We did go through a lot together ... Well, let's try to put this behind us. It's a minor occurrence that he showed up tonight. Actually, as I was talking to him, I almost felt sorry for him. It doesn't seem to me that he's changed much, even though he made a point of telling me again that he was entirely clean, and was working nine to five in an office where he had to wear a suit every day. He told me he realizes he made your life very difficult, and you know what else he told me? He said that he always knew we'd eventually end up together.'

'Good for him,' I say, trying to downplay the fact that this little premonition of Otto's does affect me in an odd way. 'Did you tell him we're moving to Lisbon?'

'Yes, I did.'

'What a strange encounter.' I shake my head in disbelief. 'I can't believe we bumped into him ...'

I look at Luca and tell him I love him. I am unsure whether it is guilt or a sincere desire to tell him which leads me to be so forthright with Luca (I seldom reveal my feelings to him), but what I do know is this: whereas with Otto, I felt an unsettling and self-destructive passion, with Luca I feel tranquil; I have finally found harmony in my life, and I'm not about to let it go.

Luca's eyes rest on mine softly, and he tells me he couldn't imagine life without me anymore. I bring my lips close to his and kiss him. He clasps me against him, his warm hands caressing my bare neck and back, while the crowd moves around us feverishly. 'I think Lisbon will be a good experience for both of us,' Luca tells me as we unwillingly detach ourselves from our rousing embrace. I acquiesce. I am looking forward to leaving New York, to living in a foreign land. I may become a diplomat's wife (I am not as yet ready to face the idea of marriage again) and learn Portuguese. I have just signed a new contract with a well-respected publishing company, to start a new book on Chaim Soutine, the French painter whom I've always admired.

'Let's finish looking at the show and then let's go,' Luca suddenly says, 'it's too crazy in here.'

'What about the dinner?'

'We'll walk around the park or something until it's time.'

'Let me help myself to another copy of the book,' I say, 'Mason sent me five copies, but I wouldn't mind a sixth one.'

I let go of his hand and walk back towards the glass case and the stacks of books. A short man is looking at one of them. I can see his back, his scruffy hair, his rumpled jeans. My heart stops. The man slowly turns

his face to the left. I can now see his profile. He has a
beard, and as his hand reaches to scratch the back of his
neck, it becomes clear to me that this could only be him.
Then, he turns around and looks me straight in the eye.
It isn't Omega.

Coda

An excerpt from the first draft of the conclusion
which was written in San Giovanni in Fiore
and which was not published

Dante Omega, A Monograph
By Laura Miller

Babylon Press. New York 1995

*It seems, that after all these years of depicting myths
and allegories. Dante Omega has come to a crossroad.
Will he move on to a new set of interests, or will he
return to his landscapes and portraits, those images
of everyday life which he has managed to convey so
powerfully? It appears that Dante Omega has finally
come to terms with Ruggero Lombani, letting his fantasies give way to reality, as rendered in his last
painting,* Isabella Climbing the Staircase, *a striking por-
trait of his wife. climbing the narrow staircase which
seems to lead up to a dimly lit room, as implied by the
subtle ray of light coming from an open door at the top
of the staircase. Here, Isabella wears frumpy gray
clothes. Her shirt slides off her shoulder, exposing the*

335

white strap of her brassiere. Her head is tilted down-wards, almost precariously so. She is holding a book in her right hand, her left hand seems to clutch the hand-rail, another indicator that she might be on the verge of falling down.

The overall mood of the painting is unlike his glo-rious and heroic mythological scenes. Here, the artist seems to have unleashed a new emotion, close to desper-ation and resignation. Whether or not this is a direct consequence of any turmoil the artist might be experiencing in his personal life, the result is one of astonishing density; where the brush strokes in his pre-vious paintings were regular and concise, here they are thick, uneven, tempestuous, waves of anguish that lure us into this destitute atmosphere where the only ray of hope seems unattainable.

Is Ruggero finally tired of Dante? Has he decided to open up his Pandora's box to the viewer, thus letting us into new corridors of his personality? And are we to forget Pandora, Aphrodite, Pygmalion, or will they return in due time?

Only time will tell. Actually, the loyalty the public has displayed towards him and his work, seems to say that Dante Omega could get away with anything. If he were to stop painting for a while, well, the public would wait for him patiently. And if he were to take on a new subject, even one which we, the public might have difficulty accepting, well, we eventually would deal with it. Once an institution, always an institution. As long as talent prevails. And until now, Dante Omega has shown us no reason to think otherwise.

A small part of the conclusion which
is now included in:

Dante Omega, A Monograph
By Laura Miller

Babylon Press. New York 1995

*Nietzsche said that the devil is the most ancient friend
of wisdom. This makes wisdom an enemy of virtue.*

*As wisdom is the result of experience, Virtue exists
in a state of innocence.*

*I suspect that Dante Omega was once a virtuous
and innocent young man. But as he grew up, pain and
suffering hardened him, and, like all mortals, he lost
his innocence. The one remaining vestige of that lost
innocence was his talent. A raw, fierce, formidable
talent, which became his weapon, a strong and unique
self-affirmation, which raised him above the level of the
ordinary man and propelled him to the spheres of power
where he learned, like all those before him, that
power corrupts.*

*Dante Omega took advantage of that adage, and
the public continued to respect him. So where can the
line be drawn, one might ask? Simply when the work
itself ceases to maintain consistency, when the power is
used up like a dried-up well.*

For now, Dante Omega has maintained consistency

and his well is full. His pornographic lithographs, however shocking and disturbing, remain works of art. Though it is difficult to distance oneself from their savage and ruthless crudity, and the moral dilemma involved, the fact is that these lithographs have artistic value.

The Renaissance painter Sodoma (1477–1549), a follower of Raphael whose real name was Giovanni Antonio Bazzi, was a notorious homosexual who was known to sodomize young boys (hence his nickname). His work was to be destroyed by order of the Pope, an order which was not systematically followed. Sodoma was considered one of the greatest sixteenth-century Sienese artists, until Beccafumi came along, replacing him as the period's main representative of that school.

I wonder if there will come a time when Dante Omega will have to put his brushes down. Not because he will perpetuate his dubious actions, but because at one point or another his past conduct will catch up with him and he will feel remorse. It might creep up on him like a ghost; one morning when he's drinking his tea, or one afternoon when he's taking a walk. It will hit him hard like a hammer, and leave him numb. This could happen today as well it could happen in the next twenty years, or not at all. But when and if the incident does occur, the artist will tell the world that he is tired and needs to retire for a while. His admirers will respect that need, and will wait patiently for him to get over his fatigue. They might have to wait a long while to see his canvases again, and some might die in the mean-time, including the artist himself.

For now, however, the artist continues to paint. He has changed his subject matter. His images of mythology have been put aside, and he has been concentrating on still-lifes and portraits again. The power that emanates from his brush is equal to what it always was: when we look at an Omega painting, we feel as if a virus is entering through our eyes and into our blood stream. It is the result of true genius. The work has such force that we cannot find the right words to speak about it; it speaks to us, like a piece of music which can only be understood through our soul, and not our mind. And as long as we continue to hear that music, there is no reason why we should keep its melody from transporting us to higher spheres.

I do not doubt that many of Omega's admirers feel angry and betrayed by what the artist is said to have done; betrayed in the sense that he has exploited their loyalty to him. They probably feel, and rightly so, that the artist abused his daughter's youth and innocence and transgressed one of humanity's basic tenets merely for creativity's sake, not to mention the issue of whether there were lucrative reasons at stake. I empathize with this feeling of anger and betrayal, because I felt the same way when I was first told about his deeds. These admirers will become his enemies; they will stop buying his work, and will dismiss his paintings whenever they are subjected to them. They have every right to feel that way, a feeling that is probably more justifiable than forgiving him. But since forgiveness isn't entirely rational, it would be ineffectual to try and defend both standpoints. Let us just say this: while all these men and women will battle on about the ethical and moral issues at stake in this matter, there is a strong chance that Dante Omega will go on painting, emerging victorious, untouched, and a hero.

The Chinese have a theory that beauty doesn't have to be good since they find beauty in cruelty. The Greeks, on the other hand, thought of goodness and beauty as being tied together; their sense of beauty defined their sense of goodness.

Once Dante Omega had trespassed into a territory that refuted the Greek notion, he had to abandon their symbols and return to those images of everyday life, safe and familiar images which carried no dogmatic interpretation. This is where he stands today. Back in today's world.